CHRONICLES OF
EVERFALL

SHADOW
OF THE
CONQUEROR

SHAD M. BROOKS

Shadiversity PTY LTD
and
Honorguard Productions LLC

CHRONICLES OF EVERFALL
SHADOW OF THE CONQUEROR
Copyright © 2019 by Shad M. Brooks
All rights reserved

This is a work of fiction. All characters, organizations, and events portrayed in this
novel are either products of the author's imagination or are used fictitiously.

First Edition: July 2019

Version: 1.0

Print ISBN 978-0-6485729-1-6

Shadiversity Pty Ltd
and
Honorguard Productions LLC

Copy Editor:
Audrey Logsdon, The Indie Editor

Proofreader:
Chris Bellomo

Final Proofreader:
Stephanie Cohen

Beta Readers:
Scott Leneau, Josiah Hanson, Jesse Adams, Isaiah O'Conner, Diego De Leon, John
Merrill, Miroslav Zivkov, Dylan Asmus, Jeremy O'Dell, Kat.

For my wife, Mary,
Without her this book would not exist.

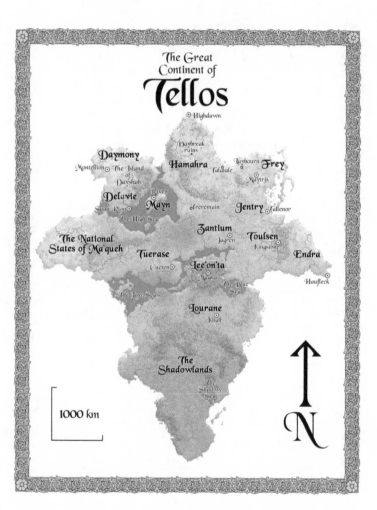

Smaller Continents
Above Tellos

The
Floating
Isles

Zuracus

Azbanadar

Ochroose

Orden

1000 km

N

CHAPTER ONE

M y name is Daylen Namaran, but most knew me as the Great Bastard, the Scourge of Nations: Dayless the Conqueror.

Yes, contrary to what everyone believes, I'm not dead.

This is no jest. Honestly, who would claim to be me? You'll find enough evidence in my home to prove what I say.

I know this revelation will distress most people who survived my rule, enraged that I escaped punishment, but I haven't. The twenty years I've spent in hiding have been torture, where death would have offered me the rest I desire.

My torment comes not from my fall from power or that I live in squalor, but because of my endless guilt.

Yes, that's right: I, Dayless the Conqueror, decree I was in every way the despicable tyrant the world claims I was. I murdered, raped, pillaged, and ravaged the world all in the name of the Dawn Empire. Would you believe that, in all my actions, I thought I was serving the greater good? Regardless, I've come to know nothing justifies what I've done.

I wish there was a way I could fix things, to go back in time and change it all, but what is done is done and I'm left to hate myself more than any person alive. I cannot express in words the depths of my shame. Every hour is agony, and I would have ended my life years ago if not for the knowledge shining through my soul that I deserve such a profound form of torture.

But now my aged body fails, and death draws near—which I welcome as a long-awaited, if undeserved, gift.

I could wait out the few falls I have left, but if I am to die, I'll see it done my own way. The world should be free of Dayless the Conqueror once and for all, and to that end I plan to cast myself from the continent.

I know, poetic.

I leave this letter so the world will know the truth. Dayless the Conqueror died hating himself and his whole life. As meaningless as these words are, I'm sorry.

I leave a world worse for my having lived in it and go to embrace the endless hell I so rightly deserve. If I am lucky, perhaps I'll be cast into Outer Darkness and my existence destroyed.

Daylen Namaran, also known as Dayless the Conqueror.
Year fifty-one of the Fifth Day.

Daylen placed the fountain pen beside his note, which lay next to the small leather-bound journal containing a brief account of his life. He had been as honest as possible, except for the part where he said the Delavian Dukes had sex with goats.

Daylen laughed to himself in long grating croaks.

Those stuck-up men were going to have a light-cursed time dispelling that one, especially when the comment was written alongside so many sincere confessions. Why would he lie about the Dukes when he was being so honest about everything else?

Because he was a bastard, of course; just not the type of bastard the world thought he was, at least not anymore. Also, the Dukes deserved it.

Daylen's dark brown eyes slowly focused to his hand, which lay on the desk. Wrinkled and age-spotted, it was a constant reminder of how old he was.

It was because of reminders like this that Daylen avoided his own reflection. In it was nothing but a haggard stranger whose blue hair had faded to a sickly gray, and whose face partially resembled a scrunched-up piece of paper.

Daylen turned in his seat to face the never-ending stream of life-giving light shining through the windows of his home—a home fighting with Daylen to see who could be more decrepit.

It was a sagging one-room structure made of crumbling brick and cluttered with the necessities of life. An aged cabinet which sat near the door held jars of dried fruit and meats. A few tarnished forks and blunt knives were stacked on the washing bench. There was a cast-iron stove for cooking and warmth sitting on a slate hearth, next to battered chests and a dusty bed. A sagging mezzanine hung out as a partial second story, made of aged milled timber and was stacked with more chests, tools, nets, and other useful things. Small sunstones hung from the roof in iron fixtures, adding to the light from the windows.

The only things in his home offering Daylen an escape from its squalor were the two benches covered in halfway-repaired clocks, children's toys, and generally anything that contained cogs.

Those townsfolk who left these things with Daylen would have to find another tinker.

Daylen sneered at the thought. Though he could find contentment in working with things, he hated the term "tinker." He was an engineer. At least that's what he would have become if his life hadn't gone down a much different path. Instead of designing bridges, uncovering new secrets in sunforging, or finding new ways of employing darkstone in automations and construction, Daylen had ended up using his passion to design machines of war. That was all a day's length from what he did now.

Daylen placed a hand on the back of his chair and forced his body to swivel out. With a concerted effort, he tried to push himself onto his feet. He failed and slumped back.

"Ya blackened useless legs!" Daylen screamed out. He had gotten into the habit of speaking to himself over these many years. It wasn't like he had anyone else to talk to. "I'd kick ya if it wouldn't hurt so much, not that you'd let me. Disloyal backstabbing bastards! Do your bloody job and let me stand."

Taking a deep breath, he heaved once, and this time rose. "Better," Daylen grumbled once on his feet.

"I really should be worried about how much I talk to my anatomy," he muttered. "But every man talks to his pisser at least a few times in his life. That I've extended the practice to other limbs isn't too strange."

Daylen laughed to himself in long croaks. "Not too strange? Light, I'm such an idiot."

Looking down to his crotch, he added, "You all right down there? Yeah, I know, stupid question considering who you have to put up with. Your family is nuts and the neighbor's an asshole."

Daylen chuckled which sounded more like he was trying to hack up phlegm.

He slowly shuffled across the floor to the large cuffed justa-corps jacket hanging next to the door. Walking was a chore these falls, and quickly drained what little energy he had. Daylen took the coat and donned it over his vest and loose-sleeved beige shirt.

Moving to a bench, he took hold of the deep black piece of cubed darkstone lying there. It resisted being picked up, as no light was touching its base. It may as well have been fused to the table. With his other hand he took a shining sunstone bead from a small bowl on the desk and quickly touched it down onto the dark-stone's top. The closer the bead had come to the darkstone the more the darkstone was repulsed by the brighter light, the table having creaked under the strain. But the stone's repulsion had been nullified as soon as the sunstone touched, which had released it from the table.

Daylen picked up the darkstone with two fingers at its corners, careful not to cover the sides from light, and dropped the sunstone bead back into the bowl.

Daylen knew he didn't really need the darkstone. Falling through the Barrier while touching sunstone would kill a person just as much, and the luminous pendant hanging under his shirt was made from just that. But Daylen was intending to kill himself, and if sunstone or darkstone would kill a man, surely touching both would be twice as effective. He never did anything by half measures.

An odd thought came to Daylen. "Has anybody ever fallen through the Barrier while touching both stones? I've never heard of that happening… Is there a chance touching both stones won't kill me?"

Daylen began to cough out a croaking laugh at the absurd thought. "Of course it will, you light-blinded fool! Thinking it won't is like believing two poisons will cancel each other out. Huh!"

With the darkstone in hand, Daylen walked to another desk and found a small wooden box. He opened it and a stream of bright light shone out. The box was lined with sunstone, the only way darkstone could be easily transported. Daylen placed the darkstone within and latched the lid. He then grabbed his coin pouch and slipped it into his coat's pocket.

Daylen took another pouch that clinked when handled, holding even more money than the first.

With difficulty, he hobbled outside.

A soft breeze ruffled his coat and the smell of fresh country air filled his lungs. Glancing to the sky, Daylen saw a black dot slowly moving westward. It was a skyship. One could always see at least a single skyship flying through the air, and they always brought a sense of awe to Daylen. He loved skyships, though he hadn't been so much as near one for years. Still, Daylen wasn't looking to spot skyships. He looked farther up and to see the faint underside of the very same continent whereupon he and everyone else lived: Tellos.

This was a result of the top Barrier of the universe. One simply couldn't exit the world when they reached its top. No, instead they reentered the world from the other side—in this case, the universe's base. This had the same effect on one's line of sight, which was how Daylen could look up and see the bottom of the continent he stood upon.

Daylen's eyes traveled along Tellos' underside to its northern edge. Then, tracing down through the sky, in between the mirror image of Tellos above and the land he stood upon, Daylen found the Plummet: the large misshaped landmass that fell through the world perpetually. A kilometer north of the continent, once the Plummet reached the bottom Barrier it would reenter the world from the top and fall all over again. This marked the length of a fall, whereby the people of Tellos measured their times and seasons.

Daylen surmised the Plummet to be only a quarter way through its fall, meaning it was mid High; or, in other words, noon.

Paradan should have arrived by now. Daylen thought, grumbling.

Daylen's thoughts were interrupted as he noticed a man sitting in front of his house on what was left of a log railing. The railing made the border between his front yard and the brick-paved road running past Daylen's home.

He wore the robes of a Lightbringer, the preachers and servants of the Light. Daylen *was* expecting someone, but certainly not a Bringer.

Hobbling to the man, who sat facing the road, Daylen called out in a disgruntled tone, "Hey, you, what are you doing?"

The man turned to look at Daylen. He was at least in his fifties, yet still looked like a pup to Daylen's aged eyes. His face looked to have been chiseled from stone for all its sharp angles, defined jaw, and prominent chin. He was clearly fit and strong, a common trait among Tuerasians—as identified by the Bringer's dark brown skin and bright yellow hair, which was cut very short and faded at the temples.

"Oh, hello there," the man said in a voice so clear and enunciated he might have been a stage actor. He spoke in a cultured Hamahran accent and, added with the fact that he was fully clothed, indicated that he hadn't been born in his native Tuerasian lands. That, or hadn't lived there for long.

The man stood, revealing that he was half a head taller than Daylen, and looked at him with some of the most discerning eyes Daylen had ever seen, their color a dark blue. "I had wondered who lived here. I don't mean to intrude, but I'm waiting for someone who'll be passing here outfall."

"Who?" Daylen asked.

"He's a young man, though I don't know his name, only that I'm to meet him here."

Daylen's home sat beside the main road from the village and it served as a recognizable marker, so the explanation made sense.

"All right, then," Daylen said. "I don't suppose I need to worry about a Bringer causing trouble."

"Indeed," the Lightbringer said with a smile. "Rather, we Bringers try to bring as much brightness as we can bring." He leaned in a bit closer and said conspiratorially, "That's why we're called Bringers."

Daylen frowned as if he had just tasted something foul. "I hope that wasn't some retarded attempt at humor?"

"Umm... Seeing as I'm not mentally disabled, I would have to say no. It was a simple joke."

"No, if you think that was a joke, you most definitely *are* mentally disabled."

The Bringer's mouth hung open and he stared at Daylen, stunned.

Daylen leaned in and, in the same conspiratorial tone the Bringer had used, said, "It was a joke."

"Insults are not jokes."

Daylen shrugged. "It depends on who you insult. I once asked the Toulsen Ambassador if his ass was jealous of the amount of crap coming from his mouth." Daylen croaked a chuckle. "He nearly choked up a lung."

"The Ambassador didn't have you arrested?"

"No. He had wanted to keep his head."

"You threatened him as well?"

"Yep."

"And he still took no action?"

"He was too much a coward."

"I hope you don't mind me asking, but how did you find yourself in a position to insult an ambassador?"

"I wasn't a tinker my *whole* life. I've seen the world."

"Yes, well, it would have surprised me if you hadn't; I mean, you're looking at the world right now, after all."

"Don't be a smartass," Daylen said, turning to make his way to the outside chair in front of his house. Each step was a struggle.

"Would you like me to heal you of your ailments?" the Bringer called out. "Consider it payment for my intrusion," he continued, walking toward Daylen.

Daylen turned back to him. "Bringers can't heal old age."

"True, but if you're not sick, a healing will still grant you some temporary vitality."

"Sure, go ahead," Daylen said, waving a hand.

The Bringer placed a hand on Daylen's shoulder. His skin began to glow softly as the light moved to his hand and then transferred into Daylen's body. A warmth rippled over Daylen that brought with it vigor and lucidity.

Any question of this man being a true Lightbringer had just been answered. Still, even with the healing—which made him feel like he had just had a good day's rest—Daylen's body was dying. He coughed. "See, you can't heal old age. But the revitalization is welcome."

"It's a pleasure to serve."

The rattle of a wagon announced Paradan's approach.

Daylen hobbled past the Bringer, surprised at the strength in his legs. The Bringer followed him down the path to sit back on the log railing.

Paradan's wagon was a very old darkstone machine, probably as old as Daylen himself, which was saying something. It pulled to a stop in front of Daylen's yard.

The man atop had large ears and a wide mouth that formed an

unfortunate appearance. Two beads hung on a length of hair to the side of his head, called a tassel: one dull white, and one a shining sunstone. This indicated Paradan had won two sword duels in the past; one against a person who had never dueled before, and another against a person who had won at least one.

"Light to ya, Daylen," Paradan said as the soft wind failed to bother his messy reed-green hair. "And Light to you, Bringer," Paradan said respectfully.

The Lightbringer nodded back. "May the Light brighten your fall as well."

"You're late," Daylen said.

"Sorry about that. Fergen Le'donner came around making a fuss just as I was about to leave, saying my son is paying his daughter too much attention. I had to deal with that old uproot before talking to Perenday. Not that it's wrong for him to pay courtesies to young women, mind you—he's marrying age, after all —but night come on me before I let any Le'donners marry into our family."

"Fergen is a Shade's tit," Daylen said. "And his kids would think half a wit is an endowment of intelligence. Light, Fergon's stupid enough to think Perenday should marry *into* the Le'donners, if such a shadow ever fell on you."

"Shade take me now," Paradan said in dread. He looked to the Bringer. "Are you to accompany—"

"No, he's not," Daylen snapped. "He's waiting for someone else. Honestly, I think I might turn this place into a skyport with all the traffic I've seen infall." Daylen ended his grumble with a hacking cough, and struggled to stay on his feet.

"Easy there, old-timer," Paradan said, jumping off his open topped wagon to help, his left hand keeping the longsword at his side from swinging.

"Off with ya!" Daylen spat, hitting Paradan's hand away. "I'm not so old that I can't stand on my own two legs!"

Paradan looked at him with insufferable concern. Daylen *hated* it. He had ruled the world, and now a peasant farmer was looking down upon him.

Grunting, he shuffled to the other side of Paradan's wagon.

"You sure you're up to travelling, tinker?"

"I'm fine, shade it!"

But Daylen knew the small energy he had from the Bringer's

healing wouldn't last; indeed, the trip would see to that. He heaved himself up onto the wagon, which was usually an impossible feat for him.

Paradan sighed and climbed aboard into the driver's seat. It was obvious the farmer didn't like Daylen—no one did—but this wasn't hatred. It was the dislike anyone had for spending time with the ill-tempered and old.

Daylen didn't mean to be so perturbed by everything; it was just that everything perturbed him. He didn't think he had been so easily annoyed when he had been young, and surely people hadn't been as patronizing.

Still, like it or not, Paradan had to give Daylen a ride. It was payment for Daylen fixing the very wagon he sat upon.

Paradan nodded respectfully to the Lightbringer and worked the wagon's control levers. He pulled on the main throttle, which opened a hatch-like door to the darkstone driver fixed at the rear. With light now shining on the back of the stone through a few magnifying lenses, the wagon lurched forward, being pushed by the darkstone's luminous repulsion. Paradan put a hand on the large steering lever sitting in front of him to direct the wagon as it traveled.

It was an amazing means of transportation, far more so than the animal-pulled wagons of old, though it was one of the simpler darkstone engines.

Even in his old age, Daylen was still enthralled by this technology. Machines powered by light, a never-ending resource. Of course, it was all thanks to darkstone's natural properties.

The wagon rattled on over one of the many brick roads Daylen had seen built during his time in power.

The bumpy trip didn't help Daylen's health, and he coughed and hacked in pain regularly. At least the weather was fine; rain would have made this trip unbearable.

They passed a patchwork of cultivated fields which sat over the rolling hills like a blanket. Many a farmer was out working their darkstone-powered plows, tilling the ground for the spring crops of barley, oats, beans, and potatoes.

Groves of varying sizes were scattered throughout the paddocks, with many tree lines bordering the fields making windbreaks.

Occasionally they passed an old ruin, most of them left over from the empires of the First Day which had ended with the First Night. It was thanks to the First Night that most of what stood in the distant past had been left in ruins.

"I've never been to the city before," Paradan eventually said, clearly trying to break the silence.

Daylen couldn't be bothered to respond.

"My son wanted to come along with us. I might have let him if not for that mess with Fergon's daughter. Light, that boy is shading my day these falls. Skipping his chores, courting air-headed nits with his own head not too far away, what with it being in the clouds so much. The lad keeps saying he wants to join the Archknights."

"You wouldn't want him to be an Archknight?" Daylen asked.

"If Perenday committed to practicing his sword more often, yes. The knights would reject him after the first week of trials with how he is at the moment. That's his problem—he keeps saying he wants all these things, but he isn't willing to work for them."

"Sounds like he just needs a good kick up the ass."

"I've tried that, too. Light, it makes me wish I were an Archknight so I could use their magic to fix the boy's head."

Daylen huffed. "Lightbinding doesn't work like that."

"But I've heard the knights can control the minds of men."

"That's a myth. I've met many Archknights in my life and as much as they've wanted to change my mind, they never could, though some of the stories are true."

"Like what?"

"Incredible strength, speed, massive jumps; some can fly, some can heal incredibly fast. I've even seen one cast lightning from his hands. But they're not invincible. I've seen Archknights die."

"You have!" Paradan said with such shock his eyes looked as though they would pop out of his head.

"I lived through the Fourth Night, Paradan. The Shade are more than capable of killing Archknights."

"I wondered about that. I mean, you look old enough, but I didn't want to be rude. So, night… What's it like?"

Daylen replied with soft-spoken words. "About as terrifying as you can imagine. Darkness all around, while being constantly hunted by flying monsters, the ever-present risk that you might turn into one if without light for too long."

"You've known people who've turned?"

"My own parents."

"*Light*," Paradan said breathlessly. "I... Daylen, I'm so sorry."

"Not your fault, Paradan, and I got my revenge. With the Archknights, we fought back the Shade, killing thousands, and we brought an end to the Fourth Night."

"Wow. Your life must have been... I can't even describe."

Daylen huffed. "That's not the half of it."

"Do you have any other stories?"

"None that I really want to share."

"Oh," Paradan said, falling silent before curiosity once again got the better of him. "So what have ya got in that box there?"

"None of your business," Daylen said, growing tired of the conversation.

Paradan pursed his lips and sniffed, looking forward.

Daylen sighed and threw a small pouch into Paradan's lap that clinked as it fell. "Here. I, er... I wanted to give you that."

"What's this?"

"Open it."

Paradan did and his eyes widened at seeing the coin. "Daylen, I...I can't accept this. It's more money than I make in a year!" The pouch was full of golden quates, worth a hundred grams each.

"Of course you can and you will," Daylen said. "You need it, what with how bad winter was."

"Daylen, I..."

"Put a rock in it, will you?"

And Paradan did, with not the least hint of annoyance. Honestly, who would be annoyed with the man, ill-tempered and rude as he was, after he gave them a pouch full of money? Daylen wasn't going to need it, and the truth was he had more stored away back home. He had more than enough coin on his person for the ship fare.

Daylen had left his home behind and he wouldn't miss it, though it was light-blindingly difficult to leave behind his sword, Imperious. If there was anything he wanted to die with, it was his sword, like the kings of old. He could have wrapped it in a cloth so no one would recognize it but he was too weak to carry the thing for the whole journey.

So Daylen had to leave Imperious, along with everything else. The townsfolk would probably ransack the place eventually.

Although, once finding out who he really was, they'd be just as likely to burn everything he'd ever touched.

Darkstone could move exceptionally fast when enough light shone on it, and the roads Daylen had seen built were still strong and smooth, facilitating faster travel. They easily crossed a hundred kilometers in a few hours, passing the six towns that lay alongside the road to Treremain, though one of the towns, Liemet, barely earned the title.

A commanding view of the land beyond revealed itself once they crested a small hill. Treremain sat far away in a broad valley.

The city was average-sized, at least to Daylen's eyes. He'd seen most of the great metropolises of Tellos in his life and Treremain didn't come close to any of them—especially not the nation's capital, Highdawn, Daylen's former seat of power. But Daylen guessed that to the locals Treremain would appear to be the largest and most bustling place they'd ever seen.

Treremain had once belonged to the Kingdom of Sunsen, which had declared war on Hamahra at the same time as the kingdoms of Daymar and Lumas did after Daylen had executed the Queen. In return, Daylen had made sure not a single a drop of noble blood remained. So devastating was his purge that many years later, when he was defeated, the lands and peoples who once belonged to those kingdoms had no royal claim or identity, and simply chose to remain with the new Hamahra.

Skyships spotted the sky like upside-down boats, though designed to be far more aerodynamic with huge variance between themselves. The larger traders and carriers queued at the registry station to pass through the city's shield net.

The shield was made from a net of darkstone anchors, large square blocks of stone that encased a darkstone core. With no light shining on the cores they were fixed in the air, the very same way the Tectonic Darkstone Mantle held the continent in place. The anchors were spaced two meters apart from one another in a diamond pattern that formed a dome over the city. The anchors were so close that any skyship larger than a dory couldn't fit between them. Any ship that tried to fly through the shield separate to the openings on the ground and at the registry stations would run into the immovable anchors and get shredded to pieces.

Shield nets had been developed before Daylen rose to power,

but he had certainly employed them to a much larger degree than times before. They were very common these falls.

Even from this distance Daylen could spot the two battleships patrolling the city's airspace from within the shield. They had very distinct silhouettes.

The smaller personal skyships, ferries and coaches, flew much lower to the city and weren't required to land in port.

What remarkable and ingenious works of engineering skyships were. Daylen had even designed a few himself, though one, the annihilator, wasn't something he was too proud of. With skyships, man had made the world a much smaller place.

It was going to be a guilty pleasure to fly in one after twenty years of exile.

Daylen looked back down to the city with anticipation.

Apart from its fine shield, the city's defenses were woeful, only having those two battleships to protect it. With a full-sized company of dragoons and a single battleship or warship, Daylen knew he could take the city in an hour. Other commanders might have difficulty with those resources; the city did have a border patrol, shield net, and would have a decent garrison, but Daylen had done more with less.

"Now that is a sight," Paradan said, looking at the city before them.

"I agree with you there," Daylen said, "but this city is nothing compared to Highdawn."

Paradan reached into a pocket at his side and pulled out some red ribbon. He began tying it around his arm, but Daylen snapped at him.

"Put that away, you blackened idiot."

A red ribbon tied around part of the body was a dueling invitation. One could be challenged to a duel without a ribbon, but unless there was sufficient cause for the challenge, there was no shame in turning it down. Ribbons also prompted official duels that would be recorded in the ranking, which were a day's length from a friendly bout.

"You sound like I'm setting up a picnic in a Shade's nest."

"The stupidity's more comparable than you give it credit."

"I'm just looking for a duel or two," Paradan said with no small amount of bravado.

Daylen sighed. In the past he had been by no means an exception to bragging, but now, having lived for so long, he saw things differently. Yes, the ever-present threat of the Shade and the oncoming Night meant everyone had the right to bear arms. Well, arms that could fight the Shade, at least, which excluded things like shotspikes and rapiers. But that didn't mean one needed to risk their life to prove themselves. If you knew you were strong, that was enough, but tradition said otherwise.

"You're not ready to compete in the lists."

"I already do."

"Not the city lists."

"I'm fairly good with a sword, old-timer, one of the best in the village. I've practiced with my brothers since before I could walk."

"A good foundation, but nothing compared to the precision that comes from being taught by a master. I'm not saying you're a bad match for most in the city, but that's because most know they'd get eaten alive by professional duelists."

"I still might win."

"You have a spare sword on you?"

Paradan looked confused. "Uh… Well, yeah, of course. There's three in the trunk."

"Stop the wagon."

"Daylen, I…"

"I said, stop the wagon!"

Paradan did so.

"Grab one of your spares and help me down."

Paradan stared at him and Daylen scowled back. That got him moving—Daylen's scowl could turn a Shade. Paradan was also probably being more accommodating than he would have been otherwise due to the money.

With some difficulty and help from Paradan, Daylen managed to get off the wagon.

His legs still felt strong, thanks to the Bringer's healing. "Give it here," Daylen said, holding out his hand.

Paradan handed him the longsword.

The sword was old and Daylen could tell by the state of the hilt and scabbard that the blade would need a good oil, but it would do.

Daylen drew the blade and threw the scabbard aside.

"Daylen, what under the Light are you doing?"

Daylen ignored him.

It felt right to hold a sword again, and yet it was distinctly heavier than he remembered. He had grown so weak.

Daylen had once been a Grand High Master of the Sword, not that he would tell Paradan that. It was the highest ranking level in the world and no more than fifty people were alive at any given time who had attained it.

With how frail Daylen was he would be orders of magnitude from the ability worthy of that rank. But he still possessed the knowledge and experience of the rank, along with the added artificial energy from his recent healing.

More than enough to deal with this misguided snot.

Daylen breathed in deeply and forced his body to move. He walked with a much stronger gait than before, though he knew would pay for it later.

That was the thing about being frail. Moving slowly and hobbling wherever he went was a way to conserve his strength, not that he couldn't force himself to exert more strength when he wanted to; it just took more effort and was bad for his body.

This was going to hurt.

"Daylen, what is this about?" Paradan said as he followed him to a clearing in the shrubby field.

Daylen pointed the sword at Paradan and said, with steel in his voice, "Paradan, I challenge you to a duel!"

CHAPTER TWO

I was born to loving parents in the city of Sunview, though now you would know it as the capital, Highdawn. My father was an educated man despite growing up under the boot of the aristocracy, so my family hadn't exactly been as poor as the rest of the country. This meant I received a good education, mostly in mathematics and engineering, the latter being my father's trade— and something I myself learned to love.

W hat!" Paradan said incredulously.

"You heard me," Daylen spat.

"Daylen, you can barely stand."

"Doesn't matter. You can't deny anyone while wearing that ribbon."

"Of course I can. Light, the ribbon means I must accept every fair challenge. *Fair!*"

"You listen now and listen good, you little snot!" Daylen said with a growl. "You'll grant me what my honor deserves and fight to first blood with the best of your ability, got it?"

"I might kill you!"

"Like that's far off, anyway! If you deny me, I'll take back that money I gave you and tell everyone how much of a light-cursed coward you are and that you piss yourself at the sight of your own shadow."

Paradan's mood darkened. "You don't need to get personal, Daylen."

"Then act like a swordsman and fight me."

"A *true* swordsman would never accept such an unfair fight."

Daylen growled and hefted his sword into Plow stance, the sword pointed diagonally toward his opponent. It took a lot of effort, but Daylen pushed himself on to advance.

Paradan drew his sword and reflexively stood in Wrath, which held the sword near his right ear, the blade pointed back over his shoulder. "Stop this, Daylen!" he said. "You'll just make a fool of yourself."

Daylen pushed his sword forward in a thrust, forcing Paradan to move.

Paradan tried to counter with a diagonal strike from Wrath, a type of riposte meant to parry and place his sword on point for a counter thrust.

Daylen stepped to his right; it was more of a stumble, but he expected his body to move like this, which was no matter as the fight was already over. By stepping and raising his sword into a hanging parry, angled down, Daylen deflected the strike to his side and stepped forward, positioning himself inside Paradan's guard.

Without pause Daylen continued to stumble past Paradan's side, his hands moving to twist the sword around and nick Paradan on the cheek with the back edge.

Daylen staggered a few more steps before regaining his footing. He let his arms drop and hunched over wheezing heavily.

Paradan spun to face him.

Daylen glanced back and smiled.

A small trickle of blood ran down Paradan's cheek, who touched the blood with stunned eyes. "Impossible!" he said.

"No: *practice*. You have a good foundation, but are still bare as a baby's ass."

Paradan's face grew red. He had just been beaten by a very old man. Not merely old, but ancient, as few people reached Daylen's years.

"Luck!" Paradan said.

"Then try to strike me, if you can," Daylen said, forcing himself upright.

He didn't even bother to raise a guard as Paradan took his sword in a Roof stance and approached. He feinted a downwards strike but pulled back into a sideways reverse cut aimed at Daylen's head.

Daylen hunched, resting his chin on his chest, and stepped forward. It was a slight movement and therefore far more manageable than the attack he had done in their first exchange, but precise. Paradan's high strike would usually be a sound move, as the other swordsman should have raised their sword to respond, but Daylen could read Paradan like an open book. His hunched step had dodged under Paradan's strike completely, putting their bodies beside each other.

With Daylen's sword pointing down, he hefted it up hilt first with both hands.

The sword passed in between Paradan's arms, where the pommel struck him under his chin.

Paradan's head swung back from the impact and he fell to the ground, letting go of his sword completely.

He lay there rubbing his chin, and when he opened his eyes, Daylen's sword was pointed to his throat.

"Swordplay isn't just about strength, speed, fitness, or precision, son. All those things help, true, but the most important thing is being able to read your opponent to react with the right move. A precise strike that gets blocked is worse than a sloppy one that connects. If you know how to read your opponents, it doesn't matter if you're like me and can barely stand. You'll still win."

Paradan lay stunned for a short time, before saying, "Teach me!"

"I don't have the time," Daylen said, dropping his sword. The energy the Bringer had given him was completely gone. "Now, get up and give me a hand before I collapse."

Paradan did, and leaning on him helped Daylen become more lucid. Light, did it feel good to swing a sword again! It was bad for his body but good for his soul, as it turned out his instincts were as keen as ever.

Once back on the wagon, an ordeal in of itself, Daylen closed his eyes and wheezed heavily. His whole body hurt.

"Will you be all right?" Paradan asked as he got the wagon moving again.

"I'll live," Daylen said. *Long enough to die, that is.*

"I can't believe you're so good—Light, you made me feel like a kid swinging a stick around."

"Then you finally have a better gauge on your *actual* ability. I hope you can see how easily you'll be beaten by a swordsman from the city," Daylen said.

Paradan response sounded disheartened: "Yeah." Then he added, "But it doesn't seem right."

"You can still carry your sword, that's every person's right, but those who wear the red ribbon in the city fight at a higher level."

"Losing isn't the end of the world. I mean, I just lost to you."

"Don't be an idiot. You know listed duels are far more intense and that deaths are common."

"Unless there's a Bringer to officiate and heal the loser."

"Sure, and what if there's not? Don't be so careless with your life. You don't need to prove anything."

Paradan didn't respond but eventually Daylen heard him untie the ribbon.

"Good lad," Daylen said, letting silence follow.

The road Paradan drove the wagon along eventually joined a much wider one that was pointed toward the city. They were joined by other travelers here: hand-pulled rickshaws meant for short journeys, wagons and carts like Paradan's bearing goods and cargo, larger darkstone-driven coaches, and those who simply walked on the side of the road. Above them flew skycoaches and the smaller dories. There was even a skyracer or two which flew overhead at incredible speeds. They weren't practical for personal transportation, but Light they looked beautiful.

Paradan eventually drove the wagon through the opening of the shield net and they soon passed the occasional brick or stone building. Most of the building were made in the baroque, neoclassical, and aristocratic styles, common through most Hamahra. Even the more plain brick buildings and warehouses had small embellishments here and there that spoke of these influences, such as an archway or framed peak atop a double-door entrance with classical-style pillars recessed halfway into a wall on either side. Stone-carved and stylized window frames and corbelling had been added wherever they could. The structures grew in number and height as they drove farther into the city, and paved sidewalks were now bordering the road. The buildings of Treremain ranged in heights from five stories to twenty.

"I've never seen buildings so big," Paradan said.

"Oh, they get much bigger than these," Daylen croaked back.

"I've read that engineers are building things called skyscrapers in the larger cities, seventy stories high if you can believe it. Then there's the Lumatorium in Highdawn, but that was built through a Lightbringer's last miracle."

"Oh I've heard of the Lumatorium, but not those skyscrapers. Light, seventy stories high! That's tall enough to reach some of the sitters and islands." Paradan nodded to the many floating buildings that either sat in the sky or on top of a tiny floating landmass, called islets, over the city ahead of them. "I'd be worried they'd fall over," Paradan added.

"They implant darkstone into the walls of the skyscrapers, much like a skysitter's foundation, to add structural support. Makes them nearly impossible to collapse."

"Smart, and I suppose they can just move a sitter if the buildings under get too high."

"No, the darkstone holding up those buildings are cemented solidly within the foundation. Very hard to affix a driver to them."

"But most of the islets were floated in."

"Islets are more stable and can survive being moved, but it's still extremely difficult. The core can't be too big, otherwise you'll need more drivers than it's worth to pass the luminous threshold. *Then* you've got to drill into the side and hope the darkstone isn't encased in granite or some other rock, and affix a large sunstone driver—we're talking several skyships in strength. And *then* you can only move it in one direction unless you drill in through the other sides and affix more. You have to fix the drivers with perfect precision as otherwise you'll miss your target location."

"Light, Daylen, you know a lot about all this."

"You don't reach my age without learning a thing or two."

They passed a factory or two and before long they were into the city proper, the smell attesting to that: coal, smoke, refuse, sweat, and the occasional scent of bread, meat, or beer.

The streets were spotted with people from every walk of life, most wearing a sword at their side but few with a red ribbon.

Those doing the most menial tasks, such as scrubbing walls and cleaning the street of trash and animal feces, were the collared slaves. Steel collars for criminals, copper for voluntary. The criminals were sold into slavery for the time of their sentence, and the date of their conviction and time of sentence etched along the collars.

There were many children running about the streets, but they worked the factories too. Daylen hated child labor. It was different to the work children did in older times, where they would help their family bring in the crops or learn their father's trade. Now they were worked to death in conditions no self-respecting person should accept. Progress, they called it; supply to meet demand, the industrialization of the world. Well, this *progress* struck Daylen as abhorrent. It was very hypocritical coming from him, perhaps, as Daylen wasn't exactly the perfect model of consistency or morality.

Still, was a time where children had to toil endlessly for basic bread much better than when he had ruled?

History considered the time of Dayless the Conqueror and his Dawn Empire to have been dark and oppressive. The history books seemed to forget his people were always fed, the children free from slave labor. He built strong roads that were still used infall, introduced a much better measurement system, he had Hamahran taught the world over, unifying the languages, though most had regressed to their native tongues once his empire was defeated. He organized and liberated the slave laws so that no one could be stolen into slavery by banditry, which the aristocracy had been happy to allow. Daylen had made child and sex slaves illegal, and no one could execute slaves without a crime fitting the penalty. He built schools and hospitals, created safety and security...but all at the cost of freedom, he knew now. He had ruled with an unwavering iron fist, killing millions of his people, not realizing that he was no better than the aristocracy he had overthrown.

Paradan jerked the wagon to the left, narrowly missing a man with curly red hair who'd walked out in front of them.

"Do you want to be run over, man?" Paradan growled over his shoulder as they drove past.

"How about you watch where you're going, you inbred country idiot!" the man yelled back.

Paradan's hand swung to grasp his sword and he started to rise, but Daylen put his hand over Paradan's, causing the man to pause.

"Sit down, lad, before you get yourself killed."

Paradan calmed himself and sat. "He was a practiced city duelist, wasn't he."

"Yes, and that would have been a duel to settle a personal dispute against a Jentrian, judging by his curly red hair."

"He was Jentrian? So what?"

Daylen sighed. "The people of Jentry fight to the death in duels to settle personal disputes. They intend to kill or be killed and are reluctant to make such challenges as a result, but rarely ever turn them down, either."

"What? Why?"

"They see it as the only proper way to determine a victor. Duels to first blood don't determine who would have won if the fight was real. There's many cases where you can take a cut and still win, as with grabbing your opponent's blade."

"I suppose that makes sense, but light, fighting to the death over a small altercation?"

"He wouldn't have challenged you over what just happened, but you were about to challenge *him*."

"Oh…" Paradan said embarrassedly.

"Exactly."

"You would think foreigners would adopt the practices of the land they're in."

"Deaths happen often enough in Hamahran duels."

"But not intentionally. Shading foreigners."

Daylen huffed, looking at Paradan from the corner of his eye. Because the farmer had grown up in the country, he had so little contact with people from other lands. The world was a very big place, filled with different peoples and cultures, many of which could be seen here in the city.

The blood-red hair of Frey and Jentry could be spotted regularly; the brown skin and bright yellow hair of the intellectual Tuerasian peoples walked into view as well, many showing off far more skin than the local Hamahrans thought modest. The dark-blue hair and olive skin of Mayn was common, and the purple hues of Dayshah's two nations could also be seen. Daymony and Delavie went about in their high-collared form-fitting suits and dresses, helping identify them from the other nation to have citizens with purple hair, the Lee'on'tese, who were rare in these lands. But it was hard to miss a person from Lee'on'ta when they did appear, due to their exceptionally long hair tied in elaborate braids, and their native robes, tanned skin, and brown eyes.

Though Daylen didn't see anyone from the countries of Ma'queh, Zantium, Toulsen, Orden, Endra, or Lourane, chances were that there was at least one person from those lands somewhere in the city. The people of Azbanadar were another story; his strongest ally during his rule, their isolation since his downfall made the Lee'on'tese look sociable by contrast.

Yet even with the mix of nationalities, green was by far the most prominent hair color in Treremain, Hamahran blue coming second, and eye colors ranged from amber to coal brown.

The rich stood out amidst the crowd. Their dress said it all; the men with their clean, prim-and-proper tailed suits with fine cravats and top hats, the women with their laced and frilly dresses and parasols. Both sexes wore finely made swords. Those women who wore hoop skirts or other wide dresses had an opening at their hips for a one-handed sword scabbard to slip through, so it wouldn't swing and tangle with their dress, and the swept hilts of their swords sat like ornamental baubles at their sides. Some women instead carried longswords with parasol scabbards that rested on their shoulders, a combination of function and fashion.

"They wear the ribbon," Paradan said, disgruntled, while looking at a couple of wealthy dandies. "But they're probably duelists, like you say."

"Not those two. Their tassels aren't long enough."

"Then why aren't they afraid of being targeted for a few easy beads? Light, I could challenge one of them right now if I wanted to."

"They both would have been trained in the best schools this city has to offer, so don't go thinking they're pushovers. Apart from that they have very little to fear of being challenged by a serious duelist if they're from a wealthy enough family."

"Why's that?"

"The family will just hire a number of duelists more skilled to challenge the winner in reprisal, making sure to knock him down the lists."

"That's rot!" Paradan said. "How is a man to learn the sword if he can't join the serious duels?"

"I suppose we should teach children to swim before they can walk while we're at it."

Paradan sniffed and said no more, directing the wagon through the streets and constantly braking for the people crossing in front of them.

It was a slow process of continuous stopping and starting, which was why it was so much better to fly across the city in a sky coach or dory. As they neared the skyport, the road widened to thirty meters abreast with hundreds of other vehicles packed side by side, many being darkstone-powered platforms floating a meter from the ground bearing great loads. A rare smile crossed Daylen's face as he gazed up. There were as many skyships above as there were vehicles below, queuing to enter the port or flying out of the city. Beautiful machines.

There were many differing designs amongst the ships, each a specific model produced by a different manufacturer, but they all had distinct similarities. Skyships mostly had flat bottoms for their landing supports and to accommodate the flat slab of darkstone that made up their core. The entire ship was fixed to that core by strong iron bracing. Those bracings would be bolted to large beams of timber which made up the rest of the ship's frame. The sides of most ships sloped inward so that their weight would rest more securely over the cores. They were sleek and aerodynamic, and looked somewhat like upside-down boats with larger rears—akin to a sea galleon.

It took a nearly an hour to move the hundred remaining meters into the port.

The skyport was a massive expanse within the city, comprising hundreds of rectangles that sat a good two meters lower than the paved ground surrounding them. Piers would extend into the rectangles along their broad sides, making separate docking bays for the ships where they could load or unload passengers or cargo. The larger rectangles accommodated larger ships.

Most of the skyships in port were carriers and cargo ships, but there were even a couple of runners. There were one or two trawlers and some whalers, too. It was odd for them, being so far inland, but bringing goods inland meant skyfish would sell for a better price, and all it cost them was a little more travel. Daylen didn't see any military ships.

"Never seen so many ships in my life," Paradan said. "They're amazing."

"They are indeed," Daylen said. "Man has yet to surpass their magnificence." He pulled his eyes from the large cargo ship they were passing, ten stories high and fifty meters long, to look at Paradan. "Lad, would you do me one last favor?"

"Light, Daylen, of course."

Clearly Paradan was still in a good mood from Daylen's gift.

"I need you to find me a carrier headed to one of the cities along the Dawn Gulf. Dirinhom, Talatale, or Lightsem should do."

"Don't worry," Paradan said, pulling the wagon to a stop and hopping off. "I'll find you a ship."

It didn't take long. Paradan returned and drove them to a particular carrier on the other side of the port headed to Talatale.

"You have a ride back, don't you?" Paradan asked as they arrived at the pier.

"I've organized everything that's needed," Daylen said. "Now, can ya help me off?"

"I can do more, if you like," Paradan said, looking to the ship.

Daylen gazed down the long pier and forced himself to swallow his pride. "That would be...appreciated."

With Paradan's support, Daylen made his way to the carrier.

"Thank you for the help, Paradan," Daylen said.

Paradan nodded, letting go of Daylen. "I'll see you when you get back. After all, I need you to teach me some of your swordsmanship."

Daylen didn't want to disappoint the man, so he lied. "I look forward to it."

Paradan left and Daylen purchased his ticket, first class, considering this was his last flight he wanted to enjoy himself, and checked in his darkstone.

There was very good cause for skyships to check in all darkstone. With the speed at which skyships flew, if someone covered a piece of darkstone from light while in flight, the stone would instantly stop its movement through space. The ship would still be moving forward, making it seem like the stone shot backward, where it would rip through the entire ship and any poor soul in its way.

Daylen looked over the ship as the tollman helped him aboard and smiled. He was so much closer to what he desired more than anything else.

So much closer to his death.

The *Denwind*, a *Lightspeed*-model carrier produced by Hammen-light Incorporated, flew through the air with remarkable silence. Only the slightest hum from the passing wind could be heard, which was amazing, for Daylen knew a *Lightspeed* could reach speeds of five hundred kilometers an hour. It was mindboggling.

Once, it would have taken eighteen falls for an army to march the distance he was now travelling in two hours. *Two hours.*

These falls, the far-off exotic lands weren't nearly as unreach-able. Light, the world had become a smaller place.

Unlike Paradan's wagon, which used normal daylight to push the darkstone, skyships used large sunstone hubs which were fixed all around their darkstone core, called drivers. With inbuilt magni-fying lenses they provided much greater control and, of course, much greater speeds thanks to the more intense and focused light.

Being only two hours the trip seemed over all too soon when Daylen felt the ship start its descent.

It had been a comfortable flight having travelled in first class and he had savored everything from the glorious views to the familiar soft hum of the wind outside.

Once at the edge of the city's airspace, there was a brief wait as the ship queued in line to pay the entry tax at one of the floating registry stations. Any skyship that wanted to enter a city's airspace had to be marked on the registry, a procedure Daylen himself instituted. They would then pass through this city's shield net.

The ship moved again and gently came into dock. The door was opened and the gangplank lowered.

The passengers began to file out and Daylen waited until last, not wanting to fight the crowd.

Getting to his feet was like trying to crank a rusted pump; but he managed, barely.

The tollman handed him his box. "Do you need any help in the city, old one?" He was a Lourian with their characteristic sky-blue hair, reddish-brown skin, big lips, and impressive height.

"I'll manage," Daylen said. "But your help down the gangplank will be appreciated."

The tollman did so and bid farewell, returning to the ship.

Being an edge city, Talatale traded in skyfish and whale mostly, though a man with half a nostril could figure that out. Luckily, the edge winds would periodically blow away the sharp scent of fish and blubber.

As was common, the skyport sat in the middle of the city; not that they were built in the middle, just that once built, the cities often grew around them. They were the centers of trade and commerce. By the look of it, Talatale's port was too small for the city's trade, Daylen noted; there would likely be other smaller ports placed throughout in an attempt to compensate.

They really should have built the docks in stacks, Daylen thought to himself, but such a thing took foresight and planning. To put stacks in the docks now, they would have to shut parts of them down, which would cause a lot of issues for the city's commerce.

Daylen found himself on a dock near the industrial part of the port, and from here he could see a few skywhales being skinned at that very moment.

They were massive creatures, the size of a skyship carrier, with broad pointed flaps on either side that stretched the length of their flat bodies. This gave them a stretched diamond shape, the flaps enabling them to steer as they fell through the endless skies.

Daylen pulled his eyes away, ignoring the sudden urge he had to eat a nice whale steak. He wouldn't be able to stomach the meat anyway. Light, was he sick of broth.

Though Talatale was an edge city, it was still at least a kilometer away from the rim.

Luckily in cities, and especially their ports, hand-pulled rickshaws were everywhere, including along the raised pathway where the *Denwind* had docked. The rickshaw pullers would have known a carrier was coming beforehand. Even with the new public transportation busses, the rickshaws were still around. They could get to places that skyships couldn't.

The rickshaws could have been powered by a darkstone pusher, like Paradan's wagon, but that would have been a waste for a small two-seater. Oh, there were two-seated darkstone carts around, but they were rare, for a darkstone pusher could power a large wagon just as well. Besides, a basic pusher cost about a hundred grams, too much for a rickshaw puller, as the trade was increasingly being taken up by the poorer class.

Daylen hobbled over to one of the rickshaw pullers, a young lanky man with an all-too-happy smile.

"Where is ya goin', grandpa?" the dirty runner asked, speaking in a lowborn Mayn accent, his dark-blue hair a mess.

"To the edge," Daylen said.

"The edge?" the runner said, looking aghast. "I can takes ya around the city, but you is better off catching a coach if ya headin' out."

Daylen didn't want to explain that once he managed to climb into the blackened thing he didn't want to have to climb out of it only to get into another one. This journey was already taking its toll.

"There's a sestus in it for you."

The man's eyes widened. "No, grandpa, that's too much."

Daylen sighed. Only a man from Mayn would haggle against himself.

"Fine, you set the price."

"Um… Four duns and five."

That was only five grams less, so clearly this man didn't object to Daylen's generosity as much as he let on—he just had to make a show of it. *Damned Maynish.*

"Done. Now, can you help me onto this blackened thing?"

The runner, whose name was Leb, helped Daylen off the rickshaw.

"Much obliged, Leb," Daylen said, feeling rotten. The bumpy trip hadn't helped his condition. He threw Leb the sestus. "You can go, I'm done with you."

"Grandpa, we said four'n'five, not fifty."

"I don't have change. Consider it a fee for helping me off."

"I'd be a bucket's rag if I charged so much for helpin' ya like that."

"No one will hear it from me."

Leb glanced about the grassy edgeside as the strong wind made a mess of his hair. "There's nothing here, grandpa. I thoughts you were wanting me to take you to an edgeside inn, or Levenfall, the little village half a step thataways."

"This is exactly where I want to be."

"How are ya gettin' back? I can wait for ya if ya like."

"Don't need it. I've made plans."

"But, grandpa…"

"Off with ya, you bloody sunspot, before I kick ya up the ass!"

Leb jumped back, looking dejected; and, after a slight pause, took his cart and began jogging away.

The Maynish were by far the loudest, most contrary people in the world, though they saw haggling and correcting others as a sign of strength and respect. The fact that everyone else did it in Mayn meant that the most basic conversation degenerated into shouting matches. At least Leb could take a hint.

Daylen sighed and walked to a tree that stood two meters from the edge, taking very small steps. Thankful for the windshield he leaned back, trying to recover his breath.

It didn't come. He needed a full fall's bed rest to recover from the trip he had just endured.

He gazed out into the endless cloud-speckled sky. The bright orb that was the sun sat high, shining brilliantly far off to his left.

"So it's all come to this," Daylen said softly, thinking back over his long life.

When still young, he had endured the Fourth Night, when the Shade had risen up and cast darkness upon the land. During the Night he had been forced to kill his own parents when they had turned. He came out of the Night as a war hero, being one of the survivors of the assault on the Shade's nest. He tried to feed the people in the wake of that war, striving to work with the old aristocracy. He had seen his wife and young children murdered in front of his own eyes. He had led a rebellion against that oppressive ruling class, overthrowing them, and becoming the new leader of his nation. He had rebuilt society, and had tried to better it.

But he had also killed kings and queens, men, women, and children, many with his own hands. He had destroyed cities, murdered millions, conquered nations, raped, ravaged, and oppressed the world.

Daylen looked high into the sky and began to weep some of the most bitter tears of his life.

It took a long time for Daylen's tears to dry.

The Plummet looked to have fallen nearly halfway between the land Daylen stood upon and the bottom image of the same landmass high above. High Fall was almost over and the people of the world, those that chose to spend their time during High Fall, would be preparing dinner. Those few who lived during Low Fall would be arising about now.

Daylen pulled his coat shut and did up the large buttons running down its front.

Still holding the small sunstone-lined box, Daylen opened it and took out the darkstone with two fingers.

He tossed the box aside.

Holding the darkstone, Daylen left the tree and hobbled to the edge of the continent which stepped down in several unmatched sections, the ground having been carried off in chunks by wind, water and storm.

It was light cursed hard to find an easy path to each lower section, Daylen even had to sit down and slide at times which caused him great pain. At least with raised earth behind him now there was cover from the wind that perpetually blew outwards from the continent, that was until gravity pulled to air down to join the Transcontinental Current.

He finally came to the very edge where no ground below him extended further out. At this place Daylen could lean out and look down without anything blocking his view except the few clouds that hung in the sky far underneath the continent.

He could just see the same edge of the continent that he stood upon far below. If he had a powerful enough telescope he could have seen himself from above, leaning out and looking down on himself and the whole world, except for the sun.

The sun was an anomaly, because it was the only thing not mirrored through the Barrier. Its position was constant with respect to the observer, meaning the sun would look to be in the exact same angle and distance to one person as it would to another who stood on the other end of the continent. It didn't matter if you tried to place yourself closer; as people had tested over long voyages, it was always the same distance away. The position itself was based on the angle to which the sun sat in the sky, and its approximate distance placed it beyond the upper Barrier of the world. This had led to the theory that the sun wasn't physically located within the universe, but that its light shone into the universe from the outside through its upper edge.

Leaning back, Daylen stood for a time looking out into the sky. Countless clouds streaked the horizon; the farthest clouds had mirror copies of themselves above and below that went on for eternity for at such a distance that the whole height of the world became a thin line.

"Finally, the end," Daylen said.

With darkstone in hand, he stepped off to fall to his death.

CHAPTER THREE

*But I loved many things my parents didn't approve of, like
dueling. I was brash and eager to prove my strength because of the
fragile self-esteem of youth. Besting others in such a socially
praised art bolstered my confidence, and arrogance, to
phenomenal levels.*

*Then the Shade rose up, casting Night on the land. Needless to
say, my skill with the sword become most useful. I was sixteen
years old, but my age didn't matter; when Night fell, everyone
fought, my parents included. If that night was to be the prophesied
Final Night where the world would end, at least we would have
fought to stop it.*

*For those born after the Fourth Night, and I would assume that's
most people who read this, it was a horror I wouldn't wish on
any man.*

Wind rushed past Daylen in a torrent as he fell limply, his
body slowing and rolling with the air. He was weak, but
still made sure to hold the darkstone tightly between his two
fingers.

Daylen had fallen through the sky many times in his life—such
was the training for any man who served on a skyship—and he
knew how to control his fall. The issue was that he just didn't
have the strength for it. Indeed, the buffeting winds made it

harder to breathe, and Daylen had enough trouble with that regularly.

He clenched his teeth as his aged weary body cried out in extreme exhaustion and pain.

"I'm not going to die before I reach the Barrier," Daylen told himself angrily. Anyway, the pain was a mere fraction of the punishment he knew he deserved. He *should* feel pain before his death.

The side of the continent raced past him in a constant blur, yet it would still take some time for Daylen to pass it; the continent was one hundred kilometers thick at the thickest part. He knew a man could fall at most around two hundred kilometers an hour, so it would take about half an hour for him to pass Tellos, the mighty landmass from which he had fallen. It would take another nine hours to reach the Barrier, the invisible point where a man stopped falling to the base of the world and fell from its top.

Daylen closed his eyes and surrendered himself to the wind which slowly carried him farther away from land. All he had to do was survive until he reached the Barrier, and then it would finally be over.

Daylen's body burned with fatigue. The air was heavy and the temperature hot. It was all he could do to keep hold of the dark-stone between his two fingers. The fact that he still held the stone meant it hadn't been nine hours yet, the time it would take to reach the Barrier. Light, it had felt like an eternity.

The wind had buffeted Daylen violently, especially when he fell into a stronger current without warning.

The stone Daylen held would disappear once he passed through the Barrier. Some speculated that darkstone and sunstone were absorbed into the body when passing through and acted like a poison, which was why they killed the bearer.

Daylen knew he had to be close; the air pressure and temperature were far greater now.

The Barrier gave a level of resistance to things passing through, like molasses being pushed through a sieve. This made the air thicken at the bottom of the world, and temperature much warmer, as gravity pushed it through and made the air at the top very thin and cold, which created a pressure and temperature differential according to altitude.

Because of this, no clouds ever drifted nearly as low as where Daylen had fallen, but rather remained much closer to the top; which, from his point of view, still looked to be beneath him. His line of sight passed though the Barrier allowing him to gaze down on the world where clouds speckled the sky much farther below.

The thick air pressure made Daylen's whole body feel like it was in a vise. The heat was already unbearable, and his breaths came with great effort. He could feel his mind drifting to unconsciousness, but it wasn't sleep that would meet him there—it would be death. The fall had taken its toll on his body.

Daylen held on to one thought as he pressed a hand onto his shirt, making sure his sunstone pendant was touching his skin: *Don't let go of the darkstone.*

But he wouldn't last much longer, and though he tried with every ounce of strength left, a part of him didn't care anymore. Dying from the fall or the Barrier—it was the same in the end, wasn't it?

"No," Daylen groaned. "I'm going to die the way I choose!"

But his body might not let him. He didn't hurt as much. Not a good sign.

Daylen closed his eyes tightly and tried to endure, but his body was failing. He could feel it. His consciousness began to fade, but Daylen knew he wasn't falling asleep. This was the final fall into death.

He had failed, but even in that there was relief. Finally, death had come; finally, he could rest.

A force hit Daylen like every part of his body had been kicked at the same time and the darkstone disappeared from his fingers.

The shock of the impact and sudden freezing temperature brought lucidity in a snap of awareness. Daylen had hit the Barrier and had felt the stone disappear... *And I didn't die.*

No! Daylen thought as the dread of failure froze his heart.

He spun about in the air to look up as he fell. Had he let go of the stone by accident?

No, he hadn't felt it slip out of his fingers. It had just disappeared.

Daylen grasped his chest to feel for his sunstone pendant under his shirt. The small brass fixture holding the sunstone to the cord was there, but the pendant wasn't. It had disappeared, too.

Daylen then realized something that should have been extremely obvious, but with his sudden shock, he hadn't noticed until now. The chilly air was very, very thin.

He could feel his breaths draw in little oxygen. It was such a contrast to the painful pressure he had been enduring only moments before.

Daylen *had* passed through the Barrier and had been touching his sunstone, if not also the darkstone. *And I didn't die*, he thought to himself again.

He looked to his hand in shock, confirming what was already obvious: the stone was gone. And yet his hands looked different...

There were no sun spots or wrinkles. Smooth, clear, strong hands were at the end of his arms, arms that felt...sturdy.

Daylen realized that since the stones had disappeared he hadn't been forcing his breaths to come, even with the extremely thin air.

Daylen breathed in deeply, trying to get more oxygen into his lungs, and was amazed at how easy it was even though the thin pressure gave little oxygen.

Daylen's lungs were definitely working better; as good as they ever had, in fact.

He hesitantly touched his face and felt no wrinkles. No haggard and loose skin. Instead, he felt a strong jaw and a smooth face.

Hesitantly, Daylen raised a hand to the top of his head and felt hair—thick, plentiful hair that flapped in the wind. He pulled a few strands out. Even amidst the flails from the battering wind, Daylen could see the strands were dark blue.

Somehow, as impossible as it seemed, instead of dying, he had become *young* again!

This was a cruel joke! Daylen had finally reached the end of his life where he could have release from his guilt, and at the very moment when the blessed end had come, his life had instead returned in full. A tease of release and then a stab through the heart!

No, not a joke, Daylen thought suddenly. *A punishment.*

This was the punishment he had chosen for himself ever since coming to truly understand the magnitude of his crimes: to live with his self-loathing and guilt. And now, it seemed, the Light agreed with him. His punishment was to live, for what else could have done this to him but the Light itself?

But did that really matter? He was falling, and the wind currents had already carried him several kilometers away from the continent. It was true that an inward wind could carry things back over the continent, but that rarely ever happened when they were cast away with an outward continental drift.

Daylen would fall for eternity and starve to death. But then why hadn't the Light just let him die when he passed through the Barrier?

The only possible answer was worse than he could imagine. The Light wanted him to live, because it was the worst thing that could be inflicted upon him.

It was what he deserved.

And the worst part about it was that knowing the Light's chosen punishment, if Daylen was truly sorry for his crimes, he was obligated to do everything in his power to see it done—even if that meant trying to survive the fall.

Daylen was many things, but never a coward, and thus he would accept every lash pronounced upon him.

Not for the first time that fall, Daylen wept.

———

It took a long time for Daylen's sorrow to dry, and even longer to steel himself to the reality of life.

Of course that still left the problem of falling to his death.

Hopefully that would still happen, but first Daylen had to try and prevent it. Then and only then would Daylen know it was the Light and not himself that had ended his torment. Giving up and letting himself be killed when he could have prevented it was as cowardly as ending his own life to escape the Light's just punishment.

Daylen growled in acceptance, forcing his faculties awake. He had to at least try and survive.

Unless he fell into a new current that blew him back over the continent, his only hope would be if he fell near a trawling skyship and got their attention.

Then as if by providence Daylen fell into a new wind which

blew in the opposite direction, pushing him back toward the continent.

Daylen could scarcely believe it. If this rare and ever so timely wind wasn't a sign from the Light, then nothing was.

Countless people had fallen from the continent before; more by accident, of course, unless they had been pushed, which was known to happen. Several procedures had been put in place to prevent or save people from the fall.

For one, every edgeside structure or village had large safety nets constructed several meters below to catch those that fell.

Daylen could try and land on one of those nets, but it would be hard to hit them from such a height. Still, even if he missed the net, he would have a good chance of being noticed by someone as he fell past. If that happened, the people could try and dispatch a skyship to scoop him up or throw a skimmer down after him; and if none of that happened, Daylen could try and stop his fall by grabbing the thick side of the continent as he fell past. That would be damned hard when falling at terminal velocity, but it was something.

Daylen needed to measure his descent to reach the edge at the same time he reached the surface. If he overshot it, he would find nothing but an unceremonious union with the ground.

It was going to be tricky, but the Light seemed to be willing to lend an unwelcome hand.

This was all light-blindingly hard to swallow. Life, after being so ready for death. It would take months to truly come to terms with it but things were the way they were.

At least he had this new body. Daylen clenched his fists and flexed his muscles to test their strength.

The energy of youth filled him.

Aside from the soul-crushing reality of his punishment, physically Daylen felt incredible—better, even. His senses were awake and sharp, no more dulled by age and fatigue, and the glorious sunlight embraced him as if he were immersed in a warm bath... But he had never felt anything like *that* before.

Daylen could *feel* the light as if it were a physical thing. He was touching it with his hands; it was like he could grab hold of it if he wanted. It felt amazing; like the warmth one feels when embracing a loved one. Daylen wanted more of it, and tried to close his fist around the light. Of course, nothing happened, as he couldn't just grab light.

It didn't matter, for the light felt wonderful, and Daylen happily let the enjoyable sensation distract him from his bitter sorrow.

Daylen stretched out, controlling his fall as he had been taught to do so many years ago, the light seeming to immerse his whole body. He breathed in deeply, wanting to take in this incredible feeling; but this time as air filled his lungs, light flowed inside of him, filling his body.

Energy surged inside. Somehow that feeling on his skin was now within every fiber of his being.

It felt wonderful, and Daylen wanted more. He drew in more light, which caused it to push on him from the inside, like it needed to go somewhere.

Hesitantly, Daylen drew in more light, and as he did a pressure grew until it began to hurt.

This might not have been a good idea, Daylen thought to himself.

Daylen tried to breathe the light out, but it didn't leave. He tensed, pushed, and stretched his limbs, but nothing happened.

The pain grew.

Could I put it into something else? he thought. *Not release it back into the world, but put it into something like I brought it into me?*

Daylen looked around, but there was nothing even remotely near. He grabbed his coat and tried to breathe the light into it. Nothing happened. Pressing his palm onto it and even slapping it did nothing.

Part of him wanted to draw in more light to see if it would tear him apart, but Daylen would fight to live, as much as he hated it. If life was what the Light had inflicted on him, he would embrace it and make sure to meet every measure he deserved.

Daylen groaned, trying to think of a way to release the light. He looked about as he thought in a vain attempt to see anything that could give him an idea, his eyes straining as they gazed down at the land far below, barely visible through the clouds and the blue haze of the air.

Suddenly Daylen felt all the light inside him flow into his eyes. His vision became amazingly clear.

He could see things at an incredible distance and make out details at least ten times as minute and fine.

The giant continent was still very far beneath him, stretching out in the distance as far as he could see, which right then was very, very far. Daylen was awed by the sight.

Then his vision returned to normal, all the light in him gone.

Daylen couldn't believe what he'd just done, let alone what had just happened to him! He was young again, though how young he didn't know until he could see his reflection; and on top of that, he had this strange new ability.

"The stones!" Daylen said in realization, but stopped at hearing his own voice.

It was muffled by the wind, of course, but it had still rung in his ears. It hadn't been old and croaky, but young and clear.

I haven't heard that voice in years, Daylen thought.

This change must have happened because he had been touching both a darkstone and a sunstone. Could that also be the reason why he'd become young?

He doubted it. There was too much poetic justice in the transformation for it to have been chance. The Light had a cruel sense of humor.

But touching the stones might have been the thing that had enabled him to feel the light and draw it into himself.

Had anyone else discovered this? Daylen could understand if they hadn't. It was a fact known worldwide that passing through the Barrier while touching one of the stones would kill you, just like knowing the bite of a jutterbug was poisonous—so who in their right mind would knowingly touch both? Well, Daylen, as it turned out.

Hesitantly, Daylen drew light into himself once more and tried to channel the light into his eyes.

It worked, and his vision sharpened briefly and then returned to normal.

Daylen tried again, but this time continued to draw in light as he channeled it into his eyes. His vision sharpened again, bringing the world into remarkable focus, and this time the clarity remained. It seemed that, for as long as he drew in the light, he could channel it into his eyes, and they would be empowered by it.

But could he channel the light into anything else?

Daylen stopped drawing in light and his vision quickly returned to normal. He drew on the light again, and this time tried to channel it into his ears.

The loud torrent of wind became deafening.

Screaming, Daylen covered his ears and stopped drawing on the light.

Okay, not such a good idea. But it had worked—he could channel the light into other parts of his body.

Still falling through the air, Daylen tested his strength; and though there wasn't really anything to test his strength on, he did *feel* stronger. He tried his nose next and was amazed at how dusty his coat smelled.

Could I do more than one? he wondered.

Daylen drew in light once more and this time tried to channel it into both his eyes and nose. His vision sharpened and his scent became keen.

He could smell the dirt on the soles of his shoes and the air had a sharp, damp scent that was nearly overpowering.

Daylen then tried to add another path for the light, and then another. It stopped at four. He could bond light to four different parts of his body.

Bond, Daylen thought. *To bind light. To* lightbind. *That's the very name of the power the Archknights possess! Do I have the powers of the Archknights?*

That should have been impossible, because a person was supposed to make the knight's pledge to fight evil for the rest of their lives in order to receive this magic. It was the same way the holy Lightbringers received their powers after dedicating their lives to helping others.

People had speculated there might be other magics in the world that would come from different oaths and lifelong dedications. None had been discovered. So far there were only three known magics: light*bringing*, light*binding*, and light*blaring*, the last being the power of the Shade.

What Daylen was doing certainly fit the description of light*binding*, but he hadn't made any vow.

Many years ago Daylen had sent spies to try and discover how the knights received their powers. All he had found was that they performed a ritual, called the Vigil, on a ceremonial skyship that flew toward the sun. He was never able to get a spy on the ship itself.

If that skyship crossed the Barrier during its flight, Daylen might have finally discovered the real way they received their powers. But they certainly didn't become young from it; indeed, many initiates died from the ritual.

Still falling, but now with greater control, Daylen tried to test his powers again. He had seen one knight fly once. Such an ability would prove most useful in Daylen's current predicament. He drew in light and tried to channel it into...flying. Nothing happened.

Maybe they flew through manipulating the element.

Daylen tried to push the light into the wind. Nothing worked. Maybe the knight had flown through manipulating gravity? Daylen tried to bond the light to gravity, not really knowing how except to *will* it. Again, nothing.

Daylen had seen an Archknight call down a storm of lightning once that had destroyed a whole fleet of skyships—his skyships, in fact, during the Empire War. Daylen didn't exactly want to strike himself with lightning by accident, so he skipped that one. In any case it appeared that Daylen could only bond light to his physical abilities and senses. If it was in his body, it seemed to work. Perhaps the Archknights' power, lightbinding, manifested differently from knight to knight. Most of them generally seemed stronger and faster than the average person, but he had only seen a couple do the lightning trick, while those same knights never seemed to do things other knights could, like lift a wagon or move incredibly fast. Maybe each knight could only bond light to one thing? But if that was the case, why could Daylen apparently bond light to any physical attribute? Maybe he wasn't a Lightbinder, but rather something similar yet different?

The constant rushing wind brought Daylen's mind back to what was happening around him. He was falling...and all the power in the world wouldn't count for squat if he became a smear on the ground.

With the continent so far beneath him, it was hard to tell how close he was to its edge. It seemed he was approaching at a good pace, but he was still too high to make out a village or town.

Well I have these powers now, so I might as well use them, Daylen thought and bonded light to his sight. Everything became so much clearer. It was like he could zoom in and see things closer than they were. With his enhanced sight, he quickly found the closest edge-side village.

"Close" was a relative term, for it was very far from him and against the wind. He had already overshot the side of the continent and now fell towards solid ground.

Well that ruins my plans, Daylen thought, and was surprised that he felt disappointed. Even though he wanted to die, surviving this fall was a unique challenge Daylen had set out to achieve, and he *hated* losing.

But from the time he had formulated his plan to land on an Edge Net, he had discovered some significant things, such as these new powers. So, could he use them to survive the fall?

He could bond light into attributes of his body, like his strength and senses, but could he channel light into more specific qualities, like his ability to heal or his weight? Though Daylen had only seen a few Archknights fly, most could jump great distances. Was it by manipulating their weight that they were able to jump so far, or was this due to brute strength?

Daylen cautiously drew in light and tried to bond it to his body's weight with the intent to make himself lighter. Nothing happened.

Thinking, Daylen remembered that weight was itself the result of gravity and he had already tried bonding light to gravity. No, if he wanted to affect his weight by altering an internal property, he would need to alter his *mass*, not his weight. So Daylen tried to will the light he drew in to infuse his mass, with the intent to reduce it.

Daylen suddenly fell faster with a great burst, a strong gust of wind smacking his face, but then Daylen felt his velocity decrease significantly from the wind pushing back against him.

"That was weird," Daylen said. "Why did I get a sudden burst of speed?" At least apart from the initial anomaly, the final result was what he expected. He knew that gravity didn't pull on him any less —gravity pulled on all things at the same rate regardless of their mass—but with less mass, he was effectively lighter, and therefore the drag from the wind affected him to a far greater degree, causing him to fall slower: the very same reason why a feather fell so slowly.

His weight must have changed significantly to produce such an effect, light his body felt like a sail in the wind.

If he reduced his mass like this and then increased the strength of his muscles, bones and fortitude, he might actually survive hitting the ground. It was a risk and would probably hurt like a bastard, but it might work.

"Amazing!" Daylen said, able to hear his voice much better now that he was falling at a slower rate. Light, he sounded like a pup.

Daylen stretched out his arms and legs, creating more drag, and this slowed him even further, almost to a gentle drift.

"But at this rate it'll take two falls to reach the ground…unless it works in reverse."

Daylen tried to switch the path of his light from reducing his mass to increasing it.

Suddenly the wind blowing in his face ceased. For a fraction of a second he had stopped in midair, as attested by his clothes which whipped down.

Then he fell and gained speed rapidly. *Very* rapidly.

"What in Light's end?" Daylen said, trying to understand what had just happened. He was moving fast now, very fast, but why had the initial increase in mass slowed him and the decrease in mass given him a momentary burst of speed?

Maybe increasing his mass was like trying to pick up a boulder from the ground while running past it. If his momentum wasn't enough to overcome his new mass's stationary inertia, he would be brought to a standstill before gravity accelerated him.

"That's it!" Daylen said in realization. "The new mass has no kinetic energy."

And now because Daylen had far greater mass, it took more wind resistance to level out his acceleration from gravity, meaning his terminal velocity was much higher and he fell faster than before.

"This is how I can survive the fall!" Daylen said. But he had to do it just before hitting the ground.

Daylen straightening his body, reducing his drag and increasing his speed dramatically.

Now he would complete the fall *much* faster, easily by half.

Daylen steeled himself and let gravity do its work.

Hours later—Daylen didn't know exactly how long—the ground finally came close.

Having fallen past the clouds, he was now under their cover and found himself amidst a slight drizzle.

With his new plan, Daylen had let himself overshoot the edge of the continent by a large degree. Beneath him, uncultivated fields of grass and trees stretched out as far as he could see in all directions.

So to do the trick that brought me to a near stop, I need to return my mass to normal, or make myself lighter, and then increase it again just before I hit the ground.

Daylen reversed the bond and reduced his mass. He was suddenly given a *huge* burst of speed. The wind resistance hit him like a wall, so much so that he was sent into a flailing spin before he leveled out to the gentle drift he had intended.

Hitting that wind resistance had *not* been pleasant. It had blackened hurt, like his whole body had been slapped, not to mention the stomach-churning spin it had induced.

Daylen rubbed the side of his smarting face. "So if I'm already moving, increasing my mass will slow me, and decreasing it will accelerate me...and I hit the wind resistance like running headlong into a wall. Altering my mass while not moving should do nothing. All good to know."

Daylen stretched out his arms and legs to let the wind slow him.

He eventually leveled out, gently drifting through the air.

The ground was very close now and seemed to approach faster as he fell—not that the speed of his descent was changing, but now that he was closer, Daylen could determine with more accuracy his speed, and he was falling far more quickly than was safe.

Taking a breath, Daylen braced himself, watching the ground race toward him. He had to switch his mass right before hitting.

Closer and closer he came, like a picture constantly increasing in size—and then just before hitting, Daylen switched his bond, increasing his mass instead of decreasing it. It was like he came to an instant stop about two meters from the ground. His jacket whipped down, but he felt no whiplash on his body. A fraction of a second later, he began to fall again from a velocity of nearly zero. He landed on all fours with a heavy thud, his hands and feet sinking ten centimeters into the ground.

He had survived the fall...

That's just. . . Wonderful. Daylen thought with agonizing sarcasm.

Daylen stood and released his bond of light, which returned his weight to normal.

He felt no increase or decrease in his velocity, for he wasn't moving. The inertia of his magical mass and his regular were again in sync.

Daylen had achieved something rather impressive: he had beaten *gravity*. He had fallen the whole height of the world and landed unassisted. No, that wasn't true; he'd had a great amount of assistance. Supernatural assistance from magical powers.

Daylen looked to his hand. It was smeared with dirt, but youthful and strong.

He gazed about. He had landed in the middle of some uncultivated grassy field, patches of small shrubbery poking up everywhere and trees spotting the rolling landscape. The cloud cover moved under the sun, periodically casting shadows which sent chills through Daylen's body. That his clothes were damp from falling through that drizzle didn't help.

Daylen wanted to see his reflection.

He had seen a lake from above that shouldn't be too far from where he had landed so he began walking in its direction.

Once he crested the nearest hill, he saw the lake and discovered that "not too far" from above meant "a few kilometers" on the ground. Still, he made his way to it. He had to know.

Eventually, he arrived at the lake having walked with singleness of mind. He knelt to gaze at his reflection.

A familiar youthful face, one he had not seen in decades, stared back at him. It was his face, his *real* face—not the one that had been marked and soiled by age, but the one he had grown most familiar with over the length of his life, if a little bit more youthful. He looked to be in his late teens.

Was he going crazy? If so, this was one blackened realistic delusion!

Daylen turned and walked up a small hill to a secluded tree. He sat next to it, leaning back with a magnificent view of wild countryside before him, and there he stayed in silence for a long time.

———

By the position of the Plummet, it was now several hours to the time Daylen had fallen from the edge last fall. His own fall had ended up being much quicker thanks to him increasing his mass, with his walk and reflection making up the rest. Oddly enough, he didn't feel tired even though he hadn't slept in more than twenty-four hours. But his mind didn't dwell on that. Apparently Daylen had the powers of an Archknight, and he was young again.

"So now what?" Daylen said softly.

He had only chosen to end his life because he had been falls away from dying anyway. He had no such excuse anymore. Another whole lifetime loomed before him, and it was almost too much to bear. Wasn't twenty years of exile, misery, and regret enough? Even though he felt more depressed than he ever had, his mind still ran the numbers.

He looked to be around seventeen years old. If he was going to live as long as he already had, that would mean he had sixty-five years of life looming before him.

Daylen cradled his head in his hand with the thought. "Oh, Light!" It was a sixty-five-year sentence of misery.

And what should he do with that time? Live in exile like he had before, helping people where he could with his natural skills, and letting his guilt eat away at his soul?

Daylen raised a hand before his eyes and gazed at it.

He had some new skills now, possessed far more than a natural inclination for tinkering and mechanics. He had *power*.

Such a dangerous thing for someone like him, but the Light would not have given him these abilities if it didn't expect him to use them...

A tiny glimmer of hope sparked in Daylen's heart and, even though it was small, his heart had been devoid of light and hope for so long that the feeling nearly made his chest burst.

Tears came to his eyes.

Maybe he had been given a chance to do some true good in the world. How poetic would it be if that good was achieved by destroying darkness of the very like he had spread throughout his life?

A purpose was kindled in Daylen's heart, and it slowly grew into a fire.

"No!" Daylen said, jumping to his feet and beginning to pace. "I've been down this path before. Last time I set out to make the world a better place, I enslaved it!"

Daylen walked back and forth battling with himself before finally stopping. "Then maybe just don't aim so high. Don't lead people. Just remain one man, helping one person at a time and fighting back darkness where I find it."

"I...I could do that and not fall back into darkness, couldn't I?"

Daylen looked to the sun, shading his eyes with a hand from the ever-present Light of the world shining beyond the universe.

That purpose within him burned once more. "If this is what you want of me, very well. I'll live out this life as you would have it... I just hope I'm up to the task."

He had a lot of work ahead of him—a whole lifetime's worth, in fact, and one of the first things to choose was where to start. Hunt down the pirates from the Floating Isles? Fight the crime syndicates? End the human sex trade? After all, who better to hunt out the evil of the world than the vilest man who'd ever lived?

And then of course there was the Shade. Sure, the knights focused on those monsters, but they wouldn't object to some help. Light, Daylen might even join the knights...eventually.

Yes, he did indeed have a lot of work ahead of him.

And surprisingly, Daylen looked forward to it.

CHAPTER FOUR

In Darkness, Lesser Shade are five times stronger and faster than any man; they can fly and see perfectly.
Greater Shade possess the power known as lightblaring, which grants them unique corrupt powers, such as killing plants by mere proximity, controlling dead flesh, taking hold of things and moving them at a distance, hearing others' thoughts, and sending horrifying images directly into others' minds. But being told of something is far different from experiencing it firsthand. I could never communicate accurately the Shade's relentless ferocity, their lack of mercy, and their terrifying hunger for destruction.

Daylen had a new life before him, and a chance to make some form of reparation for his countless crimes, but that was going to attract attention, especially with his powers.

If anyone started digging, they would find out whoever he claimed to be didn't exist on any nation's records, which were all detailed and extensive due to the Shade. Regular people turned into Shade and, by tracking births, deaths, and the population through annual census, something Daylen had pushed himself as a high priority when in power, the nations of the world could get a close approximation to the number people who had gone missing and had likely turned.

With his renewed youth, Daylen resembled his imperial self

once more. Old age had granted him the perfect disguise. That, plus the fact that he would have no recorded identity on any record, would raise some problematic questions. Light, a clever enough person might uncover his true identity. There was enough magic in the world to accept a person might regain their youth, though Daylen had never heard of such a thing. A Lightbringer could sacrifice themselves with their last miracle to bring back the dead; only a single person, true, but if that was possible, why could youth not be returned?

So, Daylen needed to get back to his home and grab those valuables he would take with him, and then head to the capital. There, he would break into the records office and falsify a birth certificate.

He hadn't needed a false birth certificate while living as the old tinker, as by his age it had been clear he had survived the Fourth Night, back when the records were not as complete. But now he looked seventeen, and the records of the current falls were very precise.

Daylen nodded to himself knowing what he had to do.

There looked to be some type of farmstead in the far distance sitting within a valley beyond.

He marched. Daylen expected to struggle as he walked, but his steps came more easily than he ever remembered. Yes, he had already walked over a kilometer to the lake, but he was a little too preoccupied to notice the difference. His old, feeble body was gone, replaced with this new one. He felt strong and full of energy.

"The young have no idea what they have," Daylen said, reveling. He ran. He couldn't remember the last time he had done this, let alone the last time he had even been physically capable of it. It felt incredible. The wind in his face, the healthy exertion of his body. It was like he was truly alive once more.

The burning purpose in his heart and the small joys like this pushed back the darkness somewhat, his guilt a soft weight on his heart, but ever-present.

Daylen eventually tired after a kilometer or so. He could have run for longer, but he wasn't exactly trying to push himself. Instead, he decided to test his powers a little while he walked.

He could channel light into four different attributes simultaneously. It made sense that this magic was called light*binding*, for binding was the most natural way he could describe what he was doing.

Focusing on one of those paths, or bonds, he channeled light into his speed and, having caught his breath, he ran. Wind rushed past him as if he were again riding on Paradan's wagon. He was easily running twice as fast as he had been before.

Stopping, Daylen looked back over the distance he had covered. "Not bad," he said to himself, and then began to think. *Increasing both my speed* and *reflexes will make me unstoppable with a sword.*

"So," Daylen said, speaking to himself, the old habit strong, "four different bonds to four different physical attributes... but can I stack more than one bond to a single attribute?"

Daylen tried to channel two bonds of light to his speed. He could feel the light passing through his body. He ran.

Daylen shot forward at an incredible pace. In fact, this second bond seemed to have doubled the speed he had run with one. The wind stung as it blew past his face and drummed in his ears.

Daylen tried to stop, skipping and sliding along the ground before finally coming to a standstill. He laughed in exhilaration.

"Okay, that was two bonds. Now all four!"

Daylen channeled his light and ran, purposely starting slow and then pushing himself faster and faster. It was *incredible*. The wind resistance acted on him like a weight on his chest, his clothes flapping about so violently that they felt as though they might rip free from his body.

Each step was separated by at least twenty meters, the grass passing under him in a blur. He ran up a rise in the land and, before he realized what he had done, had launched himself into the air like he had run up a ramp. "Whoooooa!" he cried as the wind resistance took control now that he had no traction to apply a counterforce, and he went into an uncontrolled spin.

Everything was a blur and Daylen could think of no way to correct his fall and land safely, so he pulled all his bonds off his speed and funneled the light to his mass, increasing it.

The stationary inertia of his new mass pulled him to a standstill in the air...

Then he fell like a brick.

Dirt exploded around him as he landed on the ground.

Daylen shook his head and, when the dizziness cleared, he found himself lying in a small crater.

"What under the Light?" Daylen said, stunned at the force with which he had hit the ground.

Daylen rolled over and placed a hand under himself, but when he shifted his weight to push himself up, his arm sank into the dirt down to his shoulder.

"My weight!" Daylen said. "I'm using all four bonds this time. Light, I must be as heavy as a whale, which is odd because I don't feel any heavier. Is my strength being increased to compensate for the increased mass?"

Daylen released his bonds and pulled his arm out of the ground before he stepped out of the crater. The hole he had made was about two meters in diameter.

He was covered in dirt, and brushing off his clothes only did so much.

Daylen looked up and traced the path he had taken with a finger, trying to remember the height he had fallen from when his greater mass had stopped him in the air.

"Five or six meters," he said to himself. "From that height and the force of the impact I should have broken some bones at least, but I barely felt anything thanks to the paired augment in my body's durability."

Daylen paced. "But to resist injury I could just increase my fortitude, and then I don't have to worry about greater weight."

Daylen channeled light through each bond, visualizing his fortitude. The light flowed, indicating he had made working bonds. Daylen slapped himself. He felt nothing. He then pinched himself as hard as he could, trying to draw blood. He could sense the touch, but received no injury whatsoever.

Daylen ran to a nearby tree and slammed his forearm into the trunk as hard as he could.

It tingled slightly, but the sensation was nothing close to pain.

"Huh!" Daylen chuckled. "I need a better gauge on what each bond does."

Daylen released his bonds and looked around, finding some boulders and logs nearby. Finding a large rock that he could just barely lift, he found another. Their weights were close enough to make some rough measurements. Daylen went through a process of lifting those large rocks and rock of other sizes with different levels of enhancement to his strength.

He compared those results to the enhancement he received on different attributes.

It turned out that the first bond seemed to enhance different abilities to different levels. One bond to his strength seemed to double it, yet one bond to his eyes enhanced them far more than just double. Each consecutive bond stacked after that, regardless of the attribute, doubled whatever previous enhancement was already achieved—thus, all four bonds enhanced his strength sixteen times as much. Using all four bonds on his sight was different due to the first bond having a greater effect than the single bond on strength had. It was very surreal. With his sight fully enhanced, Daylen could see the individual cell structure of things within five meters to him. And then there was the weird shimmer around everything... It made him dizzy.

"These powers are remarkable," Daylen said to himself once he had finished with his tests.

He thought of the distance he would still have to travel to the farmstead. "I think I have a solution."

Daylen channeled two bonds to his speed. Four was too extreme, as he didn't want to launch himself into the air again.

Though he covered far more distance, he still tired after the same length of time, as if he were running normally.

Daylen stopped and rested his hands on his knees, puffing to catch his breath.

He would need a couple of minutes to recover...or would he?

Daylen channeled all his bonds into healing, and after a second, his energy returned in full. "Nice."

Daylen began running again, but this time channeled a bond to his stamina to maintain his pace for longer. It worked, and this time he didn't seem to tire at all, even with one bond.

He shot across the land like a darkstone-powered coach.

The wind beat on his face, and Daylen could feel his cheeks ripple. His hair pulled behind him, as did his long coat, creating far more drag then he would have guessed.

After several minutes Daylen felt tired; yet this wasn't normal physical fatigue. His body felt fine, yet *something* felt tired—in fact it was harder to maintain the bonds he was channeling.

It was the power itself, Daylen realized. It felt really weird; like an invisible muscle he had never used needing rest. Daylen tried to push on, but with every step it became harder and harder to maintain the bonds, that invisible muscle feeling more and more stress until finally Daylen's bonds simply ceased.

Daylen leaned down and by instinct breathed heavily to try and catch his breath, yet there was no breath to catch. He wasn't winded. He felt he could go on and run with no lightbinding, like he had just woken up from a nap, yet his body was sweating. Some new part of him had been pushed to its limit.

Daylen could still feel the light around him as if it were a physical thing, yet as he tried to draw it in, his legs gave way and he fell to his knees.

"Whoa!" he said as he fell.

That was one of the odder sensations he had ever felt, his body giving way, even collapsing, while feeling physically fine. He got up without a problem.

"There's clearly a limit to how much I can use my powers," he said to himself. Whatever new ability he had that allowed him to draw in light fatigued him when used too long. "Makes sense. These powers are very intuitive."

He would have tried to use his powers in healing to help them recover faster, but at that moment his powers were gone.

Daylen walked on, letting them rest.

He had already crossed a considerable distance with his speed increased, and yet it took the remainder of Low Fall to reach the farm, hiking through uncultivated lands, wild forests, and even a few old ruins.

Before climbing over the post and railing fence that enclosed one of the nearer paddocks to the farmhouse, Daylen tentatively drew on the light. It came with a little resistance.

"So I've recovered a little, but with my power back, can I speed it up?"

He channeled the light into healing, expecting the channeling to get easier as a result. It didn't. "So healing doesn't restore my channeling ability, but can I channel light into my ability to channel and help it recover?" Daylen tried to switch the bond to his channeling ability, willing in his mind the same way he willed the light into other attributes.

The light within him was repelled as powerfully as if he had tried to drop an ice cube into boiling oil, rebounding and hitting the inside of his chest with such force it knocked him off his feet.

Daylen fell on his back like he had just been kicked by a horse, every bit of wind knocked out of him.

He writhed and gasped for air before finally managing to say, "Wow, that was weird."

After a few minutes he had recovered enough to climb to his feet. "Okay," he said, "don't touch the power with the power. Noted."

His chest ached. Daylen cautiously drew in light and channeled it to his healing ability. The light flowed through his body sluggishly, and though he could feel his fatigue disappear, the pain in his chest remained.

"Interesting. I hope I haven't broken something."

Daylen rested on the fence rail for a minute before jumping over it.

The pain spiked with exertion, but he was used to pain.

He rubbed his chest as he walked.

The farmstead comprised a quaint cottage of the old wattle-and-daub type, with a tiled roof, two animal shelters, a wood shack, a chicken coop, and a larger barn.

Smoke rose from the house chimney and flowers bloomed on vines that grew up one of the walls of the house and in garden beds near the door.

It was the morn of High Fall and a man was already up and about chopping wood in front of the shack that housed it.

Daylen approached the young man who, after noticing Daylen, leaned his axe beside the chopping block and waited cautiously.

"Light to you," Daylen said as he got close enough.

The farmer had a swollen face with sharp amber eyes. A rotund belly rested on his waistline, as round as his arms and shoulders. His blood-red hair was streaked with green; no tassel hanging from it. Had Daylen fallen into the western border of Frey?

"And light to you, lad," the farmer said in a voice as deep as his Freysian accent, which answered Daylen's question.

He calls me lad, *and the man's nothing but a pup. Who does this disrespectful sunspot think he... Oh.*

To Daylen, the man looked young enough to be his grandson—maybe forty years old—but to everyone else, Daylen himself was nothing but a hormone-addled teen. This was going to take some getting used to.

"What brings you here so early in the fall?" the farmer asked.

Daylen couldn't exactly say he had just fallen from the continent without prompting a deluge of questions.

"Well, out with it! I have work to be about."

His condescending tone almost provoked a good tongue lashing, but Daylen held back—barely. "I...um... I'm lost."

"You look it. Truly, boy, did you take a walk through the brambles or something?"

"Boy? Boy! I'm no more a *boy* than you are a goat! Why I'm old enough to be... Well, I'm plenty old, all right," Daylen finished lamely.

"Aye," the farmer said, nodding in understanding. "I was once your age, too..."

No, you most certainly have never *been my age*, Daylen thought.

"My son's going through the same thing. Wants more respect, yet shirks responsibility." The man turned and yelled, "Gaidan, you out of bed? Your chores are still needing to be done!"

"I'm sorry, sir," Daylen said. "I've had a long and complicated few falls and all I seek is a bed to rest in. Could I impose upon you for that, just for a fall?"

"Well, you're polite enough when you think to be," the man said, "and you're clearly in some need. Come, I'll show you a bed."

Daylen was shown to a loft in the farmer's barn, where two low beds sat.

"This is where my brother and I sleep when he and his wife visit. It should serve well enough."

Yep, most definitely a Freysian. That this man would give his brother's wife his own bed in the house when they visited confirmed it, what with how women were revered in their culture.

"Thank you, and my name is Daylen."

"I'm Taigo. Get some sleep and I'll find you something to eat when you wake."

Daylen fell asleep as soon as his head hit the pillow, and awoke a good twelve hours later with the sound of rain falling on the shingled roof of the barn.

Daylen rose from the cot-like bed and, looking down from the loft, saw that the animals had been brought in for the low.

Two milking cows stared at him in a way that said he wasn't welcome.

Feeling at his chest, Daylen was pleased to find the pain gone. He stretched out his hand and felt for the light. With the overcast from the rain and the cover of the barn, there was barely any light to be felt.

Daylen tried to draw in what he could, and his ability to do so responded instantly.

"Looks like they've recovered," he said, but he noted how sluggish the light came in when trying to channel in such a dark place.

Daylen bound the light to his strength and found that he would not be able to make any additional bonds without more light.

He stepped from the loft and fell four meters before landing easily.

One of the cows mooed in surprise, stumbling away.

Walking to the single door built into the two larger double doors of the barn, Daylen stepped outside.

The barn roof had an eave large enough for there to be some shelter from the rain adjacent to the wall outside.

The day was so overcast that fall that Daylen could see glowing light shining out of the cottage's windows from the sunstones within. Most people of the world despised this type of overcast, feeling it was too like the night. This showed they knew nothing about what true night was like. Overcast falls like this simply showed what a regular fall was like in the desolate Shadowlands, where the southern end of the continent sat under the shadow of itself causing little to grow and therefore was uninhabited.

He would have left the farm that very moment if not for how hungry he was. Taigo's offering of food was too much for him to deny.

Daylen ran through the rain to the cottage, knocking on the door.

Taigo opened it. "Come in, lad, before you get soaked."

Daylen's teeth grated at being called a lad, but he did so.

He walked into a brightly lit home, the light feeling wonderful. The cottage's kitchen lay directly to his right, the family's dining table to his left, where Taigo's whole family was sitting. A sitting room and laundry sat beyond the other rooms with bedrooms on the upper floors.

"Oh, you're having dinner. Sorry, I'll..."

"No, my wife has invited you to join us."

Taigo's wife, a very large woman with breasts the size of melons, sat at the head of the table, like all proper Freysian households. Her scarlet-red hair was tied in a bun, her rosy round cheeks and smile so warm they might dry Daylen's clothes on their own.

Two young girls sat at the table's left, a shuttered window at their back, and giggled whenever they looked at Daylen. One was on her way to being as plump as her parents, but the other was uncharacteristically skinny for this family, which meant she was only slightly thick of neck.

Across the table from the girls sat an older boy, very much the image of his father in girth and face. A bare seat was next to him, awaiting Daylen.

"With your blessing, Matron," Daylen said, bowing to the wife.

Her smile deepened at that, and she nodded.

Daylen took his seat with Taigo doing the same.

"By the looks of you I thought you were Hamahran," the wife said.

"I am, Matron."

"But you call me Matron with all the respect of a native-born Freysian."

"I know a lot about Frey and the world." *Light, I ruled most of it once.*

"You're a credit to your parents, then. I'm Luciana. This is Aliciana, Mariana, and Gaidan."

The pup next to Daylen, Gaidan, glanced to him and nodded. "Hi," he said, with a level of familiarity that caught Daylen off guard.

"Uh, hi," Daylen said back.

"Which part of Hamahra you from?" Gaidan asked. He must have been eighteen years old.

"The Trireme Prefecture of old Sunsen. A small town named Karadale, about a hundred kilometers east of Treremain."

"I know of Sunsen," Gaidan said. "Treremain sounds familiar, too."

"You're leagues from home, lad," Taigo said.

Daylen cringed inwardly at the use of that unit of measurement. The "league" had been used to represent so many values over the past that it was now completely unreliable, but Daylen guessed the farmer was using it in the more modern and unofficial way to mean one thousand kilometers.

Taigo continued, "How did you come all the way to Frey, and to Baisen, by all that's good? There's no main road here from the west."

"No offense, Taigo, but that's my business."

"It is," Luciana said. "Taigo, you should mind your manners."

"Sorry, my wife."

Luciana saved them from awkward silence by asking Aliciana, the larger of the daughters, to bless the food.

According to Freysian religion, called Matriology, because women gave birth, they possessed a sliver of creation and thereby shared some of the Godmother's own power, which was why only women could offer blessings. In Daylen's opinion this was contradicted by the fact that men and women could receive divine powers as Lightbringers.

According to Matriology, women created life and men took life, both necessary acts as they saw it. A devout Matrian woman wouldn't even uproot a craggot or pull a fruit from a tree and thereby end its life—that was the duty of a man. But as women created life, they were also the caretakers of life and they would see to raising the children, keeping their house in order and pleasing their husbands. This meant they would prepare the food after it had been killed, and Light help anyone who got in the way of a Matrian woman and her kitchen.

Everyone bowed their heads as Aliciana spoke, though she giggled once when sneaking a peek at Daylen.

Light, that was annoying.

"I bless this food that it will be healthy to our bodies and souls and dedicate it to all that is good."

Daylen joined them all in repeating the words, "To all that is good."

Taigo eyed him as the younger sister served the stew. "You're a Matrian?" he asked.

"No," Daylen said, "but dedicating anything to all that is good is something I'm all too happy to do."

"Hmm, would you object to learning more of Matriology? My

wife is ordained."

"Sorry, I'm a Lightseeker."

"But Lightseeking has a blatant hole in its doctrine," the Matron said.

"So I've heard. You believe there must be a specific act to purify someone of their sins…"

"Only after they repent," Taigo interjected.

"Yes," Daylen said. "And Matrians disagree with Lightseekers, who believe the Light can forgive sin by its own power without the need for a cleansing ordinance…as little objection anyone would have to Mariology's *cleansing ordinance.*"

"You mean the sacrament, which can only be properly performed in marriage," Taigo said, pointing with his spoon.

Mariana passed Daylen a bowl of stew, which he took with a nod of gratitude.

"Yeah, but you can't tell me it's not enjoyable," Daylen said.

That comment made Aliciana and Mariana blush. Gaidan huffed a chuckle.

"As it should be," Luciana said. "Redemption is a joyful thing, the very reason the Godmother made the sacrament so. And the cleansing of sin is not about power. The Godmother has all power and could make it that trees simply appear in the world fully grown. And yet she has seen fit that trees grow in the way that she has prescribed, as she has with cleansing the corruption that sin leaves within us."

Daylen swallowed a spoonful of stew. Light, it was good. You could always trust plump people to make good food. "I can agree that the Light will prescribe what it sees fit, including what one must do to be redeemed…or what one must suffer for their sins." Daylen's expression must have conveyed a measure of his feelings on the matter, for Taigo and Luciana looked at each other in concern. "Anyway," Daylen said, "we could discuss this through the fall and get nowhere. There's enough disagreement within Matriology's own denominations to prove that. You and your husband are clearly Matrian Orthodox, as Taigo claimed the sacrament only cleanses sin in proper marriage. There's enough Spousums throughout Frey that proclaim a different interpretation."

Luciana scowled. "They're glorified whorehouses."

The son, Gaidan, stifled a childish laugh.

Luciana turned to him. "And if you ever visit one of them, I'll cut off your manhood!"

"I know, Mother. You tell me whenever they're mentioned."

"Yes, and may the Godmother see that you remember."

They all returned to the food, only the casual comment or question breaking the silence.

"Remember to keep Daylen's bowl full, Mariana," Luciana said to her daughter. "When married, it'll be your honor to see that your men and boys are fed. Daylen's a growing boy, after all, and he needs his strength."

There was too much intention in Luciana's eyes as she said that, clearly weighing up Daylen as husband material.

Marianna refilled his bowl and handed it back to Daylen, who was all too happy to have another serving. Light, he was hungry.

The girls giggled once more while looking at Daylen and he snapped, slamming his hand on the table while glaring at the little nits. "What in Light's Reach is so blackened funny?"

"Now, now!" Luciana said angrily. "You'll watch your tongue under my roof."

Feeling both shame and resentment at being addressed so by a lowly farmer, Daylen forced out an awkward apology. "I'm sorry, Matron. My temper can get away from me."

If this woman knew who Daylen really was, she would piss herself and then run to the hills with her family.

"Tis a failing all young men have, I'm afraid," the woman said with a glance to her son. "Now, girls, why don't you answer young Daylen's question."

Taigo sat there silently, but seemed to be enjoying the drama.

The girls blushed and squirmed in their seats. "Um, nothing's funny."

"Then I expect to hear no more laughter from the two of you."

"Yes, Mother."

Everyone returned to their meals until Taigo asked Daylen another question.

"Your parents must be worried about you, being so far from home."

Too many questions. There was no real harm with these simple folk, but if anyone more official pried like this, there could be trouble.

Daylen needed to reach the capital sooner rather than later.

For now, he spoke the truth. "My parents are dead."

"How do you take care of yourself?" Luciana asked.

"I fix things. Most people call me a tinker."

Luciana swallowed a mouthful of stew. "Ah, a tinker. You must be good with your hands and have a sharp head to make enough money from such a trade."

"I get by."

"I hope you would tell us if you were in some form of trouble."

"No, not really."

Luciana looked at Daylen, a bit stunned. "Very well. You're welcome to stay for as long as you need, so long as you work."

Daylen looked outside and was relieved to see the rain letting up. "Thank you, Matron, but I'll be heading out after dinner. And thank you for the food. It's delicious."

Luciana beamed. "Follow the road heading east. That will take you to Aidra's Brook, a small village, but the weekly coach is two falls past. You'll have to make your way to Bukenbright along the main road. It's about a four-hour walk."

"Then that's where I'll head."

Taigo nodded to Daylen. "Now, lad, you should be carrying a sword while you travel."

These "lad" comments were getting old, and of course Daylen knew he should be travelling with a sword. Light, people weren't this condescending when his appearance matched his age. No wonder the boy next to him seemed disgruntled with his parents.

"I don't have one," Daylen said, trying to mask his annoyance.

"I can see that," Taigo said, scraping his spoon along the bottom of his fourth bowl and eating the last bit. He rose and walked to the corner of the dining room where an old chest lay buried under rugs, brooms, and whatever else this home wanted out of the way. "We've had some trouble with hillcats this summer. Now, they shouldn't pose much danger unless they're particularly hungry. Still, you should watch yourself on the road. Aside from hillcats, you might come across some wild dogs, and there's even tale of drakes flying down and grabbing people."

If they were going to lecture others, something they were more willing to direct at youth apparently, they might as well get their facts right. "Drakes don't come down to the surface," Daylen said matter-of-factly. "It's too far from the shrubs that grow on the underside of the continent."

"Shrubs?"

"That's what they eat. Drakes are herbivores."

"But the stories?"

"Myths told to scare little children."

"Oh, I didn't know." Taigo was silent for a second before pulling the chest out. "In any case, you need to be careful. Apart from what I said, bandits roam the hills and that *ain't* a story."

Taigo opened the chest and retrieved three old broadswords, one with a basket hilt, and the other two having the more common swept hilt comprised of quillons, loops, side rings, sweepings, and knuckle guard.

Daylen glanced to the side door of the home, where five other swords, in better condition, hung sideways on a rack, one for each member of the family: two backswords, a broadsword, a longsword, and a warsword. Ever since the Second Night fell over a thousand years ago, most people of the world realized that Nights weren't one-off events. Since that time, every man, woman, and child owned a weapon and was taught how to use it in preparation for the oncoming dark. These falls it would be extremely odd to see a home of any nation that didn't have a weapon for each person who lived in it, if not more.

Like Hamahra, Frey had a strong dueling culture, but the people didn't wear tassels to mark their victories.

Taigo pulled each sword out of its sheath and inspected their blades. Each one was in some state of disrepair. He picked the best and handed it to Daylen.

"It's an old sword and not too sharp at that, but it'll do the job."

"Thank you," Daylen said, taking the blade. Having a sword at his side was like a river having water flowing through it; it was just *right*. "I don't suppose it has a name?"

Luciana huffed. "It if did, it's long since forgotten. Anyway, I'd say that sword isn't grand enough to bear a name."

"Any sword that's saved a person's life deserves a name."

"Don't know if it ever has," Taigo said. "You're free to name it whatever you like."

"I might," Daylen said, rising. "Thank you for the meal and bed," he said, before placing a dun on the table.

"That's not necessary," Luciana said. "Common decency isn't worth coin."

"You're right, it's not," Daylen said, leaving both the home and his coin before they could reply.

CHAPTER FIVE

*I fought in countless battles through the Fourth Night. Worse, I
saw countless companions and friends become Shade themselves,
my parents included, whom I was forced to kill. Yes, I killed my
parents with my own sword—though in truth it was the Shade
that killed them. The monsters I destroyed only had the faintest
resemblance to my parents.
Still, it didn't make the task any easier.*

Daylen hadn't walked far from the farmstead before he heard
footsteps.

He turned to see Luciana's son running toward him.

"Is something wrong?" Daylen asked.

"What? No," the large boy said. "I…um… I'm coming with you."

"What? Light's end, you're not!"

"You don't own the road."

"Boy, it's your bedtime. Go back to your mother."

"Who you calling *boy*? You look younger than me."

"No I don't, boy! Now piss off."

The lad drew his sword on Daylen. "You watch your tongue."

"Put that away before you hurt yourself."

"You're disrespecting me and the hospitality my mother has
shown you."

"No, letting you run away would be disrespecting your mother, you ungrateful little twat!"

Gaidan raised the leg facing Daylen and he stomped it down in a dueling pose—the Freysian way to challenge.

"Oh, light's end," Daylen said tiredly.

"Draw your sword! Fight me!"

"No. That might ruffle my shirt."

"That's it!" Gaidan screamed and lunged at Daylen.

A second later, maybe two, Gaidan lay on the ground with a bleeding lip, unarmed. Daylen held the boy's sword in hand, not even having drawn his own. He hadn't thought to use his new powers, either, not that he'd needed them.

He had already found that his fighting instincts were still keen when he had fought Paradan, but now with his body as fit and as strong as it had ever been... Light, he was back to being a full Grand High Master of the sword.

"What... What just happened?" Gaidan said, dazed from his instantaneous defeat.

"You got what your light-blinded head deserved," Daylen said. "As you challenged me to a duel and lost, I'm keeping your sword. Victor's right, and all."

It was the same type of sword as Daylen's, but in far better condition. Daylen threw the old sword to the boy's feet.

"Now go back to your mother."

"But she doesn't respect me, and when I saw you, that you're on your own, all free and being the same age..."

"I AM OLDER THAN YOU CAN IMAGINE!"

Gaidan flinched again. "You got me thinking, that's all," he said. "I-I just wants to come with you."

"Look, you want respect, you want to be a man, I get that. But from what I've seen, an immature snot like yourself doesn't deserve *any* respect. You don't *demand* respect..."

Daylen paused at that comment as a torrent of memories flashed before his eyes, memories where he had forced respect and obedience through violence and brutality. He was such a hypocrite. What right did *he* have to tell another how to live their life when he had lived his own so poorly? But the truth was the truth, and it condemned him as well as the actions of this whelp.

"You're supposed to earn respect," Daylen said, looking back to the boy, "through sweat, hard work, and decency, just like your father. You want to be a man? Then fulfill the responsibility you have to your family and obey your mother while you live under her roof. Trying to leave them like you have, probably without even a word? It's despicable, and proves you're no better than a worm. Your parents are good people, and you should thank the Light for that. Do as they say, you little snot, and maybe, just maybe, if the Light is gracious, you'll become half as good as them."

The large boy's lip quivered and he tried to hold back tears.

"Now, as I said before, PISS OFF!"

This time he did, thank the Light. Daylen sighed to himself and shook his head. "Kids."

He turned and began walking down the road, but noticed off to the side that work had begun for clearing ground for another field.

Many trees lay toppled next to their sawn stumps, some having been dragged to the side of the budding paddock. A laborious process, especially if done without darkstone automation, of which Daylen saw no sign.

"I'll do good where I can," Daylen said to himself as he took off his coat, vest, and shirt. Bare to his waist, Daylen couldn't help noticing that every scar he had ever received still remained, and having been a swordsman his whole life, there were a lot of them.

"So I still possess the same body," Daylen said to himself. "Just changed." He noticed that his body was as muscled as it had been in his thirties, not his teens. "Restored to its peak strength...interesting."

Folding his clothes on top of one another and placing them on a dry part of the ground, Daylen jumped the ditch that bordered the packed dirt road and onto the grassy field.

Channeling all bonds to his strength, Daylen placed himself at the center of mass of a fallen tree, placed one hand over the trunk, the other under, and rolled the entire thing onto his shoulder, lifting it.

It didn't feel heavy at all.

He smiled giddily at his incredible power. He carried each felled tree from the field one by one.

After that he walked to the nearest stump and punched the grass next to it. Getting his hand under the stump, he pulled. Daylen ripped it up with its adjoining root system with ease.

He carried the stump to the same pile as the trunks and

repeated the process with each stump until the area was fully cleared.

A water barrel sat near the border of the field with some stools and an old firepit, clearly placed there so Taigo could find drink while he worked the field.

Daylen dunked his head in it, drinking deeply. He then washed his dirty body. Retrieved his shirt, vest, and coat, he walked topless for a time, letting the sun dry him off before dressing fully.

The nearest village was a picturesque little thing nestled within thin woodland next to a small river.

Walking by the homes and crossing a bridge, Daylen found the main road that led to the larger town where he could find a coach to the nearest city.

After an hour or so, Daylen found himself thinking about different applications of his new powers.

"There's clearly more they can do," he said, looking about.

Luckily, no one was near. He didn't want people to know that he had these powers just yet, especially considering he wasn't an Archknight.

Posing as an Archon might be a good idea if anyone saw him with his powers, but Light, what would the knights do when they learned about him?

They'd probably force him to join them so long as they never found out who he really was, which Daylen was already considering. If there was anybody who could teach him about the full extent and limitations of his powers, it was the Archknights.

But Daylen would join when *he* wanted to.

Walking to the side of the road, Daylen counted the attributes he had enhanced. Strength, speed, mass, sight, hearing, healing, smell, and fortitude.

Drawing his sword, Daylen sliced his thumb along the blade. It stung, of course, but pain was something Daylen had gotten very used to over his life.

Stacking all bonds to his body's ability to heal, the cut closed in a matter of seconds.

"Fast," he said to himself. "But will it be as fast with worse injuries?" Daylen pulled up the sleeve of his jacket and shirt and drew the sword blade along his forearm, cutting all the way to the bone.

He didn't hesitate or flinch at the pain.

Blood flowed out, but as soon as he channeled light through his bonds to heal, the large wound closed after three seconds—leaving no scar at all.

"Oh, this is going to be *very* useful. I wonder if I could regrow a limb?" He shook his head. "It's probably not a good idea to test that."

Daylen knew that there had to be a limit to this healing ability, as he had seen Archons die. Light, he had killed one himself many years ago, indicating that Archons couldn't heal from decapitation.

Daylen enhanced his scent. The first bond enhanced it to a huge level, far more than just double, and each subsequent bond seemed to double what the previous enhancement had achieved. With all four bonds channeling light into his scent, Daylen could smell that a darkstone-powered wagon bearing craggots and turem beans had passed along the road two falls ago. There had been one person who had been driving the wagon who smelled of dirt, oil and wore cotton clothes. Daylen could smell a man's *clothes* from two falls ago! There were also other scents, new ones that he'd never smelled before, one coming from himself. It smelled sweet, yet soft, and as he breathed in, focusing on the scent, Daylen instinctively realized what it was: Emotion. Daylen was *smelling* his own emotion.

"But how can I know that? Yet I do. That smell is curious amazement. These powers, it's like they also give me new instincts!"

With all bonds channeling light into his scent, Daylen could actually smell emotion!

Such discoveries like this only propelled Daylen to find out more.

The last time Daylen enhanced his hearing it hadn't gone so well; but now with no winds rushing past him, it should work better. One bond doubled the volume of every sound around: the wind passing through the trees, the cracking of the branches, and the soft breathing of some animal behind a tree. Daylen focused on that sound and as he did so every other sound faded, to the point that the soft breathing became clear and distinct. A canine-like panting, he discerned—one of those wild dogs Taigo had mentioned. The clarity was amazing.

Daylen picked up a stone and threw it at the tree the dog was hiding behind. The crack spooked the thing, and it scampered away. It was nothing to worry about unless it was part of a pack, and then only if they were particularly hungry.

Daylen could hear everything around him. The footsteps of an ant at his feet, the soft voices of Taigo and Luciana several kilometers away. Daylen focused on them and their voices became as clear as if they were speaking right next to him. Judging by the moans of pleasure, he heard that the couple were in the middle of their cleansing ordinance.

"Okay, that's a mental image I didn't need."

Daylen released his bonds and channeled one into his mass to make himself lighter. This first reduction was far greater than just halving his weight. Using two bonds seemed to make him weigh nothing at all, for as soon as the wind picked up, he was picked up, literally. Then a stronger gust of wind blew past him, launching him into the air, where he flew a good ten meters flailing uselessly before his clothes pulled him back down and he crashed to the ground.

Daylen returned his weight to normal. "Okay, that was weird—and with only two bonds. Four bonds might be dangerous... and stupid..." Daylen smiled to himself. "Then it's a good thing I'm stupid."

He ran to a wide tree to use as a wind shield and channeled two bonds, reducing his mass. Then he channeled a third, and nothing happened. Daylen shrugged and added the forth.

His clothes fell off.

No—his clothes fell *through* him, and he was standing completely naked, half translucent! He was literally see-through. Walking forward, Daylen raised his hands before staring at them in shock.

"This is very, very weird."

Daylen noticed his feet sinking into the ground. No depressions were being made; they were just disappearing into the ground!

"Light!" Daylen screamed, releasing the bonds...and then his feet exploded.

His feet *literally exploded*! A force hit him with such strength that it blew off the rest of his legs. Dirt, blood, flesh, and bone flew in every direction.

The rest of Daylen was launched head over heels—well, his heels were gone, but he spun several times through the air regardless, butt-naked and legless, before crashing to the ground screaming in pain.

Without even willing it, Daylen's body sucked in light like he was a drowning man gasping for air and channeled it through every bond inside him toward healing.

Daylen groaned in horror at seeing nothing but bloody stumps past his hips, but his fears were replaced with morbid amazement as he watched his legs slowly grow back.

It took several minutes for Daylen to find his voice. "Now *that's* a sight! And it answers my question about regrowing limbs."

It took about ten minutes for his legs to grow back completely. Once they had, Daylen wiggled his new toes.

"Okay, reducing mass past two bonds is *bad*. Very, *very* bad!"

Daylen stood and looked at where his feet had exploded. There was a crater in the ground about four meters in diameter, dirt and flesh flung all around.

"Wow," he said, and then began to laugh. "This is just too good!" Having his feet blown off wasn't at all shocking to him; he had lived too long and seen too much to be shocked by blood or injury.

Daylen walked to his clothes and shook off the countless little clumps of dirt and flesh that covered them, wondering at the specifics of what had just happened.

It was like he had lost physical interaction. Was that what happened when mass all but disappeared?

Daylen could guess why his feet had exploded when he had released his bonds. Matter couldn't occupy the same location as other matter.

"Well I was right, that *was* stupid," he said, pulling on his pants.

Having finished dressing, he walked back to the road.

"So that was reducing my mass, but how heavy can I make myself?"

The first bond increased his weight far more than just double, and like everything else, each subsequent bond seemed to double the previous enhancement. At full, the hard-packed road couldn't support his weight and he sunk up to his ankles.

Light, he had missed doing in-depth research like this. It reminded him of the months he had spent studying the device he discovered at the centre of the Floating Isles.

"I'd better hold off making myself this heavy when on softer ground," Daylen said, looking at his sunken feet. He must have weighed over five tons!

Daylen released his bonds and stepped out of the holes his feet had made.

The more he delved into how his powers worked, the more he figured out. Still, Daylen had seen Archknights cast lightning from their hands and control the wind. Maybe he could do such things and maybe he couldn't. The only way to find out was to keep testing.

Putting on his boots and standing, Daylen clapped his hands together and rubbed them back and forth smiling in delight. "All right, what's next?"

CHAPTER SIX

*None but those who lived through the Fourth Night know how
hopeless it was. I can only assume the previous Nights were the
same, but as they lasted much longer I can't imagine how
mankind survived. Without the Lightbringers and Archknights,
everything would have been lost.*

Daylen spent the next hour getting used to his powers until
they were drained.

"Well, that ends that," he said, returning to the road. "Seems like
I can maintain an hour of full channeling with all bonds." He most
certainly wasn't going to try and heal his fatigued channeling
ability again, what with how it went last time. *Don't bond the power
to itself.*

It took several more hours of walking before he arrived at the
next town. There, he caught a skycoach to the nearest city, the fare
taking his last coin.

By necessity, skycoaches were built differently to their wheel-
bound cousins, as they required a darkstone core and directional
drivers, as with a larger skyship. The coach he flew in was of a less
common design where the cabin was affixed underneath the core.
This made boarding the small ship easier, because when it was
grounded, the entrance was a single step up. Coaches that had
their cores underneath required a gangplank or fold-down stairs.

Daylen arrived at a city named Laybourn by the end of low fall, tired and hungry.

The city was distinctly Freysian, where the buildings were either plastered white or made of lighter shades of brick and stone, casting the buildings in hues of cream and pale brown, a byproduct of Frey's warmer climate. They all had flat-tiled roofs. Streets were paved in distinctive Freysian pale-brown stone, and they often bordered retaining walls, setting the city into differing elevations through the hilly religion where it was located.

With no money to purchase food, Daylen walked a decent way from the main station where the coach had docked and found a clean enough alley to sleep in. The alley was much colder, being in the shade of two buildings, but not so much to be prohibitive. As long as it didn't rain, he would be fine.

When he had ruled the Dawn Empire, there had been thousands of people who wanted him dead, so Daylen had trained himself to sleep very lightly. He wouldn't rouse from the wind or other natural noises, but the slightest hint of a footstep or breathing would wake him instantly. Doing so had saved his life many times, and living in hiding for the latter end of his life had only served to encourage the practice.

It didn't take him long to fall asleep, but a few hours later he was awoken by the sound of someone approaching.

No, they weren't approaching; they had already approached, and were looming over him—dagger in hand.

Daylen's hand shot up on reflex, grabbing the man's wrist as he tried to slit Daylen's throat.

He was a dirty beggar, obviously intending to loot Daylen's corpse, and he was strong. The beggar pushed all his weight down on Daylen, the dagger now pointed to Daylen's heart.

Daylen struggled against the man's weight, the dagger falling centimeter by centimeter. Strength against strength wasn't working, so Daylen twisted the man's wrist and brought his knee up, knocking the man off. He stumbled to regain his footing. Daylen took the brief opportunity to get to his feet and draw his sword. With that, the man was already defeated. Before the wretch could do anything, in a quick flash of steel Daylen took the man's hand cleanly off.

He screamed, falling to his knees, his uninjured hand grasping at a bleeding stump.

Rage burned inside Daylen as hot as he had trained it to, eighty years of conditioning snapping into action, channeling the rage and using it to strengthen his resolve. "You dayless son of a Shade!" Daylen hissed.

The man tried to get to his feet and run, but as he did, Daylen slashed the tendons behind his knees. He screamed again and fell.

"Try to slit my throat and rob me! *Me*! I've conquered nations, and you think a dagger from the likes of *you* will be my end?"

The man dragged himself along the ground, whimpering and trying to get away.

Daylen thrust his sword through the beggar's back, purposefully avoiding vital organs.

The man screamed.

Daylen pulled the sword free and walked in pace with the struggling sunspot.

As the man grasped at the open wound on his chest, he tried to get to his feet once more. Daylen sliced off the beggar's uninjured arm with a large swing.

The vagabond's horrified screams brought a measure of satisfaction to Daylen, but his punishment wasn't done—he was still breathing.

Daylen grasped the man by his hair and hefting him up, growled in fury and cut off his head. Daylen then took up the man's dagger and, screaming again, bashed the man's decapitated head against the wall of the alley before thrusting the dagger through the eye, pinning the head to the wall as a sign of what became of people who dared try to kill Dayless the Conqueror.

With the beggar now dead, the punishment served, Daylen's rage began to melt away, and he leaned against the other wall of the alley.

Footsteps caused Daylen to notice a young man peeking down the alleyway, obviously attracted by the screams. Daylen glared at him and the man bolted.

Starring after the man for a little while, Daylen shook his head and looked back to the alley, truly seeing it for what it was.

It was a massacre.

Daylen suddenly realized what he had done. He had not just defended himself, he had not just killed a man, he had *butchered* him. Horror overwhelmed Daylen as the reality finally settled into his mind.

"No," Daylen said in dismay as tears came to his eyes. "No, I don't want to be like this anymore! Not anymore!"

Daylen wept as he slumped against the wall and slowly slid down to lay there, crying.

He had set out to be a better person but it had only taken the length of two falls to prove that he was in every way the same man he had been.

A violent, merciless killer.

Voices of alarm sounded from down the alleyway. The authorities were finally on their way.

Daylen dragged himself to his feet, breathed in deeply, and ran away.

Daylen made his way to the other end of Laybourn and found himself on a broad open main street with crowds of people walking on either side. Carts, wagons, carriages and coaches were driving down the middle, storefront and food stalls framing the sides.

Daylen's stomach growled at the smells from the food stalls, but he ignored it.

Light, he was a fool. He shouldn't have expected anything else from sleeping in a city's alleyway. Perhaps living as a hermit for twenty years had dulled his wits.

He wanted to be alone and wished he could fly up to one of the building's roofs. He liked high places and commanding views, especially when thinking.

Hang on—of course I can get up there, my powers! Daylen had utterly forgotten about his powers; even when he was attacked he hadn't thought to use them. That wasn't a surprise; using them didn't come naturally to him yet.

Daylen sighed and turned down one of the alleyways. Paved with brick, it was wide enough for carts to pass through so they could load and unload goods, and the tall buildings on either side cast it in soft shadow.

From there, Daylen found an even narrower alley that ran behind one of the storefronts.

Daylen wondered at how he could employ his powers to reach

the roof. Could he make himself lighter and climb? Daylen placed his hand against the brick wall to test the fingerholds.

"Not enough grip…but grip is a quality of my physical body."

Daylen tried to draw in light, but only found a trickle. It was like dragging something very heavy along the ground.

"The shadows," Daylen said, remembering when he had tried to channel in Luciana's barn. The world was usually so full of light that Daylen had taken for granted that he would always be able to use his powers, but clearly in shadow and, of course, darkness, he wouldn't.

He should have realized this, for he had seen the Archknights fight through the Fourth Night and how they had relied on sunstones and Lightbringers to fuel their powers in such darkness.

Luckily there was still enough light in the alley to forge one bond. He channeled it to his grip. As he touched the wall, it was like his hand was covered in glue. It resisted all but the strongest of pulls to come off, and that was with only one bond.

Daylen looked up the wall and tried to make another bond to his weight, but couldn't. There simply wasn't enough light.

Still, with his grip enhanced so much, he was able to climb up the wall like a spider; and interestingly, his feet were affected the same as his hands, even through the soles of his shoes.

The roof was mostly flat-tiled, with countless chimneys sticking up over the cityscape before him.

Daylen walked to the low peak of the roof and sat down, thinking.

He had just killed a man. Not the first by a day's length, but the first in twenty years.

"He tried to murder me," Daylen muttered to himself. "That was why I didn't hesitate to kill him. But I did more than that. I let my rage take control and tortured the wretch before ending his life. But the beggar probably had murdered many people before trying to kill me…so the scum deserved what I gave him and more." Daylen looked at his hands. "The problem is how easy it was."

That was more troubling than Daylen could express.

If he could fall into a blind rage so quickly, he could do so against a person that didn't deserve it and pervert the purpose of his new life.

Daylen had done so in the past, had killed the innocent too

many times to count, though he hadn't believed them innocent at the time. In any case, Daylen was certainly capable of such acts.

Was this all a mistake? Choosing to hunt out darkness meant he would have to kill again, and when a man was willing to kill, he might resort to it when killing wasn't justified.

"Maybe I should never touch a sword again and help people in the little ways I have, tinkering and such."

But that didn't reach a fraction of Daylen's potential. How many Grand High Masters of the Sword were there who were also master tacticians and could wield the power of the Archknights? Daylen had a very unique and specific skill set that would be best employed against the worst and most vile parts of the world. Indeed, there was more of a need for someone to fight for those who couldn't than anything else. There were those who preyed on the defenseless, the innocent and the weak, and Daylen had great power to stop such things. *Save one person at a time.*

It was far better for him to face the horrors of the world than to expose the innocent to them. Daylen had faced such before; Light, he had even caused many. His innocence had been destroyed long ago, and with that there was nothing left that he could lose to another life of violence.

So maybe it could be a good thing that killing was still so easy for him.

He could do what better men couldn't, be the avenging knife in the dark. That was the greatest and most significant thing he could do for others, and indeed the skills he had and the type of man he was all but demanded it.

Daylen's head dropped and shoulders slumped. "Will I never know peace?" he said softly. "I've killed *so* many, and I *hate* it… But life isn't something I deserve to enjoy."

Resolve returned to Daylen's heart. "This is what I have to do… but I won't let myself darken the world any more than I have. So I vow upon the Light that if I ever kill another innocent, I will kill myself." Daylen looked to the sun. "I don't care if you want to punish me. Protecting the world from the Conqueror is more important than my misery, so if you really want me to live, help me." Daylen bowed his head and closed his eyes, speaking fervently from the depths of his heart. "Save me from myself."

CHAPTER SEVEN

When in battle, the Shade are relentless and care not for injury or loss. A Shade would sacrifice itself in an instant if it could but kill a single person, and thus through baiting and feints, we finally turned the tide. But don't misunderstand me: the Shade never retreat. We only claimed back what was lost by killing every last one in each battle, at great cost. It seems the Shade are physically unable to surrender, and I lost count of the times I should've died to a wound if not for the healing powers of a Lightbringer.

D aylen's stomach growled.

Standing, he walked to the edge of the building and gazed down to the busy street and the food stalls beneath.

He had no money, but that didn't mean he couldn't get what he needed. Do a few chores for some shop owner for a quick meal.

As Daylen walked along the edge of the ten story building the tiles he stepped on broke loose and slid out from under his feet. Daylen lost his footing completely. "Crap!" he yelled as his legs shot off the side of the roof.

Flustered by the sudden trip, Daylen quickly remembered his powers and reacted by increasing his balance and speed. But his feet weren't on anything, and before he realized that increasing his balance would do nothing, he fell, his upper body colliding painfully with the side of the roof, knocking him off in a down-ward spin to the ground.

Luckily it was easy for him to remember what had saved him from falling in the past.

Just before he hit the ground, he increased his mass, the inertia pulling him to a stop. He was upside down due to the falling spin. He released his mass as fast as possible, not wanting to fall again with it enhanced, which would be disastrous.

He was still about a meter from the ground where he fell head-first. He rolled as he landed, letting the motion bring him back to his feet—rather gracefully, if he said so himself. "Shade take those loose bloody tiles," Daylen said as he dusted himself off. "Serves me right for walking along the edge of an old roof." It was at that time he noticed the hundreds of people staring at him.

"Oh, well, crap."

He had landed right in front of a food stall that stood on the side of a very busy sidewalk.

"Light's end!" the red-haired woman behind the stall exclaimed. She had a very long neck and pronounced cheekbones.

"Yeah, um, sorry for the scare," Daylen said.

"It's Dayless the Conqueror back from the dead!" an old man screamed to Daylen's left.

Gasps erupted all around, and Daylen's heart skipped a beat. Light, he thought with a groan, someone had recognized him. Everyone looked to the wizened old man pointing at Daylen. He was clearly old enough to have lived during Daylen's time in power.

"What are you talking about?" Daylen said, trying to sound as sincere as possible. "Dayless the Conqueror has been dead for twenty years, and even if he were alive, you would think he would look somewhat older than me."

"But... But you look exactly like him...or at least, exactly like him when he was young."

"And people can't look similar to one another, you senile idiot? Piss off, and stop trying to cause a riot with your stupid conspiracies."

A murmur arose in the crowd and the old man looked truly upbraided.

"How did you do that?" a woman wearing a top hat and vested

dress from among the crowd asked, pointing to the roof Daylen had fallen from.

"Oh, that... Just a stage trick gone wrong," Daylen said haltingly.

The businesswoman frowned. "That was not a stage trick. Where are the ropes? I know magic when I see it."

Light, he had been too conspicuous; not that he could have easily avoided it, and there were only two sources of magic that people knew of.

"Can you please keep it down?" Daylen said. "I'm on an important Archknight reconnaissance survey and I've been trying to avoid notice, hence why I'm not wearing the mantle and why I was on the roofs. The tiles broke free from under my feet when I wasn't paying attention, and we're all lucky no one was standing directly beneath me. Now, with everyone's curiosity satisfied, *clear off!*"

The crowed jumped and all went to move away, though many stared at him as they left.

He was a little surprised that they all obeyed him so quickly, and that no one had questioned him on what an Archknight reconnaissance survey was. He had just made it up, and if anyone really thought about it they would have realized how stupid it was, but the knights did carry a lot of authority. Light, he hoped the Order wouldn't find out about this, some random uninitiated teenager with their powers, but even if they did, once he moved on there was no way they could track him down.

"You look awful young to be an Archon," the woman behind the stall said.

Young? What's this girl talking about... Oh. I really need to get used to that.

"Archknights recruit as young as fourteen years old, but most parents don't let their children join so young." Though Daylen wasn't a member of their order, he knew some of their basic practices.

"Oh, of course," the woman said, looking at the blood on Daylen's coat. "Is there anything we should be worried about?"

"Oh, that. No, it's all taken care of."

Blood spattered across someone's clothes might usually raise more suspicion, but Archknights were different. The people probably supposed Daylen had recently slain a Shade. After all, that's what Archknights did most of the time.

Daylen's stomach growled and, seeing that the damage was already done, he shrugged to himself and walked up to the food stall.

"I was wondering if I could have a pie. I'm *starving*."

The knights were given a privileged position in society due to the importance of their mission. A knight never needed to pay for food, lodging, or even transportation. All people honored and respected them.

"Of course, Archon," the woman said, bowing several times. She opened a paper bag and scooped three pies into it and handed them to Daylen.

"The Light shine on you," Daylen said.

"And on you too, Archon."

Daylen smiled and turned before making his way to the city's sky port. The crowd, still filled with people who had seen him fall, parted for him like he was royalty—which recalled all-too-familiar memories.

Daylen sighed and took a bite from one of the delicious meat pies.

———

Daylen decided to risk posing as an Archknight one last time to get passage on a carrier to Treremain. It was unlikely that any Archknight would hear of it, and if they did, what could they do about it? No one knew who he was or where he lived, and he was only going home to grab a few things anyway.

He enjoyed some fine food and drink and got a little rest. He also spent a little time in the water closet washing off the blood from his coat.

Once back in Treremain, Daylen began to make his way through the busy city toward home.

As soon as he passed the main exit from the skyport he heard a paper boy calling out the headlines from that fall's broadsheet.

"Tensions growing between Hamahra and Azbanadar, might lead to war! Fire in the silversmith's sky island workshop! Falling debris causes property damage, injuries, and a death. Silver Guild receives large fine, and local council representatives to submit new

safety standards on all skysitters and sky islands above the city!
Read all about it!"

Daylen would have bought the paper if he had any money on
him; but he needed to get back home, collect his effects, and make
his way to the capital as soon as possible, hard as it was, for many
other things caught his interest through the city.

Light, what he would have given to go and watch the Sky Races
again. He had always been good at picking the winners, as it was
all a matter of statistics, and he was very good with numbers. But
he didn't deserve simple pleasures like that; well, not ones that he
would go out of his way to find. He couldn't help needing to travel
on skyships, nor that he happened to enjoy flying so much. If the
Light was going to curse him with life, he would appreciate the
simple pleasures he couldn't avoid, like walking with strength and
energy. It helped him deal with his more powerful misery and self-
hatred.

The one thing that did get him to stop on his walk out of the
city was a duel being conducted on the main street. Duels
happened in Karadale all the time, but Daylen had rarely been out
and about to catch them.

This duel had clearly been spur of the moment, which was
common enough. The other kind would have a set date and location. Still, even impromptu duels attracted quite the crowd, especially if a more prominent duelist was fighting, which seemed to
be the case here.

The popular duelist was a woman with green-streaked purple
hair. Her slanted eyes and warm skin tone spoke of Lee'on'tese
decent over Delavian, though her features weren't nearly as
pronounced as a full-blooded Lee'on'tese and she certainly dressed
in high Hamahran fashion.

She faced a man of local complexion, dark-green hair and
strong of stature, who wore a tassel with fewer beads than his
opponent.

Professional swordswomen like this fine lady were less
common than swordsmen, even though the art was taught to both
boys and girls through their younger years. Boys simply liked it
more and were far more likely to continue the practice as a
pastime or profession.

Wearing a dress that identified her as coming from a wealthy
family, the swordswoman undid the snap buttons that ran down

its left side. The hoops underneath which gave the dress its volume had been made to fold together and slide open like pegs hanging on a clothesline. The material that she pulled aside bunched up to her right and was held there by a small hook. Her dress flaring out behind was quite fetching to Daylen's eyes, what with the woman's white stockings being revealed to the upper thigh, the front of her dress provided minimal modesty. She also wore knee-high black leather boots of a practical design.

It was a very elaborate and expensive dress, the height of female dueling fashion, as Daylen had heard.

The swordswoman was young, at most in her thirties, with a nose too big for Daylen to pronounce her a beauty, though some would still find her attractive.

The woman carried a longsword in a parasol scabbard, which she drew, handing the scabbard to her male companion, who also looked to be a duelist.

Daylen's dueling mind came alive as he assessed the two combatants.

The woman's longsword was well balanced and sharply tapered, a popular type among women. That type of longswords only weighed fifty percent more than the average one-handed sword, which meant that with two hands longswords were lighter for the user, which was important if strength was a consideration.

Yes, men were stronger than women on average, but once a man or woman had adequate strength to use their weapon effectively they would become better by training in technique. Swords didn't need a lot of strength to be lethal, after all, which was why women could be equally competitive in swordsmanship so long as they used a lighter weapon to offset their disadvantages in leverage, power, and speed.

The woman drew her sword and made a few practice swings. She was very proficient, but far from Daylen's own skill.

Her opponent was armed with a rapier. A dirty, blackened rapier.

There was nothing illegal about rapiers, but with their extended length and total focus on thrusting they were nothing but a specialized dueling weapon. This openly scoffed at the very reason why Hamahrans carried swords in the first place. Killing a Shade with a rapier would be like trying to peel a craggot with a toothpick, and thus a man who carried a rapier sneered at tradition and only cared for one thing: winning duels. Daylen hated people like this, and truly wanted to see this man get beaten.

The man drew a dagger in his off hand. A good pick, but Daylen preferred an armored gauntlet instead, which functioned much the same as an offhand buckler, but with more grappling options.

A Bringer had been found—it was lucky that she had been so close to the challenge and was able to officiate the duel. Duelists always wanted a Bringer to officiate. Not being able to lie, they were the perfect judges and could heal the loser.

Standing between the combatants, the robe-clad woman stretched out her arm and then brought it down, signaling the duel's commencement.

The combatants engaged and after a quick exchange of trained blows, first blood was drawn.

Duels weren't long affairs, usually lasting five engagements at most, but it was common enough for them to end on the first exchange when one of the opponents was either particularly lucky or more skilled.

The woman had been more skilled.

The man had leaned low to thrust, and the woman had used her parry motion to deflect the thin blade and strike the man's head with her back edge. An expert if predictable move.

That was the thing about sword fighting. It only took a year or so to learn the moves, but a lifetime to master them.

The crowd applauded, and Daylen clapped too. A well-won victory, especially against a dirty rapierist.

The Lightbringer approached the man to heal him. The swordswoman was practiced enough to have measured his opponent's blow so that it hadn't cleft his skull. Still, a devastating cut to the head by any means, and the blood flowed out like a river until the Bringer healed it.

Daylen turned to walk down the street, thoroughly in the mood to draw his own sword and go through some drills. Watching duels always got him in the mood to fight, but he resisted. There would be plenty of opportunity to use his sword in the falls to come.

Once out of the city, Daylen decided to run the remainder of the journey. He increased his speed eight times with three bonds while using the last on his stamina. His legs moved in a blur, and with his stamina enhanced he could push himself to run as fast as he could and not tire. He made sure to slow down when running over a hill or rise so as not to launch himself into the air.

Daylen knew that in his prime he could sprint at thirty kilometers an hour, and should be able to now. With one bond doubling that and then another doubling it again, he could run at one hundred and twenty kilometers an hour. That was *three times as fast* as Paradan's wagon.

He ran with much more care than the time he accidentally launched himself into the air and by slowing at the top of hills he managed easily. His coat flapped behind him violently as he raced along the road, slowing down as he passed the occasional traveler, cart, wagon or coach.

From what he had figured out, his powers should exhaust after an hour of continual use, but he crested the last hill to his home near the end of high fall well before his powers started to fatigue.

It took about ten meters of skidding before he could stop himself.

"Now that was a run!" Daylen said, releasing his bonds, his body full of energy.

Daylen walked the remaining distance to his home, happy for the change of pace. Running faster than a hundred kilometers an hour was exhilarating, but Light, it hurt his face. He could only imagine what his hair looked like.

With his home nearby, Daylen finally saw that someone was sitting on the log railing that ran beside the road that passed his house.

"Who could that be?" Daylen said to himself—and then he remembered his powers.

He drew in light and bonded it to his eyes, his vision becoming ten times as sharp.

It was that Tuerasian Lightbringer Daylen had found outside his home two falls past. He was even sitting in the exact same place, except that now he had his head bowed over a book, writing something.

"What in the Light?"

Daylen walked with a purposeful step toward the man and, as he did, Daylen saw that the Bringer was drawing, not writing. The book was some type of sketchpad.

The brown-skinned Lightbringer eventually noticed Daylen

and put his sketchbook away into a satchel that hung at his side. Daylen was taken aback when the Bringer stood to face him because he no longer looked to be taller than Daylen, rather they were of a height. Then Daylen realized why; he no longer hunched as he had with his aged body. It felt good to stand tall once more.

"Son, *what* are you still doing here?" Daylen asked the Lightbringer.

"Still?" the man said in that clear voice of his. His eyes narrowed at Daylen from under his short cut yellow hair. "How'd you know I've been waiting?"

Oh, shade it! Daylen thought in annoyance. "I, um..." For a little while he was at a loss for words, until he remembered the back story he'd crafted. "My father mentioned you."

"Your father?"

"Who do you think lives here?" Daylen said, waving his hand to the sagging brick cottage.

"Oh I see," the Lightbringer said. "Now that's impressive."

"What's impressive?"

"Your father, the sly old man, to father anyone as young as you."

"First of all, boy, you don't know my age—and clearly he could still get it up, as otherwise I wouldn't be standing here."

The funny thing was Daylen knew from first-hand experience that the truth had been quite the opposite—but, happily, not anymore. It appeared that with his renewed youthful body, his hormones had been given the uncontrollable kick that came with being a teenager. Daylen was already sick of the blackened, unprovoked, and rather conspicuous erections he had been getting.

The Lightbringer frowned. "There's no need to be crude, and I wasn't questioning your parentage. You're obviously your father's son. I may have only met him once, but your voice is similar. The resemblance is strong, too. No, I was admiring him. Any man would hope to retain such...um, energy."

"Oh, well, I'm just not used to people questioning or admiring the old man's plumbing."

The Lightbringer smiled and leaned in, chuckling as he said, "Then I'll try not to look at the home's drainage."

Daylen could only stare back to the man. "That might be the worst joke I've ever heard."

"Oh, come on, it was *funny*."

"Trust me, it wasn't."

"You know, your father didn't like my humor, either."

"He had good taste. So now that my parentage is out of the way, my father mentioned he ran into some Lightbringer sitting outside his home, obviously you. Now as I asked before, *what* in the Light's blessed light are you still doing here?"

"Oh. Well, I'm waiting for you."

"What?"

The Lightbringer paused and looked the slightest bit hesitant. "What I'm about to say may seem odd, but upon the Light it's the truth."

"What're you on about?"

"A week past now, the Light gave me a vision. In it, I was prompted to come to this very spot and wait for a young man. That young man was you."

Daylen was now listening intently. Though there were many people who didn't believe in the light, that Lightbringers simply tapped into some natural power much like the Archknights, Daylen knew from personal experience that the Light was very much real and that Lightbringers were indeed connected to it. Thus, he knew not to question the visions of a Lightbringer, especially if it involved him. He had made such a mistake in the past.

Lightbringers could perform varying miracles, but they could all heal the injured and create light. It was a sign of their holy calling, and proof of their personal worth and virtue. A Lightbringer received their powers purely because of their personal goodness and lifelong dedication to serving others, which also meant that they couldn't lie. If ever they did lie, as with any other immoral action, they would lose their powers.

"How do you know I'm the one?"

"You were shown to me," the Lightbringer said, reaching into his satchel. He retrieved his sketching book and opened it to show Daylen a detailed and truly perfect rendition of his now youthful face.

Daylen was stunned. He cast his mind back to the time he had first met the man. He had said that he was waiting for a young man, one in his late teens. But it couldn't have been Daylen; he wasn't even young at the time. If the Light sent this man a vision to meet Daylen in his renewed body before he had it, it meant that his transformation was preordained and not some freak accident, didn't it?

The Lightbringer put away his book. "Has anyone ever mentioned that you bear a remarkable and rather unfortunate resemblance to the Great Tyrant?"

"Dayless the Conqueror?"

"That's him. At first I worried that I was to meet the Conqueror himself! Can you *imagine!*" He chortled. "Anyway, I quickly realized that you simply looked like him. I mean, it would be impossible to meet the Conqueror in his youth after all."

"Yeah... How do you even know what the Conqueror looks like?"

"I assume you mean *looked* like. He's dead, after all."

"Whatever, how do you know?"

"I had many chances to see the *despot* while he ruled." The venom in those words took Daylen by surprise, as the Bringer had appeared to be so gentle. It was clear he hated the Conqueror, but that wasn't anything special. Everyone hated him, himself included.

"Honestly, the resemblance is so striking that if I didn't know any better I would say you were his son."

"Huh. Well, you're the first one to mention it."

"Really? You know, come to think of it, your father shares a resemblance to him too, though it's hard to tell given his age. Maybe a distant relation. In any case, you were shown to me in a vision."

"Yeah, you've said that," Daylen said, feeling dazed. The implications were profound, and he began to waver. He needed to think.

He stumbled to the old log railing next to the road and sat.

Maybe it wasn't preordained; maybe the Light simply knew what was going to happen based on Daylen's choices, a prediction of sorts—but that still left the question as to why the Light wanted this Lightbringer to meet him.

"Except that you were unclothed," the Lightbringer added with a serious yet clearly embarrassed expression.

"What?" Daylen said. "I was naked?"

"Err, yes..."

"Well, you *are* Tuerasian."

"I've never followed that tradition," the man said, clearing his throat and putting away his book. "Truly, I have no idea why. Believe me, it was one of the most awkward dreams I've ever had, especially since visions are as vivid as real life. Anyway, I only mention that awkward detail because your body was covered in scars. I don't know if the scars were metaphorical or literal."

"The scars are literal," Daylen said after a pause.

"How'd you get them?"

"None of your business," Daylen said, rising. "So, the Light sent you to meet me, to do what? To finally grant me mercy?" That was the only thing Daylen could think of. Maybe this whole new life thing was just a scare, one last kick in the balls before the Light did actually grant him release.

"Mercy?" the Lightbringer said. "No. I was told to follow you."

"Follow me?"

"Yes, and that I'm to remain at your side for as long as the Light sees fit."

"What?" Daylen said, nonplussed. "And how long will that be?"

"Until I'm instructed otherwise, I'd guess."

"You're not coming with me."

"Sorry. I answer to a higher power than you."

"But... But." Daylen couldn't think of anything to say. He had been foolish to hope for a release. No, he was truly cursed to live; yet how could he forge a new identity for himself with a blasted Lightbringer tied to his hip?

Yet how could he deny the will of the Light itself?

Could this be the Light's answer to my prayer? Daylen wondered. When he had stood atop that roof, he had asked the Light as fervently and sincerely as he ever had for its help, to protect him from himself, to guide him to be someone better. Was this Bringer the Light's answer?

Daylen looked to the man. "What's your name?"

"Ahrek," the Lightbringer said with a smile.

"A Hamahran name?"

"Oh, I'm Hamahran, born and bred. My parents were Tuerasian artists and received so many commissions from this country that they eventually moved here. They knew they had to adapt, so I was raised as a Hamahran with Tuerasian values. The best of both worlds. And your name?"

"Daylen."

"Daylen? But that's the same name as..."

"Yeah, I know. Look, it's a common enough name, so please don't bring it up."

"Very well, and well met. Honestly, I feel as lost about this as you. I don't have a clue why the Light directed me to stay at your side."

"I might have an idea or two," Daylen said.

"Really?"

"Yep."

"Well, could you *share* them?"

"Nope," Daylen said flatly.

"Light, why not?"

"None of your business."

"I think the Light's made it my business."

"Then *it* can tell you. Look, son, I'm a private kind of person, but I'm not exactly going to deny the Light. So you can come with me."

"Why do you keep calling me son? That's what I should be calling *you*."

"It's just a habit, and don't call me that. Just be happy I'm letting you come with me."

"Sorry, but I don't need your permission, as I obey a greater power."

"Trust me, if I didn't want you to follow me, you wouldn't be."

"You see, that's the funny thing," Ahrek said. "It's abundantly clear that you don't want me to, and yet you are. So what you said isn't really true, is it?"

Daylen looked at the Lightbringer for a second, before sneering. "Don't be a smartass."

"You know, you're very much like your father."

"More than you can imagine."

CHAPTER EIGHT

*It was during the Fourth Night that I met my beloved, Tara. Such
a strange time to find warmth and love.
After much fighting, we found ourselves in a position to launch an
assault on the underworld. I had never dreamed I would ever
venture into that labyrinth. Doing so would have been suicide if I
had not been accompanied by the knights who led the charge.
Somehow, they were able to sense where the Shade pooled their
powers to cast night upon the land.*

The white banner from Lyrah's mantle fluttered gently at her
back as she strode through the crowd. The people in front
parted without prompting, the mantle serving its purpose to make
her stand out.

The mantle was a thin, bright-white cape with sleeves joined
around a high collar, and accompanied by bright silvery bracers
and pauldrons. The pauldrons each bore the knights' golden sigil, a
stylized shield that bore horizontal and vertical lines interlocking
a central ring. This same sigil formed the broach that closed the
mantle around her neck and was also upon the long white banner
cape that hung down her back. A pair of white gloves completed
the Archknight Mantle. Apart from this, the knights had no other
uniform, but were expected to wear darker shades underneath to
contrast. Lyrah's choices were a black shirt with large silver

buttons, a wide, polished leather belt with an ornamental buckle, tight gray pants, and knee-high black riding boots. A large two handed warsword hung sheathed on her hip.

The knights were the protectors of the world, mysterious warriors with great magical powers, beacons of hope and justice, and thus needed to be seen and recognized as such. Hence the mantle, and why the people stared at Lyrah with reverent respect.

Lyrah had grown used to the attention, but that didn't mean she liked it.

Her archbrother, Cueseg, waited for her in the street, the crowds not daring to come within five meters of him.

Her new companion was a short-statured backward Tuerasian. Not only did he have deep brown skin and short bright-yellow hair that stuck up at the front, he had a prominent mark on his forehead from some savage branding, and wore no shirt under his Knight's Mantle, leaving his impressively muscled chest bare.

Tuerasians were considered by many peoples to be very attractive and exotic; their lack of modesty added a taboo fascination, and in truth Lyrah could admit that Cueseg was quite the physical specimen.

He stood out even for an Archknight.

Lyrah was a middle-aged Hamahran woman, though she had aged gracefully over the years. She had pale blue eyes and green hair which stood out among the more numerous Freysian reds, though her own hair had a strong line of crimson which spoke of shared heritage. Her hair was tied in a thin plait that hung down over her mantle's banner. Average in height for a woman, Lyrah was still a little taller than her Tuerasian companion.

She intentionally avoided bonding light to her ears on this occasion as she could predict what the frivolous women were saying nearby as they whispered, pointing to Cueseg.

They might have been pebbles on the road for all Cueseg seemed to care.

Lyrah felt uncomfortable with these thoughts, though it wasn't nearly as bad as when they had met. Cueseg had been completely *naked*. It had nearly brought on a panic attack, being the way she was with things like intimacy. As it turned out, Cueseg hadn't been making some type of sexual advance. Instead, he claimed to have been providing Lyrah the opportunity to master herself more fully, whatever that meant. After a *very* awkward conversation where

Lyrah could barely keep her nervousness at bay, Cueseg covered his loins, sorry that Lyrah was so weak-willed that she couldn't control her emotions. She almost knocked him out for all of that.

As if she were actually *interested* in him, or anyone in that way.

Cueseg was attractive...very attractive, with a body that looked to have been sculpted from stone. But he was also snobbish, rude, and *annoying*.

Cueseg was in the middle of eating a pie. "This is awful," he said in a thick Tuerasian accent. "The meat is too fatty." He reached into his mouth and retrieved a half-chewed piece of meat. "You see this? It is like eating a shoe." He threw the piece to the ground before taking another bite of his pie.

"Then why are you eating it?"

"I am hungry."

"You're always hungry."

"And that is why I eat."

"Makes sense," Lyrah said. "I've just spoken to the vendor. She confirms the stories we've heard. A young man fell from that building there and stopped himself in the middle of the air a meter from the ground, no ropes, no tricks. From the description it sounds exactly like a Mass Break. He had blood on his coat and said he was on a reconnaissance survey, whatever that means."

Cueseg tossed the remains of his pie to the ground. "He is asking people if reconnaissance is needed in the city?"

Lyrah tsked disapprovingly at Cueseg's waste and lack of cleanliness, but chose to otherwise ignore it. She had to pick her battles with this vexing man. "You do hear how stupid that sounds."

"I do, but you people do so many stupid things I cannot know."

Lyrah sighed. She really couldn't tell if Cueseg was trying to offend her or if he was simply ignorant. "We're assigned to hunt this city and would have been told if any other knights were given a task in our area—unless something serious happened to cause him to come here unassigned, which might explain the blood. But why in the Light's grace wouldn't he report it to the Hold? From the accounts, he didn't seem to be distressed. Quite the opposite."

Cueseg rubbed his smooth chin. "People do not like to lose so much blood."

"*Really*, are you sure about that?"

"Of course I am sure," Cueseg said seriously.

He just didn't seem to understand the concept of sarcasm. "This is why I should be the head one," Cueseg added.

"*I'm* senior, Cueseg. That's just the way it is, so get over it."

"In age, yes, but why you people be leader for age? Is not right. And what does this mean, get over it? Do you wish me to get onto you? Do you want sex?"

"No! Light, Cueseg, will you get it into your head that I don't want to have...to have..."

"Have what?"

Lyrah could feel the anxiety build. "You know."

"Sex. You cannot even say it. This is not good."

Her perpetual desire to punch Cueseg had just doubled.

"You find it hard to control. This is normal. I am very attractive and it is good that I can make you strong in this."

"*Light*," Lyrah snapped, "all I said was to get over it. Why can't you understand a simple analogy?"

"How stupid must you be if you do not understand that I would not understand the words of different language?"

Lyrah sighed, rubbing her forehead. The two of them really didn't get along. But they were assigned to each other, so they just had to put up with it.

The Order usually did this when a hunt became due somewhere. They would assign a brother, or in her case a sister, who spoke the language with another member from a foreign land. It was a way the Order diversified.

After being assigned together, and after his naked introduction, Cueseg had tried to make Lyrah play with some Tuerasian puzzles, of all things. Lyrah had refused, of course, leaving Cueseg greatly offended.

"Whatever," Lyrah said. "I suppose we could talk to the conners..."

"What does this mean, conners?"

"It's slang..."

"Do not use words I do not know to describe things I do not know!"

"A shortened name for *constable*. You know, law enforcement."

Cueseg was silent for a short time. "Then that is the way you should say it."

"Even though *now* you know what conner means?"

"No," Cueseg said, looking far more embarrassed then he should, "that is not what I mean…"

Lyrah smirked. "But that's what you said."

"By the Bright One, this is not my language. I was meant to say that you should *have* said it that way, but not anymore!"

"So…you know how you meant to say it, but you didn't."

Cueseg usually kept his face blank, so seeing him flustered was a rare event. "You… You… Be quiet, you ignorant barbarian!"

"It's okay to be forgetful."

"I said, be quiet!"

This was the first time Lyrah had seen Cueseg so embarrassed. She smiled, happy to know there was a way to shade the Tuerasian's sun and to get him back for all the drack she had to put up with from him.

It would have been rather undignified if anybody had heard the two noble Archknights squabbling, but they were speaking softly and were far enough from prying ears.

Lyrah let an appropriate amount of time pass before she spoke again. "If the blood came from some type of altercation, the patrols might have received a report of it, especially if it was a fight involving an Archknight."

"And then we will know if the blood came from his brother?"

Lyrah paused for a brief moment and decided to test her theory. "Know? It would be impossible to know from the conners. First we would need to identify the man he fought with. I thought you would have realized that."

Cueseg seemed to control himself better this time, his face passive, but his cheeks did appear to be flushed. Was he blushing? "I do not mean this!" he said with an embarrassed tone. "I mean to say that we will know who he fights with, if it is his brother or not."

"This is the second time you haven't said what you meant."

"This is not my language!" Cueseg repeated, raising his voice.

Lyrah glanced around to realize that this time their avid onlookers would have heard them. She felt embarrassed and spoke in a lowered tone. "How about we focus on the matter at hand? This young man's description doesn't match any brother assigned to the nearby regions. He didn't wear the Mantle and he didn't have a brother at his side."

"I know this. It is possible that the boy is Seerium."

"A Seerium?"

"Yes, but you call them different. Lightbringers."

"He might have been," Lyrah said, thinking over the possibility. There were Lightbringers who were members of the Order. They made up an indispensable branch amongst the knights thanks to their unique powers. "He would have the miracle of what, movement?"

"Yes."

"But I know the Lightbringers in the Order, and they're all too old."

"Yes, even among my people it takes many years to be Seerium."

"So the likelihood of him being a Lightbringer is very low."

"Also, if he is Seerium, he can ask for food as Seerium and have no need to be an Archknight. Though I do not know why he would give so much trouble to get what you barbarians call *food*."

"Cueseg, in case you weren't aware of this, people don't like being called barbarians."

"Then I will not call you this again."

"Oh…" Lyrah said in surprise. "That was easy."

"Why would it not?"

"You never admit being wrong."

"Not knowing something is different to being wrong. You do not like being called barbarian so I will not call you this. It is just the best word that I know to say what you people are."

"*Thanks*," Lyrah said sarcastically. "Good to know that's what you think of us."

"I am honor to help."

She shook her head. "We need to try and find this boy."

"Can you track him?"

"Only if I knew his scent, but there's no way for me to know which one is his. This street has had too much traffic."

"But if no one has been in the same place, you can find his smell?"

"Yes."

"Good, then you will find his smell."

"No, Cueseg, I just said too many people have passed by. I can't tell which scent is his. I mean, if I had a piece of his clothing or if he had stood in a place that no one else had recently, then yes."

Cueseg's face was blank as usual, but the tone in his voice

sounded very condescending. "Again, you do not see what is clear to see. This is why I should be the head one."

"Oh, really?" Lyrah said, before cynically adding, "So what am I missing?"

"We know where this boy stands that no one else stands," Cueseg said, pointing to the roof of the building where the boy had fallen from.

There was a clear gap at the edge of the roof tiles.

Lyrah looked and ground her teeth in annoyance, knowing Cueseg was right. It wasn't likely that anyone else had been up on the roof since that fall.

"Let's go check," Lyrah said, walking to the building.

The people on the street moved out of their way. Once at the building, Lyrah crouched and channeled a power jump, shooting up with great velocity and cresting the roof to land on the edge with ease. Careful not to break loose any tiles under her feet, she stood straight and looked down to see Cueseg rising gently up toward her, obviously using one and a quarter gravity bonds, hands held formally behind his back. Changing the direction of his bond, he floated in an elegant arch and stepped onto the roof. Cueseg had good control.

Everyone on the streets were watching them, reveling in their chance to see the Archknight magic.

Lyrah knelt down. Using her free bond, she channeled light into her sense of smell and instantly detected a person's scent. Her face must have looked confused, for Cueseg asked what was wrong.

"His scent," Lyrah said. "He smells like an *old person*, and there's something faintly familiar about it."

"Old people have different smell?"

Lyrah stood. "You're telling me you've never smelled an old person?"

"I have. They did not smell any different."

"Of course they do. Okay, not all old people, but most. You know, musty, the smell that brings on boredom and hypnotically makes people speak *really* slowly."

Remarkably, Cueseg's blank face seemed to convey that Lyrah was speaking gibberish. How was he able to convey expression while never expressing anything? It was very frustrating.

"What if he has our powers and is not a knight?" Cueseg asked.

"That's impossible."

"All he needs is to fight evil and do the Vigil."

"But no one actually *knows* what happens during the Vigil."

"Just because *we* do not know does not mean no one does," Cueseg said.

"Even outside the Order?"

"Yes."

"You know what, Cueseg...you might be right."

"Of course – it was me who said it."

"But if you are, this is far more serious than we thought."

CHAPTER NINE

*As we traversed the underworld, we passed many enormous halls
and roadways carved out of the stone by some ancient
subterranean civilization. As to who they were or what happened
to them, no one knows.*
*The Shade attacked us each fall as we traveled, and there were
many desperate battles, as the strongest of the knights was unable
to release the full force of their powers for risk of cave-ins. Of
course, the Shade had no hesitation in that regard and they used
their dark powers to kill many.*
*We were met by the largest collective of Shade once we found their
primary nest at an entrance into a great cavern. We fought with
everything we had to get the stronger knights close enough to
destroy them.*

N ow that introductions are over," the Bringer said, looking at
Daylen quizzically, "there's something I've been wanting to
ask you."

"What's that?" Daylen asked.

"Is that blood on your coat?"

Surprised, Daylen looked to his coat. He had been sure he
cleaned off all the blood, but when shifting his coat, he saw a few
streaks he had missed that were under a natural fold in the cloth.
Light, the Bringer must be bloody perceptive to notice that.

"No, it's sauce," Daylen said. "Spilled some on me when I was eating a pie."

Ahrek held a very calculating expression, and then smiled. "I see. So where are we going?"

"The capital. I just have to grab some of my things first."

"Your things? I thought your father lived here?"

"Not anymore. They're my things now."

"He *died*?"

"Yep."

"I'm sorry."

"Don't be. If you had any idea what he was like, you'd be as happy as me to see him gone."

"You didn't get along?"

Daylen laughed. "Now *that* is a funny question, because while the answer is yes, it's at the same time a profound no."

"It sounds complicated."

Daylen laughed even harder. "You have *no* idea."

"Well, at least you're here to break the news to his friend."

"Friend? I have no—" Daylen stopped himself. "I mean, my father had no friends."

"Yes he does, the farmer who gave your father a ride in his wagon. He's in the house."

Paradan—the letter! Oh, black!

Daylen ran inside to find Paradan sitting in the very chair Daylen himself had sat in before he had left. Paradan was holding Daylen's suicide letter, his face pale and expression horrified.

"Who... Who're you?" Paradan asked.

"I, um..."

Ahrek entered after Daylen. "He's the old tinker's son."

"Did you know?" Paradan asked Daylen through clenched teeth.

Daylen couldn't think of anything to say. His intent had been to burn the note, along with his life's accounting.

"Know what?" Ahrek asked.

"That the old tinker who lived here, Daylen, was really that *daybreaking*, stoned *tyrant*, Dayless the Conqueror!"

"*What?*" Ahrek said, stepping forward and taking the letter. He read, and as he did so, utter incredulity crossed his face. Once finished, his eyes were wide, and he looked to Daylen. Anger crossed the Lightbringer's face, anger that seemed truly uncharacteristic from what Daylen had supposed of the seemingly kind-hearted man. "Your resemblance is no coincidence," Ahrek said, slow and clear. "Your father was Dayless the Conqueror!"

Daylen swallowed, not sure what to do. He could pretend that he didn't know, but that would cause complications, especially with the things he wanted to grab. So, he made his decision.

"Yes," Daylen said.

Paradan spat at the floor. "That blackened son of a Shade! He's been living right under my nose for *twenty years*! I gave him a ride in my own wagon, we even had a *duel*, in which he beat me soundly. Light, I actually had a duel with *Dayless the Conqueror*."

Ahrek's face shook. He threw the note aside and paced across the floor. "This is unbelievable. After *all* this time, the Conqueror, alive! The Light truly must have a sense of humor if that was how we finally met. His age created the perfect disguise. *I* didn't even recognize him, yet now, as I think about it, I can see his face under those wrinkles. It really *was* him!"

Ahrek's eyes, like burning coals, turned on Daylen. "And this explains your namesake, *Daylen*."

"What are you talking about?" Paradan asked.

"Daylen was Dayless the Conqueror's name in his early life," Ahrek said.

"Really? He had another name, and he even had the gall to go by it?"

Ahrek sneered. "And the gall to name his son the same. He had given it up for the darker name Dayless once he gained power. Most people don't know this, which explains why he retook the name while in hiding."

"Have a look at this," Paradan said, handing Ahrek Daylen's journal. "It was under the letter."

Ahrek took the book and began to read, his brow climbing with each crossing of his eyes. He flicked through the pages reading briefly. "This is a full accounting of the Conqueror's life!"

Paradan stood and paced across the room, kicking over the chair. "We should burn this place and everything that daybreaker touched down!"

"Does that include you? He touched you, I'm assuming," Daylen accused dryly. "What about the money he gave you, or your wagon? You better burn them all."

"How do you know he gave me money?" Paradan asked.

"He told me. I was with him at the end. I'm not saying he wasn't a right blackened bastard, but his life here might still have led to some good."

"Like what?" Paradan asked skeptically.

"The *money* he gave you..."

"That doesn't count."

"Then throw the coin away, you little snot."

"*Snot*! Watch your tongue, boy!"

"If you act like a child, I'll treat you like one, so put a rock in it and *listen*. If you don't count it as good that he spent his years fixing the town's things, look at me. I'm here solely because Dayless hid himself away, and if you knew anything about my father you would know he wasn't exactly happy doing so. Living was the worst punishment anyone could have given him."

Paradan paused. "He said as much in his note, but he still escaped justice."

"At least we know the tyrant is finally dead," Ahrek said.

"But how can we *really* know?" Paradan replied. "The word of his son? How can we trust that? And how can we even know that you're really his son?"

"Just look at his face," Ahrek said. "Apart from his age, he's the express image of the Conqueror."

"I never saw the Conqueror," Paradan said, "apart from when he was hiding here, and by that time he was too old." Paradan looked closely at Daylen. "But now that I look for it, there is a lot of resemblance...and your voice is even the same, just not as croaky."

"Having any connection with...*him*...isn't something I'm proud of," Daylen said. "But the Light saw fit to bring me here, so I intend to live my life regardless of where I've come from."

"I never knew he had a son," Paradan said. "He must have fathered you after he went into hiding. But he's been living here for nearly twenty years, as long as the daybreaker's supposed to have been dead." Paradan looked directly at Daylen. "Who was your mother?"

This was a question Daylen had prepared for. "Titina," Daylen said.

"The old widow?" Paradan said. Daylen nodded. "She died... what, sixteen years ago?"

The old widow Titina *had* actually befriended Daylen when he had moved to Karadale, before she died. She had been somewhat of a recluse and had taken to Daylen seeing that he was in much the same situation as her: all alone. She was the perfect person to claim to have born a son no one knew of.

"She was able to suckle me as a babe, but after that was too old. I was sent away to the Mornington prefecture and grew up in an orphanage. Mother died not long after."

"Stranger things have happened, I suppose," Paradan said, looking about the room. His face scrunched in revulsion, he continued, "I need to get out of here. I can't stand thinking such an evil murdering *butcher* has been living so close. People gotta know, though. I'll go tell the magistrate and pass on the letter."

Ahrek passed Paradan the journal, and the farmer retrieved the letter from the floor. He left the old cottage shaking his head.

And that was it. In a couple of falls, via many phonotrack communiqués, the whole world would know the truth, or half of it anyway. Daylen *had* to reach the capital before the news spread enough to warrant further investigation, namely into Daylen's false birth.

"I see why the Light sent me," Ahrek said after a small time of silence.

"Yeah, why's that?"

"I'm to ensure that you don't follow in the Conqueror's footsteps."

"You're worried I might?"

"Honestly, yes."

". . .Me too."

Ahrek nodded slowly. "So the question is, how much are you like your father?"

Daylen laughed. "Now *that*, Bringer, *was* funny. The answer is not at all, and every bit the same."

"I don't understand."

"And hopefully no one ever will."

Lyrah and Cueseg visited the closest constabulary to find out about any violent encounters in the city. There were a few, but the one that stood out most was a violent murder in a street alley. Some beggar had been utterly butchered. They visited the alley, and Lyrah picked up the very same scent as they had on the tiled roof.

"Oh, light," Lyrah said. "Things just got a lot worse."

"You smell him?" Cueseg asked.

"That, and you just stepped in poo."

"Bieuseck!" Cueseg said, cursing in his native tongue and scraping his shoe along the ground.

"You think the water they use to wash away the blood they would clean the poo away, too. Disgusting city!"

"Oh get over it, it's just poo."

"No, it is not. I am fouled and need to wash."

"No time for that."

"I *have* to wash myself. I am fouled!"

Lyrah had enough. "If you don't get in line right now, I'll pick up that steaming turd over there and force in down your throat."

Cueseg's eyes widened in horror. "You... You will not!"

"Oh yes I will."

"I will stop you."

"You *know* my bonds are stronger. I'm senior for a *reason*, Cueseg," Lyrah bit out. "When it comes to our mandate or something that might threaten the Order, you'll put up with literal crap, blood, pain, and death."

Cueseg pressed his lips tight.

"Good. Let's go."

Lyrah and Cueseg entered the Laybourn's skyport at Low Fall to find it bustling with activity and industry.

The sight recalled memories from Lyrah's childhood, as she had grown up near the huge capital port in Highdawn.

Dockworkers raced back and forth hauling cargo, driving wagons, sweeping docks, or directing traffic. There were several whalers skinning their most recent catch in more than one dock.

Countless shipmen wearing common working clothes or the uniform of their respective ships also filled the port. They directed passengers, loaded or unloaded cargo, walked in merry groups off to a pub, or were returning to the dock to man their ships.

Most slept during this time, but as every fall was lit continuously by the sun, it wasn't much of an inconvenience to switch sleeping habits to satisfy the demands of commerce. Some didn't even follow the falls and just slept whenever they got tired.

They all gave Lyrah and Cueseg a wide berth.

The whale carcasses filled the port with the stink of blubber, but it wasn't nearly as strong as a true edge port.

"There's been too much activity here," Lyrah said. "His scent is all mixed."

"He comes here to find a ship," Cueseg said with a mouth full of pastry.

"Light, Cueseg, can you please finish your food before talking!"

"No, I find food in this place that is not awful," Cueseg said, his mouth still full of food. Holding up the pastry he was eating, he continued, "Look, it is cooked through, flaky and has lots of butter. I am going to eat."

For a man who was so picky about food, Cueseg certainly ate a lot of it—and as it turned out, Tuerasians had some very different eating habits. Cueseg always ate with his hands, made a lot of noises when eating, threw his scraps on the floor or the ground, and of course had no problem speaking with his mouth full.

"Whatever. Let's separate. Someone's bound to have seen the boy."

Cueseg left and began interrogating every person he found. Though foreign, he was still instantly recognized as an Archon with the Order's white mantle over his shoulders and arms.

Lyrah grabbed the attention of a passing dockworker.

"Lady Archon," the man said, bowing.

"I'm looking for the Portmaster," Lyrah replied.

The dockman pointed.

Now that Lyrah was looking in the right direction, the Portmaster was easily identified. She was an elderly woman wearing a business-like vest over a white shirt, a top hat, a puffy cravat, and a long-laced skirt, with a ledger in hand.

Light, what was this grandma doing being the Portmaster? Wouldn't the stress of such an office kill her? And that sword on her side should have made her fall over.

Lyrah approached the older woman.

Though surrounded by lackeys and clearly busy, the Portmaster bowed respectfully. "Master Archon," she said in a wheezy voice. "How can I serve you?"

"I'm looking for one of my brothers who might have caught a carrier out of the city," Lyrah said.

"Oh, yes, and let me be the first to officially apologize to the Order that one of our noble protectors was asked to prove his legitimacy." It literally took the woman twice as long to say this as a regular person. "Word hasn't spread too far regarding the incident and all I can do is hope that the Order will show leniency. My understanding is that the Archon wasn't wearing the mantle. He was quite young and..."

"In what way exactly did you force my brother to prove his legitimacy?" Lyrah said, unable to bear the slow discourse any longer.

The woman swallowed. "Ah. Well, just a small demonstration of his powers. Nothing too disruptive, I assure you. The Archon chose to demonstrate his speed. Once the tollman knew his mistake, the Archon was offered every courtesy, I assure you."

"What was the name of the ship in question, and where was it headed?"

The woman flicked through her thick ledger and really seemed to take her time.

Lyrah struggled to contain her growing impatience.

"It was the *Farrwhen*, headed for Treremain," the Portmaster finally said.

"What's the fastest ship currently in port?"

"That would be the *Sparrow*, a runner owned by the National Post."

"It's now headed for Treremain with two additional passengers. Make sure the ship doesn't leave until I'm aboard. The mail will have to be late. I'll collect my brother and we'll leave immediately."

The Portmaster paled, but bowed and walked away slowly.

Lyrah sighed, not feeling very proud of herself for being so brisk with the older woman. But seriously, she was in a hurry, and that conversation had taken three times as long as it had needed to.

Lyrah left thinking about how the old woman described the boy using his powers. The boy *had* to be a Lightbinder; there was no way to fake enhanced speed like that. But was he a brother? Surely he had to be, for only Archknights could obtain the lightbinding powers... Unless Cueseg was right, and the boy had dedicated his life to fighting evil and had learned the secrets of the Vigil independently.

This was worrying, but not too much, for he could only survive the Vigil if his dedication was whole and true...

But what about the deserters? Lyrah asked herself.

Knights that deserted their calling weren't common, but it

happened, and it was serious enough that a special group existed within the knights to hunt them down.

This had always bothered Lyrah. If a knight lost their dedication to the cause, they should have lost their powers in the exact same way a Lightbringer did when they lied or committed a crime against the Light. But deserted knights still kept their powers. Once a knight got their powers, they kept them for life. This was true regardless of a change of heart. It was a close-kept secret within the Order that the world didn't know, yet it still didn't make sense. If the powers came from one's dedication to a cause, they should then be reliant on that dedication, shouldn't they?

Then Lyrah had another troubling thought. *What if a person could get the powers regardless of their dedication?*

She had never thought of that possibility before, and it troubled her deeply.

If it was true, anyone could become a Lightbinder if they knew the secret, even someone wholly evil. What destruction and chaos could be wrought if that was the case?

Lyrah shook her head. It was a stupid thought. The powers had only ever been received by men and women who were willing to give up the rest of their lives to fight evil.

But then Lyrah thought of Vaytem.

Vaytem had gone through basic training with her and no one had seemed more devout than he. The knights had saved his and his family's lives from a Shade, which was why he had been so eager to join. He was the one who had encouraged the others throughout the training, and continually praised the knights. Yet when they all underwent the Vigil, Vaytem was one of the recruits to have died. Lyrah's trainer said Vaytem must have had doubt in his heart, so soft and hidden that maybe Vaytem himself wasn't even aware of it. But Lyrah had known Vaytem. No one was more committed than he. His death had troubled her ever since.

Lyrah found Cueseg speaking to a blushing young woman who was having a hard time looking at anything but the man's bare chest. "Young with blue hair," Cueseg said. "He is wearing a long coat with blood on it. He came to port last fall. You see?"

"N-no, Archon. I wasn't here last fall."

"Then go," Cueseg ordered with a palm held up, his other hand holding what was left of his pastry. He turned to Lyrah as the woman left. "I am doing as you say, but it is stupid."

"I didn't expect much."

"Then why I do this?"

"There was a chance we might have learned something. It doesn't matter; I know where the boy went."

"And how did you find this?"

Lyrah smiled. "I spoke with the Portmaster."

"You send me to ask people who would have no chance to know while you do what I need to do."

"I'm sorry you didn't figure it out."

"I was doing as you say!"

Lyrah leaned down to the shorter man and patted him on the head. "And you're a *good boy* for doing so."

Utter confusion crossed Cueseg's face. "What does this mean, the touching of my head? Are you asking to have sex with me again?"

Lyrah's heart leapt. "What? *No!*" She turned away, trying to regain control. "*Light*, Cueseg, are all Tuerasians as perverted as you?"

"How am I perverted when you keep asking to have sex?"

Lyrah's hand curled into a fist and she had to stop herself from hitting him.

She turned back and judging by Cueseg's sudden hesitant expression, Lyrah's rage was showing on her face. She hissed out her reply: "Listen to me carefully, Cueseg, because I've had enough of this. I'll *never* have…have *SEX* with you or *any* man, and if you ever talk to me about it again, I'll *kill* you."

Uncharacteristic shock hung on Cueseg's face. He blinked and then leaned forward, touching both hands to his forehead and then spreading them out before him. Lyrah had only ever seen Cueseg do this to the Order's Archerons and the High Archain. "My sister Lyrah, I am sorry from the truth of my heart. I do not know. In my culture, to master self is great above all. We only show how we feel when we want others to see. Here everyone show everything, and this is strange to me."

"What, are you saying that you can't read facial expressions?"

"I know some faces, but here there are many I do not know."

Lyrah sighed. "You can't read facial expressions."

"I can."

"But not all of them, and especially not the subtle ones."

"What is subtle?"

"Small."

"Yes, small faces, they are hard."

Lyrah was finally understanding him. Cueseg was misreading her anxiety and nervousness as attraction. That's why he thought she wanted to have—well, wanted to be intimate with him. "You've never wanted to have…relations…with anybody," she said.

"Of course not, and if they ask to have sex, they show they are weak and have no control. I show my body so people want sex, but must be strong to control. It is given honors in my home so others can learn to be strong. I am not to have sex. And you show your control in the same. I do not know you are stronger than I think."

It was light-blessed hard to keep a reign on her emotions with all this talk of sex. "That's why you go about half naked?" she asked. "Not because you want to be attractive, but to teach, or force, others to control any desires that might come from your appearance?"

"This brings honor in my home. Anyone who knows to master their body show that it does not bother them to be seen naked, and do the same for other. For me who is master, it is not right that I wear clothes."

He says he's clothed while being half naked, Lyrah thought, *but it's clear from our first meeting that Cueseg prefers to wear nothing but shoes and adornments.*

"Well it's alright when you're away from your home, Cueseg."

"Yes, I know this now."

"Good. Thank the Light that's cleared up. I've found where this boy was headed and commandeered a ship that'll take us to Treremain. Once there I should be able to pick up his scent again."

"Then let us be off."

CHAPTER TEN

*Though we destroyed the Shade nightcasters, escaping the
Underworld was another matter entirely. Thus began another
part of my life I wish I could forget. We hoped Day had returned
to the land, but until we could get back to the surface, we didn't
know. There were still thousands of Shade infesting those terrible
halls. It took a year to escape—yes, a year. It was like the passages
changed as we moved through them. Calling the Underworld a
labyrinth is apt.*

*How did we survive? Food and water wasn't an issue, for there
were ample insects and mushrooms to eat, with underground
waterways common. Sometimes we had to stay in the same cavern
for weeks just to rest and resupply. What made survival difficult
was the constant fighting and darkness, in addition to the other
horrible creatures that live in the Underworld. We would have
become Shade ourselves if not for the Lightbringers. By the end,
all that was left of the hundred-thousand-strong assault was a
mere hundred.*

Many mighty Archknights had fallen.

I t's late and I'm tired," Daylen said, looking out the window into
the shining day. "We'll leave outfall. There's some dried fruit in
that cabinet if you're hungry."

"You certainly seem to know your way around," Ahrek replied.

"My um, father, always kept dried fruit in the cabinet, and apart from that it's not hard to figure out where things are."

Daylen grabbed an old spare blanket from the sagging mezzanine that hung halfway out overhead and spread it on the floor. "The beds is yours. Oh, and I snore like thunder, so good luck with that."

"I can't take the bed. This is technically your house, after all."

Daylen lay on the blanket. "Too late, I'm already here."

"I'll not force you out of your own bed."

"Then sleep on the cold hard floor for all I care, but I'm not getting you a blanket, not when there's a bed you could have slept in."

The old wooden bed eventually creaked as the Lightbringer lay down.

Daylen lay looking up at the roof of his old cottage, letting his mind wonder.

So the Light had sent a Bringer to watch over him, either in answer to his prayer for help, or for some other reason the Light only knew. Daylen didn't know how to feel about it all. On the one hand, knowing that the Light was mindful of him enough to send a *vision* to a Lightbringer was both comforting and deeply troubling.

I wonder how I'll forge a new identity with Ahrek at my side. Maybe I could lose him in the capital long enough to do what I need?

Things were going to be very different with a constant companion, one that Daylen wasn't even sure that he liked, but it was the Light's will and he couldn't exactly deny it again—especially not after all his mistakes.

———

Daylen awoke instantly in High Fall when the Bringer began to get up.

Rubbing his neck, Daylen sat up and fully registered things around him. There was a sweet smell in the air. Had Ahrek made breakfast?

"Rise and shine," Ahrek said as he ate at the tiny dining table.

"Is that *sticky bread?*"

"Mmm, yes. It's quite good."

Sticky bread was made from fresh rolls with caramelized sugar and ground hassrum sprinkled over it, all dipped in cream. It was a damned delicacy.

"Where in the world did that come from?"

"Oh, I made it."

Daylen stood and sat on the other side of the table. "Not with the ingredients in this house, and I know you didn't leave, so where did it come from?"

"The Light."

"The Light?" Daylen asked, before realizing. "You can *perform the miracle of creation!*"

Ahrek nodded, holding out his hand over the table between them. Light began to glimmer above his palm, and then shifted to take a shape. The light molded itself into the silhouette of something on a plate—and then, as the light faded into the shape it had adopted, it stayed in place, revealing a fresh roll of sticky bread.

Daylen took the offered delicacy in awe.

He was familiar with all the miracles Lightbringers could perform, although each Bringer could only perform two. The miracle of creation was not necessarily rare—each miracle was as common as the next—but it was one of the most valued and revered. With it, a Bringer could create literally anything equal to their mass. The larger and more complex the object, the more it drained them. Lightbringers were limited to the number of miracles they could perform according to their stamina. They could even kill themselves if performing a miracle too great, though many Lightbringers at the end of their life sacrificed themselves to perform one last great miracle. No longer restricted in scope due to their safety, it seemed this last miracle had no limit, except in the types of miracle they could perform in the first place.

Daylen knew that this was how the Great Lumatorium was built, or created. One of the early Lightbringers who possessed the miracle of creation had at the end of his days sacrificed himself to perform a mighty miracle and created the Lumatorium out of an incredible burst of light. The Bringer was utterly consumed in the process.

"Sticky bread is my favorite," Ahrek said, "and because of that, it's easier for me to create than other simpler foods."

"I didn't know it worked that way."

"Yes, the more familiar I am with an object, the easier it is to create, and I can make more of them than other things."

Daylen took a bite of the bread. Light, it was good. He sat on the other side of the small eating table which was right next to one of the hovel's windows. "This is an unexpected bonus from your presence. Can I expect such fine food in every meal?"

"It depends on the type of food."

"Tuerasian cuisine?"

"I've never been good at Tuerasian food. It's very complex. The result will likely taste horrible."

"But you *are* Tuerasian."

"By blood, yes, but I was raised Hamahran."

"Yeah, there's a lot more Hamahran-born Tuerasians these falls thanks to the Dawn Empire."

"We should not credit the Dawn Empire with anything."

"Look, my father was a bastard, I get it, but that doesn't mean everything he did was terrible. The metric system is far better than anything previous. His roads, education policies, and slave laws are still in place—why? Because they work. Yes, he conquered nations, but also opened up the border to allow free trade and migration. It was because of that that your own parents and countless other Tuerasian were able to move to Hamahra. One could even say it was the open borders that enabled his downfall."

"First of all, any improvement at the cost of freedom and life is never worth it, nor does it justify the means. Also, I expect that you're referring to the fact that Rayaten Leusa was Tuerasian, implying that it was the open borders which allowed him to grow up to lead the revolution, facilitating the Conqueror's downfall. What you're not realizing is that, if it hadn't been Rayaten, someone else would have done it."

"I don't know about that," Daylen said. "Rayaten was a right persistent and slippery bastard, or so my father described him, clever enough to match wits with the Conqueror himself."

"Really? What else did your father say about him?"

"Oh, my father actually respected the man quite a lot, and was very grateful to Rayaten for ending his reign. If the Conqueror could have met him, he would have hugged the man."

"If Rayaten found out that the Conqueror hadn't died on his flagship as everyone thought, he would have hunted out the tyrant to finish the job."

"Probably."

"Regardless," Ahrek said, "from what I saw of the revolution, there were many people capable of fighting against the Great Tyrant. Not to mention the knights. The Conqueror's fall was inevitable."

"I agree with you there," Daylen said, passing his empty plate back to Ahrek.

Once Ahrek took the plate, it dematerialized into light which flowed into the Bringer's hand.

Now that was interesting, Daylen thought with a raised brow. "You can turn things you've made back into light?"

"If little time has passed. It certainly makes washing the dishes easier."

"What other miracles can you perform?"

"Well, the two miracles all Lightbringers have: create light and heal."

"And the other is creation, but can you perform any more?"

"One more: the miracle of movement."

"Oh. Telekinesis," Daylen said, sitting at the table.

"You know the miracles."

"Yeah, but how does it work? You just move things with your mind?"

"You're almost right. It's with thought that I can take hold of things and by thought that I move them, just like moving my arm, but my mind isn't the thing actually moving the object—it's light."

"So you can't move anything in darkness."

"Correct."

"But can't you just create light and then move things as normal?"

"No, my inner light is what powers my miracles, and projecting that light from my body means I can't channel it to do anything else."

"I see. How much can you lift?"

"I can lift ten times the total combined strength of my body."

"Interesting," Daylen said. "That would be what, a ton?"

"Two at the very most, though with great effort and not for very long."

"Still, that's some true power."

"It is, which is why I use them with great care."

"Like making breakfast?"

"Indeed."

"It didn't drain your powers too much?"

"My powers can't drain in that sense—no man can lose their inner light—but my body has limits as to how much light I can channel through it."

That was very similar to how Daylen's own powers worked. He never ran out of light to draw upon, but his body couldn't channel it constantly.

"Then you're not too fatigued?"

"Not at all."

"Good. Thanks for making...I mean, creating breakfast. It was delicious."

"Do you know why they call it sticky bread?" Ahrek asked.

"Please don't say it's because it's sticky."

"No," Ahrek said, chuckling. "Because it's made from bread."

Daylen rolled his eyes. "That is *not* funny."

"And yet I'm laughing."

"Well they clearly don't teach what constitutes real humor at the Lumatorium."

"I wasn't trained at the Lumatorium."

"So you became a Lightbringer naturally?"

"There's only one way to become a Lightbringer, but I understand what you mean."

"You ever been there?"

"I've served several years, though not consecutively. Everyone goes there to be healed, so it's the best place to find the sick and needy. But there are many who can't travel, and it's them that I seek out most."

"That's noble of you, but considering who you are, not surprising."

"Thank you. You'd be surprised how many animals I end up healing while traveling through these rural parts, although birds require a different *tweet*ment."

Daylen stared at the man. "Terrible."

Ahrek laughed. "I thought that one was quite good."

"Terrible."

"You are far too serious, Daylen. Learn to laugh a little."

"Oh, I laugh. You've heard me laugh, just not at your pathetic jokes."

"Okay, you tell me a joke."

"Fine. How do you make a person ugly?"

"How?"

"Ask your mother."

The Bringer didn't laugh. "That was rather mean," he said.

"It was just a joke."

"Jokes don't need to be cruel; and when cruelty is involved, it is never *just* a joke."

"Look, we clearly have different views on what's funny."

"Yet your joke didn't even make *you* laugh."

"I wasn't supposed to. Jokes are supposed to make others laugh."

"And that's my new goal. I'm going to make you laugh—not the sarcastic laughter I've heard so far, but true, *joyful* laughter."

"Good luck with that."

"Thank you."

Daylen rose from his seat, having finished his meal, and walked to the other side of the room.

He took a key that hung on a ring with several others and began rummaging through his things.

He knew exactly what he was looking for, his most prized possession. Finding the chest, he pulled it out.

The chest hadn't been touched in twenty years, the lock stale and stiff. Luckily, the key still opened it.

Ahrek's shadow passed over Daylen, the Bringer now looking over his shoulder.

The Bringer gasped when Daylen opened the chest, asking, "Light, is that *really* Imperious?"

CHAPTER ELEVEN

At the surface we were met with blessed day.
I vowed then that, if it would ever be within my power, I would
find a way to eradicate the Shade once and for all to spare future
generations from what we had endured.
We left to pick up what was left of our lives, and thus began the
Fifth Day. Fifteen years of hell and darkness had ravaged the
world, just like the other Nights before the one we had endured.
Starvation was rampant in those falls, and the aristocracy didn't
do a blackened thing about it. They made sure to feed themselves,
but not the people. I could remember my anger at that—the
righteous passion that coursed through my veins. I was a captain
due to my service through the Fourth Night, and as one of the few
survivors of the great assault, I was respected and even revered by
many as a war hero. I used my influence to reason with the
aristocracy to feed the people. I even proposed new irrigation
systems of my own design, but my designs would send the
aristocracy into poverty themselves, and they denied my proposal.
But I didn't give up. I was a thorn in their side, constantly
confronting them and telling the people of their crimes, rallying
support, and building my profile.

Yes, this is Imperious," Daylen said reverently in reply to Ahrek's question.

Imperious was the legendary sunforged sword of Dayless the Conqueror. It was a beautifully crafted swept-hilt sword that at the moment appeared to be made of polished obsidian. Being a sunucle, its oversized blade didn't match any standard sword type, as sunucles weren't restricted to the weight of steel. The sheathed blade was as wide as his hand and over a meter long.

"But it should have shattered upon your father's death…" Ahrek said in confusion. "Unless he isn't truly dead!"

"Don't be an idiot. Clearly the link has passed to me."

"What? Sunforged links can't be passed on."

"Yes, and as uninformed as you are about sunucles, you really shouldn't throw around accusations based on their function."

"Then by all means, educate me."

Daylen smiled. Ahrek was right to question him, of course. Sunforging was the process of bonding light to an object, which increased that object's power similar to how Lightbinders bonded light to themselves. The issue was that light couldn't be bonded to any nonliving thing unless the blood of a living person was placed within the object first, linking them to it and enabling it to be sunforged. The blood of animals simply didn't work. The drawback to this was that if the sunforged object, called a sunucle, were destroyed, it would severely injure if not kill the one who was linked to it; and likewise if the living link died, the sunucle would shatter.

"When a person who's linked to a sunucle dies, there's a chance the link will pass onto someone with similar blood," Daylen said.

Ahrek scoffed. "I've *never* heard that before."

"That's because such a thing is extremely rare, but it does happen. For instance, when a sunucle is linked to an identical twin, the link *always* passes to the other twin when the first dies."

"I suppose that makes sense."

"Well, Dayless's links have passed onto me," Daylen lied. "I can feel them," he added truthfully, for of course he could still feel his own links. It was true that there was a tiny chance a link could pass on to one's firstborn child, but in this case no link had passed at all, for Daylen was the original. "But I'm not surprised," Daylen said. "This is Imperious we're talking about."

Ahrek's face softened after that statement. "Yes," he said. "I've heard that it's the only sunucle ever created that that doesn't shatter at the touch of darkstone or Shade."

"Yes. Imperious is immune to the normal sunforging laws, so we might have expected the link to pass rather than it shatter." Daylen pulled the sword from its sheath. "Imperious is unique."

"Then I'm going to need a bit more proof that the link has truly passed to you," Ahrek said. "Anyone can *say* they feel the link, but considering Imperious is truly indestructible, as I think on it, it's possible then that Imperious might be able to stay intact without a link at all."

"You really know nothing about sunforging."

Ahrek's raised his brow, unconvinced, looking at Daylen as if to say he still needed to prove it.

"And here I thought you were so trusting."

"My trust only goes so far. Too many people would be willing to lie if it meant getting their hands on such a priceless object."

"Well, I won't be able to prove anything with the sword's current condition," Daylen said, referring to the obvious fact that the sword had been without light for years. As a result, the blade and hilt were jet black. This wasn't the natural state of sunucles, but rather what they became when locked away from light for extended periods of time. In its current state, Imperious was as fragile as glass, but this was easily remedied.

There was plenty of light inside, which was already causing the black color to fade. Daylen took the sword and walked outside to the more plentiful light of day.

The blackness quickly dissolved, revealing what sunucles truly looked like: softly glowing, translucent colored glass. Imperious' blade was a deep, translucent blue that shimmered like a sapphire. The beautiful swept hilt was a shining yellow made to look like a flaring sun and protected the whole hand.

The sword was originally made from ritten wood, a unique timber in that it was extremely light and hard. You could put a razor's edge on it. Ritten wood was still utterly impractical to be used for weapons—it was still wood. Or at least it was, until it was sunforged. Once an object was sunforged, it became indestructible to everything except for the Shade, darkstone, and other sunforged weapons. The most significant attribute sunucles adopted was a seemingly supernatural enhancement to whatever purpose the object was meant for. Sunforged boots gripped the ground ten times more effectively than normal boots. If a cloak was made to hide someone's identity, once sunforged it would shift colors to blend in with one's surroundings. If that same cloak was meant to keep the rain off, once sunforged the rain would streak around a person like they were protected by an invisible bubble. And of course with blades, their cutting ability became so enhanced that they could slice through steel like butter.

Daylen returned inside to where Ahrek had been watching. He put the sword on one of the work benches and walked to the other side of the room. Daylen held out his hand and pulled on the link. The sword flew off the table toward Daylen in a straight line where he caught it in his hand.

"Well, that settles it," Ahrek said. "The link has passed to you."

"Like I said," Daylen replied.

There were some interesting effects that arose from the link between a person and a sunucle. Whoever was linked to it could feel it like it was a part of their body and know when it had been touched by someone else. The linked person developed a sense of the sunucle's direction when separated, no matter the distance, and when close enough—about ten meters for most people—the linked person could pull the sunucle to them in a direct line, as Daylen had just done. The sunucle would ignore gravity and fly in the same manner as a darkstone with light. Daylen's ability to pull on Imperious had grown with practice and time to a distance of sixty meters—longer than any link he had ever heard of.

Ahrek was looking at Imperious in awe. "Dayless never shared how he crafted such a wonder," Ahrek said, "the selfish man."

Daylen sheathed Imperious. "What good would another weapon be to the world? Dayless invented the annihilator and the shooter, and how many deaths have those things caused?"

Ahrek leaned on one of the workbenches and crossed his arms. "Yes, but sunforging is used for other things than weapons. I've seen sunforged boots that never slipped on anything and hammers that drove in nails with the slightest touch. But most people are too afraid to make sunucles thanks to the few fatal weaknesses all sunucles possess—something that Dayless figured out how to overcome. With his secret we could build sunforged tools, houses, bridges, and skyships. They would all be indestructible, and last forever, never wearing down or degrading over time."

"Not skyships," Daylen said. "No sunforge in existence could forge a whole skyship." But Daylen was lying, for he knew of one forge, hidden away where no one would ever find it... An ancient artifact of incredible power that could sunforge anything of any size.

"But they could forge a piece at a time, or the most crucial parts."

Daylen walked in front of Ahrek and placed his hands on his hips, determined to argue this point. "No. If Imperious' secret got out, the first thing the governments would do is equip their armies with indestructible sunforged weapons and armor. Think of how overpowered that would be. Seriously, have you seen what a man can do in sunforged plate?"

"Not seen, but I've heard. Apart from being nearly indestructible, it's supposed to double the physical abilities of the wearer."

Daylen raised his index finger and squinted an eye. "Exactly. Even with the risks of having a full suit of sunforged plate, some people still make it because of how powerful it is, the idiots."

"It can't be any more risky than other sunucles..."

"Huh!" Daylen said. "Kid, you really don't know much about sunforging, do you? It only takes one broken link to potentially kill a man, and linking other people on sunucles you intend to use and might break is a mongrel action so despicable that Dayless himself didn't even do it. Light, he even outlawed it!"

"I know all this, Daylen. What's your point?"

"My point is that each additional linked sunucle raises the risks. It only takes one sunucle to be forged imperfectly and potentially kill, but you can't sunforge a suit of armor as one piece. You need to forge and link each piece individually."

"Oh, I see," Ahrek said in full comprehension. "Full plate has at least twenty components."

Daylen relaxed and walked to pull out a chair from the small dining table. Placing it to face Ahrek, he sat, resting Imperious on his lap. "More like forty, if it's fully interlocked. To get the full physical enhancement from plate it needs to be a full suit, so making a sunforged breastplate by itself doesn't cut it. Having forty linked sunucles is suicidal. All it takes is one mistake in the sunforging process. That, and the armor is easy to counter. All you need is a darkstone dagger."

Ahrek nodded. "I see your point. Still, it makes me wonder why Dayless didn't make his own indestructible sunforged plate."

"Who said he didn't?"

"If he did, wouldn't he have worn it? There were no accounts of Dayless wearing plate."

"Sunforged armor doesn't need to be as bulky as normal stuff. Though the physical enhancement is less, you can wear it under your clothes."

"Ah yes, he would keep that a secret, wouldn't he? Any potential assassin wouldn't account for Dayless wearing sunforged armor."

"Now you're thinking like him."

"Then where is it? The armor's link might have passed on to you, and it must be as remarkable an artifact as Imperious."

"I don't know," Daylen lied. "My father kept many secrets, and probably hid away lots of his things."

"If only he had told you."

Daylen smirked. "Yeah, if only." Of course Daylen knew exactly where his armor was—hidden away where no one would find it. Imperious was the only treasure he kept at this hovel. He would get his armor once he forged a birth certificate at the capital, if he could ditch the Bringer for a few falls at least.

"I still think the secret of making indestructible sunucles would be a great benefit to mankind, and abuses could be avoided."

"Yeah, and the sun might fall. Trust me, Ahrek, Imperious' secret would only cause more harm than good."

"I choose to have more hope for mankind."

"Then you're a naive fool."

"Or perhaps *you're* a skeptical pessimist?"

"Oh, there's no perhaps about it," Daylen said.

"What are you planning to do with the sword?" Ahrek asked.

"I don't know—dig some holes, maybe. It could serve as a toothpick, I suppose."

"Sarcasm is the lowest form of humor."

"No, *your* humor is."

"So you're just going to wear a historical artifact that once belonged to the greatest tyrant the world has ever seen?"

"And use it if I have to. From what I hear, it's a pretty good sword."

"You don't think others are going to recognize it?"

Daylen paused. Imperious would draw a lot of unwanted attention, but it was *his* sword. He was as attached to it as he was to his arm. Not only did he have a connection with Imperious, as any swordsman would, but it was also a work of his own hands, his masterpiece. He had put years of study, time, and energy into its creation, and like any artist with their greatest work, it was as if Imperious held a piece of his soul. Never touching it whilst he was in hiding had been agony, and now holding it once more was like embracing a long-lost brother. Daylen knew he could never part with it again.

Luckily, being seen with Imperious wouldn't cause too much trouble. Word that Dayless had fathered a son was probably in Treremain by now, so hiding was pointless. Imperious would just identify who he was, if people even noticed it as much as Ahrek thought they would.

"They probably will," Daylen said. "So I guess I'll be quite popular, won't I?"

"Many will think you have no right to it, the Sunforging Guild especially."

"The Guilds can go jump off the edge, the corrupt pack of bastards."

Daylen had a long history with the Guilds, as they provided a significant portion to Hamahra's wealth—and oh, how he hated them. They had been a constant thorn in his side during his rule, not to mention the endless petitions by the Sunforging Guild to know Imperious' secret. They had even tried to blackmail him once, but Daylen had executed everyone involved, as well as their families. Not his finest moment, but far from his worst, which spoke volumes.

There was one good thing the Guilds had done. They had been a main driving force behind the revolution that ended his rule, Rayaten himself being the former master of the Artistry Guild.

"The law is very clear regarding sunucles," Daylen continued. "The person linked to them always has right of ownership."

"And I support that law completely, but there still might be legal precedent to overturn it."

"If they try anything like that, they're in for a world of trouble. Imperious is mine."

"You're confident."

"Of course I am," Daylen said, rising and taking off his old justacorps coat. Coats like that were impractical to wear with a sword. One still could, of course, but being so long it would get in the way of one's leg work and might tangle with the sword at your side. A Grand High Master like Daylen moved so precisely when fighting that any obstruction was *very* annoying. He was skilled enough that his sword work wouldn't really be affected by such trivial things, but he would rather fight comfortably than not. This was why dueling jackets existed.

Placing Imperious aside, Daylen pulled out another chest. Within it were some better-suited clothes. Daylen had to shake them out a bit as they hadn't seen the light of day in some time. He put on an old, yet clean shirt, tight pants with a high waist made from an elastic fiber so they were still comfortable, leather boots that rose above his shins, and lastly his crimson stained leather dueling jacket. They still fit him perfectly.

"Now that is an *old*-style jacket," Ahrek said. "Your father's, I assume?"

Daylen looked at the jacket. It was called a dueling jacket because it had a wide belt sewn to the waist where you could easily hang a sword, and the jacket had no further length past the belt unlike the dueling tailcoats popular these days. Made of supple leather, the jacket was done up to the side of the chest by a row of shining steel tags that snapped closed. It had a line of white running along the shoulders and down the sleeves with large black cuffs at the ends to match the belt at the hem. An upturned collar sweeping behind the neck completed the look.

"Yeah," Daylen said. "I like the style much more than what's worn these days."

"You're planning to fight someone?"

The Bringer clearly recognized that, aside from era, Daylen was wearing classic dueling garb.

"No, but if I'm attacked I'd rather be prepared."

"You might as well carry a sign saying, *Challengers are welcome*."

"No," Daylen said, fixing his sheathed sword to his belt. "I'd need to wear the ribbon for that."

Ahrek smiled. "I don't think the lack of the red ribbon will dissuade everyone," he said, watching Daylen make himself ready.

The next chest Daylen sought was a much smaller wooden box. As he tried to move it, it wouldn't budge. "Oh yeah," Daylen said to himself.

"Something wrong?" Ahrek asked.

"It's my father's skimmer and gauntlet," Daylen said. "The sunstones inside have been exhausted." Daylen walked to the iron fixtures hanging from the roof that held several shining sunstones.

"The skimmer I understand, but the gauntlet?"

"It has a spring-loaded darkstone blade for countering sunforged weapons and shields."

"Doesn't surprise me that Dayless the Conqueror owned such a thing. You know it's illegal to use darkstone weapons in a duel?"

"Of course I do, but I'm surprised you know. Done some dueling in your life have you?"

"I wasn't a Lightbringer my whole life."

Having retrieved the sunstone beads, Daylen opened the smaller chest, where he found his skimmer and gauntlet.

A skimmer was mostly a shipping tool, though they were very useful outside that profession. It was comprised of a steel ball the size of a fist and a square handle protruding from it with a smaller ringed lever for the thumb. Pulling the lever would lock the skimmer's internal darkstone, making it a handhold that was frozen in the air—very useful if one was ever thrown overboard or fell from a high place. You could move the skimmer by manipulating the lever and skim through the air to wherever you needed to go.

Daylen opened the steel ball where it lay in the box, but once that was done, he could pick it up, as light was shining on the core. Daylen replaced the sunstones and, once done, he closed the ball and hooked the skimmer to his belt.

Daylen's gauntlet was a sunucle; and, having been locked away for so long, had become black like Imperious had been.

"The gauntlet's link has passed on to you as well," Ahrek said in awe.

"If one link can pass, it makes it likely that any others will, too."

Daylen carefully unclasped the main back bracer, the primary blocking part of the gauntlet, and placed the sunstones in the fixed holds around the darkstone blade before replacing the bracer. With light now shining on the darkstone uniformly, the gauntlet could be picked up and handled normally.

Daylen took the gauntlet outside and its color quickly returned. The gauntlet shone a deep blue, much darker than Imperious, and as it was mildly transparent—its spring-loaded darkstone blade could just be seen under the bracer.

Daylen came back inside and slipped his left hand into the

gauntlet. Clenching his fist with a deliberate and specific twist of his wrist triggered the spring-loaded darkstone blade. It shot out above his wrist with a mechanical sound.

"No, you're not planning to duel anyone at *all*," Ahrek said sarcastically.

"I thought you believed sarcasm the lowest form of humor?"

"It is, while also being an effective form of verbal emphasis. Seriously, Daylen, wearing a sword—and especially a gauntlet—like *that*, specifically *made* for dueling even though it does have an illegal blade, is all the encouragement any duelist will need. And then there's the fact that you bear Imperious itself! As soon as people realize this, they'll look for any reason to challenge you simply for victor's right in the hopes to claim your father's sword."

"I can deny victor's right."

"Not if it's a personal duel, and considering who your father was, I doubt anyone will have to look very hard to find personal cause. The winner still won't be able to take Imperious from you because of the link, which means according to the law you must pay the winner something of equivalent value to the sword in question. Considering that Imperious is priceless, you'll become a debt slave for the rest of your life! Once word spreads, every duelist and treasure hunter in the world will be after you."

"Not if they know they'll lose."

"Oh really, and just how good a duelist are you?"

Daylen reached in the same box that had held the gauntlet and took out a flat, round disk the size of his palm. It was a gold-plated steel disk that bore the indented steel image of a sword. This was the mark of a master, the type of metal denoting the level. Iron for Master, copper for High Master, silver for Grand Master, and gold for Grand High Master.

Daylen held up the badge. "I'm this good."

Ahrek looked stunned for a second, before laughing.

"No, really," Daylen said. "I am a Grand High Master."

"That was your father's mark," Ahrek said, wiping away a tear. "You don't deserve to wear it."

"I do if I'm actually as good as the mark says."

"Have you been tested before a panel of masters to earn the right?"

Daylen clipped the badge over his belt buckle as it was made to do. "Until I can, I need a sign to warn would-be challengers of my skill."

"You are *not* a Grand High Master."

"*Yes*, I am."

"It takes *years* of training to become a Grand High Master, years far beyond your age. Daylen, please, there's a much better way to fend off would-be challengers. Just don't wear your sword and gauntlet and wrap the sword so no one can see it."

"Son, don't presume you can tell me what to do."

"Daylen, give me the mark."

"Go stone yourself."

"Give it to me!"

"Make me," Daylen said offhandedly as he returned to rummaging through his things.

Ahrek didn't respond, clearly accepting defeat.

"Very well," Ahrek said with a stern voice. "Outside. Now."

Daylen turned to the Lightbringer. "What?"

"You wish me to make you, so I shall."

Daylen laughed. "Really?"

"Yes."

"Oh, this is going to be fun."

CHAPTER TWELVE

The aristocracy wanted to strip my military rank for insubordination, but by that time I had gained the loyalty of half the army.
So they tried to kill me instead.
The attack came during a public gathering where I was trying to rally further support. Soldiers loyal to the aristocracy surrounded us and began killing wantonly. I, with the people, fought back. We had all just endured the Fourth Night, and no one was unfamiliar to battle. They fought just as well as an army—and with my leadership, against greater numbers, we killed every last one of our attackers. Some might say we won that battle, but the truth was that only ten survived. My dearest Tara was killed in that battle along with our children: our young son, Daygen, and infant daughter, Teressa.

D aylen followed the Bringer to the grassy field beside his home.

The sun was shaded that fall by some low clouds and the grass swayed in a soft breeze.

"You can stop the charade, Ahrek," Daylen said.

Ahrek didn't reply, all humor gone from his face.

Daylen laughed. "Look, son, your bluff has failed. You don't even have a sword, not that it would have been any use. Are you going to duel me with your bare hands?"

Ahrek reached under the neckline of his robes and retrieved a medallion that had been hanging underneath. A round disk flipped out to hang in front of his chest. It was gold—and bore the image of a sword.

The mark of a Grand High Master.

Daylen nearly fell over. "*What?*"

The Bringer lowered his arms and light began to shine from his hands. The light in each hand began to grow and take shape, forming a teardrop kite shield and huge bladed broadsword, both fully sunforged that shone white. With a few masterful flourishes, the Bringer took a battle stance, shield in front, sword at the ready.

Daylen could barely believe his eyes. Not only was Ahrek a blackened *Grand High Master* of the sword, but he could create sunforged weapons out of light without the slightest sign of fatigue. Why would a stoned-blackened Lightbringer go through the extensive training to become a Grand High Master? It was true that some Lightbringers fought, especially those who had joined the Archknights, but Ahrek didn't look like a swordsman. And, on top of that, why wasn't Ahrek famous? There was only fifty or so people alive at this level of skill, and thus they were practically celebrities.

"Are you ready or not?" Ahrek asked.

No, Daylen wasn't ready. He was expecting this duel to be laughably easy, but now... Well, black! Daylen could use his light-binding powers, then he would win easily, but that simply wasn't fair. Then again, neither was the Bringer's shield.

"Are we allowing illegal arms, or would you rather I avoid using the darkstone in my gauntlet?"

"Of course I would rather that."

"What about your shield?"

The Bringer looked to his left hand and seemed to notice the shield for the first time. Turning back to Daylen, the Bringer shrugged. "Sorry, I created it on reflex. Swords only then, for a fair test of skill."

"Agreed."

The Bringer's shield dematerialized back into light that flowed into his arm, disappearing. He performed another sword flourish, taking a stance with his right side facing Daylen.

Daylen pursed his lips and took off his gauntlet before dropping it to the grass. He performed a flourish of his own and took his stance. It was surprising how quickly he had become accustomed to having a strong and healthy body once more. It had been so long since he was able to push himself physically to the level his skill demanded. His muscles quivered in anticipation.

They stared at each other for a long time.

When swordsmen reached the skill level that Daylen and Ahrek were at, they would plan their moves and predict their opponents' own moves as much as react to what their opponents did. It became a battle of psychology as much as reflexes.

Then without a word or sign, they lunged at each other at the exact same time. A blur of movement followed. Thrusts, parries, lunges, ripostes, slashes, and counters. Back and forth their swords danced with perfectly executed technique.

As the sunforged blades struck they flashed brightly in blue and white, chimes sounding from the swords' inner lights.

It was an orchestra of dance, light, and sound, each beat a step in the fight.

Ahrek truly was a master.

Few battles were fought with such perfect precision, as there were so few alive with such flawless skill. It would have been worthy of song if there was but anyone to see it.

In one last final move each sword slid down the other, to which they both countered and attacked. The combatants were forced to jump back to avoid the other's blade, which caused a pause in the duel.

Daylen stepped to the side, ready to go again, but Ahrek smiled and stood up casually, his sword disappearing into light.

"What?" Daylen asked.

"You weren't lying," Ahrek said in awe. "You really *are* a Grand High Master."

"But...but our fight?"

"We were fighting because I believed you unworthy to bear the mark. I was wrong."

"Don't you want to see who'll win?"

"Not particularly."

"*Oh, come on!*" Daylen said, annoyed.

"Very well, I concede. You win."

"That's not the same, and you know it!"

Ahrek chuckled, which only made Daylen angrier. "You're a bastard," Daylen said.

"I've never seen anyone so disappointed with winning."

"I didn't win! You *robbed* me of that."

"You're acting like it's the end of the world. This is but a very little thing in the larger picture."

"Oh, put a rock in it."

"You'll still need to be reviewed by a panel of masters, which you'll pass—but until then, as I'm a master, I can give you permission to wear the mark. Others need to be warned of what they might be getting into if they're adamant enough to challenge you, which will dissuade many from trying to steal your sword."

"I'm glad you agree," Daylen said cynically.

"You know, I'm still finding it hard to believe that you could reach such a level of skill so young, but I can't deny what I've seen."

"I wouldn't believe it either, but here I am."

"Who taught you?"

"My father."

"I thought you grew up in an orphanage."

"We visited each other when we could, and I practiced every waking minute. It turns out I inherited most of my father's natural skill."

"You're a true prodigy, then, and you've clearly dueled before. That makes me wonder, why you don't wear a tassel?"

"I, uh, lost it. I'll thread a new one before we leave with a couple of beads on it."

"You'll need red, to reflect your skill."

"That's my plan, but enough about me. *You're* a master? And you can create sunforged objects!"

"I had no reason to show the mark, as no one dares challenge a holy man. And because I can create a sword whenever I need there's no reason to carry one, which makes it doubly illegal to challenge me. I haven't fought a duel in years."

"Well, your skill hasn't waned."

"I never said I didn't keep up training. If Night falls within my lifetime, such skill will be most needed."

"Is that why you endeavored to become a master, whilst already being a Lightbringer that is?"

"I was a master before I was a Lightbringer, but what I've said is the reason I keep my skills sharp."

"I've never heard of you."

"You keep track of every Grand High Master of the sword?"

"I used to."

"Well, fame is something I've no need for. In fact, it would get in the way of my service… Another reason I hide my mastery."

"I can understand that. So how are you able to summon *sunforged* objects?"

"First of all, I don't summon them. They aren't teleported from some other plane of existence. They are created from my inner light."

"Yes, okay, so how under the Light can you create something so complex without killing yourself?"

"Well the mass of an object affects my vitality more than complexity, and if it's an object I'm very familiar with, or that I have a special connection with, like my sticky bread, they become much easier to create. Also if I'm feeling particularly emotional, the power seems to feed off that emotion before my stamina."

"I've never heard that before."

"Well, you are very young."

"I am *not* young!"

"Daylen, please. Stop getting so offended by the truth. You *are* young!"

Daylen grumbled to himself, knowing that he couldn't deny what the Bringer was saying. He needed people to think him as young as he looked, as much as he hated it. Daylen just had to swallow his pride. "Fine. I am, son."

"If you need to call me *son* to get over the resentment you have at your own age, I can accept that."

"We're agreed, then."

"Are you still planning to head to the capital?"

"Yes. I'll just gather the rest of my things; though I suppose provisions are less a priority now, considering you can just create food for us."

"I'll create what we need, but don't expect a banquet for every meal."

"Unless it's easier to create, like sticky bread."

"Well, yes, apart from that."

CHAPTER THIRTEEN

*Words will never convey the pain at seeing my wife and children
murdered. Saying my heart felt ripped from my chest, that my
soul was wracked with unspeakable sorrow and grief, reveals but
the slightest fraction of what I suffered as I knelt over the
dismembered remains of those whom I loved most in this world.
Though I still breathed, the aristocracy had succeeded in their
attempt. Daylen Namaran died that day with his family.*

Towns like Karadale held mismatched buildings ranging
between old and very old, some built from nice sturdy brick,
while others had been crafted of stone or half-timbered with faded
whitewashed daubed walls, or a mixture thereof. Every building
sat at generous distances from the others, for there was room to
spare in the country, making the streets seem more like small
trodden fields with grass growing on the edges in wide swaths.

Daylen wore his gauntlet and sword as he walked with Ahrek
down the street, a newly threaded tassel hanging from his temple
with a few red beads.

It was still early High Fall, yet most of the townspeople were up
and about. Daylen could swear that every single one stopped to
stare at the two of them as they passed. Low murmurs rolled on
the air like a distant hornet's nest.

Yes, word of who Daylen was, or was supposed to be, had clearly spread through the whole town. There he was, the son of the old town tinker—who had just so happened to be Dayless the Conqueror himself.

"You're popular," Ahrek said to him.

"Paradan did his work well."

"He hardly needed to try, considering the news."

They moved to the side of the road to avoid an old horse-drawn cart coming their way and found themselves near a group of townswomen. They were particularly invested in their discussion of Daylen, whispering frantically and pointing at him.

Being so annoyed at the unwanted attention and obvious prejudice everyone had for him, Daylen couldn't resist.

He jumped to the woman screaming, "*Raaa!*" and making clawing motions.

They screamed and ran like mice, one so frantic that her arms flailed overhead as she ran down the street long after the others had gained control of themselves, though terror was fixed on their faces.

Daylen doubled over in laughter.

The women walked away, glaring at him.

"Are you done terrorizing the locals?" Ahrek asked.

"It seems my presence is enough to instill terror, so I might as well have some fun with it. Their minds are made up. I'm Dayless the Conqueror reborn."

"And you're doing nothing to dissuade them of their fears."

"It's not like anything could," Daylen said. "Look, son, you're more naive than I thought if you haven't figured out by now that people *do* judge a book by its cover and think whatever the light they want to think about someone so long as it makes them feel better about themselves. They're going to hate me no matter what I do."

"I disagree. It's possible to earn the love of even your most bitter enemy."

Before Daylen could reply, someone cut him off. "So you're the Great Bastard's bastard."

Being in conversation, Daylen hadn't noticed that a group of young men had gathered before them.

"Huh, don't look like much," Fergen Le'donner said, head of the

Le'donner family and local twat. He looked like a dried fruit with a personality and wit to match.

There were fifteen men with him, including his sons, whose heads were as thick as their arms. The country had a knack for breeding dumb brutes. Many wore a tassel each with a few beads, and all wore swords on their hips.

"Now, men, we want no trouble," Ahrek said.

"We've no issue with you, Bringer. No, we're after the Bastard's bastard."

"Is that the best you can do?" Daylen said. "Of course, I shouldn't expect much considering the abyss of your intelligence. Don't push yourself too hard or you'll give yourself an aneurysm."

"A what?"

"My point exactly."

"Listen, you little smartass, we know who you are! The son of the Great Bastard can't be allowed to walk around freely, especially in our town."

"Piss off, Fergen, I'm leaving anyway."

"How'd you know my name, runt?"

"Everyone knows the village idiot."

"Daylen, stop antagonizing them!" Ahrek said.

"Why, I ought to—" Fergen raised his hand to strike Daylen—but then, one of his sons spoke up.

"Careful, Dah, he's wearing the mark."

"A load of drack," Fergen said. "No kid is a master or wins red beads. He's nothing but a sniveling liar, just like his father!"

"The beads are rightly his," Ahrek said, "as is the mark of a Grand High Master."

The moron hesitated as he looked to the gold disk over Daylen's belt buckle. "No. You're lying."

Daylen sighed. "Lightbringers can't lie, you stupid yoke."

"That's it!" the brute said, grabbing Daylen's jacket, about to throw a punch.

Daylen had had more than enough of this. Not wanting a full brawl in the middle of a street, he decided to end things quickly. He channeled light into his strength and speed, using two of his four paths on each, and in a blindingly fast movement of his hands he broke the man's left arm in two places and punched him in the chest. Fergen flew into the air, knocking down those behind him.

The others in the mob, those left standing, looked to their fallen companions and then to Daylen in astonishment and fear.

"Light's mercy!" Ahrek said, walking over to the fallen man who was trying to breathe, his face an image of pain.

Light shone over Ahrek's hands as he healed the man, who gasped in relief before eventually sitting up. Those he had knocked over were already on their feet.

Ahrek helped Fergen stand.

"Now leave before anyone else gets hurt," Ahrek said, waving his hand at the mob of young men. They obeyed, though they stared at Daylen, terrified.

Light, it was satisfying.

Ahrek grabbed Daylen's arm, saying angrily, "You, with me, now!"

Daylen easily resisted the Bringer's pull, as he was still channeling light to his strength. "Get off!" he said.

Suddenly a force hit Daylen so strong that it knocked him off his feet. The invisible force then grabbed him while he was still in the air and pulled him down an empty street from the view of the many onlookers.

The force released him, and Daylen crashed along the dusty side road.

He gasped for breath. That invisible blow had been so strong that it had cracked a few of his ribs. All his paths began to channel light into healing. He could breathe more easily now and he got to his feet knowing full well what had happened.

The Bringer had used the miracle of movement against him—in other words, telekinesis.

Ahrek was walking toward him, looking furious.

Most of Daylen's injuries had already healed, and he channeled light into speed, drawing Imperious.

"Put that away, you fool!" Ahrek said.

Daylen was livid with rage and tried his best to control himself. It was blackened hard.

The Bringer had actually lashed out with his holy powers against *him*. The wretch should die for that.

The Bringer walked right up to Daylen, giving no thought to Imperious in his hand. "You're an *Archknight*!" Ahrek said through closed teeth.

Daylen was so stunned by the question that his rage waned, though it was still most certainly there. "Why in the light would you say that?"

"You're channeling light!"

"You can sense it?"

"Of course I can, and so can you..." Ahrek's face suddenly switched to realization. "Unless you don't know that you can. You're a *deserter*? But then you should have lost the powers."

The surprise helped Daylen's anger come to a more manageable level. "I've never been an Archknight," he sneered.

"But only Archknights have such powers."

"Apparently *not*. And why does it matter? I have the powers of the Archknights, I can lightbind. It's not as if the world has fallen apart."

"Why does it *matter*?" Ahrek asked rhetorically. "If people other than Archknights can receive their powers, it means unworthy people like *you* might abuse them!"

"*Unworthy*! Who're *you* to say that? You just manhandled me with yours!"

"Because you nearly killed a man!"

"He attacked me, and I was far from killing the fool."

"Oh really, did you know that you broke all his ribs?"

"What?"

"If I hadn't been here, he would have died. It's obvious you don't know the slightest thing about controlling your powers or when it's right to use them."

Guilt took away the rest of Daylen's rage. He had no idea he had pushed the man so hard.

"You're like a child attempting to fly a skyship."

"Hey, I didn't ask for these powers."

"Oh, so you would be willing to give them up if you could?"

Daylen frowned. "Well, no. Of course not."

"How did you get them?"

"None of your blackened business."

"Stop pushing me away, I'm trying to help you!"

"I didn't ask for your help! I don't even want you here, but I can't exactly say no to the Light, can I?"

"But if you don't let me do what the Light wants me to do with you, then you're practically denying it anyway."

"And what do you think the Light wants you to do with me?"

"Stop you from becoming *your father*!"

The words stung deep.

"Look at your actions, Daylen. Were they the actions of a good man, or of a power-hungry tyrant more concerned about his own convenience than the lives of others?"

The reality of Ahrek's word struck Daylen.

Ahrek was absolutely right. Daylen *had* acted like Dayless the Conqueror. In other words, he was acting exactly like himself. Daylen stumbled, walking a few steps before falling to the grass on the side of the road,

"I *am* like him," he said in remorse. "I'm *exactly* like him. Is there any point in trying to change?"

Ahrek smiled down at him. "If not, the Light wouldn't have even sent me. And hopefully, if you're willing to accept my help, you won't do anything like that again." Ahrek sat next to Daylen in the shade of the long townhouse.

It was so patronizing to have a man half Daylen's age tell him what to do.

"It's not like I wanted to," Daylen said. "I just get so angry, and you can't tell me that snot didn't deserve a good thump."

"Oh, you gave him more than a thump. Regardless of his aggression, there was a hundred different ways you could have handled it."

"I was treating him with the same respect that he was showing me."

"Oh for Light's sake, you really *are* a child."

"A child!" Daylen said in disgust. He was *eighty-two years old*, black it! "I am NOT a child..."

"You're definitely acting like one, and although that man was, too, you can't afford to be so foolish! You possess too much power and could cause great harm. On top of that, people will be judging you based on your parentage before even meeting you, so you'll have to work twice as hard to gain their trust or at least show that you're not to be feared—and breaking the arms of those who accost you won't help convince anybody that you're not like your father!"

Daylen was doing his very best to listen to the Bringer, and considering the resentment he felt boiling over, it was quite the feat. He knew everything the Bringer was saying; Light, there was probably *nothing* the Bringer could actually teach him that Daylen didn't already know, but he deserved the reminder.

"So next time don't feel so entitled to respect or special treatment," Ahrek continued. "You don't demand respect, you earn it. People can be cruel and heartless, judgmental and unjust, and treating them with the same spite will only make things worse."

"Yes, yes," Daylen said, standing, reaching the end of his patience. "I'm not brushing you off. You're right, I agree with you, and I'm sorry. I acted like a spoilt brat."

Ahrek rose. "There's one more thing."

"And that is?"

"Your powers—how did you get them?"

"Why do you want to know? So you can be a Lightbinder on top of being a Lightbringer?"

"Bringers can't become Lightbinders, or at least this is what the Archknights have said, including the Bringers who're members of the Order."

"Then why do you want to know?"

"Daylen, think of the implications! The peace we have in the world is in large measure thanks to the knights. Their mandate is to protect the world not only from the Shade but from anything that threatens it, even empires if they become corrupt enough. The knights are small in number when compared to an army, but they have been able to fight because of their power. The perfect example of this is your father—if not for the Archknights, the world would *still* be under the boot of Dayless the Conqueror."

Daylen's huff was near a laugh, for he knew the truth of that more than anyone.

"And here you are, showing there's no true connection between the Order's mandate to protect and their powers."

"That's an assumption, Bringer. I could be an anomaly and the knights' powers still reliant on their oath."

"Is that what you believe?"

Daylen sneered. "Not really."

"Exactly. It's more likely that you prove anyone could receive the Archknight's powers, if they only knew how. Now imagine for a second," Ahrek said gravely, "what would happen to the world if someone like *Dayless the Conqueror* became a Lightbinder."

This time Daylen did laugh. "Oh, I don't need to imagine."

"It's nothing to laugh about," Ahrek responded crossly. "The world would fall into chaos and destruction of the likes we have never seen, and the Archknights would be ill equipped to save us."

"No. A single Lightbinder can't stand against several. The knights would take him down."

"And what if hundreds of wicked men became Lightbinders?"

"There are plenty of good people outside the Order and they'd seek the power as much as those who would abuse it; enough to balance things, anyway."

Ahrek looked to be considering Daylen's words until his eyes widened and he said, almost to himself, "Not if they might die."

"You're talking about the Vigil."

"You know?"

"My father sent spies to try and find out the knights' secrets."

Ahrek huffed. "I'm not surprised—though I am that he told *you*."

"He told me everything before he died."

"Really? Then you might possess some important information."

"And I'll share only what I choose, like the fact that the Vigil is performed on a ceremonial skyship that flies toward the sun, and that one in three initiates die."

"I knew that some die, but one in three?"

"That's the average."

"Strange that there's a consistent rate, especially since the knights say it's because one's heart isn't pure."

"Specifically that they weren't truly sincere in their desire to fight evil for the rest of their lives. Well, I can tell you my heart isn't pure, and I made no vow."

"Which means the deaths are a result of the process. This is very troubling. A good man who is content with his life has no need for supernatural powers and has little reason to risk all he has for them. But power-hungry madmen... They would gladly risk their lives for the strength to impose their will on others. Only then, when oppression reigns, would good men be willing to risk their lives for the power to fight injustice, and then it would be constant war. *If* you received these powers merely from something you did, you hold a *very* dangerous secret, one that could change the world and bring death and destruction for ages to come."

"A secret has twice as much chance of getting out when a second person knows it, Bringer. I'll not be telling you."

"But you do know the secret; the powers didn't come upon you in your sleep or something like that."

"I *might* know the secret and I'm well aware of the implications of such knowledge. No one will find out from me, just as no one has found out from the Archknights."

"Will you give me your word that you won't tell a single soul what you know?"

"I don't need to promise you anything, but I've already said as much. No one will find out how I received my powers, including you."

"Then I'm satisfied."

"Why would I care if you are?"

Ahrek ignored him. "And what will you do next—with your powers, that is?"

"Help those in need to the best of my specific and unique abilities."

"You're referring to your swordsmanship."

"A Grand High Master who can lightbind. A potent combination."

"A disturbing one. Your father set out with good intentions to help people when he overthrew the aristocracy, and look where that ended."

Daylen huffed a laugh. "Well, I'm not planning anything like that. I was thinking of hunting down pirates among the Floating Isles."

"That would be a violent life."

"Then nothing out of the ordinary."

Ahrek studied him again before saying, "You would make the skies a little safer, true, but what you should really do is join the Archknights. If you want to help people, that's where you belong, and they would be able to teach you how to fully control your powers."

"The thought has crossed my mind, but I'm reluctant to give up my freedom so soon. Besides, there are things I need to do first."

"But you do intend to seek them out, eventually?"

"Eventually."

"Good, and until that time it's best we avoid Archknight attention, as they'll be most insistent on bringing you in, so to speak, when they learn of what you can do. They're very protective of their secrets."

"You almost seem to be on my side."

Ahrek moved so his body pressed against Daylen's.

Daylen turned to Ahrek with a look of consternation. "What're you doing?"

"Now I'm on your side," Ahrek said with an amused smile.

Daylen groaned and walked back to the street.

CHAPTER FOURTEEN

I never dreamed the aristocracy would go so far as to attack their own people, innocent people, just to get at me. The aristocracy hadn't even implied that they might be capable of such violence, which is why I had thought my family was safe at the gathering. I was a fool.

Some said I rose up against the aristocracy for the people, some to fight tyranny, some for power and my own glory; but the truth is that it was all for revenge, plain and simple. They had murdered my world, and I would see every single one of them receive the same punishment.

I called on the people and gathered those in the army loyal to me, attacking every single barracks loyal to the aristocracy. It was a quick and efficient, if brutal, war. My desire for vengeance was tempered by my need for it; thus, I was methodical in my tactics and brought every skill I possessed to bear. At no time have I ever acted with more mastery over war than in the revolution.

After a few months, the remaining army sided with me and we took the capital.

Daylen found the coach heading to Treremain. It was driven by an enclosed darkstone driver and could make the trip several times a fall, though a skycoach would be faster still.

Lighteena Devashion, with her daughter of the same name, as

well as Jaram Hanathore, Daymay Frenden, and someone Daylen didn't recognize, waited to board the coach. They all eyed Daylen distrustfully, though the Devashion sprit blushed when Daylen's eyes passed over her.

At least the Le'donners had all cleared out. Daylen had only so many brain cells to lose.

Daylen rolled his eyes and turned to Ahrek. "Let's ride up top."

Ahrek nodded, but before they could pay the fare, the captain of the local Civic Guard, Edem Davenday, approached them with several constables instep. Captain Edem's brush-like epaulettes on his shoulders made him stand out.

The conners behind him looked nervous, many with a hand resting on their rapier or shooter that hung from their belts. Shooters housed shotspikes, darkstone-propelled stakes that hadn't been nearly so commonplace once. Daylen had redesigned them a few years into his rule, making the spikes smaller, and inventing the shooter housing. This made shotspikes much easier to aim and, with it, a common peasant with little training could become a deadly, effective soldier. It was partially thanks to his shooters that the Dawn Army had been so formidable. They were illegal, of course—even Daylen had the foresight to keep such dangerous weapons from the common people, though some could still be obtained through the black market.

The people needed to be armed and ready for the Shade if Night ever fell, but a shotspike was about as effective against a Shade as tickling it. To drop those monsters you needed to slash it open and let the blood flow, something that only a cut, focused sword could do. This was why carrying a rapier was at the very edge of propriety.

But the constabulary had to deal with people, and thus rapiers and shooters were standard issue. Since Daylen's initial design, others had added to it, making two, four and six shooters. Six shooters were a bit too cumbersome, which was why conners carried the fours.

"Daylen Namaran?" Edem asked. He was one of the oldest men in Karadale, being fifty-two years, thirty Daylen's junior. There were very few people alive as old as Daylen, for they would have had to have lived through a whole Night and two revolutionary wars. It was hard to escape death with so many opportunities, though Daylen had—ironic, considering he had been at the center of it all.

"What do you want, Edem?" Daylen said.

"You're under arrest."

Daylen was about to tell the snot to go and jump off the Edge, but instead he breathed deeply to calm himself and said, "Under what charge?"

"Assault and disturbing the peace."

"No harm was done, Captain," Ahrek interjected, "and it was those who accosted Daylen that caused the disturbance."

The captain looked to Ahrek, and his resolve seemed to falter. "That's not the account I heard."

"I'm perfectly willing to take this matter to a higher authority," Ahrek said. "Whose word do you think the local Magistrate will side with: the embarrassed mob who got beaten by a single youth, or that of a Lightbringer?"

"You do know who the boy's father is?" Edem asked.

"Of course I do."

"He should be locked up…"

"Since when does the law punish the children for the crimes of their parents?"

"It's been done before," Edem said. "The families of conquered rulers have been locked away in case they might try a coup. And on top of that, I saw his father punish—no, I saw his father *kill* the families of those he deemed as criminals, which was anyone who as much ruffled the bastard's shirt!"

"We would hope to prove ourselves *better* than the Great Bastard, wouldn't we?"

The captain paused, and though he tried to make his lowering eyes look like he was thinking, it was plain to see that he was ashamed.

"This boy is within my care," Ahrek said.

Oh, how Daylen *hated* being called boy, and he most certainly *wasn't* in Ahrek's care either; but Daylen let the comment slide, as he could see it helping.

"He'll not become like his father," Ahrek added.

Edem cleared his throat. "Well, I suppose there's no point in questioning the word of a Bringer." He nodded to Ahrek. "Anyway, I'd rather not have to deal with the all the blackened paperwork. If he's leaving my town, I say good riddance. Have a good fall,

Bringer." The captain then turned with his constables to walk away, but not before giving Daylen a scowl.

Light! Daylen thought. *It's a blackened good thing that I didn't have any children after I rose to power, if this is how they'd have been treated.*

Ahrek turned to him. "See, for the most part, things can be resolved peacefully."

"What, you didn't notice how polite I was?"

"I noticed that you didn't break anyone's arms. Your words, on the other hand, weren't particularly sweet."

"I didn't need sweet words; you put that idiot in his place well enough."

"He wasn't an idiot. Daylen, you need to stop looking down on everyone."

"I'll look down on those who prove themselves to be intolerant, narrow-minded sunspots."

"That description could fit well with certain actions you've performed recently."

"Bringer, did I *ever* say that I don't look down on myself?"

The coachman wouldn't charge the two for the trip, Ahrek being a Bringer and all, but Ahrek materialized a dun to pay the ten-gram fare anyway, insisting that the coachman take it.

They sat up top in the open air as the coach lurched forward, increasing speed rapidly, passing the packed dirt streets of the town to cross onto the cobblestoned imperial roads.

"I've never been able to decide if that's forgery or not," Daylen said.

"What?"

"The fact that you can create money."

"I could have just as easily created anything of value, but money can be exchanged much easier."

"I guess so. You know you could make yourself rich."

"A Bringer so desirous of material wealth would be unworthy of the calling in the first place."

"You're just supposed to help others, that doesn't exclude helping yourself."

"Not for a Bringer. The calling requires far more selflessness than that. Our desire to help others must be of such strength that we would give away any riches we already possessed in the first place."

"Okay, why don't you make *other* people rich?"

"There's a difference between giving to those that don't have enough in life and giving to those that do have enough more than they need. In fact, people who have enough in life will find far more happiness from being content and grateful than wanting more. Riches do not bring happiness."

"Wise words," Daylen said, leaning back.

Ahrek smiled and took out his sketchbook. He began to draw, though it was clear the constant bumps were affecting the quality of the overall illustration. He seemed content enough, so Daylen tried to relax.

The sky was covered mostly by clouds that fall, but it didn't look like it would rain. The country around Karadale was beautiful, with the occasional ruin standing elegantly amongst a copse or proudly by themselves, all seeming to be a natural part of the land.

"You mentioned something about sensing when I was channeling light," Daylen said, "and that I could sense it, too."

Ahrek smiled and closed his sketchbook. "Yes. The fact that you didn't know anything about it was proof enough that you weren't an Archknight. It's one of the first things they're taught."

"Why's that?"

"It can be used to sense the Shade."

"Oh. How do you do it?"

"Archknights—well, not Archknights specifically—Lightbinders and Lightbringers are similar in that we can feel light on our skin."

"That was the first thing I noticed when I got my powers."

"Well, we can do more than that; we can sense the inner light within all living things. If you reach out with this sense you will notice this light. Now, I did say this light is within all living things, but humans are the odd ones out."

"Why's that?"

"Humans are different. The light in plants and animals is bright and never wanes. Even the wolf or grif that wants to make a dinner out of you has a light within them that shines ever bright, for they cannot do the one thing humans can: make moral choices. This is why their lights can never be as dim or as bright as ours."

"Are you saying this inner light is a reflection of a person's, what, personal goodness?"

Ahrek looked at him from the corner of his eyes and smiled. "Not in all cases, but generally, the better a person is, the brighter their inner light. If they're evil, their light is barely there, but even the most loathsome person still has a measure of light within. There's only one type of human that has utterly no light inside, though you couldn't really call them human anymore."

"The Shade," Daylen said. "But this is supposed to sense light, and if the Shade have no light that would mean there's nothing to sense."

"Exactly. A living thing with no inner light is an abomination, and for those people with the ability to feel for the light that surrounds them, coming across a void in the light is as easy to notice as a slap to the face."

"I see."

"And as the Archknights are our best defense against the Shade, you can see why they teach this ability first. You should learn it too, to constantly reach out and feel for the light in all things. It's not difficult—but as you know, if one isn't taught, one might never learn how to do it."

"Okay, so what do I do? How do I try and feel with... I don't even know."

"You know what light feels like on your skin. You're feeling it right now. Well, look for that feeling, but with your heart."

"With my heart? How am I supposed... Oh!"

"See? Easy once you know what to do."

It was incredible. Daylen could feel the light around him, that light in all living things; the countless blades of grass on the sides of the road, the nearby trees, the people in the coach, and the Bringer beside him. While feeling this he literally had a sense of where they were. He could see all things around him without using his eyes. With this ability, no one would be able to sneak up on him again. Daylen realized that this was how the Archknights were able to fight so effectively in the dark and during the night: they could still see what they were fighting. This skill was *far* more useful than the Bringer had implied.

Suddenly a skycoach roared overhead, flying in the opposite direction to them, buffeting their coach with a huge burst of wind.

"Why under the Light is that coach flying so low?" Ahrek said, looking at the departing coach with deep disapproval.

"Fun," Daylen said.

Ahrek looked at him in consternation. "Fun?"

"Yeah. Have you ever flown a racer?"

"No."

"You're missing out. Honestly, I'd compete in the races if I had the time. I would probably win the championship, too."

"You know how to fly, do you?"

"Better than most."

"Well then, why don't you?"

"There're other demands in my life."

"Which are none of my business, I'm guessing."

"Look at that, you're learning."

"It's possible."

"I tell you, some of these modern coach designs are starting to impress me."

"You know, your father was considered quite the genius engineer, apart from his endless warmongering and oppression. In fact it was his keen understanding of technology that one might say facilitated his great success."

"Yeah, I know...but just because my, um, father liked something, doesn't mean that I can't."

Ahrek raised an eyebrow.

"Don't be stoned, you know what I mean. I wasn't referring to his bad tendencies."

"Which is why I said nothing. But while we're talking of your father, I should mention that even he had an inner light brighter than average."

Daylen gasped. "Impossible!"

"It's true."

"Then this sense doesn't say spit about a person's goodness," Daylen said with a sneer.

"A man who believes he is doing good will have a strong inner light, even if he is performing evil things. There have been several murderers who had strong lights within."

"How is that possible?"

"Some were mentally disabled and didn't fully understand what they were doing. Others believed what they were doing was right or had some other justification. You need to remember that a bright inner light doesn't always mean a person is good."

"But you just said it did."

"No, I said that in *general* the better a person is, the brighter their inner light. You just have to try and read people at the same time. It requires care and consideration, especially with people of weak inner light."

"What do you mean?"

"Weak light is a result of repeated actions one knows to have been wrong. It's particularly weak when the individual knows of their errors, but they don't care. A lack of empathy or kindness can result in weak light, as can dishonesty, just as well as outright murder and the vilest of actions."

"So it can be hard to tell the casual jerk from an ax murderer."

"Yes. Like I said, this sense must be used with care. You possess a great gift, Daylen—don't abuse it."

"Your own gifts are as significant, and while we're together I'll be sure to see that *you* don't abuse *your* powers, either."

Ahrek chuckled. "If I use my powers in any way that doesn't help others, I lose them. You're so quick to make sure you're on the same moral footing as everyone around you."

"I get annoyed at people who presume to know more than others or teach those who already know."

"Are you talking about yourself, or me?"

"No, I'm..."

"People can be so critical of others without realizing they're just as guilty."

"Or there could actually be a person who does know more. Life experience counts for much."

"And is that person you?"

"It's more likely to be me than others. There are a lot of idiots in the world, Ahrek, and you have no idea what I've been through in life."

"You're a fool to think that you know everything in the world."

"I didn't say that. I said I'm more likely to know something over another, and that's mostly due to experience."

"Oh, because you've lived for *so* long. There's a lot of people older than you, Daylen, so don't discount them."

"Fine, I won't discount the wisdom of anyone older than me."

"And you think the youth have nothing to offer? The words of children can hold great wisdom at times."

Daylen laughed. "I've clearly been speaking to the wrong children."

"I'm not saying everyone—yes, children included—know more than you, but they'll at least know a few things that you don't, and to discount them you'll miss those times when those precious truths come out. You need to look for those admirable qualities in others that you don't possess, look up to them for that, and try to learn from them. Otherwise, all people will seem beneath you and you'll never become a better man."

Daylen knew the Bringer was right, and was blackened annoyed by it. If Ahrek hadn't said it, Daylen would have been more inclined to adopt the advice. But if he did now, he would be acknowledging that someone else knew better than him—a young *boy*, at that, which was the very root of the issue within Daylen that Ahrek was trying to reveal.

Daylen clenched his teeth and swallowed his pride, which was like swallowing a whale. "You're...right. For so long I've presumed myself to know better than others. The truth is I don't, not in everything. I'll try and take on what you say, but don't expect night to become day in a fall."

"Oh, not at all. The very fact that you're aware of your own failings and are trying to better them is the greatest step any man can make."

"You make it especially hard, Bringer. You're all but perfect and stand as a constant reminder of my own inadequacies—in character, I mean. In looks, the constant comparison is quite pleasant."

"My, my, was that a joke?"

"Better than anything I've heard come from you."

"If I remember correctly, you believe that jokes are meant to make *other* people laugh. That one was a little mean-spirited."

"I wasn't being cruel, and you would have to be particularly sensitive to take offense at that," Daylen said, looking down the road.

Ahrek chuckled.

Daylen looked back to him. "Now, see, that *wasn't* a joke. Why're you laughing?"

"You're probably the most overly sensitive person I've ever met, taking offense at the smallest of things, like my mentioning your youth."

"Yeah, well, I never said I wasn't a hypocrite."

"And if I could clear something up, I'm *far* from perfect."

"Well, I haven't seen any particular failings, apart from self-righteousness, but that's just my insecurities grabbing at straws. People find it easier to attack a person's credibility than to accept advice and counsel."

"There! You *do* possess wisdom, when you look for it."

"Oh, I can be quite wise; it's just putting it into practice that's hard," Daylen said, looking back out over the countryside as the two of them fell into silence.

This inner light that Ahrek had taught him about was very intriguing. Using it, Daylen could sense the people in the coach beneath them. With casual sensing, he didn't feel any difference between the people's lights. When he tried to look closer with his sense, however, their different brightnesses seemed to come into focus.

The softest light there belonged to Lighteena Devashion. It didn't really surprise him that the Devashion woman's light would be the softest—Lighteena was always a stuck-up arrogant tit—but how far did it go? Was she a thief or a murderer, or was she just selfish? Ahrek was right: Daylen couldn't make judgments on people based off the light he sensed without learning more.

Feeling curious, Daylen looked to Ahrek and felt for the Bringer's inner light.

Daylen was nearly blinded. The man shone like the damn sun, except... Daylen looked closer. It was hard to describe, but there was a tiny bit of darkness in him. It was almost lost in the light's glare, but it was most certainly there, and as Daylen focused on it, he was able to see just how deep the darkness was. There was something wrong about it. Such darkness shouldn't be within so much light. It didn't belong. What did it mean?

Daylen laughed to himself as he realized it probably represented some small flaw. How many black spots were hidden in his own light? Probably hundreds.

"Something funny?" Ahrek asked.

"By now I'm very confident you wouldn't laugh at it."

"Very well." Ahrek let the silence return for a little while before he spoke again, saying abruptly, "I'm too bossy."

Daylen glanced to Ahrek, confused. "What?"

"That's one of my failings. I tell people what they should do too often, even on things that are inconsequential. I always think I know the right way to do things."

"You do at that, and I can certainly see how it could rub people the wrong way."

"I'm also too inquisitive. I've always stuck my nose into other people's business, and find it hard to judge when it's appropriate to do so and when I should have kept to myself."

"I could have told you that, but a Bringer gets a certain... allowance. It's kind of their job to intercede and help."

"But we're not really supposed to help people who don't want that help; unless the Light says otherwise, as with our current arrangement."

"It's probably why the Light picked you. Anyway, I do need help. You've proven that much...and I'm grateful for it."

Ahrek looked stunned. "Thank you, Daylen. That means a lot."

"Yeah, well, don't get used to it."

CHAPTER FIFTEEN

*With my most loyal men I cut my way into the throne room,
detaining all within. There I executed the Queen with my own
hands in front of her most loyal subjects and family, her daughter,
the young princess, included.*

*She was a girl of nine years, screaming, "Traitor, treason!" and
that she would see me hung by my own entrails for murdering her
mother. I was shocked that a child so young could speak of such
violence, but then I realized that she wasn't a normal child. She
was an aristocrat, bred to be cruel and selfish. That girl would live
her entire life with the intent to see me dead, as with the families
of all those I had already executed. I suddenly knew that if
Hamahra was to have any peace going forward, all possible
threats had to be dealt with.*

*So, I executed the girl just a few minutes after her mother, her
screams of hatred and vengeance upon me echoing through the
hall right up until I separated her head from her small body.
After that I ordered the executions of every aristocratic family.
Grandfather, grandmother, son, daughter, child, and babe, all
killed at my command.*

*After, once I was finally alone, I knelt, expecting to cry at the
horror I had just committed, but no tears came.*
I could feel nothing.

M aster Archons, we're about to arrive in Treremain."
Lyrah sat up from the bench where she had slept.

Cueseg was already awake. "Good. I am hungry," he said. "Bring me food."

"Yes…of course," the junior postman said—Hamahran-born by the look of him, and young. Probably his first employment.

Lyrah and Cueseg were in the main cargo hold of the National Post's ship, where two flat benches had been fixed to the sides in case of the odd passenger. Sacks of letters and parcels lay all around them.

It had been a very restless few hours.

"This is all we have, masters," the postman said once he had returned, and he handed Cueseg an open can of beans with a fork.

Cueseg took the can, his eyes staring at the postman and his face blank. The postman handed Lyrah the other can and fork and then returned to the helm.

Cueseg threw the fork aside and hesitantly scooped a small handful of beans into his mouth. "Ough! This is bad, this is very, very bad," Cueseg said after struggling to swallow. "If this is what putting food in metal does, I will never do it. Tastes like rust!"

Lyrah ate her beans. "There's nothing wrong with them."

"Yes, you Hamahrans think if the food does not kill you, it is good. There is more to food than this. Like *taste*."

"These beans have plenty of taste. Nothing like some good rust."

Cueseg looked at Lyrah in such astonishment that she burst out laughing.

"Why are you doing this, what is funny?" Cueseg said, bewildered.

"Your face, Cueseg! And here I thought you didn't like using facial expressions, but right then you looked like I had just turned into a goat."

Cueseg suddenly looked deeply embarrassed, or embarrassed enough, for he tried to make his face impassive. "I… This… I choose to show my face like this to show how unclean it is that you like to eat rust."

"Cueseg, I was joking."

"Then you lied?"

"No, it's sarcasm."

"Sarcasm is not to joke, you must mean what you say."

"I do…except when I don't."

Cueseg's blank expression cracked once more. "This… What… *This does not make sense!*"

Lyrah shrugged. "I'm a woman. We're allowed to not make any sense."

"*What?!*"

"Exactly."

"This is enough, you hurt my head. Strange woman!"

Lyrah chuckled to herself one last time as she felt the ship descend. It would still take a little while to reach the city and queue to enter its airspace.

Cueseg got back to choking down his beans before throwing the can away in disgust once he was finished. He picked up a handful of letters and cleaned his hand with them.

"Cueseg, you don't clean your hands with letters! Light, that's what the fork was for!"

"How do I clean my hand with a fork?"

"No, you use the fork to eat your food and then you wouldn't have to clean your hands in the first place."

"I am not a barbarian…" Cueseg paused. Lyrah guessed he had just remembered to not call her that. "I am not war maker. I do not use *fork*."

"How does using a fork make me a war maker, whatever that means?"

"Simple, it can be used as weapon. You do not bring weapons to eat. Eating is for peace. Only war makers eat with weapons."

"Your hands can be used as weapons, too."

"They are not meant to be weapons. You use hands to fight only when you have no weapons, and hands are not as good as weapons. Even *fork* better than bare hands, which is why for peace, you must not fork."

"*You must not fork?* Cueseg, fork isn't a verb."

"What is verb?"

"A word that means a type of action."

"Then I make it verb and I will never fork."

"You sound ridiculous."

"No, you are ridiculous, and you can fork as much as you like."

"Whatever," Lyrah said, waving a hand.

Cueseg huffed and stood with his back to Lyrah. He began to

go through the ritualized series of movements he did at the beginning of every fall, the same time as Lyrah usually went for her run.

She sighed in annoyance, as a long run would have done her good. She felt restless and frustrated, though teasing Cueseg had helped.

Cueseg was clearly practicing some type of martial art, but it appeared far more formal than anything from Hamahra.

The ship eventually docked and Lyrah bid the pilots goodbye.

It was the break of High Fall. Many people were just now arising, yet the city seemed to be in commotion, and it didn't take long to find out why.

"Extra! Extra, Dayless the Conqueror has been living in hiding for last twenty years! Read all about it!"

Lyrah nearly fell over when hearing the call.

"By the Bright One!" Cueseg said, looking to the paperboy in astonishment.

There was a crowd of people clamoring around, practically ripping the extras out of the boy's hands.

With her free bond, Lyrah channeled light into her voice and said, "Move!"

Bonding light to one's voice would not only increase the volume of what one said, but it also had a supernatural effect to encourage obedience, agreement, and understanding, depending on what one said.

Added that to the fact that Lyrah was an Archknight, the people parted at once.

Lyrah marched upon the paperboy and extended her hand. The boy handed her an extra with a trembling hand.

She read.

Apparently some farmer from a village named Karadale had found a note in the home of the local tinker, written by the same, confessing that he was actually Dayless the Conqueror. That he had escaped his supposed defeat twenty years ago and had been living in secret up until the last few falls where, upon his imminent death, he chose to cast himself from the edge of the world to die on his own terms.

Adding to the validity of the claim was a book found at the scene which contained an accounting of the Conqueror's life. A Lightbringer was also present during the discovery, who had both met the tinker and seen the Conqueror when he ruled, confirming their resemblance in appearance and voice.

On top of all, it appeared that Dayless had fathered a son in his old age, who was present when the Conqueror had cast himself from the continent. Also named Daylen, he was supposedly the express image of his father.

There were even two drawings which had been printed next to the article, one a representation of what the artist thought Dayless the Conqueror would look like in old age, scowling and malevolent, and another a young man who simply looked like Dayless the Conqueror in his youth.

The images nearly stopped Lyrah's heart from the shock.

The extra claimed that this was all discovered on the eve of last Low, only taking a fall for the information to reach the city and get out.

Lyrah's fist slowly crunched the extra bit by bit. She clenched her teeth and took stock. She would control herself—she was an Archon, she was strong—but Light, was it hard.

Anyone old enough to have lived during the Conqueror's reign, like Lyrah, could name one if not several things he had done to ruin their lives. There was no one in the world Lyrah despised more than the Great Bastard.

All had cause to hate him; and now, knowing that he had been living in peace for twenty years, was almost too much to bear.

His note claimed that living with his guilt had tortured the Bastard, but Lyrah didn't believe that for a second. He had been a coward to the end. If he had been truly sorry for what he had done, he would have turned himself over to the world's judgment; yet at the end of his life, he couldn't even do that.

And he had fathered another child? This son, this Daylen, could be a great threat and needed to be questioned, but that was a matter for the authorities. At least the world—and, indeed, Lyrah herself—finally had confirmation that the Conqueror, the filthy perverted wretch, was now dead.

Of course they thought they'd had confirmation for the last twenty years, so could they be sure of anything? All the more reason why the son needed to be questioned. If only to confirm the truth.

Lyrah stood for a little while with a face frozen in disgust as she took long, controlled breaths to calm herself.

Once she felt she was back in control, she tried to tell herself that it didn't concern her. She had a mission to focus on.

Lyrah threw the scrunched-up extra aside and left, Cueseg following behind.

Cueseg wanted to talk about the article—he was quite amazed by the revelation. Dayless had conquered Tuerase as well as most of the world, so the news was as poignant to him as it was to anyone from Hamahra. Lyrah couldn't handle it, however, and answered abruptly to each of his comments.

She focused on their mission and, after locating the dock where the boy had arrived, she bound light to her sense of smell and eventually found his scent. She couldn't help but constantly picture an old man as she tracked him. This frustrated her, because subconsciously she expected this boy to be moving at the same trudging rate one usually attributed to older people, which certainly wasn't the case.

They tracked the boy to a road out of the city heading south. Luckily their quarry was on foot, which made the tracking much easier, and Cueseg commandeered the fastest coach they could find: a sleek, sporty sky coach.

The coachman was accommodating, of course, and clearly nervous to serve two Archons.

They flew through one of the smaller openings in the shield net, one which sat near its base, made for coaches and the like, flying as fast as possible.

Lyrah ordered the coach to fly low and opened her side window to keep track of the scent. The sleek coach, almost like a racer in design, moved at an incredible speed, which caused the wind to whistle outside.

Sky coaches like this were built for the elite of society, and the interiors were furnished to suit. Such lavishness made Lyrah's skin crawl for several reasons, one in particular threatening to bring on a panic attack.

Cueseg on the other hand was lounging amongst the cushioned seats and pillows, eating a small cake he had found along the way, looking completely at ease.

Lyrah had thrown the cushions away from her like they were infected and now sat there gingerly, taking deep, even breaths.

"Ah, this is much better," Cueseg said. "A nice carriage, and this cake is not awful, but still not good. May the Bright One be praised."

Looking for anything to distract her from the décor, Lyrah sought conversation, as precarious as that could be with her companion. "Who is this Bright One you keep referring to? I assume it's the Light, but the way you speak of it, it's like you believe the Light is a person."

"Not a person like us, but most certainly embodied."

Now that comment *did* distract her. "Wait, you think the Light has a *body*?"

"Yes, it is clear that the Light has more substance than you Hamahrans think."

"That's ridiculous. How could the light see all things if it was restricted to two eyes like us?"

Cueseg laughed. "It is what you Hamahrans believe that is ridiculous, and we Tuerasians are not the only people who know the Light has a body. The people of Frey believe that God has a body, though it is true we differ much after this belief."

"God? What does that mean?"

"It is another name for the Light."

"God... What an ugly word. It sounds like a name for a pimple. Like, bother, I got another God on my face."

Cueseg leaned forward angrily. "You speak *blasphemy*, Lyrah!"

"Sorry. Light, I didn't mean to offend."

"Then do not speak like this again!"

"Sure, fine."

With that, the conversation was truly over. Looking out the window, Lyrah tried to make note of everything they passed. They flew over the occasional person on the road and even a ground-based coach traveling in the opposite direction. Lyrah could have seen the people clearly if she had bonded light to her eyes, but it was unlikely that their quarry would still be on the road. Besides, tracking the scent was more important, and it was even stronger now, meaning they were closing the distance.

"Nothing much can be said for the food in your country, but at least your people know how to be comfortable," Cueseg said, his body spread over the cushions.

Lyrah threw a disapproving glare at Cueseg, who took on a puzzled expression.

Oh, Light, Lyrah thought, remembering that Cueseg couldn't read subtle facial expressions and probably thought the glare was some sign of sexual attraction—or at least that's what he would have thought before they'd had their little chat.

"I can tell that you didn't understand what my look meant."

"That is because speaking through face is a sign of...no control."

"Yes, so Tuerasians don't like to show facial expressions..."

"No, this is not true. You have seen me speak with my face. Look." Cueseg put on a very pronounced look of displeasure. "We show faces that we want to show. Letting the face speak by itself is a sign of weakness. Feelings are to be controlled, so a strong mind only show the things with his face that he want to show."

"But you still can't understand subtle facial expressions."

"Yes, this is hard for me. If you do not tell me, I think the look you give me is to have sex."

"Why under the Light do you think that? It's like everything you don't understand must be a sign of sexual attraction."

"Because I show my body, and my body is strong and beautiful. Most women who look at me, and men who like men, is thinking of sex. Sex is the strongest of feelings and the hardest to master. Among my people, the feelings that most people show but do not wish to show are those feeling about sex."

Lyrah nervously curled her fist tight as Cueseg spoke so unashamedly.

"So the feelings that people show among your people," Cueseg continued, "I think must be about sex, because it is those feelings that are more shown among my people who have not mastered them. This is much more for men. You see it is the most, um...*bad* sign of weakness for a man's penis to become strong..."

"*CUESEG!*"

"What, what do I say that makes you so?" Cueseg asked with all the innocent naivety of a child.

"Stop! Just...just stop."

"You always act strange when I speak of this, which is strange, for you are very old and must have sex many times. It is just sex."

"No, Cueseg, it's not! It's *never* just...just sex!"

"I am confused. You must master these feelings, Lyrah, or these feelings will come to master you."

That comment stung more than Cueseg could ever know. Lyrah turned away to look out the window and said no more.

Thankfully Cueseg said nothing, either, and they traveled in silence.

Eventually, the scent that Lyrah had been tracking suddenly peaked.

"Stop!" Lyrah ordered the driver.

"What is it?" Cueseg asked.

"The scent, it's *very* strong here."

The sky coach circled and landed on a clear field of grass near some old brick shack.

Once out of the coach, Lyrah easily identified the source of the heightened scent. It was the hovel she had seen as they circled. It sat on the side of the road with ten Civic Guardsmen surrounding it. Several suited men stood in front of the house, conversing.

"What is this?" Cueseg asked.

The constables saluted both of them as they approached.

"Lady Archon," a constable said. "I, um… I didn't realize the Order would have an interest in this, but now I think of it…"

"An interest in what? Whose home is this?"

"You…you don't know?"

"Would I be asking if I did, constable?"

The constable was paling. "Well, um, it turns out that this is the home that Dayless the Conqueror had been living in, while in hiding."

"*What!*"

"Yes, most unsettling."

Lyrah couldn't believe what she was hearing.

"Lord and Lady Archons!" a portly man said respectfully, dressed in a tailed suit and top hat. A bejeweled cutlass hung at his side and he was flanked by three similarly dressed men, as well as a commoner. "I am the Magistrate of Karadale, Laramon of the Devashion family—and with me is Councilman Kuratail Devashion, Master Tarem of the Hanothore family, and Master Paradan, one of the local farmers. We are honored by your presence."

Karadale, Lyrah realized. That was the village mentioned in the extra.

"Magister," Lyrah said, trying to regain her composure. "You are certain of this? That this is the home Dayless the Conqueror spent his final twenty years in?"

"Um... Yes, Lady Archon," the magister answered haltingly, before continuing with haste. "Truly, none of us had any idea, and if we had, we would have taken appropriate action to bring the war criminal to the authorities!"

"Your superiors will deal with that," Lyrah replied with difficulty. "I'm looking for someone. A young man, blue hair, and he spent a good amount of time here very recently."

"Yes, the son."

This is what Lyrah had been dreading ever since realizing where they had come.

"He spent the Low here with a Lightbringer," the magister said. "Master Paradan here met the two and was the one to find the note and journal."

"Describe the boy to me," Lyrah demanded of the farmer.

"Of course, um, Lady Archon. Well, he was a surly lad with a chip on his shoulder, that's for sure. Actually a lot like the old tinker." The farmer scowled. "Dayless the Conqueror... He had blue hair, was fit, tall. Aside from age he looked and sounded just like his father. Yeah there's no question he was the tinker's son, and there's no doubt the tinker was Dayless the Conqueror, what with the things we've dug up in this old house here. Makes my skin crawl knowing who lived here."

"What have you found?"

It was the magister who replied. "There was a journal containing an account of the Conqueror's life, as well as several personal items that have been identified as belonging to the Conqueror. We also found money. Lots of money."

"Has anyone else spent time here recently of a similar description, young with blue hair?"

"Apart from his own son, no, not to my knowledge at least."

That settled it. The description combined with the scent trail meant that the young man they hunted was the son of Dayless the Conqueror, and he was *not* an Archknight. There was no way a boy who looked exactly like Dayless the Conqueror could have joined the Archknights without anyone, especially herself, noticing. This also explained why the boy's scent was faintly familiar, and why he smelled like an old man, having lived with his aged father.

Lyrah looked to Cueseg, who had a knowing expression. He'd

put it together as well, except he probably thought the boy had underwent his own Vigil after dedicating his life to fighting evil.

Lyrah didn't know if that was truly necessary anymore. There was no way the child of the greatest tyrant the world had ever seen would be selfless enough to dedicate his life to such a cause. The boy might have even murdered someone: that beggar in the alleyway. There might be *no* moral requirement to become a Lightbinder, only the Vigil. Now if *this* was true, Lyrah understood why the knights would lie to the world. Better evil men think they're morally disqualified from getting the powers than simply not knowing the secret. If anyone could become a Lightbinder, what would people do to try and learn the secrets of the Vigil?

And then where would the world be?

Lyrah had to track down this boy and stop him as soon as possible. At the very least he knew the secret of the Vigil, and if that secret was revealed, the world would fall into chaos.

"Where is he now?" Lyrah demanded urgently.

"He caused a commotion in town before leaving. The captain tried to detain him, but the Lightbringer he was with wouldn't allow it."

"Where is he?"

"He caught a coach," the magister sputtered, "headed for Treremain."

"The coach!" Lyrah spat, turning to Cueseg. "Light, we passed the blackened thing on our way here!"

CHAPTER SIXTEEN

*I had not claimed any leadership or sovereignty, but if there was
any decision needing to be made, the people came to me to make it.
I had been named leader of Hamahra without anyone saying a
single word to make it so; and, seeing that this was the case, I saw
fit to rebuild my nation.*

*The people loved me for that, and with their support I put in place
my government. I could see how things had become so bad under
the aristocracy's boot. A group of elite snobs had each claimed a
bit of the nation and held it over the rest of the larger population,
forcing them into servitude. They had a stranglehold on property
and the economy all because of greed and status. To make sure
this would never happen in my new Hamahra, I decreed that no
one could own property, not even me. Everything was owned by
the government. No one owned anything, and everything was
owned by all. I believed it to be a fair and just system, a true
communal state.*

*With the state retaining control over the land, I could ensure a
fair and even distribution of its resources, overseeing how the land
was worked, putting the effort where it was needed. This was
primarily how I fed a starving nation.*

D aylen and Ahrek arrived in Treremain by the end of mid High, their coach pulling up in the city's Grand Central Station at one of the many platforms.

The station was a remarkable construction, with each outer platform canopied by half-cylinder roofs made of iron and glass, and the main building itself constructed out of brick, standing tall and proud with a prominent domed center.

The city's skyport was very near the station, with many dark-stone-floated platforms constantly ferrying cargo between the two.

The Grand Central Station and the skyport were the main transport hubs of the city and thus the main commercial district had grown around them. The impressive brick buildings that encircled the station and port were built high and close together, bordering wide cobblestoned roads. Daylen could see that there must be high demand for space in this district, due to the many skysitters floating above with darkstone-supported staircases leading to their small terraces at their front doors; or, if the residents were richer, with fixed levitation platforms that would lift the people as high as needed.

All of the buildings on the ground had some type of storefront sellingdifferent goods or services.

Daylen and everyone else disembarked the coach, the other occupants all too happy to put distance between themselves and Daylen.

Daylen had unclasped Imperious from his belt, holding the sheathed sword in his gauntleted left hand. Ahrek and he began making their way down the platform when Daylen heard, "Extra! Extra! Dayless the Conqueror living in hiding for last twenty years! Read all about it!"

"Well, that didn't take long," Ahrek said.

"The magistrate in Karadale must have a phonotrack and sold the news to the press as soon as he heard it."

Daylen glanced to a group of well-dressed people, top hats and parasols all, who were whispering intently to one another while looking at Daylen. They were holding a single paper each. The news extra.

Daylen turned to walk to the paper boy, who was in the middle of his call. The boy lost his voice completely when he saw him.

The paperboy looked to the extra in his hand, to Daylen's face, then down to the shining mark of a Grand High Master of the sword on Daylen's belt and back to his face. His eyes were as wide as coins.

Daylen flipped the boy a gram and took an extra. When he saw it, he realized why he stood out. The paper had gone to the trouble of making two drawings, one a guess of his aged appearance—a good guess, too, though they had certainly tried to make him look as menacing as possible. The other picture looked to have simply been a reproduction of one of his older portraits, meaning a painting done early in his rule, and they had just made him look younger. Even with the loss of detail through the printing process, the image looked exactly like him.

"A perfect resemblance," Ahrek said from over Daylen's shoulder.

Daylen finished reading the extra and passed it to Ahrek. "You said yourself that I look exactly like the Conqueror. Well, apparently Paradan took that to heart, and the information was passed on. My mug is probably on every paper in the city."

"People still might not recognize you unless they look closely at your face, but then again your master's mark grabs attention."

"If anyone wants to challenge me they have a right to know of my skill, so I can't exactly take it off."

"I accept that. Just remember that with their recognition there will be many judgments and expectations. So in other words, Daylen, be on your best behavior, please."

Oh, that grated on Daylen's nerves. He looked down to the paperboy, who was still staring.

"It's really you," the paper boy said.

Daylen ignored the boy and left. *Blackened kids.*

Walking along the platform, he drew looks from every person he passed.

Yep, he really *was* going to be popular.

A man and woman dressed in the most expensive of clothes made eye contact in no other way but to say, *We intend to speak to you.* A copper-collared slave, meaning one who had entered into slavery voluntarily, stood inconspicuously behind the two.

The man approaching Daylen wore a rich tailed dueling suit, a cravat, and a top hat with an expensive broadsword at his left side. He also walked with a parrying cane in his right hand.

The woman wore a fine dueling dress. One often had to take a second look to see if a dress was made for dueling or not, for they could bear as much lace and finery as any other. But the decorated studs at the front held the dress's removable front. The elaborate swept hilt of a mastercrafted sword sat at the woman's hip, though the blade hung inside the dress, having been threaded through a purposely cut and laced bordered slit in the side.

The couple each had long tassels hanging from their hair. The man had at least two orange beads *and* a red, while the woman had three orange. They were very successful duelists, though anyone who wanted an honorable position in society had to bear tassels like these.

After reaching Daylen the two of them bowed respectfully, and Daylen had no choice but to stop, for they made sure to bar his path. The slave didn't bow, as was customary; they were regarded separate from society.

"I am Master Sunsarret of the Kon'aden family, and this is my wife, the Lady Viveen of the same."

Daylen looked at them, not replying. Kon'aden must have been one of the more powerful families in Treremain.

"Please forgive my forwardness," the man, Sunsarret, said, "but I must know, young sir, are you the one of which this article speaks? You certainly bear the resemblance."

Oh, what a stuck-up rock.

"If I am, that would be my business," Daylen replied.

"Indeed... You bear quite the mark for one so young, yet I don't recognize you from the masters."

"Are you *truly* a Grand High Master of the Sword?" the woman asked with keen interest. "It's hard to believe, seeing as we've never heard of you."

Glancing to Ahrek, Daylen replied, "Apparently there are more Grand High Masters than people realize."

"Your sword?" the man asked in awe. "It looks exactly like Imperious itself, from what I've seen in paintings. But it can't actually be Imperious, can it?"

Daylen didn't respond, his annoyance building.

The couple looked to each other nervously, and then the woman leaned forward. "Have you come to attend the tournaments?" When there came no reply, she continued, "Hundreds would pay to see a demonstration of your skill. Oh, and you *must* come to the ball! Our family is hosting this evening. *Why*, you would be the guest of honor, especially if you're indeed who we suspect. Everyone is positively beside themselves to find out more about you."

"Pray tell your name, young sir?" Sunsarret asked.

"I don't feel inclined to give it, nor to attend any ball, tournament, or function. My business is my own, to which I must be about. Good day." Daylen went to walk around the two, but was stopped as the man shot up his cane to bar the way.

"I might take offense at being dismissed so. I would implore you to offer the expected courtesy, or I would be prompted to action."

Daylen could feel the heat in his voice and his eyes locked on the man's. "You can act however you want, but just remember that I bear this mark for a reason—and unless you want a shorter life, you had better get *out of my way*."

The man wilted like a dying flower, and lowered his cane. "Upon my honor, I meant no offense. I wish you light in your fall, good sir."

"And I also to you," Daylen said flatly, his expression matching his foul mood as he stalked away.

Walking down the platform, Daylen could feel Ahrek's displeasure as if it were indigestion. "Believe it or not, Ahrek, I was holding back."

"From what, exactly?"

"Shoving that peacock's cane up his own ass."

Ahrek sighed. "While I'm *very* glad you didn't do that, you still threatened to kill him unless he moved out of the way."

"A hollow threat. I didn't mean it."

"Yet that man certainly believed it, and now he thinks the son of Dayless the Conqueror is not only willing to kill people who get in his way, but as a Grand High Master, that he is perfectly equipped to do so."

Daylen stopped walking and sighed. He actually had done his best to hold back, and it really had been a hollow threat. Yet his anger had surged, and he honestly didn't know what he could do when enraged. He needed to do better; holding back wasn't enough. He needed to do the very last thing he would ever actually do in a situation like this.

Light, this was going to be hard.

Daylen turned and walked back to the finely dressed couple and their slave.

The man's face paled as he noticed Daylen and his left hand hesitantly rose to hold his sword.

Daylen stopped before the couple and with his whole body tense forced himself to act.

"I'm sorry for dismissing you so rudely, and for any threat I might have implied. In truth, I would never harm you."

The man... What was his name? Sun-something? Regardless, his brow rose in surprise and he visibly calmed.

"I'm feeling judged enough as it is and hesitate to admit who I am," Daylen continued. He glanced about to see that nearly every passerby on the platform had stopped to watch the encounter. "My name is Daylen Namaran, son of Daylen Namaran, also known as Dayless the Conqueror." That lie was always strange to say, for it was very unnatural to think of himself as his own son. He was trying to be a different man, yet that wasn't anything new. He'd been trying to do that for years now. The fact that he was now young didn't make him a different person; he was still the same old man he had been a few falls past.

The onlookers gasped when hearing Daylen, and he turned to yell at them. "Oh, come on! It's not like you hadn't guessed." Turning back, Daylen continued, "And this sword is indeed Imperious, the link passed to me upon my father's death—and yes, that *can* happen." The couple appeared to be at a loss for words.

Thank the Light. Daylen thought and bowing, he left.

Ahrek was smiling ear to ear

"Shut up," Daylen said, walking past the Bringer.

Leaving the station, they walked onto the busy street. Thankfully most people were too preoccupied to notice who Daylen was, but they weren't too preoccupied to notice the man standing atop a box giving a very enthusiastic speech.

Soap boxing in such public places wasn't anything odd, but this particular man seemed to be truly upsetting the crowds as they booed and jeered him.

Ahrek became noticeably displeased when he saw the man. "Another one—such a despicable movement!"

"What movement?"

"Dawnism, and you're more related to it than you would like. It's those who wish to bring back the Dawn Empire."

"*What?*" Daylen said.

"Yes, that was my reaction too. It's mostly supported by discontents and those who who're too young to remember what the Dawn Empire was like. They practically worship your father."

"That's… That's insane!"

"Yes."

"But everyone in the world *hates* Dayless the Conqueror."

"Most, but not everyone."

"You think people are going to make a connection between me and this…Dawnism?"

"I think they already have," Ahrek said, nodding to the impassioned speaker.

The man on the box wore common factory clothes and shook a paper in his hand. It was the extra. Clearly he had a lot to say about the fact that the Conqueror had been alive for so long.

"I would avoid speaking to any of them if I were you. Anyone who sees you with such people will think you support their movement."

"Yeah, they'd love to have the son of their hero on their side," Daylen said, thinking about the truth of the matter. These people would piss their pants if they knew. Still, it would have been sweet poetry if he could have shown these idiot extremists that the man they idolized hated everything about them and what he once stood for.

If only.

"How could I not have heard of these idiots? There's been nothing in the papers about them."

"I suspect the government has put a gag order on the press regarding the movement."

"It's not enough. That barking fool should be arrested with the rest of them."

"No, he shouldn't, and the government shouldn't restrain the press."

"To stop lies they should. Listen to what this idiot is saying! It's enough to make me want to bash his face in."

"That was the very logic the Dawn Empire espoused."

Ahrek's comment was like a slap in the face.

"Dayless made sure to crush anyone he disagreed with and who dared speak out against him," Ahrek continued. "The freedom to express one's beliefs, no matter how good or ill, should never be censured. So as much as I despise the ideology this man promotes, I would never stop him from promoting it. Otherwise I would have no right to promote my own and give those in power the right to silence anyone they arbitrarily deem a threat."

"I don't know if I agree with that," Daylen said, feeling revolted. "Lies and hatred should never be promoted. They should be crushed."

"And that's most probably what Dayless the Conqueror said when he arrested and even executed thousands for just so much as speaking out against him."

"Yeah… probably."

CHAPTER SEVENTEEN

*Of course, every other nation saw me as a usurper and tyrant.
What else were the monarchs of the other nations to feel toward
the man who had executed his own monarchy? Light, many
neighboring monarchs were related to the higher members of the
Hamahran aristocracy. I represented a threat to their power and
stability. Thus they painted me as a villain to their people, for
only a true villain would rise up against their rightful rulers.
It was at this time that the name Dayless surfaced in reference
to me.*

W hy are we even here?" Daylen asked as he sat with Ahrek
in a cafe. "You can just create what you need."

"That's true, but in spending coin here I help the proprietors
support their family."

"I see." Daylen looked around. "We need to eat quickly. I want
to get to the capital and escape all this attention."

Everyone in the restaurant was intermittently turning to stare
at them.

"This extra is probably getting sold in every city in the country,
if not the world," Ahrek said, waving the paper. "You're going to
get noticed in the capital as much as here."

"Oh, black it, you're right."

"*Language.*"

"Sorry. What I meant to say was: Oh, shove it up a blackened motherless dracking Shade's asshole, you're right."

Ahrek frowned and his eyes stared at him from under lowered brows.

"I'll speak how I want, Bringer."

"You see, there you go again. More concerned about your own convenience than others. Using clean language is as much about showing other people courtesy as it is reflecting one's own intellect."

"Intellect? I'd be happy to match wits with anyone."

"Yes, you're smart enough to think of words that aren't crude or offensive, and yet you express yourself just so."

"But some words are stronger and cause a stronger reaction from others. When you want to express something with weight, a curse does the job better than a politer adjective."

"And how much *weight* was needed just now?"

"That's for me to decide. Honestly, what's a better world, Bringer? One in which everyone takes offense at everything, or the opposite?"

"Well, fences are essential to managing livestock."

"Oh, don't start!"

Ahrek chuckled a little before replying, "Daylen, the answer's obvious. The world would be much better if people weren't so easily offended, something you still need to practice, might I add. Also, simply expecting people to be mature isn't an excuse to abandon common courtesy."

"Whatever."

"What do you mean by that?"

"That we're done talking about this."

"Yes, that's obvious, but knowing your personality you wouldn't end any argument if you still had some rebuttal, which means you concede the point—but your pride won't allow you to admit it."

"Fine, you're *right!*" Daylen glared at him. "Is that what you wanted me to say?"

"Yes, but for your sake, not mine. You mustn't have much self-esteem if admitting personal fault is too much for you."

"I'm not hungry," Daylen said as he stood and walked away. "You can meet me at the skyport. Just look in the same direction as everyone else."

The thing that annoyed Daylen the most was that he knew the
Bringer was right. Black it, so far the Bringer had been right in
nearly every blackened thing he had blackened said. Black it all!

No one liked having their flaws pointed out. And who under
the Light gave him the right to act like that? Oh, yes: that would be
the Light itself.

BLACK IT!

*I wonder how Ahrek would like it if I pointed out all his flaws so
constantly... If I could think of any.* There were things about Ahrek
that annoyed Daylen, and in that sense they could be considered
flaws—he was preachy, intrusive, too happy, and overall *far* too
polite—yet those weren't really flaws, and spoke more of Daylen's
own issues.

Daylen stopped his brooding and sighed. A *true* man admitted
his faults and chose to work on them. A child made excuses. What
had happened to him? He used to be so much more mature than
this, in his *twenties.* Back then he had been humble yet still confident and sure; in other words, what a man was supposed to be.
Funny that the older he became the more like a child he acted.
When he had ruled, no one had dared challenge him and that had
just fostered a sense of self-righteousness and entitlement that was
now blackened hard to break.

I'm such a wretch.

Daylen looked back to the restaurant. He knew the mature
thing to do was to walk back, apologize for his immaturity and
enjoy the meal his stomach wanted so badly. But that was just too
much for Daylen, right then at least. He had swallowed so much of
his pride already, what with those two peacocks on the platform,
that honestly he felt sick.

Next time he would do better.

Daylen turned back and continued toward the skyport, doing
his best to control his self-hatred.

Daylen was practically a celebrity. He leaned against a dock warehouse wall with his arms folded, trying to keep to himself—but
with his master's mark, Imperious, and face clear to be seen,

people quickly took notice of him. They pointed, stared, walked away, and returned with more people to point and stare, who in turn left and returned with even more people.

Ahrek was right...*again*. Daylen was drawing too much attention. He should hide Imperious, take off his mark and buy a hat or something to mask his face. But he wouldn't, if only to rob Ahrek of his smug, self-righteous validation.

No, that wasn't fair. Ahrek wasn't smug or self-righteous, which only infuriated Daylen even more. How could Daylen be proven wrong by a younger man *so often* when Daylen was clearly the more intelligent one? The thing defied reason.

It was only a matter of time before one of the many onlookers approached to ask a question, which seemed to embolden everyone else.

Daylen took a deep controlling breath.

"So—so you're him, the son of Dayless the Conqueror?"

"Yes."

"What does it feel like to be the son of, well, *him*?"

"It feels like a hundred boiled eggs."

"I don't understand."

"The feeling's mutual."

"Did you know who he was?"

"He was my father."

"Why didn't you say anything?"

"Because he didn't have long to live, and besides, he told everyone anyway."

"Is that Imperious?"

"Yes, and you can't touch it."

"How did you get it?"

"How do you think I got it?"

"Where did you grow up?"

"All over the place."

"Are you a real Grand High Master of the Sword?"

"I didn't know they could come in any other way."

"Who trained you?"

"My father."

"Was he a good father?"

"No, he wasn't."

And the questions continued. Daylen tried several times to ask the people to leave—politely, of course, because Daylen was *always* so polite—but only once he had doled out enough information did they disperse. The unfortunate thing was that as soon as the crowd had recycled, the process started all over again with very much the same questions.

"You're the son of the Conqueror!" a new voice said. He was a young man dressed in a tailed business suit.

Daylen sighed, "Yes."

"You should know that your father was the greatest leader this nation ever had."

Daylen wasn't expecting to hear that. The comment made his blood boil. Trying to control himself, he quickly checked the crowd surrounding him. Everyone was watching intently. Daylen needed to act very decisively, for he would put money on this encounter being told throughout the whole city.

"Are you a Dawn Bringer?" Daylen asked as the boy, who looked to be in his twenties.

"Yes, and we want to…"

Daylen backhanded the snot and knocked him onto his ass. "Pass this on to the rest of your idiots. I despise Dayless the Conqueror with every bone in my body. He was a cruel, heartless, blackened Shade, and I'll have nothing to do with any group or individual who says or believes otherwise. Got it?"

The boy got up, pulled a dagger out and lunged at Daylen.

Daylen put him back on his ass as easy as swatting a fly, taking the dagger in the process.

The crowd gasped and then cheered at seeing the quick display of martial skill.

Now properly afraid, the snot ran away.

"Now, that was very well done!" a voice said from Daylen's side.

Looking, Daylen saw a narrow-faced man dressed in a neat black suit paired with a top hat and cravat standing a step forward from the crowd. He was flanked by four other men, one dressed much like he was, and the others wearing white shirts and slacks with long-beaded tassels. Every one of them had a rapier at their sides.

Dirty, blackened rapiers.

The man who spoke approached him, his lackeys in tow. "Those Dawnists are a despicable lot."

"What do you want?"

"I represent the Sunforger's Guild…"

"Piss off!" Daylen said.

"All I want..."

"I know what you want, and you have a Shade's chance in light to get it."

"We just want to see it."

"Piss *off!*"

"That sword is the nation's inheritance! It doesn't belong to you!"

Daylen drew Imperious from its sheath and the five men jumped back, all reaching for their swords. Then Daylen threw Imperious at an upward angle with his normal strength and pulled on the link. Imperious jerked back toward Daylen, flying in a straight line, handle first, and Daylen caught it, pointing the glowing sapphire blade back toward the man. "Want to say that again?"

"You inherited the link..." the man said in awe.

"And according to the law, this sunucle is mine. So like I said, piss off. You're not so much as going to touch *my* sword."

The man tried to hide his frustration, but judging by his tensed jaw and clenched fists, he wasn't at all pleased. He briefly glanced to the three white-shirted lackeys behind him and then back to Daylen.

He wants to challenge me to a duel, Daylen realized. *By winning, he can claim victor's right and force me to pay an equivalent amount to Imperious' value, a debt I'm sure he'll waive for a chance to study it.*

The funny thing was that even if they studied Imperious, they wouldn't figure out what Daylen had done to make it. Every observable bit of the sword was actually no different to any other sunblade. Imperious was the way it was for other reasons yet that didn't mean he would let them look at it.

The Guildsman was considering Daylen, and his eyes eventually found his master's mark, glancing from that to the red-beaded tassel Daylen wore and back again. He had to know that he nor any of his lackeys were a match for a Grand High Master. He had also watched Daylen effortlessly take care of the Dawnist who had attacked him, which gave some firsthand evidence to Daylen's skill.

"Please forgive my intrusion," the man said with a fake smile. "All the best," he added with a bow before leaving.

That's not the last I'll see of him, Daylen thought, and glared at the onlookers who stood all around.

Daylen walked away, the crowd parting for him like he was the Conqueror once more. A troubling experience. He hoped to find a place in the port where he wasn't so popular.

Thankfully none of the onlookers followed, though they talked to one another and Daylen could see with his light sense that they were also not-so-covertly staring after him. He eventually walked far enough away that they were out of range of his light sense, which seemed to be about twenty meters.

What are they saying about me? Daylen wondered.

Feeling the light on his skin, Daylen drew it in and bonded it to his hearing. As he had been practicing this, it was quite easy to focus in on those people he had left to hear them clearly above the other sounds.

"He's so handsome!" a woman was saying to her friends, and Daylen couldn't stop a smile from cracking his expression at that. He was handsome; in fact, Daylen was damned sexy if he said so himself, not that that mattered for anything in his new life.

"Poor lad, having a father like that!" a man was saying.

"Upon my honor, he's a sour one. Which suits him, considering."

"He ain't a *real* master, he's way too young. He's a liar, just like his old man."

"It's hard to believe how much he looks like the Conqueror! Have you seen the paintings? It's like they're twins!"

"The conners need to lock him up and quick, no tellin' how long before he kills someone."

"I resist the urge to judge the boy based on his parentage. Children should not be condemned for the sins of their fathers."

Daylen sniffed. It seemed a mixed bag in people's regard for him.

An odd sound caught Daylen's attention as he was still bonding light to his hearing. Focusing, the sound became clear. It was crying. A woman was crying; and with the keen precision of his sense, Daylen instinctively knew that she was around four hundred meters away.

Daylen listened to what people near the woman were saying.

"Just playing with his brother and fell."

"I tried to reach him, Light's will I tried!"

"How old was the boy?"

"Four."

Daylen's heart sunk. A child had just fallen from a window. Daylen continued to listen, the mother's heartache only growing with each minute.

If the child had called for help before he fell and I was listening, I might have been able to do something, Daylen thought in regret.

But the opportunity was lost... *No, it wasn't.* How many other calls for help were being cried at that very moment? In a large populated city like this, there would definitely be a few, and all Daylen had to do was listen for them.

Daylen realized in that moment just how much power he really had—the main thing being that he could hear those people crying for help when no one else could.

Daylen bonded all his paths to his sense of sound and focused on cries for help or distress.

He picked out three instantly.

A young girl's screams in addition to the sound of tearing of cloth caught Daylen's attention and his head snapped to its origin.

"If you stop struggling, you might even enjoy it," a voice from that location said.

It was obvious what was happening; some poor girl was getting raped.

Rage and guilt surged within Daylen with such force that he was running at a dead sprint before he even realized it.

Using a bond on his speed, careful not to move too fast so as to appear supernatural yet moving much faster than normal, Daylen ducked and weaved through the streets, his eyes locked on his target.

The sound was coming from the attic of a building several blocks away.

Ducking down an alleyway and out of sight, Daylen jumped into a crouch, where he channeled light though two bonds into his strength, the other two reducing his mass and making himself lighter.

Daylen jumped and easily pushed himself forward and up a good five meters, being able to focus all his strength to propel a much smaller mass. But with the volume of his body remaining the same it acted like a sail, the wind pushing against his chest and sending him into a flailing backward spin, stopping his forward momentum completely. He then drifted like a piece of paper to the ground.

Daylen released the bonds and thumped the brick-paved ground with his fist. Enhancing his hearing, he could hear the poor girl getting raped at that very moment. He needed to get to the top of that building, and fast.

Daylen reduced his mass and increased his strength once more and jumped. This time, after leaving the ground, he switched all his bonds to increase his mass, thinking to increase his momentum.

He stopped abruptly right in the middle of the air like he had hit an invisible wall, his clothing and sword flicking forward due to whiplash, and then he fell half a meter to land crouched on the ground, shattering the bricks beneath him.

"Inertia, you idiot! My new mass has no kinetic energy."

Increasing his mass wouldn't increase his momentum—it would do exactly what had happened when he fell from the continent and anchor him in place. He needed to give himself a great burst of speed, but shedding his mass from his normal weight wouldn't be enough.

Daylen stood, and the shattered bricks crunched underneath. He was still bonding all the light he could to increase his mass. He estimated that he weighed around eight tons, yet he could still move as easily as normal...which meant he would be able to jump as high as he normally could!

The answer came to his mind like a thunderclap.

Keeping his mass at its greatest amount, Daylen crouched, held his gauntleted forearm in front of him, looked up into the sky, and jumped.

The amount of force needed to throw eight tons into a normal-sized human jump was huge, and it was that very amount of force that Daylen had just generated due to his body being augmented to maintain his natural level of movement. Then, at the very moment his feet were about to leave the ground, Daylen switched his bonds to his body's strength, shedding the massive amount of added mass. The mass left, but the kinetic energy he had just produced remained, which was the proportional force to launch eight tons into a two-meter arch, all that kinetic energy now only pushing against his regular weight.

Daylen was suddenly propelled upward with such instant force that his shoes and socks didn't even go with him.

The bracer of Daylen's sunforged gauntlet reacted to the powerful wind resistance, creating its impenetrable yet invisible barrier the size of a heater shield on his arm, the supernatural enhancement the bracer received from being sunforged.

This was important, because Daylen expected the sudden acceleration and wind resistance would have ripped the clothes off his body otherwise. With his gauntlet making a windshield, his clothes only needed to survive their own inertia, which they did thankfully, unlike his shoes and socks.

He would go back for them later.

Within a few seconds Daylen had easily launched himself a hundred meters in a direct rising line before the wind resistance finally leveled out his momentum.

He had overshot the building completely.

"Light's end!" Daylen said, though still very pleased with the technique he had just figured out.

Daylen enhanced his mass with one bond, which slowed his velocity significantly.

Once his trajectory began to fall more directly down, Daylen reduced his mass with one bond, which again increased his velocity, but wind resistance slowed him quickly.

Daylen grabbed his skimmer from his belt, ready to lock it in place for a handhold, but he realized he'd probably be fine. Instead, he enhanced his strength while still having his mass reduced and landed on a rooftop without any problem.

Replacing the skimmer, Daylen returned his weight to normal and ran to the edge of the rooftop, where he enhanced his hearing. He easily pinpointed the building where the cries came from. They had switched to resigned sobs of misery as the vile man had his way with her.

This time, Daylen increased his mass with only one bond and jumped, releasing his bond the moment his feet left the ground.

He shot into the air, but this time in a much more manageable arch and with far less wind resistance.

As Daylen approached the building in question, his jump still too powerful, he made a mental measurement and increased his mass by only using a portion of light through one bond. He instantly slowed and his path changed in accordance, aimed directly for the roof of the building where the girl was being raped.

With increased mass, Daylen crashed through the roof and added another bond of mass just before reaching the floor of the attic, which nearly stopped him in the air. This gave him the chance to extend and stand without any issue, though the floor groaned under his increased weight which he returned to normal.

The man who was in the middle of raping the young girl jumped back, pants around his ankles, his screams of surprise joining those of his prey.

Daylen marched on the man, increasing his strength, and fended off his feeble attempts to stop him.

He grasped the rapist's manhood.

Daylen paused for a brief second, staring into the rapist's eyes and letting him realize what Daylen was about to do. He went pale, his mouth dropping and before his pleas for mercy could leave his mouth, Daylen ripped off the man's penis and threw it aside in one swift motion.

The rapist screamed frantically, falling to his knees in awful horror.

Daylen let the man enjoy his nightmare for a brief moment longer before grasping the rapist and throwing him with all his enhanced strength.

The man's screams echoed through the attic before being cut off by a loud crash as he burst through the brick wall to fall onto the cobblestoned street below.

Other screams could be heard as the man landed, but Daylen knew there was no one who could have been caught under the fall. It's why Daylen had chosen to throw the rapist in that direction, having glanced the streets before bursting in.

Daylen turned to the poor girl who had pulled her knees close and was quivering in fear. Seeing how young she was and in her torn dress made Daylen feel sick to the stomach for more reasons than he could express.

She looked at Daylen in horror. "You..." she began through heavy sobs. "You killed my father!"

"You father deserved it, or would you rather he had continued what he was doing?"

"But... But..."

"He can't hurt you anymore," Daylen said, walking to the huge hole in the wall.

"You're going? But mother will blame me. She'll say I killed him."

"She'll say you did *that*?" Daylen said, pointing to the hole.

"No, but what will I say?"

Daylen reached the hole and looked down below. There were already several people inspecting the scene and periodically gazing up. Daylen waited until several people had seen him. "Tell them the truth," he said and, increasing his mass with one bond, the timbers underneath him creaking in protest, Daylen leapt away. He didn't use his gauntlet as a windshield this time, having felt the wind resistance from his last jump not being too dangerous.

With witnesses to confirm that someone else was there, no one would be able to convict the girl.

Daylen released his mass mid-flight and simply enhanced his strength as he landed, absorbing the impact easily.

Daylen stilled himself and listened once more. Cries for help echoed in his ears. Many sounded hopeless, like they knew no help would come.

Well, it would this time.

CHAPTER EIGHTEEN

*So it shouldn't come as a surprise that the three neighboring
kingdoms to Hamahra—Sunsen, Lumas and Daymark—invaded
shortly after I came to power. Those kingdoms are no more, of
course; their former lands are now a permanent part of modern
Hamahra.*

*The leaders of these old kingdoms didn't have anything against
my people, just with me. They needed to act or lose face, to show
their own people what happens to those who fight their rulers.
Also, if they liberated Hamahra from the lightless Queenkiller and
found that there was no royalty to give the nation to, they would
then have to reluctantly take a portion of one of the most
prosperous nations in the world into their own kingdoms,
welcoming the orphaned people with open arms into brotherhood
and noble rule.*

How altruistic of them.

Daylen found Ahrek near the main entrance to the skyport.
"Where were you?" Ahrek asked.

"All over. Did you think I abandoned you?"

"No," Ahrek said, handing Daylen something wrapped in cloth.
"Your lunch," he said, smiling.

"Thanks," Daylen said, unwrapping the bundle to find some
slices of roast beef with potatoes. He ate hungrily. "I could have

left, you know. Caught a skyship," Daylen said between mouthfuls.

"Yes, but I think you've accepted our inevitable companionship, even if we do disagree at times."

"I don't disagree with you, that's the annoying thing... I know you're right."

"I'm aware of how difficult my company can be. Truth be told, it's why I haven't had many friends in life."

"Well, it's their loss."

Ahrek looked as if Daylen had just slapped him. "And here I thought my welcome was truly worn out."

"I came back, didn't I? Yes, you're annoyingly good, but the funny thing is...I like that about you. You do what you feel is right even if it offends."

"Well, I like you too, Daylen."

"I haven't done much to earn that. In fact I've treated you rather poorly, all things considered."

"You were simply adjusting to what the Light has thrust upon you."

"Trust me, I'm still adjusting. We've only known each other for what, a single fall?"

"Funny, it feels like I've known you for longer." Ahrek glanced to the many people who were staring at them as they passed. "As popular as ever, I see."

"Yeah, well, thankfully they can tell I'm with someone, as otherwise they'd all be trying to interrogate me."

"And on that note, you're lucky you weren't here. The authorities came looking for you, led by the city's chief constable. Even a pair of Archknights passed asking after you. I don't know what they were doing, but it's best we keep our distance from the Archons until you're ready to join. If you used your powers while they were near they would have sensed it."

"They've finally decided what to do with me?"

"Yes, which is to simply ask you some questions about your father's death and the time he spent in hiding."

"So you spoke with them?"

"I *was* seen with you."

"Then why didn't they stay with you until I returned?"

"Clearly they didn't think you would...after I told them that we had argued and parted ways."

"You threw them off?" Daylen asked, genuinely surprised and grateful.

"I said nothing but the truth."

"But you knew saying certain truths would give them the wrong idea."

Ahrek smiled at him.

"So you Lightbringers can't lie, but..."

"Oh, we can lie—we just lose our powers if we do, and therefore stop being Lightbringers."

"Fine, you choose not to lie, but you can still be *deceptive*."

"If it serves a noble purpose, of course. I couldn't ignore the fact that they might try to take you by force, something I don't believe they have the right to do."

"Huh, thanks."

"I know you want to avoid the authorities, but that doesn't mean I think you shouldn't answer their questions."

"Yeah, well, I'll do that when I'm finished at the capital."

"Why's that?"

"Like I've told you before, none of your business."

"And here I thought we were getting along so well."

"I'm allowed my secrets."

"Am I allowed to ask what were you doing this whole time?"

"Yes, you can ask," Daylen said, and then remained silent.

Ahrek looked at him humorlessly.

"Huh, I thought you might have laughed at that one. Look, I was doing some good."

"Some good?"

Daylen glanced about to make sure no one was listening. Several people were. Not exactly eavesdropping, but they were looking in his direction. He stepped closer and spoke softly. "I'm learning more about my powers. I realized that I can hear things kilometers away, specifically cries for help if I focus on them."

"And you endeavored to help?" Ahrek asked.

"I wouldn't be much of a man if I didn't."

"Interesting. Not all Archknights are so skilled at listening."

"What do you mean?"

"Well, all of the knights I've known could increase their listening ability—hear things through walls and such. It seems they can all increase any attribute to a mild level. But to hear things at such a distance... Well, I've only ever met a single knight who could do that."

"One bond versus many."

"What?"

"Oh, well the light I draw in can be channeled along four paths, or bonds. One bond grants a different enhancement based on the attribute being empowered, but I've found that putting more than one on the same attribute doubles the first enhancement exponentially. It sounds like the knights are only using a single bond, which doesn't make sense."

Ahrek paused and rubbed his chin. "Yes, that is odd. Well, I'm sure you'll learn their secrets when you join them."

"Yeah, but first things first."

"You look a little worse for wear. Did this helping of others involve knocking down buildings?"

"No. Crashing through walls, yes, but not knocking down buildings."

"Crashing through walls!"

"Yep."

"Daylen, what did you do?"

"Let's see... I killed two rapists and a child molester, caught five thieves, stopped a brawl, and killed two murderers."

"Killed? Daylen, you're not the judge and executioner!"

"I'm protected under the law of justification," Daylen said. After all, he should know; he was the one who had instituted that law, and the current government hadn't seen fit to get rid of it.

"Only if the guilt of those you killed can be proven," Ahrek said. "Too many people have tried to use that law to legalize acts of violence, even murder."

"The law works. And trust me, I'm not an idiot; I wouldn't kill anyone if there was the slightest doubt, but with most I caught them in the very act, and the ones I was too late to stop I followed and found damning evidence. I brought the thieves to a nearby constable, but when it comes to rape and murder, death is the punishment they...they deserve." Light, Daylen was a damned hypocrite.

Ahrek paused and seemed to try and regain his composure. "Of course I feel good those evil men were stopped..."

"I never said they were all men."

"You killed women?" Ahrek asked, exasperated. *So much for his composure.*

"When it comes to crimes this severe, women deserve equal punishment, don't you think?"

"No, they're *women*."

"I don't buy into that drack. Same crimes deserve the same punishment."

"Daylen, I'm *very* concerned that for someone so young you find ending other's lives so easy."

"I never said it was easy. It's just that I can live with it. I can do what most men can't and I've accepted that my life is going to be a violent one."

"When did you first take a life?"

"In a duel, and no, I'm not going to tell you about it or any others. They most certainly fall into the realms of none of your blackened business..."

"Please watch your language."

"I'll blackened speak how I damn well want to speak."

Ahrek sighed.

"Look," Daylen said, "I've killed before. I'm no innocent, so the way I see it, if there's killing needing to be done, it's better that someone with unclean hands do it."

Ahrek looked to be in serious thought, though his eyes never left Daylen's. "I do believe that there are crimes worthy of death, rape and murder among them, but being willing to carry out the penalty of such crimes carries a danger that you might dole it out when undeserved. Killing without just cause is *murder*, Daylen. Have you ever misjudged?"

"You seem to have a short memory. *None of your blackened business.* I told you that I intend to use my powers for good, so if you don't have the stomach for it, you can bugger off."

Ahrek was frowning deeply and seemed not able to respond. He even paced a few times before sighing. "Well...to be perfectly honest, I can't say I wouldn't have reacted the same when being confronted with such crimes."

"*You* could actually kill someone?"

A shadow seemed to cross Ahrek's face as he replied somberly, "I have a past too, Daylen."

Daylen nodded. No more needed to be said.

Silence fell between them for a few minutes.

"Tell me, Daylen," Ahrek said. "You knew who your father was before he died and of his countless crimes. No one deserved to die more than him, and you've clearly shown yourself capable enough. So why didn't you kill him?"

"Because it was obvious that living with his guilt was greater punishment than anything I could have done to him. If you want to punish someone like Dayless the Conqueror, you force them to live."

"No, Dayless deserved to meet the Light a long time ago."

"You think he deserved to go to the Outer Darkness?"

"Of course, don't you?"

"Yeah," Daylen said with hope, finding it hard to see how the Outer Darkness could be any worse than the guilt he had to live with every fall. In fact, some scripture said that those cast into Outer Darkness were utterly destroyed, and if that truly meant the end of his wretched existence, then Daylen welcomed it with open arms.

Ahrek was looking at Daylen intently. "Dayless the Conqueror prolonged his life for fear of the Light's just punishment."

"You don't know what you're talking about, Bringer."

"Then we disagree. Now, as I think of it, you must have been noticed using your powers."

"Yeah, I realized. I took off my master's mark, found some cloth to tie around my mouth, and put Imperious in a safe place till I was done."

"Do you think it worked?"

"Hiding my identity was less a priority than saving lives, so even if I was recognized, it was still worth it."

"True. So, are there no more who need help?"

"Not for the moment, not anyone close at least. With a city this size, I think if I really tried, I could always hear someone in need."

"Then why don't you?"

"Because I'm tired! My powers feel sluggish and need time to recover. I can only do as much as I can."

"It's all anyone *can* do."

"Yeah, well, I'm strung up enough over the crimes that I lack the energy to stop."

Ahrek nodded. "We best find a ship before the authorities or those Archknights return."

"Agreed," Daylen said, walking to the skyport, but not toward the main office where the carrier flight schedules would be found.

"The head office is that way," Ahrek said.

Daylen turned back. "We're not catching a carrier."

"So you plan to get us passage on a trader? I thought you wanted to get to the capital sooner."

"Yeah, most carriers are faster, but they all take the long way round."

"Because of the pirates from the Floating Isles! No one flies through those skies."

"No—some traders are willing to risk it if there's enough incentive, and that's who we're going to find."

"Haven't you heard that piracy has increased lately? Whole ships are being stolen, not just their goods."

"I read the papers, Ahrek, of course I've heard it. All the more reason."

"*All the more reason?*"

"We'll need some type of excitement along the way."

"You *want* to be attacked by pirates?"

"I'm thinking of hunting them down as a lifestyle, so why not take out a few while we travel?"

Ahrek sighed. "It's true that we possess a certain level of skill, but we're not invincible. We shouldn't take undue risk."

"Then it's good that this risk isn't undue. Now come on."

———

"You're not serious," Ahrek said, looking distrustfully at the crew of the trader Daylen had found.

"Of course I'm serious. This is one of the only traders planning to fly under the Floating Isles."

"Do they know of the increased pirate activity under the Isles?"

"Of course they would, these ship crews gossip like old women. It's just that this ship in particular has some type of crucial deadline to meet, so they're taking the risk."

Ahrek pulled Daylen a step farther away from the large ship. "Use that ability I taught you. Sense the light inside these men."

Daylen looked to the crew and stretched out to feel the light in them. He eventually found the light he was looking for. There was light there, but not much. Daylen also felt a little revolted and sick.

"You feel that," Ahrek said. "These are *not* good men. For all we know, they could be smuggling illegal goods."

"Or they could simply be dishonest jerks?"

"And that should be enough for us to find another ship, especially since their lack of light could be a result of something far worse."

"Perfect. If it turns out that they like to rob their passengers, it's better we're with them instead of others who can't protect themselves being in our place."

Ahrek sighed. "Daylen, those who look for trouble will always find it."

Daylen smiled mischievously. "That's my hope."

CHAPTER NINETEEN

*The Hamahran people rallied behind me and we met the invaders
head-on. We were outnumbered, but through military maneuvers
that everyone since have called ingenious, and the creation of our
new war machines of my own design, we fought the invaders off.
But I didn't stop there. They had sought to kill me and subjugate
my people; thus, they deserved the same treatment.*
*I chose to embrace the name my enemies had called me, Dayless,
for I would take away the light of anyone who challenged me.
Fighting the Dawn Empire would be like casting the Night on
oneself. Thus I was Dayless, and I would conquer all who dared
oppose me.*

Lyrah stood amongst several constables and two detectives
while a dead woman lay on the floor with a snapped neck.

A man lay on a nearby couch in this finely furnished sitting
room with bruises and cuts all over, while being attended by a
doctor.

"I want a full report," Lyrah demanded of a detective.

The detective, who unlike the constables was not wearing an
officer's uniform but still carried a four-shooter, had a hand
grasping the lapel of his tailed coat. Unshaven, he spoke with a
rough voice. "Well, Lady Archon, it's all very odd to say the least.
Apparently this man"—the detective indicated the man on the

couch—"was being tortured by his wife. As to the motive, we haven't yet figured it out, though it must have been something serious for the wife to do all this. We'll be investigating the husband, don't you worry. It was hard to get a lot of information out of him as he's been through quite the ordeal. What he's been saying is that some young man came crashing though that wall"— the detective pointed to the gaping hole that had been smashed through the wall, which was made of stone—"and snapped the wife's neck before she could plunge that dagger into the husband's chest." He pointed to the bloody dagger on the floor. "The man who intervened must be an Archknight."

Lyrah had to step carefully here. "People can still do remarkable things without having our powers," she said. "There's also many types of darkstone-powered weapons that could burst open a wall."

"True."

"Did you manage to get a description of this young man?"

The detective flipped back though his small notepad. "Male, young, blue hair, wore an old-style dueling coat."

"That's plenty. You may carry on with your investigation," Lyrah said, and then she walked to Cueseg. "I don't get it. He first murders a man by throwing him from a building, yet at every other point we've tracked him to, he seems to have been helping people."

"You are missing something very clear," Cueseg said, condescending as ever. "*Reason.* Why did the boy kill? The other man was missing his pants and had his penis cut off. Sex must be the reason. I am thinking that man was a rapist."

Lyrah's jaw tensed and she replied with as much control as possible. "A rapist?"

"Yes, taking a man's penis is the punishment for this crime."

Lyrah felt her cheeks flush. "No, it isn't."

"It is for my people."

"Then there's at least one custom I like from Tuerase."

Cueseg nodded once. "You will like many more as you learn. We are the most intelligent people."

"Humble, too."

"Strong and beautiful as well," Cueseg said, with such perfect sincerity that Lyrah laughed.

"What is funny?"

"Oh, just the things that go over your head."

Cueseg glanced to the ceiling, and though his face didn't change, it was clear he didn't understand. Lyrah laughed again.

"You are a silly woman, laughing too much."

"You should try it sometime. Light, Cueseg, you're as stiff as a brick."

"If I must be stiff as a brick to be as strong as one, I will be stiff."

"Don't forget thick."

"Yes, I will be as thick as a brick, too."

Lyrah suppressed another chuckle at that. "Anyway, there's no way to know why the boy killed that first victim until we question him."

"I am think he is trying to help. It makes sense. He must fight evil or he cannot have our powers."

Cueseg was right; the boy's actions *did* fit with the supposed moral requirement to becoming a Lightbinder, something she was doubting.

"Even if he is, the boy is using his powers recklessly and with no right. Taking it upon himself to be judge, jury, and executioner, just like his blackened father."

"It is what we do when we see a crime."

"A right only given to us by the nations we serve, not by virtue of our powers."

"But there is a law you teach me—what is it, to justify?"

"The law of justification," Lyrah said with a sigh. "Yes, in Hamahra, citizens can be justified to carry out punishments if they catch the criminal in the act, if they can later prove the crime through evidence or witnesses. But only if the punishment was proportional to the crime committed."

"What if this boy is justified?"

"There's not enough evidence for that. In fact, some of his acts look to be pure murder."

"Maybe, but I do not think so."

"We'll find out once we catch him."

CHAPTER TWENTY

*Many have called me mercilessly effective, which is accurate
enough. I executed all captured soldiers after each battle—better to
feed my own people than take care of enemies that would fight
against me given the opportunity.*

*I had sealed away my compassion to obtain revenge, and from
that time on no horror or atrocity I committed made me flinch, for
nothing could come close to the horror I had seen when looking
down at the massacred bodies of my family. Though I had sealed
away my humanity by choice, it was permanently severed from
my soul through action. I became a heartless, unfeeling husk.
Though I had obtained success and rule over one of the greatest
nations in the world, I was utterly miserable, and had begun to
loathe who I was.*

*So in between my acts of rule and governance, I drowned my
misery in whatever fleeting pleasures I could obtain: fine food,
fine wine, and sex. Lots and lots of sex.*

The *Maraven* was a Devendale Hauler, one of the finest
skyships ever built in Daylen's opinion. It, like many
skyships, had a large iron windshield at the fore of the deck, which
stuck up like a giant arrowhead from the bow. The edges of the
shield had been angled up and out, pointing away from the ship.
This directed wind currents away and over the deck which created

a calm air pocket where one could walk and work while the ship flew through the violent winds. The wind whistled off the sides of the ship, yet not loudly enough that people couldn't hear one another talk.

All skyships had several inbuilt safety measures to prevent sudden drops or rises that might throw a person from the ship. The navigation levers had them too, which prevented the pilot from performing such extreme maneuvers intentionally. This didn't stop accidents altogether, but reduced their likelihood considerably.

Daylen and Ahrek lounged on one of the inbuilt benches that hugged the side rail of the ship.

As usual, Ahrek was drawing in his sketchbook.

Daylen couldn't help but glance at Ahrek's work now and then and see the drawing take form. It was a portrait of a woman. Ahrek was indeed talented, and if not for the new daguerreotype cameras, he could have easily made a living off it.

Daylen held out his hand. "May I?"

Ahrek smiled, pausing his sketch. "Of course," he said, handing Daylen his sketchbook.

Daylen leafed through the pages. Most of Ahrek's pictures were portraits, all masterfully done. Daylen found the portrait Ahrek had done of him, from that dream. It was a *very* good likeness, especially from memory. As he flicked through, Daylen noticed a few recurring faces among the sketches. As he continued, those faces stood out to him more and more. Indeed, their faces were what Ahrek drew most. Then Daylen turned to a picture that had Ahrek himself with the recurring characters. It was a picture of him playing with three children, a boy and two girls, a woman at his side. Ahrek was still in his Lightbringer robes, but the woman and children were wearing normal clothes.

Daylen showed Ahrek the picture. "Who're they?"

Ahrek looked to him and hesitated before replying. "My family," he said with quivering emotion.

Daylen nodded. It was all too clear. He knew that heartache just as keenly. Ahrek had lost them, and his drawings were a way to keep them close in his memory.

Daylen looked at the picture again and felt tears welling in his eyes as the memory of his own little ones returned. He envied

Ahrek for having a way to see them, for Daylen did not. Their faces were a blur in his mind, and it broke his heart.

Daylen closed the book and handed it back.

Ahrek took it and began drawing once more. The two sat in silence for a time before Ahrek glanced at the crew of the ship. This wasn't the first time the Bringer had done this, nor the first time he had glanced at the hazy shapes of the islands that floated high above in the sky.

"Worried about something?" Daylen asked.

"I'm not worried. Just cautious. These are exactly the type of men who'd happily take advantage of anyone. I've already seen two pick the pockets of their fellow crewmen. That one keeps trying to shirk his jobs when he thinks no one is looking. And the captain has been sneaking suspicious glances toward us as he talks to his first mate."

"If I wasn't already aware of your particularly perceptive nature, I'd say you were paranoid."

"You think I'm particularly perceptive?"

"Stop fishing for validation, you know you're good at noticing things."

"Yes… If I recall correctly, you think I'm a smartass."

"And you should be flattered by that compliment."

"I overflow with gratitude."

"Careful—that's sarcasm I detect."

"I never said I can't be sarcastic. Sometimes even the lowest form of humor has its place."

"Huh, now you're being self-righteous."

"Yes, you're right. I'm sorry."

"Oh, shut up!"

"What?"

"If you're going to reveal in the smallest way that you're as imperfect as the rest of us, you could at least make it harder to admit your own fault."

"You know, you're very hard to please."

"I've got to keep you on your toes."

"Then why are we sitting?"

"Pathetic."

Ahrek chuckled. "So pathetic that it's *hilarious!*"

"No."

Ahrek sighed and glanced again at the crew.

"All right, what is it?"

Ahrek closed his sketchbook and put it away in his satchel. "I'm simply wondering what could honestly make these men risk flying through these skies."

"First of all, it's not nearly as risky as you think. We're flying as low as is safe and at a decent clip which is hard to spot from up at the Isles. So unfortunately we're probably not going to see any pirates."

"Yes, a *tragedy*, but still a great risk—and is it really worth saving half a fall's time?"

"Depends on schedule and demand. If this trader gets to a buyer that can only purchase a cargo's worth before another trader...well, they'll get to sell their goods and the late arrival will be left out of pocket. If a trader has debts, and by the look of this once impressive ship I'd say they do, making it to a deal is often the difference between success and bankruptcy."

"Life is ever more valuable than money."

"That's too simplistic. Money facilitates the ability to live, so don't judge people for seeking it."

"Oh, but I *will* judge for that very reason. What point is there for money to support life when that life is risked in its pursuit? Such a contradiction reveals a very unbalanced set of priorities."

"Yes, these men have skewed priorities. For whatever reason, they need to get to the capital as soon as possible, and we're here to benefit from that. So stop whining."

"Very well. My concerns will be contained."

"Thank you."

"Might I ask a question instead?"

"Might you?"

"How do you know so much about pirates, as demonstrated by your confidence that they won't attack? Or is this another thing that falls into the realms of none of my business?"

Daylen considered the question. "What I will tell you is that I've visited the Floating Isles before. Light, I've even traveled to their cities: Deadend, Freelife, and Raidaway."

Ahrek looked genuinely surprised. "When under the Light did you visit those awful places, and more to the point, how did you survive?"

"You're lucky I've said as much as I have."

"Yes, with how secretive you are with your past, I suppose I should be grateful for any small offering."

"Good. Anyway, the cities are interesting to say the least," Daylen said as he thought back, "but not exactly what you expect. They go through phases of law and lawlessness, depending on who's in power at the time. Of course their version of law isn't what the word implies; it's more an unspoken code that might get enforced if any particular person feels so inclined."

"It's a wonder no one has thought to do something about those lawless havens."

"Dayless the Conqueror tried to."

"Yes, well, apart from *him*."

"He *was* called the Conqueror for a reason, so do you really think anyone else is going to have a better chance than he had? Dayless wiped out each of those cities, but the ruffians who lived in them just hid in the thousand other islands, hunkered down and fought back like the bandits they were. It was literally impossible to root them out with all the places they could hide. The Isles are like a never-ending three-dimensional maze. No one has ever been able to completely chart the place. So even with their cities destroyed, the people in them were never defeated. Dayless eventually abandoned his mission as a lost cause. One might say it's the only battle he ever lost."

"Again, you're right," Ahrek said. "I suppose if someone as ruthlessly effective as the Conqueror couldn't clean out the Isles, no one can. And now I hear that the bandit cities have been rebuilt larger than they ever were."

"Yeah, I've heard the same."

"Hmm..."

"What?"

"Oh, just a personal thought. I'm going for a walk. You're free to join me if you wish."

"No, that sounds a little too gay for me. I'm sure that at least one of the crewmen here might swing the other way, if you care to find out."

Ahrek shook his head as he left. "Truly, your humor needs a thorough reeducation."

"Huh, you're one to talk!" Daylen called out after him as he leaned back to gaze up at the soft, island-spotted sky.

There were several hundred thousand individual islands

among the Floating Isles, all ranging from the size of a skyship to kilometers in diameter, all at varying yet relatively close heights and localized to a hundred-kilometer radius.

The prevailing theory on where the Floating Isles came from was that they were all once joined as a much smaller continent that floated above the mainland, much like the smaller sister continents of Orden and Azbanadar. Daylen had lent credence to this possibility many years ago when finding that most of the Floating Isles fit back together like some massively complex puzzle. Something incredibly powerful had blown it apart, and that was one of the things Daylen had looked into during his attempts to eradicate the pirates.

He had found an ancient device buried in one of the center isles. After giving up on the invasion as a lost cause, Daylen returned to study the device, discovering that it was an incredibly advanced sunforge. It could make sunucles far easier and quicker than any forge in the world. But Daylen had suspected it could do more. Finding it at the center of the Floating Isles was too much of a coincidence. Daylen thanked the Light he didn't discover its full function until after his defeat, as otherwise he might have been tempted to use it.

Once in hiding, he had all the time in the world to study the device, and after a few years he had figured it out. Its sunforging ability was unlimited. It could sunforge a whole skyship...or continent. But when trying to sunforge a continent, as some idiot had tried to do so long ago...well, the Floating Isles had been the result. The device could sunforge darkstone, something thought impossible, but from testing tiny granules Daylen discovered that darkstone exploded when sunforged, and the yield was thousands of times more powerful than anything else—hence the Floating Isles.

But that didn't matter anymore. Daylen had hidden the device away and it was far better the thing was lost once more, considering its incredible destructive potential.

Daylen leaned back and was feeling good, invigorated even, and he realized why. He had now recovered from the overuse of his powers.

With access to his powers once more, Daylen decided to test

them again. The light came to him as easily as ever. Smiling and reveling in how wonderful it felt, Daylen bonded it to his eyes and gazed above.

It was amazing. He could see so far, and easily gazed through the haze of the air above. Now the islands were perfectly clear to him, and in very fine detail.

Daylen enjoyed the view for a moment before channeling all bonds to his eyes.

Daylen raised his hand in front of his face. With his eyesight enhanced so much, he could see the individual cells of his skin. Looking up at the isles was something else—not only could he see the underside of each island in his field of vision as if he were next to them with a magnifying glass, but he could see all those things in his field of vision in that level of detail at the one time. Normally a person could only focus on one thing at a time even though there were many things in their field of vision. That was not the case anymore. It was as if, with the enhancement of his eyes, his mind was also enhanced to be able to process and comprehend all the information.

Smiling, Daylen was content to enjoy a view of things he had never dreamed were possible. After a few minutes he released two of his bonds, wanting to see how long he could maintain his powers at half strength. An hour passed, and where his powers would have been exhausted by then if used to their maximum, he didn't feel fatigued one bit. It was at that time a skyship flew out from above an inconspicuous island kilometers overhead. With his eyesight still enhanced, Daylen saw it immediately.

Daylen maximized his sight to get a better look at the ship. It had once been a Hammenlight switchback, one of the faster carrier models, but had been aggressively retrofitted with iron plates, harpoons, and a rammer fixed to the bow.

It was a pirate ship.

Daylen smiled to himself. "Well, this trip isn't going to be nearly as boring as I feared."

CHAPTER TWENTY-ONE

*It started with the finer ladies of ill repute, but with the pleasure
of bedding them came a feeling of filth. I loathed myself enough as
it was, and soon couldn't stand to be in their presence. I wanted
something pure and innocent, such a contrast to what I was, so I
called for a willing young woman. A virgin.*

*Many girls came forward, believing that I sought a wife, an
empress to rule at my side. My people still loved me at that time
and the one I picked thought it as a marriage proposal. She
deserves to be remembered. Her name was Deena: sweet, kind,
beautiful, and in all ways perfect.*

Daylen couldn't help but laugh as he thought of what it
would be like for pirates to attack a skyship that he was
aboard.

No one else had noticed, of course—the pirates were still
several kilometers above them—but it had certainly spotted them,
for it was flying their way like a shotspike.

Daylen stood and casually made his way to the captain,
noticing that Ahrek, who looked to have been deep in thought this
entire time, had seen Daylen rise.

Ahrek met Daylen as he reached the captain.

The portly captain's clothes looked much like his ship, a
respected fashion that must have been expensive to purchase, but

were now worn and tattered from continual use and neglect. The captain himself had neatly combed hair, but needed a shave.

"And what can I do for my esteemed passenger?" the captain said, who had been offering Daylen every possible courtesy thus far. Daylen suspected this was mostly due to his master's mark, sunforged sword, and the staring crowds surrounding Daylen as he had bartered for passage.

"We've been spotted by pirates."

"What?" the captain said with dread as he searched the skies. "I can't see anything."

Daylen pointed. "Right there to the left of that small cloud. Use your telescope."

The captain did so. "Son of a Shade!" he cursed and turned to his first mate. "All hands on deck! We'll outrun the bastards."

"Not a chance," Daylen said. "That pirate ship is a Hemmenlight switchback carrier. If it can reach even eighty percent of its max speed, it'll be on us in minutes. You have no hope of outrunning it."

"How can you blackened see that?"

"Trust me."

"Told ya this was a bad idea," the first mate said to his captain.

"Don't start with me! We're behind schedule because of your stuff-up, so if those pirates catch us, I'll be sure to introduce *you* to them first." The captain turned back to Daylen. "We should be fine. We'll just have to break out the weapons."

"No. Get everyone below deck. I'll deal with the pirates."

The captain and first mate looked at each other and then back to Daylen in dumb surprise. "Are you crazy, boy?"

"Don't call me *boy*," Daylen hissed. "I'm a Grand High Master of the sword. Now—get below deck!"

"If he is," the first mate said to the captain, "he'd be able take a few of them out before they stick him and pry open the doors."

"Fine," the captain said. "If you want to kill yourself, go ahead. We'll prepare a few surprises inside. Are you coming, Bringer?"

"No, I'll be staying with my friend."

"What, you want to die too?"

"We'll be fine, Captain."

"You're both as blackened brainless as a beggar from Mayn!" the captain said as he left to get the crew beneath.

Daylen calmly walked to the center of the deck and watched the pirates approach.

Ahrek joined him, saying, "This is rather noble of you."

"Not really. It's not like I'm sacrificing myself."

"But you're risking your life."

"As little light as these men have, I don't know of any reason they deserve to die. As far as I'm concerned, they warrant my protection like anyone else. Regardless, it's not much of a risk. Even without my powers I could have taken on a good number of these pirates; added with some tactical positioning, I might have even won. With my powers, there's no contest."

"You're good with tactics?"

"Yes."

"Even so, there's always a chance of defeat."

"I'm not an idiot. I know that, but it doesn't mean I can't be confident."

"True."

A few moments passed before Daylen spoke again. "So what's your plan? Are you going to fight alongside me?"

"Only if I have to. My first act will be to try and resolve things peacefully."

"Peacefully? These are pirates, Ahrek! They need to be stopped. If we scare them off or simply convince them to leave us alone, that still leaves them to hunt the skies."

Ahrek sighed. "You're right. So we need to make them surrender to us and then turn them in to the authorities."

Daylen laughed. "The punishment for piracy is execution! There's even a standing bounty for turning in pirate heads, so if you're worried about the legal right I have to kill these scum, I have it."

Ahrek frowned. "Yes, you have every right in the law to kill the men that are about to attack us; but please, if any of them surrender, show mercy. What if there's some lost soul on that ship who's only there because of bad luck? Don't think of them as faceless pirates. They are still people, Daylen, and some few of them might be redeemed of the life they have found themselves in."

"It's a bit hard to tell who that might be when trying to stop them from killing me."

"Not for us."

"What?"

"Light, Daylen—look for their light."

"Their inner light…" Daylen said in realization.

"You can be confident that any among these criminals that still possess a brighter light within has hope of redemption."

"Would you say that about Dayless the Conqueror? After all, he supposedly had light within him."

Ahrek didn't reply right away. "No. There was no redemption for your father."

"Well, I can't argue with that."

"Then we are agreed. You shall show restraint if you can?"

Daylen nodded. "Agreed."

The pirate switchback was very impressive, decked out with outer armor and weapons, and it came in fast. Several men stood along the deck manning old-style harpoon shotspikes. As soon as the lethal looking switchback flew aside the *Maraven*, the pirates fired. The shotspikes launched forward with such great speed that they easily penetrated the *Maraven's* hull. The ropes must have been fixed to darkstone pulleys, for the floor under Daylen heaved, but the *Maraven* stayed on course.

Daylen could hear the iron supports inside the *Maraven* groan, for the darkstone core was still spatially locked except for its forward movement. The entire ship would be ripped from the core before darkstone moved without sunlight.

Instead, the pirate's switchback was pulled in toward the *Maraven*, which must have had its core unlocked along that axis, as otherwise it would have run into the same problem. The harpoons would have been pulled free, or one of the ships entirely ripped from their heart.

The switchback crashed into the *Maraven's* side, causing another great heave in the ship—but, impressively, the *Maraven* held strong. As Daylen suspected, the ship was far sturdier than a casual glance would indicate.

Pirates jumped aboard easily, the two ship's windshields merging their air pockets, meaning there were no dangerous wind currents between them.

They had weapons drawn and murder in their eyes.

A few of them were even armed with shooters. The others held either swords or the older and larger handheld shotspikes, which were the size of thick short spears. Daylen hadn't seen those things in years.

These pirates have a better chance of flying without darkstone than having enough inner light for me to spare them, Daylen thought, but as Ahrek had asked, he reached out with his new sense.

Sure enough, their lights were faint indeed, about the same as many of the crewmen of the *Maraven*—the difference, of course, being that these pirates were trying to kill him.

Three of the pirates shot their spikes at him, one toward Ahrek.

Daylen's heart leapt in fear—not for himself, but Ahrek.

The Bringer was far from defenseless, but even a master would find it very difficult to dodge a shotspike in flight.

Spikes flew about twice as fast as an arrow and with far more force behind them. Daylen's speed and reflexes were already enhanced, so he dodged the spikes easily as they whistled past.

Ahrek raised his hand before the third spike reached him and light flashed from it, materializing into a familiar-looking sunforged kite shield.

The spike hit the shield, which chimed from the impact and ricocheted off at another angle, where it arced and fell to bounce along the deck. Shotspikes were designed to disengage their internal drivers upon first impact so that they could be collected and used again.

The pirates hesitated at seeing Ahrek's powers, and then charged toward Daylen—a good twenty-five men.

Daylen drew Imperious and walked to greet them.

Ahrek's warning voice echoed on deaf ears as he cried, "Men of the skies, we don't want to harm you!"

Daylen channeled two double bonds into his speed and reflexes, dodging the other spikes shot at him and then deflecting the first attacker's blade with his gauntlet. He sliced the pirate in two as if he were made of paper with the sunforged blade while dodging three other sword strikes.

Daylen moved with truly supernatural speed as he felt for the light in his enemies, seeing their positions and actions as if seeing out from the back of his head. In seeing and thereby predicting each attack, he moved through the flurry of swords like a leaf on the wind, stabbing, slicing, and at one point grabbing the skimmer that hung from a pirate's belt. Switching one bond to strength, Daylen pulled the levers and broke the safety lock, which locked the inner darkstone in place. As the switchback and the *Maraven* were flying at an incredible speed, the skimmer, now not moving at all, seemed to fly backward into the pirate's stomach. The pirate cried out in pain and horror, for the skimmer nearly ripped through his entire body before carrying him to hit the back cabin wall, where it did rip through his body and the rest of the ship—though it was just as likely that the skimmer had broken into pieces after the first few walls it crashed through, releasing the darkstone and exposing it to light.

Daylen dodged and weaved as if performing an acrobatic dance, Imperious lashing out to dismember a pirate with each move.

Blocking a blow that came from behind with the sunforged bracer of his gauntlet, Daylen thrust his sword backward without even looking, seeing the pirate with his light sense as clear as day and running him through.

Daylen sensed another attack and easily dodged it—and even though he realized in that instant that this particular pirate was a young woman, he didn't hesitate to take off her head. She had chosen a life of piracy, and had as little light within her as the rest of them.

As Daylen continued to fight, he spied a single pirate who thought it best not to take him on. He charged at Ahrek.

This is going to be interesting, Daylen thought as he kept his eyes on Ahrek, relying on his light sense to dodge and fight off his opponents.

Ahrek stood calmly, his shield having disappeared. As the pirate neared, Ahrek waved his hand like he was swatting a fly, and an invisible force suddenly ripped the skimmer from the pirate's belt before hitting him with such power that it knocked the man entirely off the other side of the ship.

The moment he left the calm pocket of air made by the ship's windshield, the powerful air currents blew him backward like he had been yanked by a hook, his cries of astonishment and fear echoing in the distance.

Huh. That'll do the job, I suppose.

Daylen finished off the last pirate with a clean decapitation—there had been a lot of those. Those pirates he had run through held their bleeding bodies as they moaned in pain or tried to crawl away. Daylen finished them off before looking to Ahrek and, with accentuated mock concern and dramatic body language, said, "Oh, Ahrek! You just killed a man, whatever will you do?"

"Have I ever told you my opinion about sarcasm?"

"*No*, you've *never* mentioned *anything* like *that* to *me* before."

Ahrek smirked.

"I almost had you, then."

Ahrek quickly removed his smirk and cleared his throat. "Almost. Oh, and technically you're wrong."

"About what?"

"Me killing a man."

"But you just did!"

Ahrek looked to the side and smirked. "No, I didn't. Well, not yet at least."

"What?" Daylen said, before connecting the dots. Almost laughing, he continued, "Ah, I suppose so, for the next few minutes at least."

"I almost had *you*, then."

"Not even close."

Daylen leapt aboard the enemy ship, leaving Ahrek to stop any pirates who might try and board the *Maraven*.

Several pirates were in the process of cutting the harpoon ropes. Having watched Daylen dispatch those pirates who had tried to take the ship, they must have thought it a much better idea to flee. They ran as soon as Daylen hit the deck, several ropes still in place.

With lightning speed, Daylen took out the nearest pirate, then picked up his sword and threw it, skewering another. The next pirate was a young man who tried frantically to get below deck, but it appeared that the other pirates had bolted the door.

Daylen marched on the lad, but before his sword fell, he noticed something. The boy, who looked to be in his late teens, had an inner light that shone much brighter than a normal person's—and a normal person's light would have been odd enough to find among these scum.

Seeing Daylen, the boy grabbed two skimmers from his belt and used them in unison.

Daylen was almost too shocked to stop the boy, for using two skimmers took a remarkable level of coordination. The skimmers pulled the boy to the side and into the air at a great speed but Daylen caught him by the belt and increased his own weight and strength. The boy now had an anchor attached to him, and the two skimmers flew out of his grip—and then their ropes, which were attached to the boy's belt, snapped free.

Daylen had spared the boy's life by grabbing his belt; for if he had grabbed, say, the boy's foot, those ropes would have ripped the boy's belt free from his pants and nearly flayed his skin before breaking several bones; or if the belt had held, it would have ripped his leg from his foot.

Still, those ropes yanked brutally on the belt before they burst, and the boy screamed out in pain as his belt suddenly crushed in on his sides.

He fell limp, hanging from his pants. Daylen carried him to the edge of the carrier.

"Just kill me already," he groaned.

"No."

The boy tried to free himself but was too hurt for a true effort.

"We'll talk later," Daylen said and, throwing him into the air, he shouted out to Ahrek. "Catch!"

Ahrek promptly caught the boy with his own power and floated him to a corner.

"He might need healing," Daylen called out, "but be careful, he's a wriggler!"

Daylen turned and scanned the deck of the pirate ship. There were a few other pirates left, but one in particular stood out. He was at the ship's helm, his arms folded, staring at Daylen with serious eyes. He wore a gold-trimmed tricorne hat and a fashionable justacorps coat of a modern cut. Under the coat he wore formal dueling garb, its cleanliness standing out in stark contrast to the rest of the crew, as with his discipline. This man had to be the captain.

What was most shocking about him was that, for a moment, Daylen thought he was looking at himself, for the man had blue hair under his hat in the exact shade as Daylen's, and there was significant resemblance in the face. But the shock was short lived —the man was not some phantom doppelganger. There were significant enough differences in facial features, and though he was still very youthful to Daylen's aged eyes, the man looked older by at least twenty years compared to Daylen's new physical appearance.

The pirate captain strode confidently down the stairs to the main deck, taking off his coat and throwing it aside. He drew out a side sword and fixed a center-grip kite shield that had hung from his back, both sunforged, shining faintly in a transparent ruby red. No formal duelist would ever be allowed to use a sunforged kite shield in a proper duel, but this man was a pirate; fair play meant nothing to him, and nothing gave as much protection as a sunforged shield.

On top of that, Daylen spied two shotspikes fixed to either side of the captain's sword blade near the hilt. This man had made his sword into a two-shooter. Clever. Dirty, unprincipled, and illegal, but still clever—Daylen could see himself coming up with the idea. He would never use it in a duel, of course, but for battle he wouldn't hesitate.

This fight was going to be interesting.

"I wonder how many of us bastards are out there?" the captain said as he approached.

"What in the Light is that supposed to mean?" Daylen said derisively.

The captain spoke in a mocking tone, "Can't you tell? With how damn good you are with that sword, and with your hair and looks, it's clear that we're long-lost brothers."

Daylen laughed at the absurdity of the comment. "You're blackened stoned, mate. Yeah I can see some resemblance, but trust me when I say there's no chance under the Light that we're related. Seriously, what have you been sniffing?"

"Only the finest snuff money can buy, or I should say, sword can steal."

"Whatever," Daylen said as the two of them sized each other up, weapons in hand. Daylen was of course wearing his dueling gauntlet, but it didn't offer nearly as much protection as a sun-blackened-forged kite, so in terms of arms, Daylen was outmatched.

The captain smiled, astoundingly overconfident. He had no idea who Daylen really was or the true extent of his skill. Still, Daylen was wearing his master's mark, which didn't seem to faze this man. Perhaps this captain was far more skilled than the regular slob, or he simply put too much stock in his sunforged kite and dirty spike-loaded sword.

Kite shield or no, Daylen knew that with his powers he could wipe the floor with this man, which is why he decided not to use them. Daylen was simply too much a duelist at heart, and honestly since fighting Ahrek a fall or so ago, Daylen had been craving another bout as good and exhilarating as that, and one that would actually conclude properly.

So when the captain attacked, Daylen didn't use his powers. He was forced to block with his sunforged gauntlet, for this captain was indeed skilled—very skilled.

Strike after strike came and Daylen dodged, parried, and blocked, all the while attacking back with his own.

Daylen guessed the man was at least a master, and with his large advantage from the sunforged kite, the bout was indeed even.

The musical chime of clashing sunucles filled the air as the blades and shields crossed, clashed, and countered in bright flashes of light.

The captain locked their swords and shields together, twisting and angling so his sword pointed at Daylen's head.

A click sounded from the man's sword and Daylen just managed to jerk his head out of the way of the shooting spike.

"Good!" the captain said with a large grin. "No one's ever survived that before."

"That was your best?" Daylen said as their weapons clashed back and forth. "And here I thought I might break a sweat."

"Oh there's better, trust me." The captain switched his style to rely more on his shield, and due to it being sunforged, it effectively put an impenetrable wall between them.

Daylen spun around and struck back, but it hit the invisible barrier extended by the captain's shield. That thing was going to be blackened hard to get around.

The sunforging process enhanced the purpose of the shield, which was to protect, and thus it blocked anything that threatened the one who wielded it and allowed the wielder's own attacks through—and that was the trick to get around it.

Daylen feinted an attack, spun around, and pushed himself into a low slide. He skidded through the invisible barrier of the kite, for his slide wasn't an offensive attack against the captain. Once past, Daylen spun back around and struck.

The captain brought his sword over and blocked the attack,

which Daylen had to admit was a damn fine move, and then another click sounded.

Daylen wasn't fast enough, and the shotspike pierced his shoulder. He grunted in pain as the captain bashed at Daylen with the corner of his kite.

Daylen caught the edge of the shield with his gauntleted fist, but as his wound was on the same arm, he had no strength to push back and get the angle he wanted—otherwise he would have triggered the spring-powered darkstone dagger in his gauntlet. That would have shattered the shield with the merest touch.

Daylen had to let his opponent push him back, so he heaved, something his current positioning helped with a great deal. Daylen had forged the hand pieces of his gauntlet separate from the main bracer, which meant the sunforging process had enhanced a different property: specifically, the grip strength in his hand. Thus, even with his wound there was no way the shield could get wrenched from his grasp.

Pulling backward, Daylen placed his boot onto the captain's gut and kicked as he rolled, launching the captain overhead.

Daylen rolled onto his feet in an acrobatic flip and, with another jump using the same momentum, he flipped through the air to slash down at the fallen man.

The captain rolled out of the way and sprung to his feet with as much acrobatic grace as Daylen.

Imperious slashed through the deck as if it wasn't even there.

The captain was short of breath and he smiled. "Haven't had a fight like this in years. You're pretty good, kid. That master's mark is well deserved."

"From the way you've been fighting you deserve one, too. Not a Grand High mark, but you're at least a master'."

He scoffed. "I'm not a noble, fair-playing duelist. I'd rather surprise my opponents with a sword in their back."

"A good tactic."

"I haven't become the most feared pirate in the skies from dumb luck."

"Oh, was I supposed to know who you are?"

"If ya spent time near any dock you would. I'm Captain Blackheart, terror of the skies!"

"And master of cliché titles."

The captain pointed his sword. "Watch your tongue, boy."

Daylen's anger surged. "Or *what*, you pathetic little snot? You're nothing but a wretched, despicable thief who preys on the weak and helpless." Daylen switched his bonds to heal his wound as he spoke. "You're worse than a worm, you miserable piece of drack. So yeah, this has been fun, but I'm done. No more playing. I'm going to make you suffer. I'm going hurt you slowly and deliberately until you realize in horrifying clarity that you're about to *die*—and then, and only then, when you plea for mercy, am I going to do the very thing you've done to others. I will rob you of your heart's most desperate desire by killing you in the most unholy way I can think of!"

With every word the captain's face grew redder. "Why, you... I'll see you gutted!"

He charged.

Daylen had meant it when he'd said it was fun, and that now it was over. With light flowing through him, Daylen channeled it into his speed and strength. He deflected the captain's attack with casual ease and he switched one bond of speed to his weight to anchor him as he kicked. The captain blocked with his shield, of course, but with Daylen's enhanced strength, the kick launched him into the air and back a good ten meters. He crashed to the ground with none of the finesse he had shown himself capable of. Groaning, he rolled and forced himself to his feet, but Daylen was already there.

Grasping the captain's sword arm, Daylen channeled strength and crushed the bones underneath. The captain screamed, releasing his sword. Daylen then triggered his darkstone dagger from his gauntlet and punched it into the captain's shield, which shattered into a thousand brilliant shimmering pieces.

The captain was chuckling.

"You weren't linked to the shield," Daylen said with a sinking heart.

"No. You just killed the daughter of Senator Terain. I'd kidnapped her a few years ago. Was a good way to ensure the Civic Guard stayed off my back, don't ya think?" And then Daylen heard a tap against his sword. A chime of shattering glass sounded in the air as Daylen's sword redirected the blow. Looking down, Daylen saw that the captain had pulled out a darkstone dagger and had touched it to Imperious.

The captain looked to the sword in shock. "What? That can't be possible...unless that's Imperious itself!"

Daylen punched him, making sure to break a few ribs, then grabbed him by the throat dragged the captain to the side railing.

"If...if that's Imperious," Blackheart wheezed out, "he must still be alive. But how did you get it?"

Daylen dropped the captain and ripped off a long piece of the side railing of the ship. He then stomped his foot through the floor and thrust the railing through the hole to leave a pointing pike of wood jutting out of the deck two meters tall.

The captain lay there, trying to move, but making very little progress considering his shattered ribs.

Daylen grabbed Blackheart by the shirt and pulled him close to whisper, "I never *got it*—I've always *had it*. I *am* Dayless the Conqueror, you pathetic little worm, and now you're dead."

Blackheart's eyes widened in fear. "No—wait!"

Daylen hoisted him up.

"What're you doing?" Blackheart asked in fear, and then he saw the pike of wood. A sudden awareness seemed to bring horrifying clarity to the captain's mind. "No, you wouldn't—wait! If you really are the Conqueror, that means I'm your son! Can't you see that? I have money, gold! I can pay you! Don't—"

He screamed as Daylen impaled him by the rear end, slowly, the captain wailing in agony with each penetrating inch.

CHAPTER TWENTY-TWO

*I was at war with Daymony at that time, and Deena was a much-
appreciated distraction in between my battles. Poor Deena took
my lust as affection, but the truth was I had none left within me.
And yet still she fell in love. She probably fell in love with the idea
of me: the champion of the Fourth Night, the tragic hero who rose
up after the death of his family to conquer tyranny, the majestic,
unapproachable Emperor. As soon as I realized Deena's
attachment, I discarded her like a soiled rag and called for
another. The last thing I wanted was attachment.*

*My people simply believed that the engagement hadn't
worked out.*

*Several girls later, Deena managed to sneak back into the palace,
broken and distraught, and she lashed out at me. I fought her off
easily but saw her attack as an attempt on my life, and thus I
ordered Deena's execution.*

*Now, as I think back, I can see that she hadn't truly tried to kill
me—she was just heartbroken—but that didn't matter to me. From
then on, any girl that grew too attached and tried to rejoin my
side, disrupting whatever I was doing at the time, was sentenced to
the same fate.*

D aylen felt tired and sickened. Truly, what he had just done *was* an unholy way to kill somebody, but it wasn't his first, far from it, and that wretch most certainly deserved it.

Besides, Daylen was, if anything, a man of his word.

What was that stupid stuff the captain was saying? That he was his son? *Ridiculous*. Daylen hadn't fathered any children after he had lost his little ones. Oh, he'd had sex, lots of sex, but he had made sure measures were taken to avoid such complications.

Daylen looked at Imperious to find it in perfect condition. His legendary sunforged sword could even resist the touch of darkstone.

"What's that make it?" Daylen said to himself as he cast his mind into his memory. "Ah, that's it. Seven hundred and ninety-two."

By this time, any last remaining pirates that had been on deck had chosen to jump from the ship to skim down to the surface. They were the lucky ones, for Daylen would have killed them too.

Daylen needed to stop the ships—with no one at the helms, they might crash into something.

He walked to the helm of the switchback and disengaged the ship's main driver. Momentum still carried the ship forward, but eventually those harpoons would rip free from the stress as the *Maraven* was still in flight, which Daylen didn't want to happen.

He quickly jumped over to the *Maraven* and also disengaged its driver. Now both ships would eventually slow and then stop from wind resistance.

Back on the switchback, Daylen kicked down the door that led inside the carrier and dispatched those behind it with lethal effectiveness. His anger had subsided, which made the ugly task a slow dredge of slaughter, for he truly did hate killing people, but these men were loathsome murderers and deserved no mercy, except for the one he had found before with the bright inner light. The rest had barely a glimmer.

By now, the pirates were doing their very best to hide from Daylen. He sighed, not being in the mood to dig them out one by one. His light sense could detect them, of course, but it appeared the walls had reduced its range to the point that he could only sense things five meters behind other obstructions.

Then Daylen suddenly realized he could look for them an easier way.

He channeled all his bonds to his ears, focusing on the softest of sounds. He instantly could hear the heartbeats and breaths of every single creature within a kilometer's distance. Light, he could hear the flapping wings of a flock of birds eight hundred meters from the stern of the ships. Just like when he enhanced his eyes, it was like his mind was also enhanced to comprehend all the new input. He could hear every single thing at once and know of their locations. Interestingly, Daylen could hear a large collection of heartbeats all gathered together back on the *Maraven*. With these heartbeats were clear and distinct sounds of whimpering and crying—each from a young and feminine voice.

"No... " Daylen said in disbelief as his anger surged to a far greater degree than the captain had stoked previously.

Turning Daylen marched back to the *Maraven*. Once on the other ship, Ahrek pointed to the dead, impaled captain. "That was *completely* unnecessary, Daylen!" Ahrek bellowed.

"Then why didn't you stop me?"

"I've only just noticed, what with all the pirates dying over there that man's screams weren't out of—"

Daylen cut him off. "That's about to appear tame if I find what I expect."

Ahrek stopped, his eyes widening slightly through his anger. "What's wrong?"

"Follow me and you'll find out," Daylen said through gritted teeth.

Daylen kicked down the door, scaring the life out of the *Maraven's* captain and first mate.

"Fire!" the captain said as a man pilled a lever to the housing-unit of a warhead. A Light-blackened *warhead*!

Channeling all four bonds to his speed, Daylen *just* managed to dodge the flying warhead, which had been aimed at a slight upward trajectory and flashed by in an instant to disappear outside.

A warhead was like a giant shotspike with a melon-sized chunk of splintered iron as its head. It was pushed by a powerful dark-stone driver and, when launched, would fly with incredible speed to explode upon impact from the sheer force of the kinetic energy, throwing deadly shrapnel everywhere. *Where under the Light did these idiots get a military-grade warhead?*

"Oh, Light, it's you!" the captain said. "I thought you were the pirates. Wait a minute—you actually beat them!"

Daylen ignored him, as he had a much more serious concern. He walked past the men standing behind the door.

"Hey, where are you going?"

Daylen continued through the skyship, the captain following with Ahrek in tow.

"Stop! You're not allowed back there," the captain said, drawing his sword as he reached the cargo holds.

A sudden force pushed the captain flat on the side of the hallway and held him firm.

"Thank you," Daylen said to Ahrek as he broke the lock and opened the door. The light from the hallway illuminated the darkness of the hold. It was the size of a large room and had no source of light within.

It was filled with young girls.

They had all been very poorly treated. Most wore nightgowns, dirty and tattered, and the others who were in dresses weren't faring any better. The horror and despair in their haunted eyes said it all. These poor young girls had been kidnapped and were on their way to be sold into the underground human trafficking market as sex slaves. It couldn't be anything else.

"By the Light, no!" Ahrek said in sincere dismay and then spoke to the poor girls, "Don't fear, young ones. My name is Lightbringer Ahrek, and my friend and I are here to help you." Ahrek turned to Daylen. He regarded him and spoke softly, but with the most anger Daylen had ever heard in his voice. "I'll stay to help them and leave you to do what needs to be done."

"My pleasure."

Daylen made his way through the crew of the *Maraven* and methodically killed each one of them. None possessed even the slightest amount of redeeming light. Ahrek had been right about these men.

The hypocrisy wasn't lost on him, either. Here he was killing men for a truly loathsome crime, and yet he had committed worse.

There was just no one there to stop him, or rather those that had the power to stop him took too long to act. That someone so unworthy as he held the blade this time didn't really matter so long as evil was destroyed.

Daylen made sure to do his dark work cleanly so that no more blood would stain the ship, snapping necks with enhanced strength and speed. Those poor girls would have seen more than enough horror recently. Of course, that standard didn't apply to the captain. No, the captain of the *Maraven* received the same treatment as Blackheart himself. They now hung on the pirate switchback, impaled side by side.

It had been horrible, killing man after man, and even a woman here and there. After the first few had tried to fight him, the rest had given up and pled for mercy.

Their desperate screams found nothing but death.

A better man, like Ahrek, would have found the task far too distasteful, but Daylen was different, and he had the strength to do what needed to be done when others couldn't.

During this time, Daylen also finished cleaning out the pirates from the other ship. Afterward, he grabbed Blackheart's sunforged sword and took a look in the dead captain's quarters. The room was comfortable enough, but not lavish, scattered with maps, clothes, and other odds and ends. Daylen couldn't find anything that might shed light on who Blackheart really was, found nothing about his past victories—including the poor girl he had linked to his shield—and nothing of his plans for the future. So Daylen left and collected the bodies of the *Maraven*'s crew into one of the unused cargo holds before returning to Ahrek.

Ahrek was in the middle of treating a girl while summoning light in one hand.

"The ship is safe and clean," Daylen said. "The girls can come out."

Ahrek sighed and gave Daylen a soft smile. "Thank you, Daylen." Ahrek then helped the young woman he was attending, sixteen years old or so, to her feet. "Come now, child. Come into the light."

Those girls who were faring better helped the others that were still struggling.

They swept away tears as they walked into the sun once more, several collapsing to the deck in relief and joy.

"How many?" Daylen asked Ahrek in a whisper.

"Fifty."

"Were any of them close to turning?"

Ahrek's reply was laced with disgust. "Yes. The wretched traders were fools. It seems they only knew the most basic facts about turning and thought they would be safe giving the girls light at intermediate intervals."

"Well, with a few falls of constant light, they should recover."

"From the turning process, yes, and I can heal the physical injuries. But the emotional scars... Oh, these poor girls. From the looks in their eyes, I can guess many of them have been raped several times already."

Daylen felt sick. "It was the crew. They do it to break the girls in, so they won't have an emotional collapse once sold to their new owners."

Ahrek's face quivered with rage. "I...I just can't understand how people can do things like this!"

"I can, and that's why I killed them."

"You killed them? When I said for you to do what needed to be done, I meant for you to capture them to be tried and punished!"

"Where they'd be executed anyway, we would hope. Can you imagine if any of them got free? This way, we save time. Regardless, I was justified under the law."

"But there were so many, and surely they didn't *all* resist?"

"No. Most surrendered and begged for mercy."

Ahrek looked horrified. "And you *still* killed them?"

"Without hesitation."

Ahrek was unable to say anything, his face a mask of dismay.

"Did I do wrong in my actions?" Daylen asked. "You think they deserved any better?"

"No. It just troubles me deeply, very deeply, that you're capable of such things."

"Me too, but the ugly truth is there needs to be people like me in the world so those who can't stomach such brutality need not lose their innocence."

"I know... But what under the Light have you gone through to make you like this?"

"Ahrek, I told you, that's none of your business."

Ahrek stared at him and nodded. He patted Daylen on the shoulder and left to see to the girls, attending them one at a time, healing when needed, but mostly consoling them and letting them cry on his shoulder.

Daylen walked to the side of the deck to look out at the sky and land below. The ships had slowed to a stop and the air was still and quiet.

Killing so many in such a short time made Daylen feel dead inside. He knew he would be faced with violence in this new life—Light, he even went out of his way to look for it—but he hadn't really been expecting to perform a massacre so soon.

Just another one to add to the list, he thought to himself as his heart broke and he fought back tears.

Such was the tale of his life.

"Thank you," a young voice said from Daylen's side. "Thank you for saving us."

Daylen wiped away a stray tear and turned to see one of the girls. She was a beautiful thing with big dark blue eyes and blue hair with streaks of scarlet throughout.

Daylen didn't know what to say. His instinct and natural reaction was to berate such a comment—common decency didn't deserve thanks—but he couldn't bring himself to be so harsh to this poor pretty creature. She had been through a horror and needed no more negativity.

"It's nothing."

The girl wept as she replied, "No, it's not. You *saved* us."

She suddenly dived into Daylen's arms, hugging him as she broke down, crying, "Thank you, *thank you!*"

It felt *very* awkward.

When Daylen could bear no more, he gently pried the girl, who must have been around sixteen, from his side and told her to see if Ahrek could help her. She wiped away her tears and smiled at Daylen as she left.

Oh, Light! She thinks I'm some blackened savior, Daylen thought before looking to the other victims. Though still distraught, many of them were looking at Daylen with as much gratitude and hero worship in their eyes as the first.

Why aren't they looking at Ahrek like that? Daylen wondered. Ahrek looked much more the hero than Daylen's old grumpy scowls. Seriously, if Daylen was completely honest, Ahrek's youth was far better looking than Daylen's old, haggard...

Daylen sighed. He *still* hadn't gotten used to his new appearance. Daylen was eighty-two years old and he was used to looking his age. He might not physically feel that old anymore, but mentally he certainly did. Yet to these girls Daylen would look to be very close in age to many of them, as well as strong and admittedly attractive. A heroic figure if there ever was one, like those only found in romance novels.

Daylen sneered at the repulsive image. He had to get away from the attention, so he made his way over to the pirate he had spared.

The young man was still tied up.

Refreshingly, he looked at Daylen in nearly the exact opposite way the girls had. He'd had a front-row seat to Daylen's treatment of both captains, after all, so to this sorry sod Daylen might as well have been the Herald of Night in the flesh.

"If I were going to kill you, I'd have done it by now."

The young boy, maybe eighteen or nineteen, slowly stopped cowering, though he was most certainly still afraid. "What…what do you want with me?" he said with a Hamahran accent—which was odd, because his messy hair was a deep purple, the common color of the Dayshan peoples of Daymony and Delavie. There were a few streaks of green, though, which meant he had some Hamahran blood. He had a square face with handsome features, a strong jaw, and sharp, discerning green eyes.

"Why was someone like you with a bunch of pirates?"

"Someone like me?"

"You're not as bad as the other pirates, not even close. So…how did you become one?"

"Why would you think I'm any better?"

"Are you?"

The boy stared at Daylen for a time before glancing away. "Yeah."

"Exactly. So, why did you become a pirate?"

"I didn't really have a choice," the boy said rudely. "I grew up in Raidaway. If you don't steal or kill, yeah, you die, it's as simple as that. Joining a pirate crew seemed my only way out of the place."

If this was true, the boy would have lived a very rough life. It wasn't hard to see how he'd ended up where he had. "Well, you're not a pirate anymore. Try to steal from me and I'll kill you, got it?"

"Yeah, so I'm your slave?"

"Exactly. A prisoner slave, until I feel it's safe to let you go. Until then you'll do exactly as I say, or I'll make sure to turn you over to the authorities for piracy. You'll either be executed or given a nice steel collar where you'll become a real slave, spending the rest of your life in the mines."

The boy looked at the girls across the deck and, sneering, spat at Daylen's feet. "I might be a pirate, but I'll never be a part of sex trafficking, you rapist scum."

Daylen leaned down and backhanded the boy across the jaw with his natural strength, knocking him to his side. "You're in low light as it is, so don't push it," Daylen said—and then, enhancing his strength, he hoisted the boy into the air. With his other hand, he grabbed the boy by his cheeks and forced his face to look at the two impaled captains over on the pirate's switchback. "See the other captain? That's what I do to those who take part in human sex trafficking. I bought passage on this ship and only discovered what was going on while cutting all your mates to pieces. Now, with everyone else dead, I guess these ships are mine for the time being. So, do you have a problem working for me now?"

The boy mumbled his reply through his squeezed mouth. "No."

Daylen dropped him back to the deck, and the boy rubbed his face.

"How are you so strong?"

"I eat my vegetables."

"No one becomes that strong naturally."

"You're right," Daylen conceded. "In fact, with only a thought, I can turn your gut into flesh-eating worms that'll devour you from the inside out. So *don't* cross me."

Interestingly, the boy's face paled but he did his best to hide it, throwing a disbelieving sneer Daylen's way. He must have wanted to change the subject, judging by his next words. "They weren't my friends. Blackheart was a bastard and deserved what you did to him."

"Look at that, we've found something we agree on. So, what's your name?"

"Sain."

Daylen leaned down and untied Sain's bonds. "You can call me Daylen. Now, Sain, you're going to show me where your crew's hideout is."

CHAPTER TWENTY-THREE

My attendants did a good job at keeping things quiet, but it didn't take long for the girls to stop volunteering. I was never gentle with them, yet I still believed they came willingly—at first. The truth was that my attendants coerced the girls that caught my eye. Whether out of loyalty, a lust for my favor, or a belief that a happy ruler led to a happy empire, my servants saw to my every whim. They bribed at first, but eventually devolved into threats and acts of violence.

As my people slowly started to fear me more and more, often through acts I did to achieve that very purpose to ensure obedience, a nightmare slowly began to grow among the young women that they might catch the eye of the Emperor.

Lyrah continued to follow the scent of the boy vigilante, the blackened son of Dayless the Conqueror.

"I think he went to the skyport," she said to Cueseg beside her.

"Then we find which ship they take and follow."

"That's the plan," Lyrah said as they quickened their step. The people continued to part before them, more so now as they moved with obvious purpose.

As they came close to the skyport, Lyrah noticed a man standing atop a box and speaking passionately to a crowd of people.

She stared at him.

"What is it?" Cueseg asked.

"Go ahead and find the Portmaster. I'll catch up."

Cueseg looked to the soapbox man. "Ah, this again. Do not make too much trouble," he said, then left for the port.

"It was the Conqueror who made our nation strong!" the Dawnist bellowed over the boos and jeers, though there were a few in the crowd who seemed to be truly listening. The young man wore a dirty buttoned shirt and slacks, but no sword and especially no red ribbon, as wearing one would justify people challenging him to a duel just to shut him up.

Lyrah couldn't help but listen to a little of the tripe.

"Indeed, Hamahra would have been destroyed by our own aristocracy—but it was the Conqueror who liberated us! And then after that, the other nations flew in like drakes to take our lands. Who was it that fought them off? We all know who! The same man who saved us from starvation and ensured we were always fed. These days, we regular people starve and the Senate not only does nothing—they are complicit! Why? Because their pockets get lined with gold crowns by those who force us to work in their factories like slaves."

The Dawnist pointed to the well-dressed people in the crowd booing at him. "Of course *they* don't want the Empire back, because people like them couldn't exist in it. In the Empire, everything was owned by all, not the greedy few that steal money from our own pockets. Not that it's much, barely seven measly rupenies an hour while they *hoard* all the wealth that *we* make for them!" he roared to the crowd. "Then there's the Guilds, who don't allow the common man to learn their trades and charge a fair and honest price for skilled labor. The Emperor fought the Guilds to regulate them properly, and what did they do? They rose up against him! Under the rule of Dayless the Conqueror, each man got his fair share and no man could make himself better than another!"

"Except for the Conqueror himself," Lyrah said calmly; but with Light bonded to her voice, it carried over the crowd, silencing everyone.

The Dawnist gulped. It seemed he hadn't noticed Lyrah until this moment.

"He put himself above everyone and killed for the slightest inconvenience," Lyrah added, her controlled tone resonating powerfully. "Anyone who thinks to bring back the days of the Dawn Empire is a fool. You say everyone got their fair share? I lived through that time, and you did not, so let me tell you what it was truly like. The Great Bastard took everything from everyone and returned the barest portion. Yes, all were equal: equally oppressed, poor and starved. No one could own property or land, not even their homes, and thus when the Great Bastard felt a population had outgrown the resources of their land, he forcefully relocated countless families, and executed any who resisted— women and children included."

Lyrah began to walk toward the man. "Later, he ordered his men to execute the family members of anyone he deemed a criminal, killing innocents for the most inconsequential actions that he thought rebellious. You glory in the privilege of attacking the government while espousing a way of rule that would have you executed for the same. Even those that didn't speak out against him were forcefully conscripted into his armies and sent to die in the unjust wars he declared on innocent nations."

Lyrah was now standing directly in front of the Dawnist. "Most people think the Archknights are only sworn to fight against the Shade, but our true mandate is to protect the peoples of the world. We, the Knights of the Arch Order of Light, declared *war* on the Dawn Empire! Do you know what that means?"

The man was failing to look defiant, though he tried. He stumbled back off his box.

"It means that The Dawn Empire had grown to threaten all of Tellos, and the Archknights, for the first time in their existence, entered into a political conflict. The Dawn Empire drew every nation into war. It became an enemy to all that is good, and you want to bring it back?"

Every other Dawnist Lyrah had confronted like this had said no, claiming they were only supporting the good that the Dawn Empire did, not the bad. But this man forced himself to stand tall and replied, "*Yes*! And you Archknights betrayed yourselves in fighting against our rightful ruler! The impure elements must be purged, and I cast night upon you and your order!"

Lyrah couldn't believe what she was hearing. This young man actually had a measure of light within him, meaning he honestly thought what he was doing was the right thing.

Which made him *very* dangerous.

"Then you have a powerful enemy," Lyrah said, and turned to the crowd. "I can see that most of us here wish this fool would stop speaking his hate, but taking away his freedom to do this would make us as bad as the Great Bastard himself. We cannot stop him from speaking, but it's our choice to listen. Like a disease, our displeasure brings him joy, and I've done this, too, by confronting him. I see that I was mistaken. What I do now is what I hope you all do: ignore him! Take away his power, and let the fool cry to the empty air."

Lyrah left and, thankfully, most left with her, the Dawnist calling out after them in a frantic voice.

"You cannot stop us! The Dawn Empire will return, and though you choose to leave, others will listen and join our cause! Long live the Dawn Empire!"

The people ignored him but the disappointing thing was that Lyrah knew it wouldn't last. Most people were so insecure in their beliefs that they couldn't resist defending them, sometimes violently, in reaction to the smallest disagreement. Thus as soon as more people heard the Dawnist preach such offensive dogma, they'd stop and argue, fueling the fool's ego. Then, with a crowd there, like a herd of goats, more people would come, including some who'd actually be susceptible to the Dawnist's lies.

Yet there was no more Lyrah could do unless the Dawnists broke the law. Considering their patron, they might be capable of some truly terrible things. If that was the case, she and the Archknights would be there to oppose them.

It was easy to find Cueseg within the skyport. *Just look for the only dark-skinned, yellow-haired topless man with muscles like rocks.*

"They are on a skyship…" Cueseg began, but then stared at her. "Lyrah, your face is different, and even me who is bad with faces, it is big enough to know. You are angry."

"It's the Dawnists."

"Yes, they need to be killed."

"They can't be *killed* for controversial opinions, that would make us no better than the Conqueror."

"Belief becomes action and their belief is to kill people who do not agree. It is better to stop a crime before it happens."

"But you can't punish a person who hasn't committed a crime, even if they want to commit it."

"This is stupid. If they want to do bad, they are guilty as if they did."

"Only if you can prove it, and though it's clear what the Dawn Empire was, most Dawnists try and paint a much nicer picture. Everyone knows that they're preaching hate, but unless they incite criminal activity, it's not right to act against them."

"No. If they are left to grow strong, it will be hard to stop them, and I will be there to tell you so."

"I'm sure you will," Lyrah said with a sigh. "What were you saying before about the skyship?"

"The boy we are chasing, he is on a skyship to the head city of your land."

"The capital," Lyrah said.

"Yes, the head city."

"It's not called the head city. It's the capital, Highdawn."

"Yes, your *head city*."

She shook her head tiredly. "Whatever. Did you find out what type of ship they caught?"

"A trade ship called *Maraven*."

"Then it's slow... Good. All we need is a fast ship, and if we fly under the Floating Isles we should overtake them."

"Yes, and we might find pirates as we fly," Cueseg said, smiling.

"Feeling a little restless, are we?"

"Our powers need to be used; if not, we should not have them."

"Yeah, with how frustrating this blackened chase has been, I'd like to hit something, too."

Lyrah found the Portmaster, a short bearded man, and enquired after the fastest ship destined for Highdawn.

"There's a Tuerasian trader destined for the capital," the man said. "Name's the *Tecato*, or *Taybato* or some such. They're fast, those prig ships..." The man suddenly paused and looked to Cueseg embarrassedly. "Ah, my apologies, Master Archon. I, ah... It was a slip of the tongue."

Cueseg simply glared at the man.

The Portmaster swallowed.

"We'll see to the ship," Lyrah said. "Thank you, Portmaster."

Lyrah looked to Cueseg once the man had left. "A Tuerasian ship. Should I expect the captain to be as difficult as you?"

Cueseg face was still. He glanced at Lyrah, saying nothing.

"What, are you really that upset about the Portmaster saying prig?"

"No."

"Then why so sullen?"

"What does this mean?"

"Upset."

"I am not upset."

"You could have fooled me."

"Which is something too easy to do," Cueseg said without any emotion, turning to walk out of the office.

Lyrah was shocked. Cueseg had said offensive things before, but this was the first time he had actually sounded cruel. What under the Light had upset him so much?

Lyrah caught up to Cueseg and they walked to the ship, not saying so much as a word to each other.

The ship was crewed totally by Tuerasians in varying levels of undress, a few not even covering their private parts, with one or two women among them.

Lyrah's anxiety surged. "Oh, Light, *really?*" she said to herself, purposefully looking at anything other than the crew.

Rubbing her forehead, she sighed. "Cueseg, I need you to sort things out here."

Cueseg didn't reply.

Oh, Light, I don't need this right now.

"I will do," Cueseg finally said before walking toward one of the crew.

The individual that Cueseg approached wore slim Tuerasian-styled boots that hugged his calves, which the man's extremely baggy pants, thank the Light, were tucked into. Tuerasians seemed to prefer strong colors in their clothing, and the man was no exception, his pants being a deep red. He also wore a strange yellow half jacket that covered the shoulders and upper back but left the chest, arms, and waist completely bare. Although this Tuerasian had short yellow hair like Cueseg, he wasn't nearly as fit, which was easy to see considering Cueseg wore no shirt under his mantle, his chest as bare as his countryman's. The other man's belly was round and pronounced, sitting happily out in the open for all to see, which surprised Lyrah, for she had expected being fit was a cultural thing. His chest was still smooth, free of any hair, and shimmered in the light as if slightly oiled.

The man was in the middle of loading some sacks aboard the ship. He noticed Cueseg approaching and put down his load. He started to bow but stopped halfway once he looked to Cueseg's face, his expression blank.

He straightened, still staring at Cueseg's face, then at the Archknight mantle, and then back at his face. It was like the man didn't know how to respond.

Cueseg spoke to the man in their native tongue. The man, face still blank, backed away and boarded the ship.

It was a very odd interaction, but then again, everything about the Tuerasians was odd.

Cueseg returned to Lyrah and even though his face was blank, Lyrah sensed a hint of satisfaction in his bearing.

Shortly thereafter, a woman descended the gangplank from the deck of the ship, and she was naked.

Well, mostly naked—for she wore the same styled Tuerasian boots, and there was jewelry all over her body. Brightly colorful embroidered lengths of material looped from bangles at her wrists to thin golden chains around her waist. Yet nothing covered her private parts; and indeed, everything she wore, from the design and shape of the silver jewelry to its positioning, seemed to draw attention to those prominent features. She was slim and toned. Her brown skin was smooth and clean, devoid of all types of body hair, and her straight, shoulder-length, bright-yellow hair was combed back to fall elegantly past her shoulders.

She was beautiful.

Still, the flagrant disregard for modesty made Lyrah feel *very* uncomfortable, but not nearly to the anxiety-inducing level of the men's state of undress.

Light, these Tuerasians are backward!

The woman approached Lyrah, utterly ignoring Cueseg, who was standing beside her, and smiled.

A Tuerasian...smiling?

Lyrah hadn't expected that.

The woman touched her fingertips to her forehead and then opened her arms out before her. When she spoke, it was in a very respectful tone without the slightest hint of an accent. "Lady Archon, your arrival and interruption is irritating, but because of your station, I offer you all the courtesy it deserves and will not express my profound annoyance beyond what I have said. Age has not diminished your physical beauty too much, though you are not as beautiful as I, and you do not appear to manipulate your appearance to influence men to your advantage, as is common among Hamahran woman. Instead, it appears that you rely on the authority of your station for influence. I respect this."

"Ah…" Lyrah began, nonplussed. "Thank you?"

The captain smiled in a very expressive way, and indeed her face was more expressive than what seemed natural. "Excellent. I see we're good friends."

"Um, if you say so."

"I do."

Lyrah looked to Cueseg, whose face was blank, and then back to the female captain. "We're here because we must commandeer your vessel."

The woman sighed. "This is profoundly irritating and has the possibility of affecting our friendship. In what capacity do you need my ship?"

"We must get to Highdawn as soon as possible."

"Ah, this is much more acceptable. You've chosen my ship because we are already headed to your capital."

"Yes, and because it's one of the fastest ships in port."

"I am very pleased that you know this, and it makes me like you more."

"Also, we must fly under the Floating Isles."

"That, my friend, is very troubling. Regularly I would never risk such a flight, but with an Archknight's protection I see no reason to fear."

"Two."

The captain tilted her head slightly. "Two?"

"Two Archknights' protection," Lyrah said.

The captain sneered, glancing at Cueseg. "I find it despicable that one as shamed as you is a knight, forcing me to show respect that you do not deserve."

Cueseg's face was stone yet his tone betrayed strong emotion. "Yet I *am* Archon. You will show respect or be shamed."

The captain continued to sneer. "I will show every courtesy as is expected, but I will continue to despise you regardless, *Master* Archon."

Cueseg's mouth curled into the slightest grin, a triumphant shout by Cueseg's standards. "Good," he said in satisfaction.

What was going on? Why was Cueseg shamed? This was all very odd. Lyrah had been expecting this woman to be the same as Cueseg; but, Light, she couldn't have been more different and yet so distinctly *Tuerasian* at the same time. She used expressions in a very pronounced yet calculated way, whereas Cueseg rarely used them at all, and she voiced every thought. Cueseg never hesitated to tell her what he was thinking, but compared to this woman his comments were positively *subtle*, something Lyrah never would have considered to be a possibility.

The captain looked back to Lyrah. "Please, come aboard. I am eager to reinforce your knowledge that Tuerasian skyships are the best in the world. I'll see that we embark at once."

They followed the captain aboard the ship and Lyrah had to keep her eyes on the deck as they walked to their cabin with so many privates on exhibition.

Once inside and alone, Lyrah spun on Cueseg. "All right, what under the Light is going on?"

"It does not matter. It is a thing of my people."

"She said you're shamed. What does that mean?"

"That I am shamed."

"You know that's not what I'm asking!"

Cueseg walked past her and sat cross-legged on one of the large cushions, facing away from her. "I will not talk."

"It's that branding on your forehead, isn't it? None of the other Tuerasians have it."

"This is my shame, Lyrah. I will not talk."

"Okay... Fine."

Cueseg didn't reply, and Lyrah collapsed on one of the low and heavily cushioned beds, totally fed up with backward Tuerasians and their strange customs.

CHAPTER TWENTY-FOUR

My stewards noticed that I enjoyed the younger girls more than any others, so that's whom they sought.
Some of the girls grew attached to me, misunderstanding my lust like Deena had. They were naive, and apart from my own actions they were treated very well whilst in the palace at first. Those that came from poorer homes were overwhelmed with its luxury. But as soon as I noticed their attachment, I discarded them and called for another. And it wasn't just attachment that caused me to want the next; all it took was for me to grow bored, something that happened more often as time progressed. Toward the end, I even forced the girls into depraved acts with one another and denied them clothes, no matter the setting or who was present, only letting them wear jewelry and ornaments like the outfits of some Tuerasian woman so that their appearance would please me at all times.

Y ou want to go to their hideout?" Ahrek asked dubiously.

"That's what I said," Daylen replied as he stood at the *Maraven's* helm.

"Daylen, these girls need to be taken to safety."

"They are safe."

"Taking them into the Floating Isles most certainly is not!"

"With the two of us it is. Look, Ahrek, when I fought Blackheart..."

"Blackheart! That was *Blackheart?*"

"Oh, so he *is* famous."

"Uh, yes!"

"Not anymore," Daylen said, and held out Blackheart's sword. "Ahrek, his sword is sunforged, and his shield was too. During the fight I shattered the shield. It didn't affect him. The bastard said he had linked the daughter of some senator he had kidnapped. Said his name was Terain. Ahrek, if he had linked some poor innocent girl to it, she's either dead from the link or in a whole world of pain right now."

"You're right, yes," Ahrek grumbled. "If she's alive, we have to help her. This most certainly takes priority."

"Not only that, this sword didn't shatter upon his death, so it too is linked to another. Judging by his actions, it's likely another innocent person he's using as leverage."

"Agreed," Ahrek said, "we need to find them. Shall we scuttle the pirate ship?"

"And lose a whole ship? Light, no! I'll just rig the core so we can tow the switchback from the *Maraven*."

"You can do that?"

"I'm good with that kind of thing," Daylen said, handing Blackheart's sword to Ahrek. Leaving, Daylen walked over and grabbed Sain by the arm. "You're helping me," Daylen said, dragging the boy over to the switchback.

Daylen didn't need Sain's help; he just didn't want to let the little snot out of his sight.

Daylen reached out to feel for the light around him and found he could sense every living person aboard both ships. Thus even while not looking at Sain, Daylen knew where he was and what he was doing. *I really need to use this sense all the time*, Daylen thought to himself.

Sain took a step toward the cabins.

"Don't even think about it," Daylen said.

"Think about what?"

"Running to the stores in the ship to grab a skimmer and escape."

"So you can read minds, too?"

Daylen turned to Sain and, with the authority fostered from his years as Emperor, said, "Yes. And I can see all things around me, so if you put one foot where I don't want it, I'll know."

Once Daylen turned to walk to the helm, he sensed the boy make a rude gesture at him with his hand.

Daylen turned and slapped the boy off his feet.

Sain rubbed his jaw as he rolled to look at Daylen in horror.

"Do you want to test me again?"

Sain shook his head.

"Good," Daylen said. "Now, stay within five meters of me at all times or I'll introduce you to some exotic levels of pain. Got it?"

Sain nodded quickly.

The helm of the switchback was much like that of any other skyship: a series of identical control rods. When pulled, these levers opened specific sunstone hubs around the darkstone core of the ship and thereby controlled every which way the ship moved.

Daylen knelt down to open the cabinet just under the levers.

"What are you doing?" Sain asked.

"Looking at the levers."

"Yeah, I can see that. Why?"

"Huh, so *now* you're trying to make conversation?"

"If I had any say in it I'd like to *never* speak to you again... I was just wondering."

Daylen glanced at him thoughtfully. "Why?"

"Why what?"

"Why were you wondering?"

"I thought you could read minds?"

"That's only when I split open their skulls and write words with their brain matter."

"You're sick."

Daylen chuckled. "I thought it was quite funny."

"You're proving my point."

"Oh, Light, you're as high strung as the Bringer."

"Better to be like him than you."

"I won't argue there. So are you going to answer my question?"

"What question?"

"Why were you wondering what I'm doing here?" Daylen said, pointing at the lever mechanics.

Sain suddenly looked embarrassed. "I was just wondering. No one's ever told me how this stuff works." Sain suddenly laughed bitterly. "Because no one I've ever known knew anything about them in the first place. Raidaway doesn't exactly have schools or anything." Sain glanced around and scratched his head. "I guess I figured I could get some information out of you but now that you know I want to know, I can guess you're not going to say anything." Sain looked to his side and added under his breath, "Bastard."

Daylen stared at Sain for a little while, mostly to let the wave of anger at the insult subside. It was true, after all. He turned back to the lever mechanics—a system of rods, springs and cogs under the main helm counter—and spoke as he inspected the configuration. "Most people understand the basic principles of darkstone mechanics," Daylen said as he worked. "No light, and the darkstone is locked in space. Directional light makes it move in the direction the light is shining, whereas uniform light or the touch of the right sized sunstone makes it behave like a normal rock. Which is odd, because if light applied force to darkstone, you would expect uniform light to lock it in place, having equal force from all sides. But no. Darkstone doesn't exactly conform to classical mechanics."

"Classical mechanics?"

"The laws that describe how things move. Darkstone throws most of those laws out the window and functions under its own set of equations. What most people don't know is that darkstone is actually affected by levels of luminosity; the larger the darkstone, the more light it takes to move it."

"Yeah, I don't get it."

"A hunk of darkstone the size of, say, the core of this ship, isn't going to move from a small beam of light, if that's the only light touching it. Such low levels of luminosity aren't strong enough to reach that stone's specific luminous threshold. Every stone has one, determined by its overall mass. L equals M times 1DL squared."

"*What?*"

"You've never been taught math?"

"What do you think, smartass?"

"That's the light-to-mass equation in determining a specific stone's luminous threshold. It can also calculate the minimal sunstone size needed to nullify the darkstone's luminous repulsion if it touches."

"Why does this matter?"

"Because when you shine light on a stone just *under* its luminous threshold, it's still locked in place. It'll float, but an external physical force can now move it. The closer to the luminous threshold, the easier it is to move. So what *we're* going to do is lever the sunstone hubs around the ship's core equal to a little under the luminous threshold, subtracting any force already on it, like the weight from the frame of the ship, and in so doing the *Maraven* will be able to tow this ship without having to carry the whole thing on its back."

"You can tow a skyship?"

"Yep. The math can be tricky as you have to be very precise, otherwise there'll be way too much drag, or the ship will slowly fall out of the sky. Because you have to work so close to the threshold, there's always a danger you'll cross it entirely, and when doing so on the vertical plane the stone will be affected by gravity in all its normal ways."

"Which means we might plummet to the surface."

"Exactly."

"Yeah, this is a great idea!"

It took a few more minutes to figure things out. Daylen also took Sain to inspect the darkstone core, to see if there were any broken hubs. There were a few.

Sain, of course, tested how far he could push things, falling back to just under five meters and eventually going over to see if Daylen truly could sense it. Daylen gave him a good thump in the gut, which dropped the snot like a sack.

"How do you do that?" Sain forced out as he struggled to catch his breath.

"Magic—and next time you'll get a broken bone."

Returning to the helm, Daylen drew out the math with a pencil on scrap paper he got from Blackheart's cabin.

Sain was watching with avid curiosity.

Daylen returned to the internal mechanics of the control rods.

"What are you doing now?" Sain asked.

"These ships are made to *not* fall out of the sky, and what I'm doing is close enough. Each ship has safely locks and redundancies inbuilt, such as gradual hub shifts."

"What's that?"

"Darkstone will move as proportionally fast as the strength of light shining on it. Too much light and the acceleration will be nearly instant. Any idea what could happen?"

"Sudden speed without gradual acceleration?"

"Yep."

"Whiplash?"

"Keep going."

"If you're not in a seat, you could get pancaked on the back wall."

"Better, but keep going."

"What, the core couldn't rip free of the ship, could it?"

Daylen nodded. "I've seen it happen. If the sudden speed of the core is greater in energy to the strength of the braces holding it to the ship, the core will rip free. The same will happen if you try and slow the ship too fast when in flight."

"In that case the ship would rip itself free of the now stationary core," Sain said.

"You got it. The safeties are to prevent things like that."

"Which you're about to disengage."

"Fun, isn't it?"

"Yeah, not the word that comes to mind."

"Well, I'm only going to loosen those safeties. The main things I need to disable altogether are the altitude regulator and the lock."

"Altitude regulator?"

"Stops the ship from free falling."

"How does the ship know the difference between falling and descending in normal flight?"

"Good question. The ship doesn't know a thing. The engineers who designed it knew that if all vertical hubs are opened, the ship will freefall. To fix that, each hub has a gauge, which is connected to this gearbox." Daylen pointed to a wide-riveted steel box under the helm with multiple small rods connected to the main levers and twenty driveshafts that ran down into the ship. "This is the main safety regulator. It prevents the vertical hubs all being opened at once, or opened to the core's luminous threshold. It also forces the levers to tick through stages when opening, which controls the ship's rate of acceleration."

"So do you just rip it out?"

"Nope, the control levers pass through this gearbox. Rip it out and you rip out your ability to fly the ship."

Daylen drew Imperious and deftly cut through the rivets

holding the thick front case of the gearbox, which fell clanking on the deck.

Within the gearbox was a maze of oiled cogs. It was like looking inside a large and even more complex pocketwatch.

"Light, that looks confusing," Sain said.

"Only if you've never worked with them before," Daylen said, putting Imperious back before reaching in, enhancing his strength. He didn't have the right tools to unscrew the gear, so instead he ripped it from its thread. "Regulator springs are now disconnected." He then grabbed a series of gears all lined up next to one another on the same shaft and ripped that entire component free. "And that's the safety lock."

Daylen stood and handed Sain the components. "Here, a present."

"Uh, thanks," Sain said and threw them over his shoulder. "So now you could close all the altitude hubs and we'd plummet."

"No, closing the altitude hubs would lock the core from vertical light, which would lock our altitude."

"So yeah, to free fall, all the vertical hubs have to be *open*, and then we'd plummet to our deaths."

"Like I said, fun."

"I can't believe the amount of stuff inside these things. They're so complex."

"It's all based off simple principles, but it's incredibly sophisticated. Skyships are amazing feats of engineering." Daylen looked to the piece of paper he had made his notes on. "So, according to my calculations, I need to set the longitude and latitude hubs to this and this." Daylen pulled the levers a degree at a time until they were in the right place, and then locked them there. "Now the tricky one: altitude."

Sain leaned in and was visibly nervous.

"There's a lot to calculate," Daylen said. "Like the ship's weight, which is very hard to figure out considering cargo. So if I get it wrong… Well, you get the picture."

"Just…just don't be wrong, yeah?"

Degree by degree, Daylen released the altitude lever until he simply pushed the levers fully up.

The ship suddenly fell out from under them, and Sain screamed.

Pulling the levers back down, the ship stopped instantly and Sain landed on the deck with very little grace, falling on his rear.

Daylen laughed hysterically. "You just soiled yourself!"

"You..." Sain tried to say, but was quivering in fear and rage. "You *bastard*!"

"That," Daylen replied, "I don't deny."

A voice called out from above them, "Is everything all right?"

Daylen called back, "Oh, it's fine, Ahrek! I'm just teaching our new friend here how to cure constipation."

"Oh, well, make sure he wipes himself properly. We don't want him stinking of poo the whole trip."

"Get stoned, the both of you!"

CHAPTER TWENTY-FIVE

The possibility of what was happening, that the girls were being forced into my bed, had always been in the back of my mind, but I was happy in self-imposed ignorance. The truth was that I really didn't care. I was getting what I wanted.

"There's little danger in falling," Daylen said. "I was just pulling your leg. Even though what we're trying to do is very close to the threshold, we'll feel the ship slowly sink before it freefalls. Finding the altitude threshold is actually the easiest, because you can measure off the movement of the ship."

Daylen began to nudge the altitude lever degree by degree until the switchback began sinking very slowly.

"See? Now that we can feel that we're just over, we nudge the lever a degree at a time back until the ship stops, and that's the sweet spot." One nudge later, and the ship halted. "Done. This switchback is good to be towed."

Sain grabbed the scrap piece of paper Daylen had been writing on. "What was with all the math, then?"

"I still needed to calculate the longitude and latitude hub positions. You don't need to factor in the weight of the ship, just the size of the core. I still might be a few degrees off, but I'll be able to tell when we try and tow."

Daylen walked forward and grabbed Sain.

Because Daylen had let the switchback fall a bit from his joke to scare the boy, it was about ten meters lower than the *Maraven*.

"What are you doing?" Sain asked, as if expecting another beating, but before he could finish, Daylen had scooped him under his arm. Daylen crouched, his strength already enhanced, and he increased his mass. The timber planks groaned as they now supported a near ton of weight. Daylen then pushed up, ready to release his mass to propel himself.

His feet pushed through the deck under him. Daylen instantly released his enhanced mass but still fell with a yelp of surprise. Sain hit the side of the hole Daylen had just made, Daylen hanging halfway through, holding himself up by leaning on Sain and bracing himself with his other hand.

"Get off!" Sain tried to yell, with Daylen's now normal weight on him.

"I'm a blackened idiot," Daylen said as he climbed out of the hole.

Sain was looking at the hole in the deck. "The ship is falling apart."

"No, the ship is fine," Daylen said, grabbing Sain and channeling light through all of his bonds to his strength.

"This again?" Sain said, frustrated.

"Oh, this time it's going to be a little different," Daylen said as he took Sain from the back of his belt and neck of his shirt, picking him up like a bag of grain. Spinning around to build momentum, Daylen tossed Sain up to the other ship.

Sain screamed the whole way. Daylen had measured the throw well, as the boy crested the railing of the *Maraven* with only half a meter's clearance. He obviously landed on the deck without a problem, as there were no cries of pain—but there were some curses.

"You're a light-cursed bastard, you are!" Sain called out to him.

Daylen chuckled and looked about.

Clearly his enhanced jump through mass manipulation was too powerful; indeed, it wouldn't serve all the time because it easily launched him fifty meters on a single bond. He could experiment with half bonds, but now wasn't the time.

He needed another way to jump a more modest superhuman distance.

Well, he could make himself sixteen times as strong. That

should grant him a significant jumping distance. It wouldn't be anything near what he could achieve with his mass-manipulated jumps, which was exactly what he wanted.

Daylen walked to a more supported point on the deck, as there was still a small chance he might kick through the floor again.

Once in place, Daylen enhanced his strength and jumped with all his might.

The height of his jump was only a little more than usual, even though it felt like he weighed nothing due to his greater strength.

"Well that's odd." Daylen said, placing his hands on his hips and thinking. "I need momentum to jump, which is a property of mass and *speed*, not strength. Enhancing my strength increased the rate I could extend my legs marginally, which had a lesser effect on the height of my jump. So instead. . ."

Daylen crouched, channeling two bonds of light to his speed and then jumped. He shot into the air a good fifteen meters and slowly arced over the *Maraven*'s railing and landed easily.

Interesting that my speed jump must have required greater strength to extend my legs so fast, Daylen thought. *Or at least more power. It must be another tangential augmentation in the same way my body's durability increases with greater mass.*

"You're an Archknight!" Sain said, staring at Daylen in awe.

"No, I'm not. And five meters, remember?"

Sain hopped forward to keep close. "No, that's it. I thought you were just really strong and weird, but seeing you jump like that... Only Archknights can jump that high."

Daylen shook his head. "I'm not an Archknight."

"You have to be!"

"Would you tell him, Ahrek?"

"Daylen is not an Archknight," Ahrek confirmed.

"Thank you," Daylen said, looking at Sain.

Sain was looking at Ahrek, clearly knowing he was a Light-bringer and thus couldn't lie. "So how can you do what you do?" Sain asked Daylen.

Daylen sighed impatiently. "How can the Archknights do what they do? It's just magic."

"There's more to it than that."

"And you really think I'm going to tell you?"

That finally shut him up, the petulant whelp.

Daylen left the snot under Ahrek's supervision while he dug up some strong rigging straps used to strap cargo containers to the undersides of skyships when their standard cargo holds were insufficient.

Not all carriers were built for such stress, but the *Maraven* was a hauler; and, well, the name said it all.

Daylen moved the *Maraven* to sit directly above the switchback and fixed the straps to their fittings. He then jumped from the *Maraven* to swing under and around the switchback and then fixed the straps on the other side.

It was incredibly fun, like flying on a giant swing.

Daylen repeated this for every strap that had a fitting, eight in all, which held the switchback firmly underneath.

"We're good to get underway," Daylen said, approaching Ahrek. "How are the girls?"

"They're doing better than when we found them," Ahrek replied.

Daylen looked to them and realized from their stares that they were probably watching him the entire time as he jumped and swung around the ships. Black, there was even more adoration in their eyes than before. Daylen groaned inwardly.

"They're still coming to terms with the relief of their rescue," Ahrek added. "Some look to scarcely believe it."

"They're lucky," Daylen said. "There's a whole lot more girls stowed away in other carriers meant for the market."

"It sickens me."

Daylen nodded slowly. "We might have a chance to dig out the scum who run the larger operation. The former captain of this ship must have some notes in his cabin about the drop off and sale."

"I guess we'll know what we're doing after we search for the pirate's hideout."

"If there's no more surprises... Have you told the girls that we're not taking them home straight away?"

"Yes, they seemed more than willing to wait if it meant saving other kidnapped girls."

"Good," Daylen said, looking toward the Plummet, "but we need to sleep before winding our way through the Isles. I'll fly us to the underside of one of the lower islands. There's bound to be a good bay to shelter us for the rest of the Low. While I'm doing that, you conjure us something to eat."

Daylen did indeed find a good bay underneath a near island which covered much of the ship from hostile eyes. Lower cloud cover intermediately masked them from the surface underneath, but being so high up, anyone would need a damn good telescope to see them anyway, after the miracle of actually finding where to look.

Ahrek made sure the girls were well fed before finding them appropriate sleeping quarters. Daylen dragged Sain below deck and locked him in the brig.

"Are you kidding me?!" Sain protested.

"Nope."

"Come on, I'm not going to escape."

"What a load of drack. You'll be gone at the first opportunity, and though I wouldn't exactly be *particularly* upset to lose your company, I still need you to guide us to your former friends hideout."

Sain punched the bars and screamed angrily.

Daylen laughed. "That's sure to achieve a lot. Keep going. I'll see you at the fall."

"Get stoned!"

CHAPTER TWENTY-SIX

*What I did to those girls was a true and terrible form of
psychological and sexual torture. Many broke, so young and
unprepared for the horrors of life, their minds snapping like twigs,
and so I put them out of their misery. I saw no point in sending a
mindless girl back to her family that couldn't contribute to society.
To me, they were already dead. They had killed themselves.
It's funny how we can go on thinking that there's a line we would
never cross whilst having long since crossed it. I thought rape a
thing so evil that it was far beyond my capability, and I made sure
death was the penalty of that crime. I may have never physically
forced a girl into my bed, but the truth was that they were all
forced, just not by me directly, but rather at my command, and I
had in every way become a compulsive rapist of young women.*

Daylen ate with Ahrek, finding the Bringer
uncharacteristically quiet. When probing to see what was
wrong, Ahrek simply replied that there was a lot on his mind and
that he would sleep on the deck, as the fall was bright and warm.

Daylen couldn't be bothered arguing and made his way to the
captain's quarters.

No expense had been spared, it seemed, for the quarters were
truly lavish. It was the size of a regular master bedroom, and being
on a skyship that meant it was comparatively huge. The room was

carpeted, with patterned wallpaper on the walls, a coffee table with couches on either side, a sunstone chandelier, a large study desk, a glass cabinet filled with expensive spirits, bookshelves, armoires, a side washing room with toilet, and a large four-poster bed sat in front of massive lead-lined windows that stretched the entire length of the aft.

"Figures," Daylen said to himself. "The only thing he bothered to maintain on his ship was his own room."

Daylen walked to the drinks cabinet and found a nicely aged scotch. Pouring himself a glass, he sat at the desk and began rummaging through the old captain's notes. It didn't take long for him to find what he was looking for: the captain's journal, ledger, and itinerary.

Daylen began reading, being utterly meticulous so he wouldn't miss any important details, even though he knew what he really wanted would be near the ends of these documents. After a few hours and learning some important information, he came to it—the delivery of the current cargo.

Unfortunately there was no address, just a place somewhere in the city called the "Meat Market." There was a note describing the need to get the goods there by the end of High Fall on the sixty-third fall of summer, which happened to be right then. Well, it was clear they weren't going to make that appointment.

How were they going to get past the inspections? Daylen wondered. All skyships that entered a city had to be inspected at its skyport, even the ships with a permit to anchor at private docks. The *Maraven*'s captain must have set up a drop-off outside the city. Things were much easier to smuggle in on the ground than the sky, regarding large cities at least.

Unfortunately Daylen could find nothing about the drop off, which meant all he really had was the name of the market. Knowing criminal organizations, they would definitely change the location of this market constantly.

Still, Daylen was confident that he could track it down. He would spend his life doing good, and this was as good a place to start as any.

A soft knock came on the door. It clearly wasn't Ahrek—the knock wasn't right—so then it had to have been one of the girls.

What could they want?

"Come in."

Sure enough, a young girl with blue hair streaked with red wearing a dirty tattered white dress entered. She was the one who had first thanked him up on deck. Big blue eyes, dark lashes, a button nose, and flushed lips—no wonder she had been targeted by the traffickers. She nervously shut the door behind her.

"Is there something wrong?" Daylen asked.

"My...my name is Sharra."

"Oh, of course, Sharra," Daylen said, getting up and walking toward her. "What can I do for you?"

"The Bringer—he called you Daylen."

"Yes," Daylen said, growing suspicious.

"Where are your parents, Daylen?"

"They died a long time ago."

"I see. That's why you're alone, why you're able to be so strong... I was living with my family when I was taken, but I can't go back."

"What do you mean?"

Sharra began to weep as she continued, "I'm...I'm ruined now. I'm no longer pure..."

Daylen took Sharra by the shoulders and looked right into her eyes. "That's a load of drack!"

Sharra was blubbering by now. "But who'll marry me now? My...my parents won't want me anymore."

"If your parents love you, that isn't true."

"But they *don't* love me," she whispered forlornly. "They've said as much. I'm a bastard. My true mother died, my stepmother hates me, and my father is shamed by my existence. The only reason they accepted me into the family was because I'm pretty. They intended me to marry, but now no one will have me. I have nowhere to go."

The sad thing was that this story wasn't too uncommon in the world, especially with wealthy families.

"You could hide it."

"And say that I just ran away?" Sharra said, wiping her tears but still distraught and sniffling. "They'll think I ran away with Heneran, a boy that I liked. They'll check and see what has happened to me and throw me out!"

"Well, you'll have to find your place in the world," Daylen said as he turned away. "That's what most people have to do."

"Can... Can I stay with you?"

Whirling, Daylen replied incredulously, "What?"

"Please. Let me stay with you."

"No. That's impossible."

Sharra began to weep once more.

"Go back to your quarters," Daylen said. "Things will be all right." With that, he walked back to the desk.

Leaning on it, Daylen rubbed his head. *Oh, what a mess. Poor girl.* Sharra's sniffling had stopped, but the door didn't open. She was still in the room.

Turning, Daylen saw that indeed Sharra hadn't left, but now her dress lay at her feet. She stood completely naked there and looked at him nervously from under long lashes.

Oh, Light!

"No... No," Daylen said, looking away. "Sharra, get dressed right *now*."

"If you let me stay with you, you can have me..."

"Stop!"

"It's not like I haven't done it. I mean, they made me do it... They did it to me, but I know it now. I'd rather let someone like you have me than anyone else. You're a hero, and I want this. Just let me stay with you," she begged.

Daylen's young virile body had reacted the only way it could. *Damn it all! Why does she have to be so blackened beautiful?* Daylen clenched his fist as he struggled with a now surging desire. Out of *all* the vices of his past, why did this one have to cross him? Why did it seem so less wrong now that his physical body was the appropriate age, even though he was still eighty-two years old?

She must be only sixteen years old, you wretched old scum, Daylen told himself. "Sharra, this is wrong. You're too young and you should never... You need to leave."

"You're not that much older than me. It's all right."

"No, it's not."

Daylen felt a hand on his back. She was so close, the warmth of her body radiating. Another hand took his own and Sharra pressed it to her breast. "It's okay if you haven't done it before. I...I can show you."

Daylen's strength to resist had been crumbling with each second and this was too much.

He had lost this battle.

Daylen turned, giving into his desires and was about to take

Sharra with all the passion his young body possessed; but looking upon her, upon her innocence and beauty, it was impossible to not see all those young innocent girls he had ravaged in his past.

There had been so many, all a reflection of Sharra in one way or another. He had told himself that their tears had come from fear and nervousness, not from the truth that he willfully ignored: that they had been coerced to his bed. And here he was, about to commit the same crime, for Sharra clearly felt that this was her only choice. She was as coerced by her circumstances as much as the young girls of his past had been coerced by his servants.

And Daylen was still willing to take advantage of someone's vulnerability.

Suddenly Daylen felt revolted at himself. He was truly the most despicable thing that ever wormed its way out of a mother's womb. Self-disgust surged inside with such power that he felt sick to the core. Daylen pushed Sharra away and lunged for the waste bin, where he threw up everything he had just eaten.

"Daylen, what's wrong?" Sharra asked.

"Get out," Daylen spat.

"But…"

With murderous rage Daylen turned, and screamed with such ferocity that it would have given an army pause: "Get *out!*"

Sharra gasped in fear, and after a few hesitant steps backward, took up her dress and fled.

Daylen lay spitting the vomit from his mouth before lying next to his waste, where he cried bitterly, hating everything about his existence.

CHAPTER TWENTY-SEVEN

After I had conquered Daymony, my people were already becoming discontent with life in the Dawn Empire. They had gone from being grateful for having food to complaining that they weren't being given enough, even though the quantity I allotted to them hadn't changed. The empire produced far more food than was necessary, of course, but I stored all the excess away for my armies, potential famine, and my larger plans.
I saw their complaints as threats to the stability and safety of the nation, so I punished anyone who spoke out against me severely.

"Sleep well?" Ahrek asked as Daylen met him on deck at Early High.

"I didn't sleep."

"Hmm, if you're not feeling well…"

"I'll manage. Has everyone had something to eat?"

"Everyone except our guest in the brig."

Daylen nodded, glancing to the few girls up and about. Sharra was among them and was looking at him pleadingly.

Guilt surged inside him, making Daylen feel sick once more, and he groaned, cradling his forehead.

"Not liking the attention?"

"You've noticed?"

"It's rather hard to miss. If these girls weren't so distraught I'd expect they'd be throwing themselves at you. You're their dashing young hero, after all."

Daylen sneered. "They're a bunch of doe-eyed immature nits who need to grow up."

"Daylen, they've been forced to *grow up* far quicker than anyone else their age. How could you forget what they've been through?"

"I haven't! I'm just in a bad mood, all right?"

"Very well."

"I'm off to retrieve our guest," Daylen said, making his way below. Daylen dragged Sain out of his cell and made sure the snot followed behind him, but before climbing even one flight of stairs, Sain edged his way over Daylen's imposed five meters mark.

Daylen broke his arm.

Falling to the deck and crying out in pain, Sain managed to scream at Daylen, "I just *forgot!*"

Daylen dragged Sain the rest of the way. "No, you didn't! You were testing me—did I pass?"

"Go screw a goat, you Shade's tit!"

"I told you what would happen if you tried that again."

Sain continued to scream in pain.

"If there's one thing you should remember about me, it's that I keep my word."

"You broke my arm!"

"Ahrek will heal you, so stop your whining!"

Sure enough, Ahrek met Daylen at the door to the deck. "What under the Light happened?"

"Just teaching someone a valuable lesson."

"Light, Daylen, you didn't need to break his arm!"

"I told him what would happen. So, actually, he broke his *own* arm."

Ahrek healed Sain and asked, "Is that better?"

"Thanks," Sain said, testing his arm.

"The girls should all remain inside throughout the journey," Daylen said to Ahrek.

"Yes, I agree," Ahrek replied as he left to gather the girls, sending one last look of disapproval Daylen's way.

Sain quickly got to his feet as he saw Daylen leaving.

Good, he's finally learning.

"This is only temporary," Daylen said to Sain. "You'll be free to go when I'm finished with you."

"Get stoned."

Daylen laughed. The kid really had balls to show such back-bone even after what Daylen had done to him. The strength of growing up in one of the roughest places in the world, Daylen supposed.

Reaching the helm, Daylen began working the flight levers and the ship sunk out of the bay it had been docked in. "Now, my fine navigator, point the way."

"You know we'll get attacked, right?"

"Well, that depends. Your old ship, the switchback now strapped to us—was it well known?"

"The *Bloodrunner*? Of course it was. Blackheart made sure of it."

"The *Bloodrunner*? That's its name, really?"

"Yeah."

"Light, Blackheart really liked cheesy names. Anyway, because of his reputation, would any other pirates try and attack him?"

"Not unless they had some big brass balls and thought they would win. So no. No one ever attacked us."

"So what do you think they'll do when they see the *Bloodrunner* strapped to us?"

Sain nodded. "Yeah, I get it. They'll simply think he's captured another ship, only that the *Bloodrunner* was damaged."

Daylen's brow leveled at that. "Another question: did Black-heart steal the ships instead of merely robbing them?"

Sain shrugged. "Not at first, but recently he was focused on capturing any ship that he could. We flew off much farther than usual to find them. The captain was pretty happy to have spotted yours so close. Didn't turn out well for him, though, did it?"

"So he was trying to build his own fleet?"

"He didn't have *that* many in his crew. No, Black sold them off."

"He must have gotten a blackened good price to make it worth his while."

"Yeah, as much as if they were sold second hand."

"He had a buyer that would pay retail in the Floating Isles? But that means the buyer is keeping the ships; they'd never pay so much if they planned to resell them. What would they want with a small fleet of stolen ships?"

"I don't know."

"How many ships did Blackheart steal and sell off?"

The boy paused, thinking. "Twenty or so."

"And the crew of those ships?"

Sain didn't reply, but he pursed his lips and looked away.

"Right…"

"I didn't kill anyone. Black didn't trust me to hold a sword."

"Still, twenty… That's a lot when it comes to skyships. Whoever is buying them must be running a big operation of some sort, but there wasn't anything in Black's cabin."

"He did most of his planning in his room at the hideout. None of us were allowed in."

"Then we'll make sure to take a good look there. But until then, you better be hoping we don't run into any trouble, because I'll have no other choice but to blame you if we get attacked."

"Blame *me*?"

"I'd have to assume that you led us into an ambush, and then I'll have to kill you."

"What?" Sain asked in a panic. "Even with Black's reputation, we still might get attacked if they think we're vulnerable. Especially if they think we took a hard enough hit that his ship can't fly!"

"My, my, that would be an unfortunate turn of events—for you, that is. I suppose you're going to have to take us along the safest route to your hideout and hope we meet no one along the way."

"You really are a bastard!"

Daylen smiled. "Yes, yes I am."

Sain paced back and forth a few times. "There's a crew in the hideout."

"I already figured as much, but that you told me just saved your life. Well done." Sain sneered. "Well as soon as they see you, they'll attack."

"Really? When I first saw Blackheart, I thought I was looking at myself."

"Yeah, that is weird. You two do look alike."

"You think your friends…"

"They're not my friends!"

"Fine, your former crewmates. Do you think they could tell the difference from such a distance?"

"Probably not."

"My thoughts as well. And for added security, you're going to guide us so that we approach the hideout from above, so no one will see anyone on the deck until it's too late."

"What's your plan once we get inside? Kill them?"

"Do you want me to?"

"Yes," Sain replied coldly.

"They really *aren't* your friends, are they?"

"They're a bunch of blackened sons of Shade. Like I said, I was only with them because I had no other choice."

"No, there were other pirate ships you could have joined. Also, if you really tried, you could have found your way out of the Floating Isles. So Blackheart had something on you to make you stay. It's obvious that he liked blackmail."

"So what if he did? I'm not going to tell you."

Daylen smirked. "You think I'd blackmail you?"

"Yes."

"Well, that's not exactly hard to guess. Is there anything else I should know about Blackheart's den?"

"He's got some angry dogs locked away in case anyone tries to sneak in. Nothing you shouldn't be able to handle."

"Still, good to know. Anything else?"

"Not that I can think of."

"Well, the more I can be aware of, the better for the both of us."

The boy paled. "The...the *both* of us?"

Daylen chuckled. "You think I'm going to leave you on the ship? Don't worry, I'll do all the fighting."

"Yeah," he said, swallowing. "Just don't mistake me for one of them."

Ahrek soon joined them at the helm after all the girls were safely below deck. Sain directed their way and Daylen steered the *Maraven* with the switchback in tow through the maze that was the Floating Isles. Sain did seem to take them a roundabout way, but Daylen expected this, as they were trying to avoid any other ships.

Sometimes they flew directly up for whole kilometers, weaving around islands both large and small.

It took a whole fall for the *Maraven* to reach Blackheart's hide-out. They weren't exactly flying fast, what with the weight of the switchback they were towing. Any turn, stop or acceleration that happened too fast or sharp would burst the straps. Combined with the fact that they had to constantly weave through the isles, while also taking the safest route Sain knew of, their progress was slow indeed.

Impressively, Sain seemed to know exactly where to go. The Floating Isles were a maze of incredible complexity, especially considering that some of the isles floated in fixed circles, and knowing even a vague way to get to one location in it was a feat beyond most people. It wouldn't have been hard at all for anyone to claim they had no idea where to go, yet Sain had simply accepted Daylen's command to guide their path. Daylen suspected that this was an unintended concession on Sain's part that he was still unaware he had let slip. Sain's ability to navigate the Isles spoke of a much greater degree of intelligence than he let on. He would have easily made it into a university if he had been born on the mainland.

Blackheart's hideout was a cave that opened to the side of a rounded and unevenly shaped island. It was about two hundred meters in diameter, medium in size compared to the other islands. Because the island had a rounded top, it was extremely unlikely that anyone would ever think to build something atop it. It was also surrounded by a whole bunch of smaller islands, providing a great level of concealment.

"How far away are we from the cities?" Daylen asked Sain.

Sain pointed. "Deadend is a few hours flight that way, if you're flying fast. For us while towing the Bloodrunner, it would take us half a fall."

Daylen looked back down to the cave entrance. "It's a nice and secluded spot. Had I known of it I might have even picked it for a hideout."

"Well, Blackheart is dead," Sain replied. "I suppose you can take it once it's cleared out."

"You know, I might, if I could remember the way back."

Ahrek was looking at Daylen curiously. "Why under the Light would you need a hideout?"

"Well, um, to *hide*, maybe? Though I could be wrong about that."

Ahrek sighed and simply looked at Daylen, unimpressed.

"You never know when you might need a good hideout or supply cache."

"Your father thought the same. He was famous for his hidden

weapon stockpiles and secret bases of operation. In fact, he had an Imperial Reserve that was never found."

Daylen ground his teeth, looking to Ahrek. "Look, I get it. I have a *lot* in common with my father, and every time I do something that's the same, you get worried that I might be too similar and follow the same path. Trust me, if I do, I'll kill myself."

"No, Daylen, if you truly become anything like your father, *I* will kill you."

At first Daylen was speechless, and utterly shocked at the serious intensity in Ahrek's voice. Ahrek was such a happy man most of the time, and yet there was this darkness in him. Perhaps this was the very reason the Light had sent Ahrek to Daylen in the first place. Unlike other Lightbringers, Ahrek truly would kill Daylen if he judged that he was too much a threat to let live, and this gave Daylen such comfort.

"Thank you," Daylen said earnestly. "You're a better friend than I thought."

Ahrek smiled and replied in his normal, pleasant voice. "You're more than welcome."

"You two are completely insane!" Sain said, looking at the both of them. "And who in the Light is your father?"

"Dayless the Conqueror," Daylen said casually.

"*What?*" Sain said. "So you and Blackheart were *brothers?*"

Daylen huffed at the ridiculous question. "Of course not."

"But Blackheart was one of the Conqueror's bastards. He boasted of it all the time."

"He was obviously lying," Daylen said. "Dayless never had any children."

"Except you," Ahrek said.

"Well, of course, but he had no *other* children."

"Blackheart said there were heaps," Sain replied. "That he had met at least seven of them."

Even though Daylen knew this was impossible, his heart began to sink. "No, Blackheart must have noticed how similar he looked to the Conqueror and used it to boost his own reputation."

"But what of the Conqueror's harem?" Ahrek asked curiously. "Your father had a taste for young women, virgins to be precise."

"He never had a harem—it was one girl at a time, two at most by the end, and none of them had any children!"

Ahrek's brow rose. "You can't truly know that."

"No, but it's what my father said."

"And he was such an honest, trustworthy man."

"He never had any children!"

Ahrek replied tentatively, "You and Blackheart looked *very* similar, Daylen."

"People can look alike."

"*That* alike? You've used your own resemblance to the Conqueror to help prove your parentage. On top of the unnatural resemblance, Blackheart was an exceptional swordsman and a tyrant as well." Ahrek turned to Sain. "I think you might be right. It only makes sense that at least some of the Conqueror's women fell pregnant, especially with the number he went through. He must have tried to kill the babes to hide them away."

Daylen's rage flew free. *"He never killed any infants!"*

Ahrek raged back with ferocious passion. "He killed *hundreds* of infants, children, women and innocents, Daylen! Or have you never heard of the Daybreak Massacre? Don't try and convince yourself that your father was anything other than what he was: a murderous, genocidal tyrant!"

Daylen's rage died as fast as it had grown, and he was left standing there wishing oblivion upon himself, because Ahrek was right. Daylen had only screamed because speaking of Dayless the Conqueror was speaking of himself, and *he*, with his current understanding and regret, would never commit such a heinous sin as murdering an infant. That was what he meant: that *he* would never do such a thing.

But he had. When he had overthrown the old aristocracy, he had executed every aristocrat regardless of age or gender. He had destroyed many cities of the nations that fought him. And then there was Daybreak. How many children had he killed throughout his life? How many babies?

Ahrek spoke in a calmer voice. "Very well, perhaps killing his *own* children was something that even he couldn't do. Tyrants can still love, after all; but to prevent any challenge to his rule, they were hidden from him."

Ahrek's words came like hammer strikes to Daylen's mind—for what he said was, in part, possible, only that the children must have been hidden from Daylen himself. Daylen had ordered precautions be taken to avoid any pregnancy to prevent a legitimate challenge to his power. He also hadn't wanted any children, not after the ones that had been taken from him. Nothing could replace his little ones. But he *never* would have killed any child he had accidentally fathered. If those contraceptive precautions weren't nearly as effective as he had been told, he would have executed his doctors and anyone else he could blame without a second thought. So, to save their own lives, they might have hidden the truth. Kerkain, his ruling second, would have known... but he had been executed by the revolutionaries.

If the contraceptive didn't work Daylen could have fathered hundreds of children, literally *hundreds,* without ever knowing, and Blackheart's uncanny resemblance was very, very strong evidence to that.

Daylen began to feel sick. The possibility of this was an unbearable nightmare, for if this was true, Blackheart might very well have been the bastard son of Dayless the Conqueror—which meant that Blackheart wasn't Daylen's brother.

Blackheart had been his own son. And Daylen had not just killed him, but had butchered and tortured him until death.

"No!" Daylen said in horror, stumbling over to the rail, shedding tears of bitterness and self-loathing. *"No!"* he screamed, falling to his knees. He might have killed his own son, a wretched tyrant who had turned out to be just like his father. But what if Daylen could have helped him? If Dayless the Conqueror was capable of learning the error of his ways, anyone was, so what right did Daylen have to kill him? Indeed, if Blackheart was his own son, which was becoming more and more likely in Daylen's mind, did Daylen then have a responsibility to him, an accountability for his actions?

Daylen thought of Blackheart's words.

"I really wonder how many of us bastards are out there?"

"Can't you tell? With how damn good you are with that sword, and with your hair and looks, it's clear that we're long-lost brothers."

"Wait! If you really are the Conqueror, that means I'm your son! Can't you see that?"

Blackheart had really believed he was the bastard son of the Conqueror.

Ahrek knelt at Daylen's side. "Would you have still killed Blackheart if you had known he was your brother?"

Oh, Light, Ahrek doesn't know the half of it. "Of course not," Daylen said, his voice trembling with emotion and distress.

"That's good that you care for anyone who might be family, but Blackheart did deserve to die. He was a plague on the world."

"You don't get it."

"Then help me see."

"You can't, for both our sakes," Daylen said, dragging himself to his feet before stumbling away to his quarters.

CHAPTER TWENTY-EIGHT

For the most part I believed my system to work, and I strived to give all of my people the necessities of life. The problem was that even though my nation esteemed all people as equal, people are never the same, especially in regard to what they contribute to society. How just is it to reward the indolent as much as the motivated? Not at all, and my dream of an equal society failed with disastrous results.

You see, by nature people are both lazy and greedy. Unless driven by an ideal or passion, when given a choice they'll always choose the easier option or the one that will benefit them most. Seeing that my people lost the vision of the empire I was building and that I ensured everyone the same wage few were motivated to perform the harder jobs or those ones that required more training and education, unless they were members of the guilds. So, I took away their choice and forced those people that showed ability into the professions I needed and punished anyone who didn't meet the quotas I set.

I took away their freedom to maintain productivity, stability and equality and believed it justified.

L yrah found the flight to the capital very awkward and long. Cueseg wouldn't speak about the tension between him and the crew.

Then a fall into their flight, the captain, of all people, had asked to speak with Cueseg in private.

Several hours later, Cueseg returned, and though he kept his face devoid of subtle expression, his bearing and countenance was even more depressed than before.

It was interesting how easily Lyrah had come to interpret Cueseg's mood through body language as opposed to his blank and mostly expressionless face.

Cueseg sat on one of the large cushions with his head slumped.

"What happened?" Lyrah asked in concern.

It took a while for Cueseg to reply. "I am shame. I will never have Rien."

Cueseg's face might have as much emotion as a puddle, but his voice always carried expression. Lyrah had never heard him sound so miserable.

"What are you talking about?"

"Tishlue…the captain. She called me to have sex…and I did."

Lyrah's heartbeat doubled its rate. She had to sit on the bed and close her eyes to try and hold off a panic attack as Cueseg spoke.

"I say I am strong of will and in most things I am. My mind is strong and tell my body to work and become strong too. But in sex, I am weak. This mark on head, that is what it means. It means I have sex with woman who is not my Rien; with a woman who has Rien with other man. Now I have no Rien and this mark is for all Tuerasian to know that I am to never have Rien. It is shame on me forever."

Lyrah tried to listen. Cueseg had never acted like this before, and she wanted to help in whatever way she could. Indeed Cueseg had never appeared more, normal, to her than right then. It was just so hard while trying to deal with her own issues. Still, she managed to keep the panic at bay, focusing on the social meaning rather than the act itself. "So, you committed adultery?"

"If that is word for it, then yes. I have this mark because of adultery. It means I am weak of will, that my mind does not control my body. There is no greater weakness."

Lyrah had absolutely no idea what to say. She wanted to comfort Cueseg, but she couldn't talk about intimacy without hyperventilating; and even avoiding those topics, she didn't know a thing about backward Tuerasian customs and why they would savagely brand and shun adulterers. Adultery was of course severely frowned upon in Hamahra, but people weren't branded and cast out for it.

Cueseg eventually spoke again. "The captain, away from eyes and ears of people, cares not for my mark and my shame. She has come to live like you Hamahrans and want me even with my shame. I am without Rien for so long and I think Tishlue ask to have sex because she want to be Rien. This make me happy, but after, she tell me she just want sex and not Rien."

And then for the first time Lyrah heard anger in Cueseg's voice: fierce, hot anger. "Without Rien, sex is *shame*. She give me *more shame* and I am *shame enough*!"

Lyrah's anxiety disappeared instantly, replaced by worry. She stood. "Cueseg, what did you do?"

Cueseg looked at her from the corner of his eye. "I follow law of my people."

"Which was?"

Cueseg turned to her and slowly pointed to the scarred brand on his forehead.

It took a second for Lyrah to figure out what he meant. "You *branded* the captain?"

"I am shame for weakness. Now she is shame, too."

She would have asked how he did this, but Cueseg's powers enabled him to burn people and more. "Oh, Light, Cueseg, that's called assault and mutilation. You're an Archknight!"

Cueseg stood and growled back. "I am Tuerase! This is law of my people."

"But we're not in Tuerase, and you represent the Order!"

"We are on ship that is Tuerase, and in sky it follow Tuerase law."

Lyrah sighed. "Yes, you're right about that, but what gives you the right to dispense Tuerasian law? Don't your people have some type of judiciary?"

"What is judice'ery?"

"A legal system, an official organization that dispenses and oversees your nation's laws."

"Of course we have this, but I am Archknight. I have right to punish in law."

"Yes, but the governments get very upset if they would've ruled differently to what an Archknight decided. We must be very careful in overstepping our authority, otherwise it will be withdrawn."

"I did not step over. I did what is law."

"Okay, okay, but Light, what if the crew turns against us?"

"No, they will turn on Tishlue for her shame. I am shame, but I am also *knight*. My people must show respect or they break the law."

Lyrah paused as the implications of Cueseg's words sunk in, which brought on a troubling thought. "That's why you became an Archknight, isn't it?"

Cueseg didn't answer.

"I'm right. You were disgraced and outcast amongst your own people. So to get around your own culture's social order, you became an Archknight, which forces them to show you respect and gives you a higher status than you ever could have received otherwise. That's why the crew has been acting so strange with you."

"This does not matter."

"Of course it does! Light, do you even care about the Order?"

"I have given oath and will keep my oath."

"But did you truly want to fight evil for the rest of your life when you undertook the Vigil, or were you more concerned about obtaining a higher social status?"

"It not matter. I make oath to fight evil and I keep oath. That is enough."

"That's not how it's supposed to work. You're supposed to *want* to fight evil with all your heart and soul, for only the pure will be accepted."

"No, I do not want to be knight like that. Being knight helps me and makes a better life, but I make oath, so oath is enough."

Lyrah sat down on the bed, overwhelmed with the fact that now all her suspicions had been confirmed. *Anyone can become an Archknight.* This boy they hunted, Cueseg, and even a tyrant, if he learned the secrets of the Vigil.

"Oh, Light, this is so much worse than I imagined," Lyrah said softly to herself. Now she had to find that boy, and she would make sure he never revealed what he knew.

By the next fall, Cueseg had returned to his normal self, or so it appeared. They didn't see the captain at all, even when they landed within the Capital Skyport.

Disembarking, Lyrah marched straight to the massive skyport's main offices, where the Portmaster would be located.

The main office was an impressive ten-story building made of decorative brick and several interconnected buildings. A horde of people moved through its many doors. Though the people outside the building took notice and made way for them, the crowds inside were so preoccupied with whatever task they were about that they didn't notice the two Archknights who had entered.

The first room was large and open with countless lines of people in front of raised and walled-off reception desks. The fact that an organization could process even half of the submissions, complaints, fines, inquiries, ship inventories, and countless other procedures that the Capital Skyport required was remarkable. Yet the administration handled it well enough to see the port run efficiently, though one might not say smoothly. It all looked so chaotic.

Lyrah bonded light to her voice and called out, "Silence!"

Everyone in the room became quiet and turned. When seeing two Archknights they parted as Lyrah and Cueseg walked to one of the reception desks.

"I need to see the Portmaster at once!"

They were promptly shown to a formal sitting room on a higher level within the building and shown every courtesy. On their way to the room, Lyrah asked that the Portmaster find out if a ship by the name of the *Maraven* had dropped anchor recently before meeting them. She also requested that word be sent to the Hold, the official Archknight headquarters within the city, that she and Cueseg had arrived and that they needed to speak with a superior. Their attendant nodded and left.

The muffled sound of the frantic bustle in other rooms could still be heard within the sitting room, yet it was still comparatively quiet.

Cueseg lounged on one of the couches.

"This is a formal meeting, Cueseg. You should be standing when the Portmaster arrives."

"In my culture, we sit to greet people."

"But we aren't *in* your culture, Cueseg."

Cueseg sighed and stood.

Lyrah's stress gnawed at her while they stood there waiting. Things had been so intense recently, what with the threat that this boy posed and their lack of progress in catching him. What she wouldn't give to have a good game of Rattan Ball to unwind, go for a long run all by herself, or take a day off to watch the Races. But there was no time for any of that.

The Portmaster of the Capital Skyport arrived shortly after, flanked by four Harbormasters. He was an older man, but not nearly old enough to trigger her aversion. Indeed, the man looked full of energy, ready to get anything done that needed doing. He had faded blue hair, graying at the sides, the wrinkles on his facing adding character.

Walking to Lyrah, the Portmaster bowed respectfully before sweeping off his top hat. He was dressed in an embroidered tailed suit coat and wore a cravat and appropriately beaded tassel with a bejeweled backsword at his side. Very fine dress; but considering that the Capital Skyport was the largest skyport in the world, any managerial position in this port indicated a prestigious career indeed.

"Lady Archon, I am Mr. Tellfen," the Portmaster announced formally. "I've just checked through the logs and with every registry station around the city. The *Maraven* has not seen port in the city for four months. I've also sent word to the Hold as you requested, and a member of your Order should be on their way."

Cueseg stood to Lyrah's side, holding a firm, blank gaze on the people before them, and it was clearly making them feel a little uneasy.

"Thank you, Mr. Tellfen," Lyrah said. "I'd expected we might have beaten the ship here. Please place a standing alert for the *Maraven* at all registry stations. Also, the Hold must be alerted as soon as it's spotted. Let the ship enter, but I need to know in what dock it does."

"That's impossible to know, as the docks are occupied and vacated constantly through the fall," Mr. Tellfen said. "All captains know they're free to pick any vacant dock within the area of the harbor they were directed to. We record and inspect the cargo of each ship after they land, as well as their length of stay, but knowing what specific dock, in even an hour's time, simply can't be done."

Lyrah raised an eyebrow. "But you can keep a specific dock free, can't you?"

The Portmaster considered this. "If we moved some boom gates in, yes. The dockmen would need to be on watch for the ship to raise the gates in time, and the ship would have to be ordered to that specific dock, which would be highly irregular."

"Yes, and that would create suspicion," Lyrah said. "We don't want to tip them off. Have the registry stations on alert, but admit the ship as normal. Then have them sound an alert once the ship has passed through the shield as it will be too late for them to escape. We'll inform the Border Patrol to approach and escort the ship to a specific dock when hearing the alert."

Tellfen nodded. "Excellent plan. Should I be concerned about this ship? Does it pose a threat to the city?"

"The knights will keep everything in order. What dock will they be escorted to?"

Mr. Tellfen looked to one of his Harbormasters, the only woman among the four.

She was similar in age to Lyrah, the knight noted as the woman looked through her ledger. A Harbormaster's role in Highdawn was easily as broad as a Portmaster of a smaller city. "I'll keep dock two clear on the twelfth stack," the Harbormaster said. The Capital Skyport was large enough to have skyships dock above one another, and thus each dock was grouped in stacks according to harbor.

"Is the second dock the highest in a stack?" Lyrah asked.

"In the First Harbor it is, Lady Archon. There's only two docks to each stack, as it accommodates for the largest of ships."

Though Lyrah didn't know much about skyport procedures, she did know that the First Harbors were regularly reserved for the more important ships.

"Have it put in the lower dock, the first, and the patrol ship will anchor above," Lyrah said.

"I'll see it done," the Harbormaster said, bowing.

"Then dock one, stack twelve of the First Harbor it is," Lyrah said.

"Excellent," Mr. Tellfen said. "You may use my personal office once your brother arrives from the Hold for your meeting. And if there's anything at all, please…"

"Thank you, but this sitting room will be sufficient," Lyrah said.

"Please keep everyone from entering while we're here, except our brother, of course," Lyrah said with a dignified smile.

Mr. Tellfen smiled back, bowing. "Yes, of course. Good day, Lady Archon, and if there's anything you need, please don't hesitate to ask."

Lyrah and Cueseg watched the men and woman leave the sitting room. Once the doors were closed, Lyrah turned to Cueseg. "You didn't need to glare at them the whole time."

"If they think we unhappy, they try and please us more."

"But you're not exactly good at subtle facial expressions, Cueseg. You looked like the men were constantly farting throughout the conversation... Wait, that's a bad example. You Tuerasians don't find farting offensive."

"That is because it is not."

"What do you find offensive?"

"Having dirt on face and clothes, but the most offensive thing a man can do in my culture is to have his penis be strong when others can see."

"*What!*"

"The most offensive thing a man can..."

Lyrah could feel her anxiety rise. "I heard, Cueseg! But... *Light.* Speaking about things like that makes me really, really uncomfortable."

"I was thinking you better at this now. When I speak of Tishlue and sex, you not uncomfortable."

"No, I was, believe me, but that was different. You were depressed and...and talking about it with me seemed to help you."

"So you do for me?"

"Well, yes."

Cueseg was silent for a moment and then touched his fingers to his forehead and opened his arms to bow. "Thank you, Lyrah. You are noble and strong."

"Oh, well... Um... You're welcome."

An awkward silence followed, though Lyrah was getting more accustomed to them recently. She eventually let herself collapse onto a couch.

"I am hungry," Cueseg said.

"That's nothing out of the ordinary."

Cueseg walked to the door and spoke to someone outside,

Lyrah couldn't see who, and eventually a large platter of assorted cheeses, crackers, and fruits was brought in.

Once the attendant left, Cueseg picked up a small block of cheese and looked at it with a horrified expression. "This has mold all over!"

"It's blue cheese, supposed to be a delicacy."

"Mold is *delicacy*?" Cueseg exclaimed incredulously. "It is *mold*!" Cueseg threw the cheese at the door in disgust, saying, "You Hamahrans make me sick," and then carefully examined every other cheese block with a look of distrust.

Lyrah sighed and grabbed a grape from the platter. "Then eat the fruit. Surely Hamahran grapes can't be worse than Tuerasian?"

"That depends, do you wait until it is moldy?"

"No."

"Only with cheese."

"Not all cheese. Try some of the others. Light, you might have even liked the moldy...I mean, the blue stuff."

"If the mold is good, then *you* eat."

Lyrah pursed her lips. She had never tried blue cheese and couldn't say she really wanted to, either. It *was* mold, after all.

"Exactly," Cueseg said with a hint of humor in his voice.

———

Several minutes passed before the door to the sitting room opened and a man walked in wearing the Archknight's Mantle over black dueling clothes. Lyrah recognized him. He was Archallion Kennet, commander of the Archknight Hold in Highdawn.

Lyrah stood and walked to greet her superior, while Cueseg reclined in his chair, eating a cracker.

"Archonair," the brother said, nodding to Lyrah, calling her by rank. "Archus," he added, nodding to Cueseg. Cueseg sat up and touched his forehead with the tips of his fingers and swept them out. He then reclined, continuing to eat.

"Sister," Kennet began in a stern voice, "what're you doing so far from your hunt?"

"We're still hunting, brother, but a different quarry. Cueseg and I have come across a young man who can lightbind—and he isn't an Archknight."

Kennet looked like Lyrah had just told him the world wasn't

flat. "That's impossible," he said. "This young man must be a brother who's also left his assigned area for some reason. Or he's a deserter."

"Is the son of Dayless the Conqueror a member of the Order?"

"What?" he asked, flabbergasted.

Lyrah pulled the extra from her pocket that announced the Conqueror's death and the existence of his son. "I assume you've seen this?"

"Yes, and the stories printed in the broadsheets," Kennet said cautiously. "What of it?"

Lyrah pointed to the depiction of the son who supposedly looked exactly like his father, just younger. "This is the boy we chase, and I'm fairly certain the Order would know of a member that looked exactly like the Conqueror, let alone if he was his son."

Now Kennet looked as though Night had fallen. "Are you certain?"

"There's no doubt."

"Then we must detain him immediately!"

"That's exactly what Cueseg and I have been trying to do."

"Do you know where he is?"

"No, but we know where he's going to be, and I suggest we make a little surprise to greet him."

CHAPTER TWENTY-NINE

I was a hypocrite, wanting all people to be equal but granting privileges to my soldiers. I needed to incentivize military service to maintain the strength of my armies. This eventually created a class distinction as real as the aristocracy I overthrew—but I didn't care. I rewarded loyalty, which secured my military and thus my power, which I used to suppress and punish all discontents.

"Y ou can leave if you like," Ahrek said across the aged table as he sat in the ship's mess, sketching in his book.

Sain, sitting across from him, sneered. "Yeah, how exactly?"

"Take the pirate ship. It's still perfectly capable of flying."

"You would let me go with a whole skyship?"

Ahrek looked right into Sain's eyes. "Yes."

"And what would your friend think of that?"

Ahrek put aside his sketchbook to eat another piece of sticky bread, speaking between mouthfuls. "Oh, he would be livid, I'm sure; but I'm not his servant, I'm his friend, and friends don't always agree. You've done exactly what we demanded from you—led us to your former associate's hideout. I see no other reason to force you to stay with us."

"And what if I've led you into a trap?"

"I trust you."

"No, you don't."

"Actually, I do. I'm a Lightbringer, remember? I don't lie."

"And what if I want to stay?"

Ahrek's brow rose and he felt genuinely surprised. "You actually want to stay?"

Sain looked away. "Don't tell him that, whatever you do...but yeah."

"Why? You haven't exactly been treated well."

"I'm used to that," Sain said, turning back to Ahrek. "Look, you're a real Lightbringer and I've seen that you mean to free the girls aboard. You both have no reason to find Blackheart's captives or clean out the rest of his crew, yet you are. Why?"

"Because it's the right thing to do, and in our case, we have the ability to do it."

"Exactly, and that's why I want to stay. I've been forced to do some really bad things, but now that Blackheart's dead, I have the chance to do something right for once. I figure sticking with you two is doing just that. I might even learn something."

"Hmm..." Ahrek nodded. "Well, I see no issue with another companion, and Daylen will be fine so long as he thinks you don't want to stay. It's when he thinks you want to stay with him that he will try and get rid of you."

"That's stupid."

"No—you just have to understand him."

"And you do?"

"I'm beginning to."

"Must take a while. I mean, he seems like such a stone-cold...I don't know, warrior, and then he learns that he killed his half-brother and he cries like a baby and hides away in his room for a fall."

"You wouldn't cry if you found out you had killed your brother?"

"If I didn't know him, and if he was a bastard like Blackheart? No. I wouldn't."

"Well, as cold and heartless as Daylen might try to act, he is a man of deep passion and feeling."

"So he's secretly a softie?"

The Lightbringer smiled. "Deep down, yes."

"Why are you following him? I mean, you're a Lightbringer! I get it that he thinks he knows what he's doing, and he does have those powers he likes to show off. But he *is* still just a kid. By the looks of it, he's even younger than I am."

"Aside from how old he looks, Daylen possesses the intelligence, maturity, and burdens of someone much older... I still don't know how, and he's very guarded about his past, but he must have endured many things that have forced him to grow up faster than most." Ahrek's voice softened as he reflected on his mysterious companion. "You can see it in his eyes. It's almost as if there's a whole lifetime's worth of suffering behind them."

Sain didn't reply right away. "Yeah, there is a look about him. Still, that doesn't answer why you're following him when it should be the other way around."

"The Light told me to follow him."

"*Really?* The *Light.*"

"You don't believe in the Light?"

"No."

Ahrek sighed. "Then I can see why I've crossed your path."

"Why?"

"To help."

Sain looked cynical. "You going to convert me?"

"Only if you're open to it, but that's not my purpose. Like I said, I'm here to help."

Sain harrumphed. "Well, I'll take any help offered."

"You haven't had much of it in life?"

"No, not really."

Daylen had lain in his quarters for a fall. He had barely felt the ship move shortly after his seclusion; Ahrek was taking it to a safe cove, most likely.

His mind was in turmoil, his self-hatred having taken over. He would have cast himself from the cabin's window had he not known to his very core that he deserved to be tortured for eternity. A lifetime would have to suffice, or two in his case.

"I've been a plague on this world," Daylen said to the Light. "And now I might have spread my own spawn to plague it in turn."

Daylen had vowed forty-five years ago to never have another child after his first two were murdered. Nothing in his life had caused such profound sorrow as that. He thought he could never live through losing another child... and yet if Blackheart had indeed been his son, Daylen had not only seen the death of another child he had been the one who killed him. His own child, and in a most unholy and merciless way.

The thought caused him to wail in agony.

Yet Blackheart had been a vicious murderer and had needed to be stopped. Who more appropriate to stop him than his father? If Daylen was indeed his father.

"If I've sired more children," Daylen said to himself, "they are my responsibility. I'll have to hunt them down and see if any others are like their brother. . . like me, and put an end to them. Daylen's tears returned as he spoke. "How many more of my children's deaths will I have to see?"

It was so clear why the Light hadn't let him die when he had reached the end of his years. His punishment was far from over—it had to be, when there were such profound and intimate ways to yet prolong his torment.

"Let me go to oblivion," Daylen said pitifully to the Light. Suddenly he roared, "Consign my soul to Outer Darkness and be done with it!"

Nothing happened, of course. He was left lying on the large bed, being crushed by the guilt of a million sins.

Yet after a time, a new thought entered Daylen's mind.

If Daylen did have more children, maybe, just maybe, there might be one of them that had become good. Unlikely; but oh, if there was, it might mean that Daylen could actually have left *one* good thing in the world. If he did, he had to find that one. If the others had turned out like Blackheart he would have to find them too and see if any might change their ways. If not, then. . .

And with that thought, the small, vain hope that one of his potential children might be good, Daylen felt he had the strength to return to his feet.

He ate some bread, and even though he despised the fact that he hadn't died when he should have, he could still appreciate being free of the burdens of old age. Not even two weeks ago, eating solids as simple as bread would have utterly ravaged his bowels for a fall.

Daylen left the cabin to be about his work, which in this case was the cleansing of a pirate's hideout where an innocent person was being held captive, having been linked against their will to a sword which had been used by a now-dead tyrant.

Daylen found Ahrek and Sain up on deck.

The skyships locked anchor in a shadowed cove of a floating island, Ahrek obviously having moved the ship away from Blackheart's den.

The old priest and young pirate noticed Daylen as soon as he emerged.

"I don't want to talk about it, so don't ask," Daylen said, walking past the pair.

Ahrek nodded with an insufferable look of compassion and Sain seemed compliant enough. Daylen was half surprised Sain was still here. He had guessed Ahrek would have let the snot go free by now.

Daylen made his way to the helm and the two followed.

"I'm confident we haven't been discovered," Ahrek said, "but a side effect of our seclusion is that we haven't been able to keep an eye on the den."

"What has fallen has fallen," Daylen said as he worked the ship's levers. "You might want to get those girls below deck."

The girls seemed to be doing better. Thankfully, Sharra wasn't among them—Daylen really wouldn't be able to stand seeing her right now. The adoring looks that the girls were sending his way were insufferable enough, and they began to trigger another blackened damned erection. This young body of his had its downsides. No wonder teenage boys were so retarded, what with all this blood flowing in the wrong direction!

Daylen glared at the girls. He really was their *handsome young hero*, he thought bitterly. What would they would think of him if they learned he was once the greatest tyrant the world has ever known? Could saving their lives be enough to convince them that he had changed?

No.

"So we're going in right now?" Ahrek asked.

The question pulled Daylen from his thoughts. "Yes. I'd say grab a sword, but for you that would be redundant."

"Can I have a sword?" Sain asked.

"Not a—" Daylen started, but his words were interrupted by Ahrek.

"Of course."

Daylen looked to Ahrek, stunned. "We're not giving him a sword!"

"Sain isn't our captive," Ahrek said calmly. "I trust him. He's kept his word and co-operated with me completely while you locked yourself away."

"I said no!"

Light shone from Ahrek's hand, materializing into a swept-hilt broadsword. Ahrek handed it to Sain. "I'm your companion and friend," Ahrek said to Daylen, "not your servant. We're going into a dangerous situation and Sain has the right to defend himself."

Daylen was furious, even if in the back of his head he knew Ahrek was right. *I have to get used to this*, he told himself as he gripped the two levers and forced himself to breathe in deeply and evenly. *I'm not an Emperor anymore, and if there's any hope for me becoming a new man, I have to* stop *getting so angry with everyone. There's not a soul in the world that I have a right to command.*

"Fine!" Daylen said. "But if you're going to give him a sword, you might as well give him Blackheart's old one."

"But it's not linked to him."

"It wasn't linked to Blackheart, either," Daylen pointed out. "He's not going to come across anything that will break the thing, so we might get some use out of it before we find whomever it belongs to."

"Very well," Ahrek said, holding out his hand to Sain.

Sain returned the broadsword and Ahrek turned it back into light, then materialized a copy of Blackheart's sunforged sword.

"I said to give him Blackheart's sword, not to make a copy."

"This *is* Blackheart's sword."

"It's a duplicate."

"No, this is the very same sword."

"But you just made it!"

"Only because I had stored it within me previously."

"*What?*"

"It's a little ability that comes from the miracle of creation," Ahrek said casually. "You think I create things from light, but technically I just reform light into a different state—but it's still light. This is the same with all creation. Everything is actually light, just in different states of being, or spheres of organization. I can technically return anything to light, but only those things that don't have true identity, and came from myself, can be fully absorbed back."

"True identity—what does that mean?" Daylen asked.

"All physical objects, though they cannot truly think for themselves, have an inherent sense of being. They know what they are. They have identity."

"Interesting, so the things you create don't have this true identity."

"Only for the first hour or so from the time they are created. Within that time I can un-create them, if that makes sense. It's as if they become more solid the longer they remain as they are, gaining an understanding of what they are, and then are not willing to change. When that happens I can still return it to light, as readily any other object, but it remains a separate thing inside me for as long as I keep it. That light will forever be what it was created as."

"And as a result you have an invisible bag to hide stuff in," Sain said, looking impressed.

"Essentially. Anything that I've recently created can be uncreated. I can store anything else, though only so much. The object's weight remains, making me heavier."

"Light has weight?" Daylen asked.

"After it permanently becomes a physical thing, yes."

"Why didn't you tell me you could do that?"

"It hasn't come up, but evidently it's not something I try to hide. It's merely a useful byproduct of my power."

"Just a byproduct! You could smuggle anything anywhere and no one would know."

"Because smuggling is such a noble pursuit."

Daylen waved his hand. "Whatever," he said, and Ahrek handed Sain Blackheart's sword.

"You have anything else stored away?" Daylen asked.

"Of course."

"Like what?"

"Huh," Ahrek said, smiling.

"What?"

"I just didn't expect I would get to say *none of your business*."

Daylen laughed.

"I did it!"

Looking to Ahrek in confusion for a second, Daylen groaned.

"Did what?" Sain asked.

"I have achieved the impossible," Ahrek said in genuine amazement. "I made Daylen Namaran laugh!"

"It doesn't count," Daylen said.

"Of course it counts."

"No, that wasn't one of your terrible jokes. I was laughing at the irony!"

Ahrek paused. "Perhaps, but it was still an achievement."

"Whatever flies your ship, Bringer. Now, did anyone see what happened to Blackheart's hat?"

They approached Blackheart's den from above. Daylen spotted spy holes which had been carved into the sides of the island. They had shadowed faces within that seemed to watch their every movement.

Daylen glared at them from under Blackheart's tricorne hat. No alarm was sounded.

They reached the mouth of the cave and Daylen adjusted the control levers to guide the ship forward.

They entered a dark, stalactite-riddled passage that was damp and cool. There was light at the other end, about forty meters away, but it was far from reaching them.

The moment they had crossed the threshold into the darkness, a cold rippled over Daylen like his clothes were being peeled from his skin.

Daylen gasped and looked back.

"Yes," Ahrek said knowingly, barely visible through the thick shadows. "This would be the first time you've been entirely without light since receiving your powers. It isn't pleasant."

"I've been in shadow, but not such a stark contrast from light to dark. I hadn't realized the feeling was so normal to me."

"What is it?" Sain asked worriedly from the darkness to Daylen's right. "Is something wrong?"

"Calm down," Daylen said. "Everything's fine."

"I am calm!" Sain said, contradicting his words by the tone of his voice. He had walked to Daylen and was still only just visible.

"Haven't you flown through this passage a hundred times?" Daylen asked.

"Yeah, and I hated it each time. The dark—it's *unnatural*. You telling me you're not bothered by it?"

"Any sane man should fear the dark," Daylen said. "Just don't let it control you."

Ahrek chuckled. "Then Daylen and I should be feeling fine, seeing as there's only one Sain man here."

Daylen groaned. "Really, Ahrek?"

Sain was chucking nervously. "That was a pretty bad joke, Bringer."

"They're his specialty."

"You should strive to be good at your craft," Ahrek said, smiling, "whatever it is."

Sain looked to be much calmer—and, after a short pause, he asked, "So what were you two talking about before? Powers and light?"

Ahrek answered, "I am a Lightbringer, and Daylen's powers work in a similar way. We both feel light as a physical thing, like we're constantly immersed in warm water."

"Weird," Sain replied.

"We'll it's normal to me by now," Daylen said.

"And now you can't feel a thing?"

"Not on my skin at least," Daylen replied. "I can still sense the light outside, the light further within, the soft light in the timbers of the ship, the light on the cave walls, and the light in you and Ahrek." He didn't add that in sensing the light in living things, he could effectively see everything around him without the use of his eyes.

"Wait, there's light in me?"

"There's light in everything, with one exception," Ahrek said. "The light's strength is reflected by the person's desire to do good, their sense of right and wrong, and their knowledge of truth."

"So the better a person is, the more light they have inside?" Sain asked skeptically.

"Not always," Daylen said, thinking of himself. "But it's the reason I didn't kill you when we met. Unless you think it means something else and I should get back to killing all pirates on sight?"

"Nah, it's definitely a measure of their goodness," Sain said flippantly.

"Yeah, I thought you'd say that."

"Screw you."

"Sorry, I don't go for boys. Why don't you ask the Bringer? He dreams about naked young men."

"Daylen," Ahrek said, "that is *completely* out of context."

"So...you *do* dream about naked young men?" Sain asked teasingly.

"I'd rather not talk about it."

Daylen and Sain laughed.

It wasn't long before the passage opened to a softly illuminated cavern with a high toothy ceiling and deep jagged floor. The light shone from natural skylights and sunstone formations that made the damp rock shimmer in brilliant colors.

Around sixty meters away, the cavern climbed back up, forming a natural flat that was more or less in line with the passage they had just flown through. The flat became the new floor of the cavern and extended much farther in from the expanse that Daylen was guiding the ship across.

Daylen knew that caverns like this didn't form naturally. He guessed that in the initial explosion that had formed the Floating Isles, a chunk of shattered landmass had fallen on top of another that still had a good amount of stable darkstone within, making the cavern's roof. Water drainage and time had eroded the rest.

The flat provided a perfect natural formation to set up a dock, which was exactly what had been done. The dock was built from a ragtag assembly of wooden scaffolding and structures that continued farther into the cave, their sheer volume enough to impress the eye.

Pirates slowly began to appear along the main dock's ramparts.

Daylen counted twenty-five of them. They all had their swords drawn, one or two with hand-held shotspikes, and all were standing nervously.

"This all of them?" Daylen whispered to Sain.

"Not by half. I wonder when they're going to realize that you aren't Blackheart?"

Daylen pulled a lever to lock the anchor alongside a jetty. "Oh, I'd say in a few seconds."

Walking with focused steps, Daylen reached out with his light sense. He could feel that those men on the dock had barely any light within them, which wasn't a surprise; they were pirates, after all, who murdered, raped, and pillaged as a way of life. Sain was the exception, however, proving it was still worth checking.

Daylen began to run across the deck, a sensation that still felt odd to him, as a week ago he hadn't been able to run in years. *Light, walking had been hard enough.*

Daylen bonded light to his speed and performed an enhanced jump from the bow.

His powers were sluggish. There was far less light in the cave than there was outside, but enough to draw upon thanks to the nearby sunstones and skylights.

Cries of alarm sounded as Daylen soared through the air and drew his sword, Imperious—yet those cries sounded too late to save the three men he landed amidst.

Interestingly, the lack of light in these despicable men was as noticeable as brighter lights in others, even more so. There was a wrongness to them that made Daylen feel sick, and he couldn't help feeling satisfied as he ended their abominable lives.

"We're under attack!" a voice called out.

"The dogs!" another replied. "Release the dogs!"

Dogs? Daylen thought mockingly. *These worms haven't a hope.*

The pirates near where he had landed rushed Daylen with their weapons drawn.

Daylen smiled and let his instincts take control. With his powers and natural skill it didn't take long for Daylen to dispatch everyone that attacked him, dancing like the wind around the deadly weapons. He still wore his sunforged gauntlet for defense, but he didn't even need it in this fight.

Any battle with sunblades resulted in a horrifying mess due to how easily they sliced through material. Blood pooled around Daylen with each opponent's body lying in several pieces.

Daylen glared at the remaining pirates who were clearly rethinking their options.

One of them launched a shotspike at Daylen, and in response he enhanced his mass and fortitude.

The spike hit him, stabbing through his jacket but barely even depressing his skin. The tip bent sideways and the whole thing broke apart.

The pirates stared at him in stupor and then ran.

Daylen smiled, very pleased with how that last combo had worked out. He had noticed that increasing his mass made him more resilient in the same way as did increasing his fortitude, only that he was also heavier. Daylen had been wondering what would happen when they were combined; he had tried it more for experimentation, as he could heal easily enough from the spike if it had pierced him. It appeared that increasing his mass while at the same time his resistance to injury made him far more resilient that if he had just stacked all his bonds on either mass or fortitude respectively.

He had no idea why, but it certainly worked.

Daylen heard someone running down the jetty from the docked ship. It was Sain. As was agreed, Ahrek would stay with the ship to protect it and the girls aboard. Sain would accompany Daylen to offer any help, as he was far more familiar with the hideout.

Daylen began to make his way further into the den along a timber walkway which provided a much surer step than the damp stone.

Sain joined him.

"Stay behind me and keep out of trouble," Daylen said.

"No argument here."

This section of the massive cavern had a relatively flat base and was divided by wooden structures separating parts for supplies, tools and living quarters.

Natural light streamed out of the holes spotted along the cavern's roof, which were either lined with crystal formations reflecting the light from outside, or had natural sunstone growths within.

The stone, comprised of differing colored hews of rock, had large patches of moss growing on it, thanks to the natural light, and a few clumps of mushrooms here and there. Light shimmered off the many small beads of moisture. It was a beautiful sight, but Daylen gave it little heed. There were pirates to kill.

Daylen skewered two more pirates along the wooden walkway before he reached a flat and open part of the cavern. It was filled with tables, chairs, and some couches. Clearly this was some type of common room.

On the far side of the area, bathed in shadows, was a large metal door that several pirates had just unlocked.

"That's where Blackheart keeps the dogs," Sain said, panting.

"That's an awfully big door for a bunch of dogs," Daylen replied cautiously.

All but one pirate ran from the door as the last swung it open, revealing a dark cave behind. He, too, began to run before something grabbed him, pulling him into the darkness.

Bloodcurdling cries of pain sounded from the cave, which was black as night inside, before being silenced by a sound of wet ripping.

Daylen whirled on Sain. "That's not a pack of blackened dogs!"

Sain looked utterly shocked. "No... I swear they're dogs. I've seen Blackheart throw in new ones."

"No—Blackheart was feeding dogs to whatever he's really been keeping locked away!"

A high-pitched, horrific, and unnatural shriek echoed from the room.

Daylen's heart felt like it had stopped. He turned to the smaller cave, saying, "No, that insane *fool*! What has he done?"

"What?" Sain asked, wide-eyed. "What is it?

"Run back to the ship, get Ahrek, and then hide with the girls!"

"What—"

But Sain stopped speaking.

Suddenly, from a quickly growing circle of darkness emanating from the room, all the light in the cavern was being pushed back, plunging everyone inside into complete, whole, and consuming darkness.

"The Shade," Daylen whispered.

CHAPTER THIRTY

I eventually discovered the duplicity of the craftsmanship Guilds,
charging more for their services than my set pricing which
explained why they had such ease in keeping their members. I
tried my best to suppress them, but they unionized against me.
They knew I needed their skilled labor, so instead of punishing
them, I executed their wives, daughters, and sons. This brought
them in line, but sowed the seeds of hatred that would eventually
lead to my downfall.
There was a middle-ranking Guild member, from the Artistry
Guild, that took particular grievance to my actions. You all know
his name.
Rayaten Leusa.

Men screamed as they were ripped apart, the others
stumbling and running into things, utterly crippled by the
loss of light.

"What's going on?" Sain called out in a panic.

"It's a black damned Shade, two by the sound of it."

"Oh Light!" Sain said. "I can't see where I'm going."

But Daylen could see, not with his eyes but with his Light
sense. With it Sain was as visible as in day. In fact, as Daylen fully
relied on this power, he could see everyone and even the faint
outline of his surroundings. But there was something else; some-

thing wrong and unnatural. The wrongness had form, and Daylen could see them, like two darker parts in the blackness, and it made him feel sick.

The Shade.

They flew with lethal speed from man to man, slashing and tearing with their vicious claws. The men floundered helplessly.

Most Shade could fly when bathed in the black of night, but hopefully these would be too new to have developed any greater powers.

Daylen ran to a source of light that he could sense through the darkness. This light didn't come from a living creature, but rather one of the sunstones in the many sconces of the cavern.

He entered a small area of light, for the darkness that the Shade cast couldn't extinguish it, only push it back. They weakened the light and restricted it to glowing only a meter or so from its source.

Within the light, Daylen himself was illuminated, as was the ground under his feet, but everything else was bathed in darkness.

Daylen grabbed a sunstone the size of a large marble from the sconce and held it between two gauntleted fingers, Imperious in his other hand.

Grabbing a second sunstone, Daylen ran to Sain, finding him easily in the darkness with his light sense. Daylen gave Sain the second stone. "Get to the ship and grab Ahrek! I need him!"

Sain nodded quickly and moved much easier now, having some light to guide him.

Daylen ran forward and attacked one of the monstrous Shade.

He had fought Shade before—Light, he had fought thousands of them, having survived the Fourth Night—but it had never been easy.

One of the best weapons to fight the Shade was a torch, a sunstone-powered light that looked like a telescope. By focusing and magnifying the light, it could pierce the Shade's unnatural darkness to an extent. If you shone enough intense light on a Shade, they lost all their unnatural powers, like their ability to fly, but not their strength. Of course, Daylen had no torch with him.

Luckily, from how these things moved and attacked, they were both only lesser Shade; but lesser by no means meant weak or harmless. They were still more deadly than any natural thing in existence. A Greater Shade, or the worst, a Lord Shade, would have meant his doom, given how unprepared he was.

Daylen took off his sunforged gauntlet and threw it aside. It wasn't like Imperious and would shatter as soon as the Shade touched it.

Daylen drew in the light from the sunstone he held and bonded it to his speed. As he drew upon the light, the sunstone dimmed greatly.

Daylen charged at the monster.

It noticed him instantly, as they could see perfectly in darkness. It shrieked and flew up, avoiding Daylen's attack.

With his sense, Daylen could make out the Shade's form and see that it had once been a young teenage girl, her dress hanging in tatters. In their early forms, Shade looked mostly like they had in life, except corrupted and foul. Blood was ever seeping from their eyes and mouth, their skin a decaying white, their hair black as night, their teeth jagged, their fingers ending in vicious claws; and, devoid of all life, their eyes were as red as blood.

The Shade dived toward Daylen, its claws ready to rend him apart. Daylen leapt to the side and rolled before rising, only to be struck by the second.

Its claws sank into his shoulders, pulling him into the air with it and trying to rip him in two.

Daylen enhanced his fortitude to resist the Shade's unnatural strength.

The light from Daylen's sunstone enveloped them both, but it wasn't strong enough to nullify the Shade's powers.

It shrieked as it tried to rend him, but Daylen's power kept him in one piece.

The Shade held Daylen's sword arm at bay, but he did manage to raise his left fist and push the small sunstone into the Shade's face. The stone's light alone might not have been bright enough to affect the Shade, but making physical contact was different.

The thing shrieked in pain and they fell.

Daylen directed their fall, forcing the Shade under him, and managed to pull his sword arm back enough to drive Imperious through the monster's gut as they landed.

Shattering glass sounded as Imperious resisted the Shade's touch. *Seven hundred and ninety-one*, Daylen thought in the back of his head.

The Shade screamed and, with one arm, threw him away. Daylen was still bonding light to his body, so the landing didn't break any bones.

Getting to his feet, Daylen's bonds suddenly switched to healing without him causing them to do so. In a few seconds, the deep cuts in his arms from the Shade's claws were healed.

The sunstone felt noticeably smaller than when he had found it. Indeed, when looking at it, Daylen saw that it was half its original size. His powers were consuming it.

The two Shade circled him in the air. It took a lot more than a mere impaling to kill a Shade. Cutting them in half or a proper decapitation would do the job. The problem was that a Shade's flesh was twice as tough as a boar's.

Then suddenly Daylen was surrounded by light.

Ahrek.

"Thank the Light!" Daylen said, sighing in relief. Ahrek was using his powers and light was streaming off of him, though he was only able to illuminate a five-meter radius before the darkness fought back. It was like the shadows were trying to press in on them.

"This is certainly unexpected," Ahrek said.

"Blackheart. He must have thought this was a nice security measure."

"The fool."

"That's what I said."

Ahrek looked up and to his left, possessing the same light sense as Daylen even though their powers were different. "Any more than these?" Ahrek asked.

"Only the two, both lesser, one injured, with no unique powers as far as I can tell."

"Then let us end this quickly," Ahrek said, stretching out his hand, the light emanating from his body being drawn to it. Bright, intense light suddenly shot in a beam from Ahrek's outstretched arm. It pierced the darkness—and though it grew weaker the further away it was from Ahrek, it was still strong enough to strike the nearer Shade, which then fell from the air.

Daylen raced forward while channeling light through each of his bonds to speed, spinning and slicing the thing in two, Imperious chiming its sound of breaking glass. Yes, a Shade's flesh was tough, but for Imperious it was butter.

"Seven hundred and ninety," Daylen said softly.

"I've seen you before," a grating voice whispered softly from the darkness.

"The Shade, it speaks!" Ahrek called out, from where Daylen couldn't see.

"Lesser Shade can't speak, Ahrek! Not for themselves, at least. A Greater Shade is speaking through it, using their hive mind."

"Yes. You know us well," the Shade said. "I remember fighting you."

This wasn't good. Daylen had to kill the thing quickly. "You're remembering my father," Daylen lied. "He fought you the last time you things tried to end the world."

"Oh, but we remember—we remember everything, and we remember *you*. Yes, you say we tried to end the world, yet you have done more in bringing that about than anything we have ever done…Dayless the Conqueror."

"Silence!" Daylen screamed, enraged.

He drew on the light from his sunstone, but he wanted more. He wanted to kill this thing as fast as possible. Pulling on the light, like sucking in as much air as he could, Daylen absorbed the whole stone and his powers suddenly surged. In a blindingly fast motion, literally a fraction of a second, Daylen sped forward and cut the Shade in two.

The chime of breaking glass reverberated through the cavern as light flooded the cave. Daylen managed to think, *Seven hundred and eighty-nine,* but was then quickly distracted by what he had done. Somehow he had absorbed the whole sunstone, which gave him a brief burst of heightened power.

"I was ready to send another beam of light," Ahrek said, "but clearly you didn't need it."

"I, um…I just did something strange."

"I saw. You surged your powers with the sunstone."

"I what?"

"Absorbing a whole sunstone for a large but brief burst of power," Ahrek said, walking to Daylen's side. "It's called surging. I can do it, too, but if we absorb a sunstone that's too big too quickly, it will kill us."

"And you didn't tell me!"

"I'm still waiting to see you use your powers responsibly. You're doing better, but I've yet to see you control yourself when angry.

Breaking Sain's arm didn't help. With that in light, I think it's obvious why I don't tell you how to get more out of your powers."

"Even if it might save my life?"

"I didn't know we would run into the Shade, Daylen. Still, the knowledge you had of your powers is perfectly adequate for anything you need."

"And what if I had been holding a sunstone that happened to be bigger and accidentally killed myself?"

"Very few people figure out surging on their own."

"Well, I'm one of those few."

"Obviously."

"Is there anything else you're not telling me?"

"When I was a teenager, I liked to draw naked women."

Daylen ground his teeth in frustration. "*Ahrek.*"

"It's true. Oh, puberty," he said with a sigh, "a very difficult time."

Daylen glared at him.

"Someone's not in a laughing mood... Okay, you need to be touching the stone to surge from it. A sunstone about the size of a fist is as large as you would want to go. Surging a whole stone of that size will give you a massive burst of power and won't kill you, but you'll feel like a horse kicked you in the chest for the length of a fall. Alternatively, if already in regular light, you can draw on the stone at a slower rate for a small but consistent enhancement on top of your regular powers but that will fatigue your body's channeling ability much quicker. You might find yourself quickly exhausted and unable to channel at all for several hours."

"Anything else?"

"Look, Daylen, I only know so much about lightbinding—specifically those things that overlap with my own powers. Right now, there's nothing else that comes to mind."

"Well, I guess I know now," Daylen said, grabbing his gauntlet from the ground. He walked to a few nearby sconces, where he took their sunstones. This surging thing could be *very* useful.

"You handled yourself admirably," Ahrek said, looking to the dead Shade. "And you were right to call for me."

Daylen was pulling on his gauntlet. "I did what needed to be done."

"You've clearly fought them before."

"Yeah. Even in day, the Shade lurk under any dark rock. A lot of people find themselves against them."

"But few survive."

Daylen looked down on the Shade he had just killed. It was the female one, and indeed she had been a young girl when turned. "Most likely it was Blackheart that turned them," Daylen said. "Locked them away in that dark cave. I bet this one would have grown into a Lust given enough time, and then no weak-willed red-blooded man could have resisted its sexual compulsion, especially not these brainless pirates. Light, Blackheart was a fool."

"More arrogant than foolish, though arrogance can make many intelligent men fools," Ahrek said. "Interesting that the Shade thought you the Conqueror."

"Is it?" Daylen said, preparing to spin some bull. "You picked out that I was the Conqueror's son the first time we met. I look just like him, and my father was my age when he fought the Shade during the Fourth Night. It's an easy mistake, considering."

Ahrek was silent for a few seconds. "Yes, clearly."

"This thing," Daylen said, nodding to the dead monster, "can't have been the captive Blackheart linked to his sword, otherwise it would have shattered when she turned."

"Then we best search this place thoroughly."

CHAPTER THIRTY-ONE

I didn't even know who this Rayaten was at first, for he was still a young man and did his work in the background. He was not even a Guild Master. However, it was his efforts to oppose me through enriching the Guilds and circumventing my policies that earned him the position of Master of the Artistry Guild. If I had known of his actions at that time I would have executed him without hesitation, but he was subtle in all his dealings, as with the other Guild Masters. They had learned to do nothing too conspicuous. I thought I had the Guilds mostly in check, though I couldn't have been further from the truth.

G rab Sain," Daylen said. "He'll know where the captives are held."

"You're not joining me?"

"I'd rather you be the hero, thanks. Anyway, I want to take a look through Blackheart's quarters."

Ahrek nodded and left.

Daylen scanned his surroundings and noticed a very fancy door, like one you would see in a manor house. It was on an upper level of the cave and a walkway had been carved out of the stone leading to it. The timber frame around the polished door was of rough workmanship, as were the structures strewn all around, making for a stark contrast.

"Subtle," Daylen huffed to himself, walking toward the door.

Enhancing his strength and weight, Daylen kicked the door in. The door's lock was so strong that it held firm, causing the door to split in two down the middle as it burst open.

Beyond was a short sunstone-lit tunnel that led to a large room-sized cavity. Once inside, Daylen whistled low and long. The room was filled with the finest comforts money could buy, putting the captain's cabin back on the *Maraven* to shame. A great, opulent bed, gold-trimmed armoires, satin couches, a massive sunstone chandelier, a large window built into what was a natural opening to the outside of the island, a huge open fireplace, patterned rugs lining the floor, shelves and shelves of books, an ivory-key grand piano, gold-and-silver-trimmed chests, a fully stocked liquor cabinet with some of the finest of wines, statues, paintings, and a large cushioned chair behind a chestnut desk.

Daylen looked back to the tunnel, knowing that these things couldn't have fit through it, but then remembered the window. It was four meters in breadth and must have been removable.

Daylen kicked open a nearby chest. It was filled with coins and Daylen guessed the other chests were just as full. All that loot from the skyships Blackheart had robbed and then sold. He really had been raking it in.

Daylen poked through the chests, looking for the golden coins known as crowns, the largest and most valuable coin in the Hamahran currency. Interestingly, the chests only contained the less valuable coins, mostly rupenies, making the total worth of all these chests far lower than it appeared. A few crowns would be worth more. So it seemed that the coins actually worth something were too valuable to be left out in the open, even here.

But why were all these rupenies on display?

"It's a misdirection," Daylen realized out loud. If someone found Blackheart's den while he was away and tried to rob him, they might just think this was all his wealth and not bother to look further. This meant that Blackheart was indeed hiding the larger portion of his wealth, and where his money was would be anything else he truly valued.

Looking about the lavishly furnished room, Daylen knew he didn't want to spend the time ripping it apart.

If only my powers could point out hiding places, Daylen thought, and then paused, realizing something. Maybe they could? His ability to find things was a result of his own natural perception.

Testing, Daylen drew in light and tried to bond it to his perception. He noticed things instantly: like the fact that there were more bottles of Summerside wine in the liquor cabinet than anything else, and that the bed sheets had recently been changed.

Daylen smiled and channeled all four of his bonds which would enhance his perception sixteen times more than his natural ability.

It was incredible. He noticed everything that could be noticed. With the slightest glance at the desk Daylen knew it had four hidden compartments, was made from three separate trees, all oak, and was fifty-two years old counting from the time of its construction. Daylen could deduce the age of the trees that had been used to make the desk and when they had died, where they would have grown, the lacquer used to polish the thing, and knew the number of all the dents and scratches that were on the sides that faced him, twenty of which had been made with a dagger, one with a side sword, and another with a cutlass—and there were still more things that came to his mind with that one piece of furniture. He was noticing just as many things about every other item in the room.

Daylen gasped at all the information flooding him and broke the bonds. It was just too much.

Clearly there's even more ways I can use my powers, Daylen thought.

Interestingly, when the bonds broke, Daylen forgot most of the information that he had in his mind only moments ago. Not too surprising; the natural mind wouldn't be able to remember so much, in fact he had a soft headache now which might have been some type of side effect. That or his poor sleep was finally getting to him. At least he retained the most important things he had noticed.

Daylen walked to an armoire and pulled on it. The whole thing moved forward and opened like a door. It slid easily, as it was built onto a railing that sat in the stone floor—and, once opened, it moved aside to reveal a two-meter-tall steel safe that had been built into the stone behind it. But this wasn't what Daylen was looking for. No, his powers had revealed something else: something ingenious and elaborate that would have taken a long time to set up.

It was a very clever little trick Blackheart had engineered to hide his most valuable things, and Daylen knew he wouldn't have noticed the clues without the help of his powers. Like the rope holding the chandelier: it was actually a painted steel cable. Steel cable was a more recent invention that was only now becoming more industrially used. The pulleys guiding the cable were made to bear massive weights. Daylen might not have noticed the hidden weights in the chandelier, that its frame was made of reinforced steel, or that the cord wrapping around the winch to raise and lower the chandelier was redirected into the stone wall. The railing supporting the armoire was made for something *much* heavier than a cedar cabinet.

The crank attached to the chandelier's cable also functioned as a combination lock. Pulling on it, the crank slid out a little, releasing it from the cogs, but engaged a combination system. Enhancing his hearing and focusing on the crank, Daylen easily noticed each click as he turned it, letting him know he had hit the right pin. With all pins pushed, Daylen reengaged the cogs of the crank and began turning. The chandelier lowered as would be expected, but this time it functioned as a counterweight and the whole safe he had just found was pushed forward, swinging from a large reinforced steel arm out of the wall.

The safe was real enough, but Daylen knew that nothing truly valuable was inside. It functioned as another misdirect, a deception, and as it turned out, a door and bulwark for the real safe.

Blackheart seemed to know that the best way to keep something from others wasn't to barricade it behind steel, but rather to ensure its location was so well hidden that no one would ever find it.

There was no door to this second, real safe, for the first safe *was* the door. Inside was a brightly lit room filled with workshop desks, equipment, shelves, and chests, but what caught Daylen's eye most was the fully equipped sunforge. Daylen had suspected this, since Blackheart had linked his sunforged sword and shield to other people as a perverse kind of leverage. Most sunsmiths insisted on taking the blood needed to forge the links themselves so they could ensure no one was being linked against their will, which meant that it was unlikely Blackheart had gotten a sunsmith to link his captives. No, Blackheart *himself* had been the sunsmith.

The room was lit by large piles of sunstones, which were needed for sunforging.

The side shelves and small chests were filled with loot and valuables, many of which held quate and crown coins. Daylen noticed that just one of these small chests held more money than all those outside.

Daylen walked casually through the room, inspecting everything. He found a medium-sized chest on a desk filled with what looked to be shattered pieces of dull yellow glass—but Daylen knew it wasn't glass. They used to be sunucles, and the shards were dull yellow because they had been common wood before the forging process. The sunucles had either been shattered by darkstone or the people they were linked to had died. Daylen also noticed many larger pieces of sunucle amongst the smaller shards that looked to be intact.

Pulling them out, he found that they were tags, the size of bookmarks, with a hole in the end where a slip of paper had been tied with string. Each piece of paper had a name written on it.

Daylen inspected the tags one by one and found a name he recognized: Sain. This was the leverage Blackheart had over him. It appeared that Blackheart used sunforged linking to blackmail everyone, even his own crew, and all the shattered tags in the chest were a result of the crew Daylen had killed. But ten other tags were still unbroken. Did Blackheart have more crew that weren't here in the den?

Regardless of who they were linked to, no one deserved to be linked against their will.

Daylen took all the tags to the sunforge and began adjusting the circular focusing lenses that were held above by steel levers. It had been over twenty years since he had done this and it brought back many memories. Just like swimming, his skills hadn't waned; in fact, they might have been sharper. He didn't have to pause and fight to recall anything, something he'd had to do with every second thought when he was old. Well, he was still old, he thought, just not physically. The doors to his mind were open, everything there ready to be used. Did being young help him recall information and facts? If so, that would be ironic. The age when a person possessed their greatest mental capacity just happened to be the age when they were the most stupid!

Reverse sunforging was a very delicate process that few

sunsmiths had ever attempted, as failure meant breaking the sunucle and possibly killing the one linked to it. But Daylen was more than a master sunsmith; he had forged Imperious.

With the right lenses affixed, including the most precarious darkstone lenses, Daylen placed a sunstone behind them, the opposite of regular forging. Light began to drain from the first tag and its translucency faded until it looked as black as obsidian. This stage alone required tremendous precision and would have shattered the sunucle if the luminosity was off by a fraction of a degree. Daylen carefully felt for the hidden lid which held Sain's blood and, with tweezers, opened it. Dried blood was within and Daylen carefully dribbled a bit of spit onto it. He then broke up the dried blood with the tweezers and mixed the spittle through. By tainting the blood while the sunucle was lightless, the link would end and the reverse sunforging process would be done.

Tossing the tag aside where it shattered, Daylen repeated the process with the others.

Once finished, Daylen walked to the small chests and filled one of his belt pouches with crowns, which was more money than he would need for a very long time.

He then grabbed every ledger and journal he could find, including anything else that might contain information on Blackheart's operation.

Daylen returned to the main room and sat at the desk.

He opened the hidden compartments in the desk just to see what was inside, and the most valuable thing he found was snuff: finely ground, processed, and aged tobacco, to be sniffed through the nose for a buzz and hit of flavor. It wasn't cheap.

Snuff never really did anything for Daylen, and besides, it was very addictive.

Daylen shut the drawers and began to look through the books. Daylen scanned several and found nothing. He hoped that the information he sought wouldn't be there—but then, to his dismay, he found it.

Footsteps sounded from the passageway. By their pace and weight, it was Ahrek approaching.

Daylen didn't look up as he heard Ahrek enter, not to be rude, but rather because of the heartache he felt from what he had read.

"Light," Ahrek said, "the man certainly had gaudy taste."

Daylen couldn't reply.

"What's wrong?" Ahrek asked with concern and approached the desk.

Daylen held up Blackheart's journal. "Blackheart *was* the Conqueror's son. He mentioned his mother's name, Bethenen, who was a girl the Conqueror had for a time."

Ahrek seemed to have trouble replying. "You could only know that if your father told you of the girls he raped."

"He never saw it like that!" Daylen snapped, but then closed his eyes to calm himself, breathing deeply. "Her name came up when my father was talking about people he missed. Apparently there were a few girls he liked more than the others. Bethenen just so happened to be one of them."

Ahrek nodded, looking barely satisfied, but he didn't push the subject.

Daylen felt revolted at himself. Though he'd had his favorites like Bethenen, they had really meant nothing to him. He had been too blinded by the loss of his wife and children to care about anything, at least not emotionally. It was as if he had lost his soul and humanity after they died, especially after taking his revenge.

But that was no excuse for his actions, he reminded himself harshly, and he deserved to burn in an endless hell because of them.

There was no other way Blackheart could have known of Bethenen, and if there was one, there would be more. *Many, many more.*

The darkness of misery and guilt that Daylen kept locked away, the very darkness that had crippled him for two falls, began to surface again. He had children—potentially hundreds of them.

He shook himself. It wasn't the time to sink into misery, but it was hard to avoid, and he sat in silence for a time waging an internal battle. He almost lost that battle more than once in those dark moments, but eventually he opened his eyes and looked to Ahrek, who had been standing there patiently.

"Did you find the captives?"

"Yes," Ahrek said.

"By your mood I'd say we were lucky and found them both alive."

"Five of them, actually. They're all children of important people."

"The one that was linked to the shield is lucky to be alive. How is she doing?"

"Fine, now that I've healed her, though she was in tremendous pain."

Daylen looked aside. "I'm sorry for delaying things. She wouldn't have suffered for as long had I not been so focused on my own misery."

"You needed the time, and now the girl is safe. They're all very grateful."

"I don't want their gratitude," Daylen said. "Please don't let them know I had anything to do with it."

"As you wish, though I expect they'll figure it out."

"Did you find who Blackheart's sword is linked to?"

"No, that had slipped my mind, though I suspect it's one of the captives. Thank you for reminding me."

"I guess it doesn't matter. There's a full sunforge in the hidden room, so I'll just reverse the sword and undo the link."

Ahrek's reply came after several seconds. "You can *do* that?"

Daylen was too miserable to care about the unlikelihood of an eighteen-year-old snot being a master sunsmith, or to care what Ahrek thought about it. Besides, Daylen wasn't going to let a poor innocent girl live her life in fear thanks to the risk of being linked against her will. "Yes, I'm a sunsmith."

"You might think you are, but only *master* sunsmiths can reverse forge."

"Then I suppose I have luck to thank for the twelve sunucles I just reversed," Daylen said, pointing to the secret room.

"You what?" Ahrek said, walking through the false safe into the hidden room.

"Blackheart linked his entire crew to sunforged tags as extra leverage over them," Daylen called out. "I found Sain's name among them and reversed every one that was left."

"You *are* a master sunsmith!" Ahrek said as he returned, clearly having seen the black, shattered shards of the reversed sunucles.

"If it's any consolation, I can't cook worth a damn or sing a solid note to save my life."

"Actually, it is rather nice to hear that you aren't good at everything."

"Then add making friends, being patient, gardening, and poetry to the list."

"Done."

"Anyway, I'm not as good as my father was at it," Daylen said, the lie coming to him easier now, "but he still taught me a thing or two. He did make Imperious, after all."

"I... I just didn't think you spent that much time with him."

"I told you that he visited my orphanage whenever he could. When I was old enough to leave it, I basically lived with him. My father tried to pass on every skill he knew, so if there was something he was good at, I'm probably good at it too."

Ahrek pressed his lips thin and held a concerned gaze on Daylen, saying nothing.

"You know looking at me like that is just as bad as saying it."

Ahrek sighed. "I know, and in truth your heroic actions have proven you different to the Conqueror, even with your unnatural similarities. You're a better man than he by far."

Daylen huffed. "I'll hold you to that."

"Are you living your life like this to atone for what your father did?"

"No. He could never be forgiven by the Light or those he oppressed...or even myself. But he brought so much darkness to the world I might as well try to remove some of it."

"His sins are not on your head."

Daylen's frown deepened. *Oh, but they are. Every last blackened one.* But nothing could come to his lips as he stared at the Light-bringer, because denying that statement was a lie too perverse, even for him.

Ahrek looked back, his face seeming to weigh Daylen and the concern in his eyes slowly grew. His eyes glanced to his right, and something seeming to dawn on him.

Did he just figure it out?

Ahrek was silent for another second before looking back to Daylen, asking, "Did you discover anything about Blackheart's operation?"

"Yes," Daylen said cautiously, choosing to not pursue whatever the Bringer had just been thinking about. "The group he's been dealing with are the blackened Dawnists," Daylen said with a sneer.

"The Dawnists! What would they want with illegally obtained skyships?"

"They want to bring back the Dawn Empire, but I don't see any logical way they could do that with twenty or so civilian ships."

"They don't seem particularly violent, so refitting the ships for battle in the hopes of some future revolution doesn't make sense."

"And even then," Daylen said as he slowly rocked back and forth in Blackheart's fine desk chair, "refitted civilian skyships wouldn't stand a chance against proper military vessels. So they must want those ships for something else. According to these figures they've been paying full price, so it's no wonder Blackheart had been snatching up every skyship he could find. That also means the ships aren't being resold. There's no profit in it, and considering the money they've been throwing around, they don't need it."

"I didn't think they were so well funded."

"Neither did I. They might have a very wealthy backer, and with their money they could have easily purchased brand new ships legally; the difference is that they would be registered and their every flight logged. So whatever the ships are being used for, it must be illegal." Daylen sighed. "I guess I'll have to pay the Dawnists a visit after we get to the capital."

"How do you know that it's the Dawnists from the capital that have been purchasing the ships?"

Daylen took out a crown from his belt pouch and held it up. "Apart from how clean this coin is and the lack of scratches, the date that it was minted is stamped near the edge. It's not even a season old, and most of the others are exactly like it."

"And that means?"

"While you can find newly minted coins in circulation in the outer cities of Hamahra, so many from the same batch being together means it's very likely that someone withdrew them directly from one of the larger banks in the capital, with the national reserve being so close and all."

"I see," Ahrek mused. "So the money that purchased these ships came from the capital. What exactly are you planning on doing to the Dawnists once there?"

"You know me, Ahrek. I won't do anything to them that they don't deserve."

"That's what I'm afraid of."

CHAPTER THIRTY-TWO

*It was during this time that I set out to conquer the Floating Isles,
and we all know how that ended. Blackened pirates.
There was another reason to all my warring, aside from protecting
my people and unifying the world. The Shade. I had seen their
butchery firsthand. Vile and merciless. It was foolish to simply
wait around for those monsters to grow in strength and cast night
on the land when we could strike at them preemptively. But to
eradicate the Shade once and for all, I would need the collective
strength of every nation on Tellos. That would never happen
through diplomacy. Could you imagine the Lourian Empire ever
being willing to work with Lee'on'ta?
So yes, some might say I conquered for power and revenge, but
those goals were merely a means to an end—that of eradicating
the Shade.
But the ends never justify the means.*

T he *Maraven* flew over the farms and fields that blanketed the
land around them like a patchwork quilt. It was the middle
of High Fall and Daylen had been flying the ship for eight hours
straight, having risen early.

Ahead in the distance, the fields were broken by a speckling of
small towns which grew larger and closer together until finally

forming the broad and mighty metropolis that was Highdawn. The city dominated the view ahead.

Highdawn was an edge city and thus the land before them simply ended, falling off into the endless sky.

As they were flying northward, the Plummet was falling slowly off to the left in the distance. The blindingly bright orb that was the sun sat to their right, high in the sky.

Floating above the countless buildings of the ground-level city was a flat disk, like an enormous dinner plate several kilometers in diameter, which was completely covered in buildings. Above this disk were three others, each one smaller than the one below, crammed atop with buildings too, the top disk bearing the two largest and most impressive structures of all: the Senate, once called the Dawn Palace, Daylen's former residence, and behind it the Great Lumatorium.

The disks sat off center from each other, their sun-facing sides in line, and because each lower disk was bigger, their southern side extended farther out from the one above.

A great ramp-like road built of marble rose from the ground to each disk in a straight line, its design fashioned after the aqueduct structures of old. It was called the High Road.

Highdawn wasn't the only city in the world built on islands that floated near the ground, but it was the only one with islands as flat as disks that were so perfectly arranged. The disks were created with the Lumatorium.

Most of the rescued girls stood along the sides of the ship, leaning out to look at the city ahead. They seemed very excited, and happier than Daylen had seen them in falls. Maybe they would be able to return to normal lives.

There was a sharp briskness to the air that fall, and the girls were all wearing warm coats which Ahrek had found in store on the ship. Ahrek was now talking to each girl in turn, writing down the names of their families and home addresses so that the information could be handed over to the authorities when they landed.

The soft, high-pitched hum of wind whistled in Daylen's ears as he piloted the ship. Daylen loved that noise, for it meant that he was truly flying, not just gliding or floating, but *flying*. It made him feel free.

Daylen looked to his left. Clouds floated low that fall over an endless landscape under the blue sky, the faint outline of the continent high above. It seemed so calm, though Daylen knew the truth of it. That beautiful hum told of strong wind currents beyond the calm air pocket over the deck, created by the ship's windshield.

They were flying at two hundred kilometers an hour, not the *Maraven's* top speed due to her towing the *Bloodrunner*, but still far beyond anything that could be achieved on the ground.

Sain climbed the stairs to the helm and joined Daylen's side. "Wow," he said, looking at the city.

"Yep," Daylen replied, "there's no greater city in the world." And one of the reasons for that was Daylen himself. Once named Sunview, he had made it his capital after the First Revolution. He was born in that city, he had fought and bled in that city. Once making it his capital, he had made it truly grand. Still, it was hard to look upon Highdawn without being overwhelmed by guilt, for it was in that city where he had committed, or ordered, his greatest crimes. He would love and despise it forever.

"What's that dome over the city?" Sain asked.

"It's a net of darkstone anchors fixed in position around the city to prevent unwanted skyships from entering the city's airspace. Usually a shield net's anchors are spaced two meters apart, but Highdawn's are spaced one meter apart, and it has five layers. That's essentially five shields in one that are each twice as strong as normal. It took years to put them all in place, and is why this shield is so visible at such a distance."

"So how do we enter?"

"There're openings in the shield, specifically at the registry stations."

"Wow," Sain said. "They're the perfect defense against skyships."

"Yep. Shield nets are remarkably effective…except against annihilators."

"I've heard of those. They're the biggest skyships ever made, aren't they?"

"It took a genius to design them in a way that they could still be maneuverable. An annihilator can punch through a regular shield net, but not Highdawn's."

"You really know a lot about this stuff."

"Oh, I know a lot of stuff," Daylen said and pointed. "Do you see that large building on the Fourth Isle?"

"The Fourth Isle?"

"Highdawn is divided into five parts. The Ground City, the

First Isle, the Second Isle, and so on. So do you see the large building on the Fourth Isle?"

Sain squinted. "Yeah, what is it?"

"The Lumatorium, the grandest building in existence. The thing defies physical laws. There are even doors on one end that open to rooms on the other side of the structure."

"Wow," Sain said in true awe.

The kid was far more amicable now than he had been a few falls before. Apparently teaching him how to pilot a skyship was enough to win the boy over—oh, and freeing both him and his mother from the sunforged tags Blackheart had linked to them.

Sain seemed truly grateful to Daylen for that and had opened up along the flight, and had told him of how he had ended up in Blackheart's crew. The kid had tried to steal from Blackheart, but had been caught. His punishment was to be a lifelong sentence in Blackheart's crew, his life in the bastard's hands through the forced sunforged link. Sain said he would have run away and let the bastard kill him if not for the threat to his mother, who had also been forcibly linked and became Blackheart's favorite whore when he dropped anchor in Raidaway, her face rarely free from bruises and cuts ever since.

It was a sad tale, but remarkably Sain had grown strong and resilient from it. Through it all he had never broken. Daylen was right about the kid; he certainly had some balls.

"Do you think we'll get to see it?" Sain asked, referring to the Lumatorium.

"You don't need my permission; I'm not your keeper."

"No, I'm your prisoner."

"Not after we dock."

Sain didn't reply and Daylen turned his head to see frustration on Sain's face.

"I thought you'd be jumping for joy."

"It's not that."

Daylen looked back to the city and thought about what Sain meant. "Yeah, it can be hard to find your way in the world, but you'll figure it out. The truth is you're a resourceful kid and could do well in life if you make the right decisions."

"Don't call me a kid," he said scathingly. "We're the same age."

"Trust me, you're a kid."

Silence hung for a moment before Sain said anything. "I want to come with you."

"No, you don't."

"Yes, I do."

"Kid, if you knew who I really was, you would want to get as far away from me as possible, if you didn't want to kill me first."

Sain seemed to be studying Daylen. "Who are you?"

"I can't tell you, but if you stay with me, you'd just get in the way. You need to live your own life, Sain."

"What do you expect me to do, get a job in a port or work in some factory? Screw that! Apart from getting stuck with Black-heart, there was one good thing about my life: I was free."

"And you'd think you would be free with me?"

Sain shook his head. "But without you I'll be stuck in High-dawn just like I was stuck in Raidaway."

"Then it's a good thing you'll have a skyship."

"What?"

"Blackheart's ship—it's yours. I'm keeping the *Maraven*, but you can have most of the loot we loaded up from the den. You've picked up how to pilot well enough. Do whatever you want, go wherever you want to go."

"I... But..."

"You're welcome."

"You're really giving me the loot?" the boy asked, his eyes wide.

"A tenth of what's there is more than I'll need for years. The rest is yours."

"But that's enough to buy, like, three mansions."

"More like twelve. I suppose you're going to live a very nice life. Don't be stupid with it, okay? Once we're docked, organize a secure transfer of the money into a bank through the skyport office."

Sain's mouth hung open and he stared into nothing. Eventually he turned and walked from the helm, finding a seat on the long bench that had been built along the siding of the ship. There he sat in stunned silence for a good while.

Daylen smiled to himself.

This must be a dream, Sain thought to himself. *Nothing like this happens to me. How can Daylen give me a whole skyship and a fortune on top of that?*

Sain looked to Daylen at the helm. The man could act like a right bastard, but Sain had come to see what the Bringer had been talking about. Acting like an unfeeling bastard was all show to hide his true feelings from others. Maybe the act was to protect those feelings.

Sain looked down to his hands. Whenever speaking to Daylen or even thinking of him, he couldn't help but see Daylen as older. Like, *way* older. It was the way Daylen acted, the way he spoke and carried himself. Like he had seen everything and knew everything. Nothing could faze him. How in the Light did a person become like that? It was impressive, though Sain would never tell Daylen that, or how much he secretly wanted to be like him.

And now he's made me rich! Nearly all of Blackheart's loot... Blackheart had been boasting that he was close to retiring, that he could live like a king for the rest of his life.

Sain didn't know what he should do with it, apart from going back to get his mother and buying her a nice place, probably in Highdawn. Wow, what was that going to be like? His mum, in Highdawn! Sain laughed. Well, at least she wouldn't have to be a whore anymore.

Someone's shadow moved across his line of sight.

Sain glanced up and saw one of the girls Daylen had saved standing before him. He had noticed her before—she was hard to miss, considering the girl was the most beautiful thing he had ever seen. Deep-blue hair with crimson streaks running through it, a perfect face, and alluring curves. She wore a white dress that was a little worse for wear under a long fur-lined flight jacket.

"Hi. My name is Sharra."

"Ahhh...I'm Sain."

Daylen hadn't let Sain even be close to any of the girls, but that was when he hadn't trusted him. Things were far better between them now.

Sharra took off her coat and sat on the bench next to Sain. "I've been trying to figure out how you fit in with all of this."

"I've been trying to figure that out my whole life."

Sharra smiled at that. *Why did that make her smile?*

"I mean with Daylen and the Lightbringer. The first time I saw you was after we had been rescued. You were tied up and Daylen really didn't seem to like you. But now you seem to be friends."

"I guess maybe we are friends. If what he says is true, then he's done really good by me. Better than I deserve."

"Will you be going with him?"

"No, he doesn't want me around. I don't know what I'll be doing...but I guess I'll have a lot of options. Why do you want to know?"

"It's just that I'm alone, too," Sharra said, shrugging, which caused the shoulder of her dress to fall down over her arm, revealing a slender neck and the sensuous lines that led to her breasts.

Whoa, she just put her hand on my thigh, Sain thought in alarm. It was really close to something that was reacting the only way it knew how.

"Could you follow me?" Sharra said with a smile, nodding to the cabin door. "I'd like to show you something."

"Ahhh...sure," Sain said, feeling too stunned to process anything.

Sharra stood and walked to the door, looking back over her bare shoulder at Sain and smiling sheepishly.

Sain followed, wondering what under the Light this beautiful girl could want from him. Whatever it was, he was keen to find out.

Daylen was guiding the ship to line up with a few other skyships toward a registry station at the border of the city's shield. Before them were four small fancy structures that had been built atop darkstone foundations and were floating in place as solidly as if they were on the ground. Spaced out from one another by generous distances, the stations had been placed at the side of openings in the city's shield. The left sides of the buildings had long hallways extending out with box-like rooms on their ends. The small square rooms—supported by darkstone, of course— were called tollbooths. They were made to stretch out to skyship decks where they could receive the entry tax.

The registry station to which Daylen was aligning the *Maraven* had a much smaller and age-worn skyship called a dory docked next to it. Clearly that was how the tollman had gotten to the station in the first place.

Ahrek climbed the stairs to the main helm where he joined Daylen's side.

"It feels as though we're about to complete a grand adventure," Ahrek said.

"If that's how you want to see it."

"How do you see it?"

"That we're not done. We still need to figure out what the Dawnists are up to and stop whatever they're planning. After that, I'm thinking to end the sex trafficking trade that exists in the city."

"Noble goals, though not small in the least."

"Are you going to be sticking around?"

"Of course. The Light sent me to you for a reason, and if that's to help you stop the criminal activities of the Dawnists as well as the sex trafficking trade, I shall see it done."

"And what if you didn't want to?"

"But I do."

"Would you be picking a fight with the Dawnists if you hadn't met me?"

"Probably not, but I want to do what the Light directs me to."

"And as a result you really don't have any free will."

Ahrek raised an eyebrow.

"Don't get me wrong," Daylen said, "I've learned enough from my own mistakes to know that I need to do what the Light wants, but that doesn't mean I don't resent it for that. Sometimes I just want to tell the Light to bugger off."

Ahrek stifled a concerned groan at Daylen's blasphemy. "But you've clearly learned that it's always better for you in the long run to obey."

"Yeah," Daylen said with a sneer.

"And in relation to your first point, nothing is *forcing* me to obey the Light. I choose to obey."

"No, you're coerced to obey because of the implied consequences."

"Really? Would I be struck down by the Light if I left and never saw you again?"

"No, but you would be punished eventually. Trust me, when the Light calls a man to answer for his crimes, it makes him pay in *every* degree."

"I agree, but justice is most often held in store for the afterlife. If the Light punished men for their every crime and directly rewarded them for their good deeds the moment after they were done, no man would ever sin. And where would free will be then? That, Daylen, is true coercion, and we must realize that in life evil men will often get away with being evil and good men will still suffer. Yet every one of man's actions is seen by the Light, and they'll be held accountable for them once they are dead."

"Yeah, I know all that. My point is that, even knowing that...it still bothers me. I still find it hard to swallow my pride and heed the Light, and you're just annoying as *anything* for how easy you make it look."

"I never said I found it easy."

"No, but you show it."

"Daylen," Ahrek said with a heavy sigh, "I honestly wish I'd never become a Lightbringer."

Daylen's eyes went wide. "What?"

Suddenly, Daylen saw that the man was struggling with some clearly powerful emotions as he tried to hold back tears. "I only gave up my life to serve others after losing my family... I had nothing left. It was either that or die. Being who I am, doing what I do, has *never* been easy."

Realization hit Daylen with profound significance. Ahrek wasn't an easygoing man of perfect selflessness. Oh, he was selfless of course, but he found life difficult. Maybe even as much as Daylen himself, and he knew why. No man should ever have to suffer the loss of his wife and children.

Daylen lowered his eyes. "You're an amazing man, Ahrek."

"No," Ahrek said, his self-control having returned, "I'm just a man."

They stood in silence as the *Maraven* moved the rest of the way through the queue. Daylen eased the ship under the tollbooth and then brought it up so the tollbooth rested half a meter above deck.

A suited middle-aged man wearing a cravat and tricorne hat sat inside the booth. "Two ships, the second in tow. Are you claiming...?" He trailed off, his mouth opening wide. "Oh, blessed Light, you're *him*!"

Daylen rolled his eyes. "The milkman?"

"N-no," he stuttered. "The one that's been talked about in the papers. The son of the Conqueror, the one who stopped all those crimes in Treremain."

Light, so he *had* been recognized when he was leaping about in Treremain, or else a reporter had figured it out. "You must be mistaking me for someone else," Daylen said.

The tollman pulled out a paper and held up the front page. Daylen's face had been printed on it, a perfect likeness. They must have been working from the countless paintings there were of his older self. The headline read: *A New Hero*.

How could they be regarding him a hero? All he had done was stop a few thieves, rapists, and murderers... Okay, that might have done the job, but he certainly didn't deserve the recognition. It's not like he had risked his life. Any regular soldier was a hundred times the hero he was.

"No, it's you," the tollman insisted, "it has to be. The papers say you've got some new type of power, seeing as you aren't an Archknight or Lightbringer."

Daylen looked to Ahrek, who said, "The secret's out now."

"Not really," Daylen said, relieved that people hadn't figured out he bore the same powers as the knights.

This also raised a significant problem. He had attracted so much attention that somebody must have already dug into his past far enough to find that there were no records of him. Forging new ones that magically appeared after it had been discovered that they didn't exist would just create more suspicion.

"Light damn it all!" Daylen said. He had arrived at the capital too late. He had failed. Now he would just have to see how things turned out. He needed to change his story at the very least. Maybe his father, Dayless, had destroyed the records before they had been sent to the capital, making sure there was no way anyone could trace it back to him and discover who he was.

Daylen turned to the tollman. "Are you going to do your job or not?"

"Oh, of course... The ship in tow. Are you claiming the right of salvage on it?"

"On both ships, actually," Daylen said. "This is the *Maraven*. We bought passage on her from Treremain to Highdawn, but were attacked by pirates. The crew were all killed"—Daylen didn't mention by who—"but the Lightbringer and I were able to defeat the pirates in the end."

The tollman's mouth was hanging open.

"Powers," Daylen said, pointing to the paper resting in the Toll-booth. "In taking the ships and inspecting the cargo on this trader, we found these girls." Daylen pointed to the girls on the foredeck. "They had been locked away and destined to be sold on the sex trafficking market. They've all been kidnapped and need to be returned to their families. They can also bear witness to the crimes of the *Maraven's* crew and our actions in fighting off the pirates. The second ship is the *Bloodrunner*, which belonged to the pirate captain Blackheart. We killed him, too. Oh, and found a few of his captives. The Class-A illegal activities conducted on both ships void all ownership rights. We'll alert the authorities once we find port to sort out all the legalities."

The tollman's face was an image of amazement. "You killed *Captain Blackheart?*"

"I can grab his head, if you'd like?"

"No… That won't be necessary, though you will need to show it to the authorities."

"That's why I kept it."

"You really *are* a hero."

"No, currently I'd say I'm an adequate human being, and then only barely."

"But…"

"The entry tax? We need to get the girls to their families."

"I… Ah, yes. And you said the ship is the *Maraven*. Yes, that makes sense."

"What makes sense?"

"Oh, slip of the mind," the tollman said, chuckling nervously. "It makes sense because the ship *is* the *Maraven*, so you wouldn't exactly call it by another name."

Daylen handed him a leather envelope containing the ship's registration. Daylen had found it in the captain's quarters.

The tollman took it with a shaking hand, and saw that Daylen noticed. He cleared his throat while inspecting the registration.

He was certainly nervous, but Daylen was a bit of a celebrity, it appeared, and he did just claim he had defeated one of the most notorious pirates of the skies while towing proof in the form of the scoundrel's own ship. Perhaps the tollman was just intimidated.

The tollman handed back the registration "Typically the tax

would be two hundred for both ships, but I can understand that you might not have the money on hand."

"Well, we weren't exactly expecting to have claim over two skyships, but I can pay regardless." He took out a crown, handing it over.

The tollman nodded, taking the coin. "Very well," he said, but then he paused briefly. "Um, to save you searching out the authorities once you land, I...uh... I could alert the Border Patrol to escort you in... I mean, you *are* a hero, after all! Towing the *Bloodrunner*, too. This will mean you skip the queue waiting on the port's traffic controllers ahead."

Daylen's brow rose. "Sure, that's very generous of you."

"Oh, it's my pleasure, sir. Just don't mind the siren you'll hear or the patrol vessel that comes in. Do exactly as they say, because the patrol won't know why I've flagged you for an escort. That could mean I suspected you for smuggling illegal goods or have seen you as a threat. You can sort everything out once you land."

"Thanks."

"Good day."

Daylen walked back to the helm, pulling a lever to move the ship on.

Sure enough, soon after leaving the station, an alert sounded.

A patrol ship in the distance responded and flew close.

Daylen waved to it as it flew up beside them, to let them know their escort was expected.

Like all military ships, it had a steel rammer built at its tip with side portholes to launch warheads and any other darkstone-powered projectile.

"They're going to recognize you," Ahrek said, "and I'm sure they're going to have as many questions as the authorities in Treremain did."

"Yeah, I know."

"So whatever you need to do here in the capital should be put off. I suggest you let them take you in, Daylen. Running from them will only create suspicion."

Daylen sighed. If he was lucky, the local authorities might not have looked into his past, or at least not seen the significance of the missing records. The best course of action was to play along for now.

"You're right," Daylen said. "It's time to turn myself in. They won't be able to hold me for long, and once I'm done with them we can get to those other loose ends."

"Meaning the Dawnists and sex traffickers?"

"Yep, and I'm sure our meeting is going to be... *engaging*, to say the least."

CHAPTER THIRTY-THREE

*Through all this time I had been waging constant war. Right after
conquering Daymony, now the Daymon Republic, I declared war
on their neighbors in Delavie, which I justified through the
ancestrally contested lands they had fought over with Daymony
for thousands of years.*

*As a side note, I also found out the Delavian Dukes had sex with
goats. Seriously, goats! The lot of them. They're goat buggers.
They invited me to join in, the sick bastards.*

*Anyway, Frey had a treaty with Hamahra to back each other if
one of us went to war with Delavie. Frey thought my declaration
of war was unjust, however, and pulled out of their treaty. I made
sure to plan something special for those oathbreakers, especially
their young Head Matriarch, Quallandra. You've probably heard
about my affair with her, and the rumors are true, but
Quallandra only consented after I had promised her marriage and
an alliance. She did it for the sake of her kingdom.*

Daylen flew the *Maraven* through the sky buoys with the
patrol ship alongside. The buoys directed all ships entering
the city to the Capital Skyport. The city below had a wide path
walled off that had no buildings or people within. It mirrored their
path. This way if anything accidentally fell from a skyship while it
flew over the city, it wouldn't harm anyone or cause property

damage. This was yet another policy that Daylen had instituted. Skyships hadn't been as prominent in his youth, but he had known their use would just continue to grow, and that provision needed to be prepared in the city's infrastructure.

Ships could obtain permits to fly freely across the city, of course; and the smaller the ship, the fewer the restrictions.

Although dwarfed by the four greater islands above, countless sky sitters and sky islands floated in the air, some on the same level as the *Maraven*. Light, he could look right through the windows of the closer ones.

"Where's that snot disappeared to?" Daylen asked. "I thought Sain would like to see the city up close."

"Maybe he wishes to avoid being seen by the authorities." Ahrek nodded to the patrol ship escorting them. "He is a former pirate, after all."

"Good point," Daylen replied as he adjusted one of the control levers.

It wasn't long before the Capital Skyport came into view, and what a view it was. Essentially, the Capital Skyport was an enormous square, over five hundred meters to each side, framed and pierced by large structures of timber, stone and brick making up the countless warehouses, skyship hangars, and company offices. Each building that bordered the port was at least five stories high with a few skyscrapers among them.

Hundreds of straight broad roads ran into the main square of the skyport with two additional roads stacked above. All were built of stone with darkstone foundations so that they simply sat in the air.

Those roads, called wharfs, had hundreds of triple-stacked piers sticking out on either side like the teeth of a comb. Buildings often stood where the piers met the wharfs, all of them at least three stories high, lining up with the roads.

Daylen had designed the docks to be modular so that they could be added upon as the need arose, which they had. Because skyships could stay in place permanently once they'd locked anchor, most piers had another two built atop, matching the levels of the triple-stacked wharfs. This meant that a skyship could simply dock above another, multiplying the space that could be obtained, and more could be built in the future. Each individual set of docks that was built on top of another was called a stack.

The docks were not equal, however. There was one set of wharfs that had much longer piers sticking out, which were spaced farther apart from one another with a single level stacked atop the first. Daylen recognized that set of wharfs with its larger docks to be the First Harbor, reserved for the larger shipping companies, freighters, and the few cruise ships.

Daylen couldn't help feeling a surge of pride at seeing how one of his works had grown in grandeur over the years he had spent in exile. It appeared that his designs were working perfectly. One more good thing he could leave the world, though he would never be remembered for it. His crimes overshadowed everything else in his life.

Pulling his gaze from the glorious port, Daylen continued to guide the ship through the buoys until coming to the line of ships that waited on the skyport's traffic controller.

The traffic controller was a man who stood on a floating platform and directed the ships coming in to a specific harbor. He would judge each ship according to size and the capacity of the harbors on that specific fall and use flags to convey messages.

Luckily, Daylen only needed to follow the patrol ship and they flew over the line straight on in. The patrol ship guided them to the First Harbor. Special treatment indeed, considering the *Maraven* was a small trader.

A soldier standing on the deck of the patrol ship called out, "Dock One, Stack Twelve, First Wharf."

Daylen frowned, wondering why it should matter which dock they used. Knowing which harbor to dock in was important, but after that any free dock on that specific harbor should have been fine. But then Daylen remembered that there were always a few docks reserved for suspicious arrivals, and the patrol ship didn't know why they had been called in for an escort, of course...except that those reserved docks would not have been in the First Harbor, *especially* the docks so early in the stacks.

"We're expected," Daylen said.

Ahrek glanced at him. "What do you mean?"

Daylen tilted the ship so they could see the dock they were headed toward and pointed. "The stacks usually fill up in order, as the first ones are closer to the port's sides. Easier to unload cargo. Every stack before and after twelve is taken, which means someone's been keeping it clear."

"Yes, I see," Ahrek said. "Our destination would have been logged in Treremain's skyport well before we left."

"Yep," Daylen said. "Apparently the authorities are far more determined to get their hands on me than I thought. I bet there's at least a squad of constables waiting for us."

"Then I suppose it's a good thing you've already decided to turn yourself in."

"Yeah," Daylen said, though he still felt uneasy about all the obvious preparation that had been made for him.

Daylen guided the ship into the lowest dock of the stack.

The stacks in the First Harbor were built to accommodate large freighters, so the Maraven, with the Bloodrunner under it, fit easily within the dock's borders.

The patrol ship locked anchor in the dock above them.

Daylen walked to the left of the helm to glance down at the pier they sided.

Sure enough, there were two squads of constables waiting there. "Time to face the sun," he told himself before walking to Ahrek.

As they made their way to the stairs that led off the helm, Daylen heard the door that led below deck open.

It was Sain. Daylen reached him a second later.

"It's best if you stay out of sight for a while," Daylen said, nodding to the pier they sided. The *Maraven's* main deck sat just a little above the level of the pier, and because they stood on the far side of the ship, they couldn't be seen by those who stood on it. "There's a heap of conners over there who're going to be asking a lot of questions. I think you should avoid any close scrutiny considering your past acquaintances."

Sain nodded anxiously. In fact, the boy looked flushed.

"You all right?" Daylen asked.

"Yeah," Sain said, scratching his green-streaked purple hair, which looked a little more disheveled than normal. "It just...umm, the conners, you know."

"All right, we'll see you in... Well, I don't know how long this is going to take. You better get below."

Sain nodded and closed the door behind him.

Daylen turned to Ahrek. "I trust you'll see to the girls and sort out the salvage claims. I have a feeling I'm going to be occupied."

"I'll see it done and meet you at the constabulary."

"Don't bother waiting around for me—this could take a while. Once you're done here, head to a hotel named the Fallton."

"If you're going to meet me, why at a hotel when there's plenty of rooms on the ship?"

"Which are all cramped except for the captain's," Daylen pointed out. "Besides, the skyport isn't exactly central, and there're too many eyes here. I'll be staying at the Fallton whether you head there or not."

"Very well."

"Try and get one of the penthouses if you could."

"A *penthouse?*" Ahrek said with a raised eyebrow. "I'm not particularly inclined to such extravagance."

"Would you just do it? It'll be much easier to find you in the penthouse if we get separated than it will in the hundreds of other rooms. It's not like we can't afford it."

After a moment, Ahrek replied, "Very well," and followed Daylen as they lowered the gangplank.

As Daylen stepped onto the pier to meet the constables waiting for him, a powerful feminine voice called out from his left. "Daylen Namaran!"

Daylen turned to see two Archknights approach. One was clearly a Tuerasian man like Ahrek, but this one was a born-and-bred prig, as evidenced by his impressive physique and bare chest. The other knight was a beautiful middle-aged woman with dark-green hair that had a strong line of crimson running through a long plait. There was something powerfully familiar about this woman, but Daylen didn't know why. He was also extremely annoyed at himself for not realizing that the Archknights who had been tailing him in Treremain would have followed him here. *I'm such an idiot!*

"You are hereby under arrest for murder, assault, and impersonating an Archknight," the female said harshly.

Ahrek looked to Daylen in disbelief. "You impersonated an Archknight?"

Daylen shrugged, saying embarrassedly, "Eeeh yeah, maybe."

"Why would you do that?"

Daylen rolled his eyes. "*That's* the charge you have an issue with?"

"I know you're innocent of the other charges!"

"Careful, he's a master," one of the conners announced, looking at Daylen's mark.

They all drew their shooters and pointed them at him.

"My actions were justified!" Daylen called out. "It's explained in every blackened paper in the city!"

The female Archknight interrupted, "Small claims trumped in the papers don't clear you, pretender!"

"Hey, I was protecting people!" Daylen growled back.

For some reason, the woman flinched at that, her face looking vulnerable for just an instant, but it was long enough for Daylen to recognize her—and his gut sunk.

"Lyrah…" he said in sorrow.

She hesitated. "H-how do you know me?"

How could Daylen answer *that*? He should have no idea who she is.

Lyrah's expression suddenly hardened. "It doesn't matter. You're under arrest!"

Letting the authorities take him was one thing, for they would eventually let him go or he could escape. But the Archknights could properly detain him against his will, as they had the same powers he had. They'd make sure Daylen would never leave their sight for the rest of his life. Yes, he would join them eventually, but on *his* terms, and when *he* was ready.

"Sorry, not this fall," Daylen said, getting ready to increase his mass and soar away.

He was then struck by lightning.

It had come from the Tuerasian knight—he had stretched out his hand and shot a blackened bolt of lightning at him!

It hit Daylen in the chest and it was like his heart had just been pounded by a hundred industrial hammers. Daylen was knocked backward at least twenty meters down the pier where he crashed, rolling to a stop.

Every bond instantly switched to healing.

"What under the Light do you think you're doing!" Daylen heard Ahrek demand.

"This doesn't concern you, Bringer," Lyrah said.

As the healing neared completion, Daylen began to get to his feet but a hand grabbed the back of his jacket. It was the muscled Tuerasian again, and he was *strong*—but nothing compared to Daylen once he used his powers.

Daylen was about to switch his bonds and give the prig as hard a knock as Daylen had just received, but the Archknight pressed a black marble of some sort to the back of his right hand, which he held with two fingers.

Suddenly, all the light Daylen was drawing in couldn't be channeled into any of his abilities; it was being sucked back out of him and into the marble, he could feel it. Daylen tried, but couldn't channel the light into anything, for as soon as he drew it in that black marble pulled it out. Then Daylen felt heavy; *really* heavy. It came in a wave and he struggled to remain on his hands and knees. Then the weight seemed to double, and Daylen was crushed to the ground, barely able to move.

It was gravity. The gravity on him had been increased.

This Tuerasian, this Archknight, he could do things that Daylen had seen certain other Archknights do in the past, but that Daylen himself couldn't. As he'd suspected, there was a lot more to lightbinding than he knew.

"If you fight more, it will be worse," the knight said in a thick accent, simply holding the marble on Daylen's palm.

Judging by the glove that the Tuerasian wore on the hand that held the marble, it would affect him as much as Daylen if it touched his skin.

Daylen stopped drawing in light, as it was achieving nothing. Interestingly, at the very moment he did this, the stone that the Tuerasian was holding to the back of Daylen's palm pressed down with twice as much force. It hurt!

Thanks to that, Daylen knew exactly what it was. *Darkstone.* Daylen drew in light again to let the stone suck it back out, relieving the pressure. The light it sucked out of Daylen acted on the darkstone exactly the same as regular light, pushing it on that plane. That's why the Tuerasian was holding it on him the way he was, letting as much natural light touch the stone so that it wouldn't lock.

Darkstone nullified lightbinding when touched, apparently. Well now he knew, and because of that he knew exactly how to get away.

Even with the massive gravity crushing him, Daylen managed to slide his left hand along the ground, edging it toward the Tuerasian knight.

"You still fight? You must see that you have lost."

"*I—don't—lose!*" Daylen said, and triggered the darkstone dagger in his gauntlet. It sprung out and stabbed the knight in the side of his foot. Daylen's weight returned to normal as the darkstone nullified the Tuerasian's powers. Daylen snapped the dagger off from his gauntlet, which it was designed to do, and pulled his hand out from under the Tuerasian, who was growling in pain and frustration.

The Tuerasian lifted his foot and reached for the dagger. He shouldn't have been able to do that, as the part of darkstone in his foot was shielded from light... but he was a Lightbinder. The dagger was sucking the light out of him and therefore still had uniform light on all sides, unlocking it in space. The knight would be able to pull the dagger from his foot like it was a normal blade, something that normal people couldn't do. Darkstone weapons were usually very nasty.

Before the Tuerasian could do anything, Daylen sprung up and kneed the knight in the face with enhanced strength. The Tuerasian fell back, flinging up blood from an obviously broken nose. He landed on the ground, knocked out completely.

"Shoot me with lightning, you blackened little prig!" Daylen spat, and the command to shoot was given to the constables,

Several shotspikes pierced him.

Such wounds would kill a normal man, but with Daylen's healing at full they didn't even make him flinch.

Then he was punched in the side of the face.

It was the female Archknight, Lyrah, and *Light*, was she strong! No, more than strong; the bottom side of Daylen's face caved in, bones crushed to powder, and he was knocked a good five meters off his feet. This, too, would have killed him if not for his healing powers, which Daylen suspected the knight knew of, for it had been such a severe blow that it would take a good few seconds for him to recover. It took a lot of force to take down someone who could lightbind, or Daylen's kind of powers at least, for the Tuerasian's brand of lightbinding didn't seem to include healing. The Tuerasian remained still in the ground where he had fallen.

Daylen was very grateful that his healing ability reacted automatically in these cases.

Unfortunately Lyrah had already jumped toward him, her fist back ready for another blow.

Oh, Light, this is going to hurt.

Then she stopped midair, like an invisible force had grabbed her.

"That is enough!" Ahrek's voice called out in fury. He turned to the constables. "Put those away this instant!"

His voice echoed with such authority that the constables lowered their shooters.

Light-blessed light, thank you, Ahrek, Daylen thought as his face healed.

Lyrah struggled against her invisible bonds, her arms and legs kicking out, but her waist remaining perfectly in place. She glared at Ahrek and then slowly drifted down. The moment this happened, Ahrek strained in difficulty.

She's increased her mass, Daylen realized.

Ahrek reached into his robe and the tension in his face left as he pulled out a sunstone, clearing surging from it to increase the strength of his power.

The woman reached for a pouch, but Ahrek flicked his hand and the pouch was ripped from her belt. It hit the ground, spilling sunstone marbles along the dock.

Daylen got to his feet, his face finally having healed. Light, it had hurt.

"What do you want us to do, Lady Archon?" the constable lieutenant asked.

"Leave this to me," Lyrah growled.

Ahrek nodded to Daylen, and he got the message. He was about to jump away when Lyrah stretched out her right hand. Light burst from it in a line, forming a huge yellow sapphire two-handed sunforged warsword that was easily as long as she was tall with a blade as broad as two hands.

Daylen couldn't believe what he had just seen. Was she a Lightbringer as well as a Lightbinder? She had just created a sword out of light!

As astounding as what she had just done was, Daylen couldn't understand why she needed it. She had a regular steel warsword hanging at her side that was just as useless to her, being restrained by Ahrek's power.

She threw the sword at Ahrek, blade first.

Ahrek raised a hand and caught it with his powers, holding the sword in the air between them.

Lyrah smiled and raised her fist before pulling it back through the sunforged link. Her whole body jerked forward and the sword was ripped from Ahrek's hold with a loud cracking sound that split the air. Ahrek screamed in pain, grasping his chest and falling to a knee. Lyrah was released, falling to the ground where she caught the sword as it flew toward her.

Daylen stared at her, wide-eyed. No link could be so strong!

The sword in Lyrah's hand turned into shining light that seemed to flow inside her.

She looked at Daylen and drew her steel sword with a sneer.

Oh, black. Daylen had been so stunned and amazed at seeing what the woman had done to realize that he should have been running. It was too late now.

Lyrah charged and Daylen's frustration at this injustice exploded. He drew Imperious.

"*Fine!* You want to fight? It's your funeral!"

Before Daylen could attack, an invisible force knocked Lyrah's feet out from under her with such power that she spun in the air, and when her body was sideways, another force hammered her down, pummeling her into the pier.

An explosion of debris, rocks, and dust flew out everywhere from the impact.

Daylen was shielding his eyes from the dust, but could still see Ahrek kneeling with a hand pressed on the pier before him. He had recovered quickly from whatever injury Lyrah had inflicted, though he still looked to be in pain and was clutching his chest with his other hand.

"Light's end!" Daylen said to himself. Ahrek could really do some damage with his powers when he wanted to. Did he kill her? The impact was *huge*—in fact, it had far greater power than it should have, unless the knight had increased her mass. If so, it meant that several tons had just been knocked into the dock, and it might also mean that she wasn't incapacitated as increasing mass gave a resistance to injury

Lyrah groaned, and with the dust already clearing Daylen could make out a human shape starting to move from within the small crater.

"Daylen," Ahrek's voice called to him, "go!"

Daylen nodded. Using his powers, he leapt high into the sky and away from the port.

CHAPTER THIRTY-FOUR

The Lourane Empire honored their treaty with me, and they were easily the strongest nation after my own at the time. They were all too happy to use the might of the Dawn Empire to settle their disputes with Lee'on'ta. But the Lourians were growing too powerful, and I had been betrayed too many times by the other nations to let it happen again.

Thus, after I subdued Delavie and Frey, I chose to engage the Lourians on my own terms and turned on them during a large battle in the Great Rift—an act now called the Great Betrayal.

Ahrek struggled to his feet as the dust began to settle.

The constables held their shooters with both hands, looking utterly stunned.

Ahrek could understand their hesitation. Both Archknights and Lightbringers had certain privileges in society, and thus things got very confusing when an Archknight or Lightbringer broke a law, or as was evidently possible, fought each other. What was the legal recourse?

Ahrek's chest ached. Normally it would take a fall to recover from what had happened, his invisible hold having been overpowered. Luckily, he could heal himself. Ahrek did so, and the pain left.

What the female knight had done should have been impossible. Somehow she possessed the miracle of creation. That was the only way she could have created that sunforged sword, wasn't it?

And how did Daylen know this woman's name?

Ahrek stood and walked to her. She was just now getting to her feet, covered in debris and dust but otherwise appearing uninjured, which was incredible considering how much force Ahrek had put into the blow.

She glanced about intently.

"He's gone," Ahrek said.

"You," she hissed. "What have you done?!"

"Assisted a friend, if not saving his life," Ahrek said, walking to the other fallen knight.

The woman's blue eyes shook with rage. "I *wouldn't* have killed him!" she growled.

"You had lost control."

"And you *hadn't*? Bringer, you attacked an *Archknight*."

Ahrek knelt and began healing the other knight, feeling his inner light being drawn upon and channeled through his body. His inner light couldn't be exhausted no matter how much he drew upon it, but his body was limited by how much light he could channel *through* it. It was possible to reach a point where he wouldn't be able to channel at all until he rested.

"I used enough force as was necessary to the task," Ahrek said to the fuming woman.

"And because of that you're guilty of assault and obstruction!"

"Actually, guilt is determined by a trial, which I'll happily attend to explain my actions."

"You honestly think what you've done was *justified*?"

The Tuerasian knight sat up, speaking in his native language. "Argh, I'm so stupid!" It had been a while since Ahrek had heard his parents' tongue spoken aloud. The now-healed knight looked to his companion and asked in Hamahran, "Where?"

"The Bringer knocked me down, and the boy escaped!"

The Tuerasian knight looked to Ahrek, horrified. "Seerium, why?"

Ahrek rose. "Because my friend is guilty of no crime, apart from pretending to be a member of your Order—that I wouldn't put past him. Still, even then, there was no need for the Order's presence."

"With his powers, there's no chance that regular law enforcement could subdue him."

"You would only have to subdue him if he resisted, which he wasn't intending to do until he saw you."

"You think he would have turned himself in if I wasn't here?"

"Well, he seems to know who you are. Do you have some reputation I should be aware of?"

"No more than any other knight. The boy clearly would have resisted regardless of my presence."

"No, we had agreed before disembarking that Daylen would turn himself over to the authorities."

"I don't believe you," the woman said to Ahrek's mild surprise.

What was the name Daylen had called her? Lyrah?

"You think I'm lying?" Ahrek asked.

"No, I think you've been misled."

"About what Daylen would have done? Interesting, because I would assume I know him much better than you."

"Get out of our way, Bringer," Lyrah said, attempting to walk past Ahrek, but he interrupted her. "What's the real reason you're here? As I see it, Daylen is charged with no crime that falls under your jurisdiction."

"It's not what he's done," Lyrah said, leaning in to speak softly, "it's what he *is*. His very existence is a threat to the Order!"

Ahrek whispered back, "You would only think that if you knew Daylen hadn't dedicated his life to fight evil."

Lyrah's face twitched in shock, confirming the truth of Ahrek's statement, but her anger quickly returned.

Her Tuerasian companion stood beside her and looked back and forth between Lyrah and Ahrek with a blank face, but Ahrek was Tuerasian himself, and had grown up understanding his people's subtle body language thanks to his parents. The man was very conflicted. Tuerasian culture held Lightbringers, or Seeriums as they called them, in very high regard, and it was clear the man didn't know whether to side with Ahrek or his companion.

"Ah, and that's the *real* reason you're after him," Ahrek said to the woman. "Your fear for the Order's safety doesn't justify taking away a man's freedom, especially when your fears are unfounded. If Daylen intended to..." Ahrek glanced to the crowd of people around them. Apart from the constables, all the girls aboard the *Maraven* were standing along the railing and watched everything.

Ahrek leaned in and spoke softly as Lyrah had. "If he intended to tell anyone how he received your powers, he would have done so already. I tried to get him to tell me; I'm his only friend, and he won't speak a word of it. And you *know* I can't lie while keeping my powers."

Ahrek raised a finger and shone light from the tip to drive the point home.

"He is the son of...of Dayless the Conqueror!" Lyrah said with venom. "He cannot be trusted."

"Daylen despises the Conqueror, and his relation to that tyrant does more to make him a better man than anything else! He is keenly afraid of making the same mistakes."

"So he thinks he might make the same mistakes?"

"And he guards his actions as a result."

"I don't care," she replied harshly. "His parentage, powers, and knowledge make him far too dangerous to be free. You can't stop us, Bringer."

"No, probably not," Ahrek conceded. "But I will see him freed, as you have no true legal right to detain him."

"Legal right?" Lyrah said, waving a hand to the constables. "He is wanted for several crimes!"

"Yes, and he will turn himself in to the constabulary for those charges. The Archknights have power of arrest, but this is to deliver criminals to the local judicial authority."

"We're empowered to make judgments and carry out sentences too, Bringer. The Archknights protect the world, and your friend stands as a legitimate threat to the Order, making him a danger to the world. I have every right to take him in!"

"No you don't," Ahrek said calmly. "You cannot prove Daylen threatens the Order based on a subjective accusation. You're overstepping your authority here, and I can guarantee you the Senate will be very upset."

"This isn't something we'll drop, regardless of how many senators dislike it," she said distastefully.

"And would the Order be willing to go to war against Hamahra for one boy? To fight and kill the very people they're sworn to protect?"

Lyrah scoffed. "Don't be an idiot. Hamahra would never take the issue so far."

"I'll see that they do, and we both know the Archknights would never go to war for such reasons, unless the Order has truly fallen from its noble purpose." Ahrek shook his head. "No, what'll happen is that the knights will hand over Daylen before going to war, losing a profound amount of respect and influence in this nation."

"You really think you could convince Hamahra to declare *war* on the Archknights? We protect this nation as well as the rest of the world. No nation would attack the very thing that keeps them safe."

"They would if the Order begins to oppress the people they're sworn to protect."

Lyrah seemed to calm a little. "You're right, of course. We would never fight the innocent, but regardless, you're only fear mongering. The boy isn't valuable enough for Hamahra to even think of fighting us."

"He is the only known son of Dayless the Conqueror."

"Fine, we let the senators question him about his father, and then they'll have no reason not to hand him over."

Ahrek leaned in, speaking softly. "That's probably true because they don't know what Daylen does. The knights have done well in hiding the secret. Most people think their powers are directly connected to being an Archknight, in devoting one's life to fighting the Shade. I thought that once, as being a Light*bringer* is directly connected with living one's life in serving others." Ahrek stared at her intently. "But we both know that's not the case, don't we? Anyone can actually become a Lightbinder regardless of how they live or who they are, and the Archknights have no power to stop them apart from hiding the secret. I wonder how valuable Daylen would become if the government knew he could tell them how to make an army of Lightbinders?"

"You wouldn't *dare*," she seethed. "You're a Bringer, and that would throw the world into chaos!"

"And yet if the Arch Order of Light is willing to intimidate and take away the freedom of the very people they are sworn to protect due to its own self-interest, it's not worthy of the power it holds, and I can see we will need another group with equal power to oppose them. If that is a nation's army, then so be it!"

The middle-aged knight bared her teeth at Ahrek. "You're a son of a Shade, you know that?"

"Lyrah!" the Tuerasian knight said reproachfully. "You do not speak to a Seerium this way."

"He's threatening the Order, Cueseg!" she hissed to her companion.

"I know this, but he is also Seerium, and we must give him honor."

Lyrah's fist clenched and she looked like she was about to hit her companion.

"You know I'm right," Ahrek said. "Live up to your Order's true ideals instead of acting out of fear and prejudice. The local authorities will handle the charges against Daylen, and you won't so much as touch him until he chooses to join your ranks. It's the best course of action."

The woman turned and angrily paced back and forth. "Fine!" she said.

Ahrek smiled, truly gratified to see that at least one knight still showed that they were worthy of their powers. Even here, when fearing for their Order's safety she showed that they could live up to their ideals and mandate over their own interests.

"But we'll be accompanying him wherever he goes until he finally chooses to join," Lyrah added after stepping in close. "After all, the best person to ensure that your friend doesn't give away the secret of the Archknights is an Archknight."

"He won't accept that."

"He doesn't have a choice. I trust *your* word when you say he'll turn himself in, but I can't trust *him*. So I need to ensure he does what you say. If he's cleared of all charges as you believe he will be, the Order won't simply take it on faith that he'll eventually join us, that he won't abuse his power in the meantime, or that he might inadvertently or purposefully reveal what he knows."

Ahrek certainly hadn't expected this, yet he couldn't fault the knight's request, for truthfully he would probably have asked the same if the roles had been reversed. "Well, I suppose that is reasonable enough, so long as you don't try to control him."

"Except in the cases where he might do those things I've mentioned."

"If he does, it wouldn't be on purpose."

"But you just admitted there's a chance, which makes our presence all the more necessary."

"Very well, and I'll be there to ensure that you don't abuse your powers or act in any way unjustly toward him."

"Good. We're in agreement."

Ahrek looked away from her and toward where the Conqueror's son had been. "The problem is that I highly doubt Daylen will be."

CHAPTER THIRTY-FIVE

*Due to my betrayal of the Lourian Empire, both Zantium and
Tuerase declared war on me.*
*I had crippled the main Lourian fleet, but needed to call back my
armies to protect the Hamahran border from my new enemies,
which gave Lourane time to recover. The threat of the Dawn
Empire was so great that Lee'on'ta, instead of striking at Lourane
while they were weak—which was my hope—put aside their
centuries-long dispute and made peace, turning their attention
toward me with Tuerase and Zantium at their sides.*
*Lee'on'ta and the Lourians working together: I could barely
believe it.*
*Azbanadar, the Endren Kingdom, the Orden Empire, and the
divided city states of Ma'queh saw they needed to choose a side by
this time, as it was inevitable they would be dragged into the war
eventually. Endra, Orden, and half of Ma'queh sided with my
enemies, who called themselves the Allied Empires. Azbanadar
and the other half of Ma'queh sided with me.*
Thus started the First World War of Tellos.

Daylen sat on the small brick fence that encircled the top
terrace of a high-rise building. The building sat on a darkstone foundation and floated above the Ground City several kilo-

meters away from the skyport. A darkstone elevator led to it in the sky.

Daylen dropped his head into his hands. For an instant, during the fight with the two knights, he had lost control. If not for Ahrek, he would have fought to the death with that Archknight... *Lyrah*.

It was impossible to not recognize her. She had become an *Archknight* of all things. The guilt from the memory was almost unbearable—but even having been face to face with that poor girl once more, Daylen had let his rage overtake him. He had been ready to kill her. Of course, with how strong she was, Daylen might have been the one to die. *Oh, how wonderful that would have been*, Daylen thought bitterly, *to be finally released from this torturous life*.

Daylen growled to himself and stepped off the fence, letting his mind dwell on less emotionally taxing thoughts, like how under the Light the girl had created a sunforged sword.

Lyrah. Guilt surged within Daylen as he saw her in his mind.

Daylen growled again. He didn't have the strength to face that yet, so he tried to focus on what she had done, not who she was.

She had *created* a sunforged sword. Ahrek had said Light-bringers couldn't become Lightbinders, and he couldn't lie, so at least Ahrek honestly believed it.

Daylen remembered what he had sensed during the battle. He could feel the woman using her powers, and there was a familiarity about it. But her companion was different. The light he had drawn in had left his body. Indeed, when Daylen was struck by that bolt of lightning, there was something in it: light. The bolt of lightning had been controlled, or called forth, by light. Daylen had no idea how the Tuerasian knight had done that, but considering that the knight hadn't bonded any light to his body—and in contrast the woman hadn't bonded any light to anything other than her body—meant that there was at least two types of light-binding. Daylen and the woman must share a type, while the Tuerasian was the other.

Still, that didn't answer the question as to how the woman had created a sword from light—if Ahrek was right in that she couldn't be a Lightbringer, then it *must* be an ability from the lightbinding power, and if Daylen's powers were of the same type as hers, then Daylen should be able to do it, too.

Daylen tried to recall what he had sensed as she did it. Such a specific thing was hard to remember. If only his memory were better…

Daylen rolled his eyes, smiling to himself, and channeled light through each of his bonds into his memory.

The clarity was crushing. Everything he had ever done in his entire life was before him in full and awful comprehension; and considering all the horrific sins he had committed, the utterly perfect recollection of every instant within every instant of those sins caused Daylen to *scream* in agony and turmoil.

He let go of the bonds as soon as they had formed and fell to the ground, crying.

He had just relived his entire life in flawless detail, every crime, every mistake. He had seen the face of every person he had ever murdered, every girl he had raped, their tears and cries for mercy, the sorrow of their loved ones, his heartless carelessness for anyone or anything apart from his own power. His memory had returned to normal, but the clarity that had just been inflicted upon him remained. It was the most profound proof of how wretched his life had been: for what could condemn a monster more than reliving his own life?

Daylen wailed in heartbroken agony. To go on living he had forced himself to not think of his past sins. He hadn't forgotten them, he never could, but recalling even a few at a time had over-powered him with guilt. Now, having every sin come before him… No, it was worse than that, for the clarity was so strong and perfect that he had just relived his entire life.

And now, with all that, it was too much.

Daylen cried in unbearable pain and anguish, writhing on the ground as if assaulted by some terrible force. Wherever his mind turned it was confronted with one of his past sins, and he recoiled both mentally and physically, only to be assaulted by another. His back arched and his whole body tensed, his face growing red from the mental anguish. He screamed and screamed.

It was an assault on the mind and the senses too torturous to bear. Daylen could *feel* himself swinging the sword that took off the nine-year-old princess's head, and even worse, he could remember how he had felt about it, how he had felt that it was actually the right thing to do. He remembered his feelings and hatred for the people of Daybreak when he ordered the city's destruction, he remembered watching on with satisfaction as he murdered millions. Some vile, dark part of himself back then had actually enjoyed performing those heinous acts.

His body tensed and writhed even more, reflecting the torment of his mind to the point that blood began to seep through the pores of his skin. And then, in that instant, Daylen's mind snapped, unable to cope—and Daylen Namaran died.

Death has many stages, yet they happen so fast that most people don't realize this. The heart stops and blood is no longer pushed through the body; then, with a lack of oxygenated blood, the brain suffocates and shuts down. Yet even then there are vestiges of life in every cell of a person's body, though many would still call this— the stopping of the heart, the shutting down of the brain—death.

Yet if those cells have an unbidden reflex to draw in light to heal, if enough of them are still alive, and if the light they can draw in is strong enough, death can be prevented from taking over.

Thus Daylen did truly die when his mind snapped under the unbearable load of all his memories, and he would have died completely, for the body cannot live without the mind as the mind cannot live without the body. But his body pulled in light through the four paths that existed within Daylen and were bonded to his mind, healing it. Four healing bonds of light are powerful indeed, and after a few seconds, Daylen's eyes, though already opened, moved with life.

What just happened? Daylen thought, sitting up.

His whole body ached, but the ache was fading. He was healing himself for some reason.

Daylen wiped the sweat from his brow to find it tinged red, like it had been mixed with blood.

Daylen wiped again and, thanks to it being mostly water, it came off easily.

There was something in his mind, something locked away, a memory; yet the very moment Daylen even considered recalling it, fear overwhelmed him. Whatever he did, he couldn't allow himself to remember it. The odd thing was that he knew what it was, as if it were a basic point of academic knowledge, without truly remembering it. It was the knowledge of what had happened: he had bonded light to his memory and accidentally relived his entire life. He knew it without truly thinking of it or recalling anything in regard to how it had felt. The memory was locked away tight, and for good reason; it had almost killed him, hadn't it?

Daylen climbed to his feet. What had he been doing? That's right: trying to figure out how the female Archknight had created a sword from light.

Daylen's light sense had felt what she was doing, and in fact Daylen thought he had sensed something different from the woman when she had summoned the sword, but he couldn't remember... Yes, that was why he had bonded light to his memory in the first place. To try and remember more clearly what the woman had done.

Well now he knew that, for him at least, bonding so much light to his memory could be extremely dangerous, but that didn't mean he wasn't going to try again. Daylen had never claimed that he was incapable of being a reckless idiot.

This time, Daylen started with one bond, focusing specifically on the event he wanted to recall. It became clearer instantly. He could remember finer details, and even what he had felt from his light sense during the fight.

Daylen could tell that he had the capability to remember other things from other times, but he didn't want to remember any other moment apart from the time he was focusing on. With that focus, the memories didn't overwhelm him. Daylen tried two bonds, and the events he was focusing on became clearer while everything else remained safely locked away.

Feeling much more secure, Daylen channeled light though all his bonds to his memory, focusing specifically on that one time, which became vividly clear. He remembered things he hadn't even realized he'd noticed—in fact, it was as if he were walking through that fight as a third-party observer while it played out at a fraction of the speed.

It was amazing.

Daylen focused on his light sense as the woman called forth the sword. The first thing he realized is that he sensed a separate light within the woman; there was her inner light, which shone with pure brightness, revealing how good a person she was, but there were other lights inside there, separate but present. What were they?

Then one of those separated lights moved when the woman stretched out her hand, and it flowed out, forming into her sword. Daylen sensed the action in exactly the same way as he had when the woman had bonded light to one of her abilities, like her strength. It was then that Daylen sensed something different about the bonds she was using with her strength—they were twice as big as his own. He could sense two of them, and the light they could channel was easily twice as much as he could with any one of his own bonds. Her third bond, the one she was using to channel the sword through, was the same size as normal, and then Daylen had realized what he had just thought. The only way he could describe what he was sensing in regard to the sword was that the sword was being channeled *through* the woman's third bond, the exact same way as light was channeled.

Daylen released his memory bonds, which was like stepping out of another world but as soon as he did this his head burst with pain.

"Ouch!" Daylen said stumbling forward and cradling his head. It wasn't the worst headache of his life, but light it had come on suddenly. He quickly channeled to heal himself, the pain subsided but didn't disappear completely.

"That's not good," Daylen said, for never had his powers failed to heal him fully, and why did enhancing his memory give him such a headache in the first place? Yet that wasn't the first time he had gotten a headache after using his powers. His head had hurt after enhancing his perception back in Blackheart's hideout, too.

"But it's also not the time to worry about it," Daylen added as he cast his mind back into the interactive memory he had just walked through.

"How could that sword have been channeled like light?" he asked out loud, and in answer to that, Daylen asked another question. "What had Ahrek said about the miracle of creation?"

He had said that all things were technically light, which was why he could absorb them.

"Well, I can draw in light, and if all things are actually made of light, shouldn't I then be able to draw any object like Ahrek?"

Daylen pulled a coin out and focused on it. Yes, he could sense it—very faintly, barely noticeable in fact—but he *could* sense it. There was light in it.

Daylen tried to draw in the coin as if it were normal light. Nothing happened, and it felt like trying to walk through a solid wall.

It really seemed like Daylen could only channel and bond normal light, whereas Ahrek could channel, just not bond, anything that *was* light, even light that had taken form—or adopted identity, as Ahrek had put it.

Then how had that Archknight done it?

Well for one, she hadn't channeled a normal object. It was a sunucle.

Daylen paused as the difference dawned on him, a difference that should have been obvious: a sunucle was an object that had light bonded to every cell of its structure to the point that it was a solid light object.

That fact struck him a little strange now, for according to Ahrek all things were made from light, and Daylen's light sense seemed to confirm that otherwise he wouldn't be able to sense inanimate objects. So a sunucle was an object which was light, and one that had more light bonded to it—maybe that was why sunforging was possible. So could a Lightbinder who could draw in light draw in sunforged objects?

There was an easy way to find out.

Daylen drew Imperious from its sheath. He could sense the sword as it was linked to him, but now he realized there was something profoundly familiar about that sense. It felt *exactly* the same as the light he could sense anywhere thanks to his light-binding powers; just stronger and focused into a single location, the same as the light within people. But he knew the light he sensed was Imperious, and for some reason he couldn't mistake it for something or someone else.

Holding Imperious, Daylen tried to draw on it in the same way he could draw in normal light. Imperious suddenly lost its form, turning into bright white light that flowed inside him, disappearing.

Daylen stood there, amazed.

He had just drawn Imperious into himself. Indeed, he could feel it inside, a separate something, which seemed to indicate that the sword had not actually *merged* with him, but rather it had only been stored. If it was anything like Ahrek's own ability, Imperious's weight would still be present.

Daylen tried to draw the sword back out—the problem was that he didn't know how. Willing the thing to leave him did nothing. He stretched out his hand and tried to draw on the light inside that was Imperious. Nothing.

Then Daylen realized that he was still thinking of Imperious as light that he needed to draw in, but it was already within him. What did he do with light already drawn in? He channeled it into an ability. Okay, so what would happen if he channeled it into his hand? Daylen did this and light suddenly shone from his hand, forming into Imperious's shape before fully materializing.

This was how the female Archknight did it. She didn't have any light*bringing* powers—she couldn't create or absorb inanimate objects—it was simply an extension of lightbinding, a remarkable and extremely useful extension at that.

Daylen turned over the sword in his hand. When he had been Emperor and had just ordered the destruction of Daybreak, one of his worst atrocities, the Archknight that was his advisor had attacked him upon seeing that Daylen was set on committing such a terrible act of genocide. Daylen recalled that the knight had been unarmed one moment, but when Daylen looked again he'd had a sunforged sword in his hand.

This was how that knight had hidden his sword: Lightbinders could absorb and store sunucles within themselves!

Still, this didn't answer every question Daylen had. The female Archknight had pulled on her sword through the natural link with *far* more strength then she should have been able to do.

Daylen hefted the sword in his hand, its weight being far lower than a regular sword, and felt the link. It was prominent, and he tugged on it, feeling the sword pull back in his grip.

Daylen walked to the back of the terrace where another level of the building loomed over him—a penthouse by the look of it. Daylen threw Imperious over the lip of the roof and then pulled on the link. He heard Imperious drag a little forward before hitting the small brick barrier at the lip. Daylen felt himself get tugged up but with nowhere near enough force to lift his weight. Sunforged links only ever had enough strength to pull on the sunucles themselves, and only if one was close enough.

Daylen tried to pull harder, but nothing changed. He lay on the ground and pulled. His chest rose a little, as if an invisible rope were pulling on him, but there was still nowhere near enough strength to lift him off the ground, let alone overpower Ahrek's invisible force—which had been enough to pick up full grown men and throw them about like ragdolls.

Well, this appeared to be the extent of his link in its normal state, but that woman wasn't a normal person, and neither was Daylen.

"The question now," Daylen said, "is can I bond light to my link with Imperious?"

Daylen tried. Light seemed to flow into the link. Daylen's awareness of the sword became *far* stronger; in fact, he could feel the roof. Not the ground where he lay, but rather the roof where Imperious was. He could feel the breeze and hear the wind that hummed over the building. It was like he had another set of ears that picked up noises from his sword's location. Daylen channeled his other bonds to the link and it became even clearer. In fact, a double image appeared in his vision. Daylen closed his eyes and found that the image was a view from the perspective of Imperious itself—like a second set of eyes that sat inside the blade. He was able to gaze out from his sword and even turn his view to look in other directions.

"Incredible," Daylen said. He was constantly finding new possibilities for his powers. Channeling light to a linked sunucle meant one could see and hear out of it at a distance!

Then Daylen gently pulled on the link, and he rose a little off the ground. He swung as if tied by a rope to the closed door of the penthouse.

Lowering himself, Daylen stood and stepped away from the penthouse to yank on the link. His whole body shot up into the air, and Daylen crashed into the lip of the penthouse's brick roof chest first—Daylen's ribs shattered. Gasping in pain, he fell back down to the terrace, his head cracking on the tiled patio, knocking him out.

Daylen regained consciousness as his powers healed him. "This is becoming a habit."

He rolled onto his back. "Looks like I need a bit of practice with that one," Daylen added before getting to his feet.

Stepping away from the penthouse, Daylen channeled two bonds to the link, one to his reflexes and another to his strength.

He yanked on the link, which again pulled him into the air with half the force as before—yet it was still very fast.

With his agility enhanced, he easily raised his hands to grab the lip of the roof, his enhanced strength absorbing the impact, and he let the momentum carry him over, where he flipped in the air, pulling Imperious up into his hand and landing on his feet feeling rather happy with himself.

Daylen was about to sheath Imperious, but then smiling to himself he absorbed it instead and walked with a skip to the side of the building. No wonder the knights hid this little trick.

Daylen leapt from the building to go and buy another sword, a fine steel one. Daylen did have an empty sheath at his side, after all, and it was always good to keep one's options open.

CHAPTER THIRTY-SIX

The disorganized city states of Ma'queh didn't bring me much value—they simply fought the other Ma'qains, as they have been doing for centuries.
Azbanadar, on the other hand, brought a mighty army.
For my part, I had the combined strength of the old kingdoms of Sunsen, Lumas, and Daymark, as well as the larger nations of Jentry, Daymon, Delavie, Mayn, and Frey. The Dawn Empire had grown mighty indeed, but to wage war on six fronts against Zantium, Tuerase, Lee'on'ta, Toulsen, Orden, and Lourane, I needed all the resources my people could produce. I believed that it was for them and their safety, not realizing that I was constantly sending their sons to die in my battles, squeezing them for every drop of productivity and coin I could get.
The fighting went on for many years, though I made sure to take Tuerase as fast as possible, attacking them from Azbanadar—which provided the perfect staging platform.

Daylen soared through the air. His mass-manipulated jumps were so great that they felt like flying.

Instead of reducing his mass, which wrought havoc on his velocity, Daylen found that he could land much easier by increasing his strength. Sometimes he would land on the side of a building and enhance his grip, which let him stick to it as if he were covered in glue.

Daylen leapt again, arcing through the sky, his gauntleted left hand holding his new backsword to prevent it flailing too much at his side.

He had guessed it would take a while for Ahrek to sort things out at the docks, so Daylen had taken his time looking for a new sword. The one he had now was a fine spring-steel backsword with a broad blade, a different sword type from Imperious, for steel functioned very differently to sunucles. Daylen was a traditionalist and felt swords should be carried in case of Night; the dueling culture was just a byproduct, not the reason. Thus the backsword he purchased could easily cut a Shade in two, as all swords should.

After purchasing his sword Daylen had done a little searching and found a darkstone vendor to replace the dagger in his gauntlet. It was quite the revelation that darkstone could nullify lightbinding, and having that dagger had just gotten him out of a very sticky situation.

Daylen had never even heard rumor that the knights bore such a fatal weakness, even from the spies he had sent to infiltrate them. Just another secret the knights kept—and for obvious reason. Had he known this when he had been in power... Light, he could have defeated them easily. If he'd just tipped shotspikes with darkstone, he would have reigned night down on them. It was a troubling thought. The knights weren't nearly as invincible as they acted, which wasn't good. The world truly needed them, especially because of the Shade.

Daylen would keep their secret, but that didn't mean he couldn't use this secret to his advantage.

After replacing the dagger Daylen had stopped for dinner, all the while wondering how Ahrek would deal with those Archknights. *Oh boy, would that have been a sight!*

Now he was making his way to the hotel where had had planned to meet Ahrek. He landed on the Fallton's penthouse patio. Instantly, he sensed a bright inner light from within the next penthouse over. That light had to be Ahrek's, Daylen knew, as there were very few people as bright as he. Jumping to the next terrace over, Daylen saw that this penthouse was much larger than the others; indeed, this must have been the Imperial Suite.

Daylen wondered why Ahrek, who was so reluctant to even rent a penthouse, would purchase the most expensive room among them.

Then Daylen sensed the two other inner lights inside.

Ahrek wasn't alone.

Hotel attendants? Maybe some constables waiting for him?

Or it could be the last two people Daylen wanted to see?

Daylen walked across the terrace and opened the double glass doors that led to the Penthouse's sitting room.

The two Archknights stood inside with Ahrek, who was relaxing on a coach and drawing away in his sketchbook.

Daylen's eyes were instantly drawn toward Lyrah, and seeing her brought a sharp stab of pain and guilt which quickly turned to caution. These two knights *had* just attacked him half a fall earlier.

"They're not here to fight," Ahrek said, clearly noticing Daylen's defensive posture.

Daylen glanced to Ahrek and then looked back to the knights distrustfully.

"He can't lie, remember?" Lyrah said.

"Then why are you here?" Daylen asked accusingly.

"We've come to an arrangement."

"Funny how I'm clearly not included in the *we*, even though I'm the one the arrangement must be about."

"The arrangement will require your acceptance too, Daylen," Ahrek said, "but I do believe it's the best option."

Daylen glared at the Archknights. "All right, let's hear it."

"Lightbringer Ahrek has convinced us to not take you into Archknight custody," Lyrah said, "though you *will* turn yourself over to the constabulary to face the charges against you. If you're found guilty, I'll see that your sentence be carried out. If you're innocent, we will remain with you to see that you don't abuse your powers or give away any secrets until the time comes that you keep your word and join our ranks."

"This is the only peaceful possibility," Ahrek said, answering Daylen's frustrated expression.

"No, another possibility is that you knights could go and shove all this up your..." Daylen's heated words died in his mouth the instant he looked back to Lyrah's face. Guilt and heartache came upon him instead.

"Archon Lyrah has already spoken to her superiors, and they've agreed," Ahrek added.

Lyrah's face flashed with deep displeasure at that comment, but her very presence was recalling such terrible guilt within Daylen that he had barely noticed.

In fact, it was hard to think anything at all, standing face to face with one of the young girls that had been forced into his bed more than twenty years ago. One of the young girls he had raped...again and again.

The more he looked at her, the worse his guilt grew.

Daylen tried to fake composure. "Fine, I suppose we're going to have to get...to get used to each other. Nice to meet you," Daylen added as he turned abruptly and walked to one of the rooms. He closed the double door behind him and leaned on it, slowly losing the strength in his legs, sliding to the floor.

There he remained as the pain of past memories grew to consume him, his eyes seeing only those things in his mind—and there they found nothing but torment.

———

Ahrek kept looking at the double doors that Daylen had closed. "Hmm... I thought he would have kicked up a bigger fuss than that."

"Yet he did not look happy, not at all," Ahrek's Tuerasian kins-man, Cueseg, replied.

"Good," Lyrah said. "It's only fitting that he hates this situation as much as we do."

Ahrek frowned. "There's no need to be petty."

"Petty?" Lyrah spat. "You've strong-armed this whole situation, Bringer! Who's being petty here?"

"And now we're companions, so we'd best find a way to get along."

"It can be hard to get along with this one," Cueseg said, nodding to Lyrah. "But she is good."

"Oh, great way to show loyalty, Cueseg!"

"I do not find this as bad as you. My Seerium brother is right that we cannot arrest the boy. It is not justice. Now the boy knows we will follow him until he joins the Order and he is not fighting us."

"But babysitting isn't what we should be doing. We should be hunting out the blackened Shade!"

Ahrek cleared his throat. "Surely a woman who bears such a sacred duty would use more civil language."

"This is what I say to her," Cueseg chimed in.

Lyrah rubbed her forehead. "Yes, I know, *thank you!*"

"It is you who said we will follow the boy," Cueseg said to Lyrah, "and now you say you do not want to? Is he a danger to the Order, or is he not?"

"Of course he's a danger," Lyrah said.

Ahrek chose that time to interject. "I think you'll see differently as you get to know him."

"Argh! This whole situation stinks," Lyrah said. "I need sleep. Cueseg, keep an eye on the brat and make sure he doesn't sneak off without us. Wake me by mid Low."

Lyrah walked to another bedroom and shut the doors behind her.

Ahrek looked to his Tuerasian brother and asked in their native tongue, "Would you like some company?"

Cueseg looked at him with a blank face. "Seerium, you wish to be in my presence?" The Archknight's Tuerasian speech was of the formal prestigious accent. Clear and perfectly spoken.

"Of course," Ahrek said. "It's been a while since I've been able to spend time with anyone from Tuerase."

"It's my responsibility to explain to you," Cueseg said, "as you're obviously more Hamahran than Tuerasian, that I am a lowsum and shunned by our people, but as a knight you must also show me respect."

"I know what your mark is; my parents were full Tuerasian, after all. But I grew up in Hamahra and I couldn't care less."

Cueseg's face barely changed, but from his experience with his father Ahrek knew that Cueseg was pleased. Cueseg also seemed to relax and took a seat on one of the couches. "I can't express how good it is to speak in our language. Whenever I speak in Hamahran I feel like a dribbling idiot barely able to make myself understood."

"Oh, you do fine," Ahrek said, creating some plates of sticky bread on the low table in front of the couch. "Please, help yourself."

Cueseg looked at it with a blank face, but the tone of his voice conveyed distrust. "I've never seen a dish like this."

"Then you're in for a treat."

Cueseg sighed. "I don't think so. It's clearly Hamahran, and the food of this land is horrible."

Ahrek smiled in reply but didn't say anything.

Cueseg sighed and took a piece of sticky bread. After chewing a little, his eyes brightened. "Seerium! This is actually *good*."

"That appears to be more of a miracle than the fact I created it out of light."

"But it is!"

Ahrek laughed. "You must have been starved of fine food for some time."

"Yes!" Cueseg exclaimed. "Everything I've purchased in this land is either too bland, lacking any spice, or so overpowered that it's as if the ingredients are at war." He held up the sticky bread. "This has been the first truly good thing I've eaten since coming here."

"Where has your food come from?"

"From the vendors, of course, and the regular meals from the Hold."

"Ah, *that's* why."

"What, have I been doing something wrong?"

"Unlike Tuerase, anyone allowed to publicly sell food in Hamahra doesn't have to undergo formal training or meet a certain standard apart from the health and safety laws."

"Yes, I've learned that."

"Instead, the master chefs work in places called restaurants. They're like a formal supply store that sells cooked meals. It's there that you'll find the true heights of Hamahran cuisine."

"So, Hamahran restaurants are like Tuerasian street vendors?"

"In terms of quality, yes."

"Oh…"

"Your companion would have told you as much."

"You have no idea how hard it is to communicate with that woman."

"You don't get along?"

"No," the Tuerasian replied stridently. "I like her very much. She is a strong woman, has a kind heart, and wishes to help anyone in need. But whenever I try and help her overcome her weaknesses, all I do is manage to offend. She has such amazing strength that she hasn't embraced, having given in to her fears too easily.

The Tuerasian way would help her greatly, for she *needs* to master herself. I tried this when we first met…"

"Oh dear, you weren't naked, were you?"

"Of course I was. She, more than *anyone* I've met, needs to confront the weaknesses of her flesh and learn to master them."

"Hamahrans view the body *very* differently."

"So I've learned, as backward as it is. By hiding their nakedness they make it taboo to one another, making their bodies like hidden prizes that must be earned. And because they rarely ever see a naked body, when they do, their own bodies take control. Do you know how much *rape* is in this land? Because the body is held as a prize, those who cannot earn it choose to take it by force. It's horrendous!"

"I wonder if the lower rate of sexual assault in Tuerase is more due to the penalty rather than cultural differences of modesty."

"The penalty is as bad here."

"Many men would rather die than publicly lose their manhood," Ahrek pointed out. "And there are other regretful cultural practices here in Hamahra that might inflate the difference."

"Such as?"

"Social shame. Women who've been sexually assaulted here can, unfortunately, be seen as 'damaged goods.' Because of this, there're many cases where women choose not to report the crime."

"*What?*" Cueseg said in disbelief.

"I know, it's horrible."

"It's *unforgivable!*"

"Every land has unfortunate elements within their culture," Ahrek said, pointing to his forehead and giving Cueseg a knowing look.

Cueseg sniffed.

"What was your profession?" Ahrek asked at length.

"I was a chef."

"Ah, that explains it."

Cueseg nodded. "My standards are very high… I haven't had the opportunity to cook in so long. But that was my choice. I am an Archknight now. Not that anyone would ever accept food from a lowsum."

"Hamahrans don't care about that."

"Then they don't know my shame."

"I'd happily eat anything you made," Ahrek said. "In fact, judging by Tuerasian standards, if you really were a qualified chef, I would be delighted."

Cueseg's brow rose.

"There's a kitchen right here. I would love to taste some genuine food from our homeland; it has been quite a while."

For the first time since Ahrek had met this serious man, he smiled—and it was a true, genuine smile. "I would be honored, Seerium."

Daylen hadn't moved a fraction from where he had slumped against the door, his body frozen as his mind drowned in misery.

He kept drifting in and out of troubled sleep, but now his internal body clock was telling him a new fall had dawned.

Daylen still didn't move.

He couldn't face her again; he was simply unable to bear the guilt and pain. He was such a coward. But she wasn't going anywhere. What was Daylen going to do?

Truly, the Light hated him. It wasn't enough to lengthen his torturous life; now Daylen had to face what was likely the most terrible and significant reminder of his crimes, one of his past victims. And not just any victim, but one of the most innocent and vulnerable souls that he had ever violated.

Lyrah hadn't changed much, yet at the same time she seemed like a different person. She carried herself with such strength. *Light*, she was more than just strong, she was an Archknight! Yet still her face, though aged, was exactly the same as that of the poor frightened young girl that Daylen had taken such pleasure in abusing.

Lyrah had been one of the youngest at fourteen years old. Hard to believe that back then he'd thought he had standards, fourteen years being the legal age of marriage and consent during the Dawn Empire. Dayless the Conqueror made sure that no girl he took was under that age, like that made what he had done any better.

Daylen remembered how he had convinced himself that each girl he took had come willingly, though deep in the back of his mind he really knew the truth, he just didn't ever admit it to himself—not until much later, at least. In fact, any honest man would have found the truth impossible to miss, for it was in the fearful eyes of each girl, Lyrah far from the least among them. She had been so innocent, so scared.

In his later years Daylen didn't even let the girls wear clothes for the length of time they stayed in the palace, dressing them up like Tuerasian women. Just another type of humiliation and abuse he had inflicted on them.

"I've been such a Light-cursed monster!" Daylen said to himself, recoiling from the memory, which seemed clearer and more vivid than ever before.

He couldn't help but recoil, as any sane and good person would, when thinking of such a perverted and foul a thing as raping a frightened fourteen-year-old girl. The problem was that Daylen couldn't recoil away from *himself*, as much as he might try, for wherever he turned he would find another vile perversion he had committed which only compounded his guilt.

Daylen moved a shaking hand in front of his face. Though young and strong, they were still the hands that had committed the crimes. How could he have done such acts? How could any man do such evil? Yet he had.

And now he was being punished for those crimes, and he deserved every bit of misery and torment that tortured him, including this new one, a constant reminder of his past sins.

It was true that Daylen was unable to bear the full force of his guilt and self-hatred; he had been crushed by just a fraction of it that low fall. But even so, there eventually came a point where Daylen found that he could move again. He could bear it and keep on going, as the only other option was to lay down and die. Perhaps this was thanks to his infinite stubbornness and pride; he just couldn't allow himself to give up, regardless of how much he wanted to. Or perhaps it was a curse from the Light, for it simply wouldn't let him die before his punishment was over, even if that meant giving him the strength to stand when he honestly felt that he was unable.

Daylen grasped the door handle above him and with one hand dragged the rest of his body up. He grunted under the strain. There was no physical resistance, but the emotional effort he had to exert at that moment was like pushing back against a mountain of guilt and loathing.

Daylen found his feet eventually and stood strong.

So, what was he going to do with a constant reminder of his worst crimes following him wherever he went? *Suck it up and take the torture.* Daylen knew that he was scum and deserved everything he was given. Such was his life.

Lyrah hadn't slept much that low. Thankfully she didn't need to; by bonding light to her body's ability to heal while she slept, three hours had the same effect as nine. The unfortunate thing was that this had left her a lot of time to think about the recent events.

She had left her room and relieved Cueseg from his watch. Cueseg and the Bringer seemed to have had a great time together. The Bringer had gone to sleep at the same time Cueseg did, finding their own rooms—the penthouse had six of them—which left Lyrah alone with her thoughts in the bright sitting room as she stared at the closed doors to the boy's bedroom.

When demanding this arrangement she had acted out of duty and anger. After chasing that boy for so long, her instinctive reaction was to *not* let him go, which was why she fought so hard against the Bringer's defense. This was right, of course, as the Order's needs were paramount: that boy *had* to be watched. Of course the best thing would have been to simply force the boy into the Order, or execute him, but that damned Bringer was right. If the Archknights were willing to commit such a crime to protect themselves, even for the greater good, then the Order wasn't worthy of their power.

That didn't mean her superiors agreed with her. Archallion Kennet had ordered her to go back and bring the boy to the Hold by force. He had figured out, or he simply knew, being of higher rank, that the Vigil could actually be performed by anyone, not just Archknights. What she suspected he didn't know was that the vow to fight evil wasn't necessary, either. Still, Kennet's belief was enough to insist that the boy be brought in knowing that if the governments learned the truth, they would do anything to learn the secrets of the Vigil and try to make Lightbinders themselves. Vowing to fight evil didn't mean that a man wouldn't serve the unjust interests of his own nation.

Kennet understood this, and therefore the Bringer's threat to tell the government that the boy knew the secret of the Vigil was enough for even Kennet to relent and admit, as much as he hadn't wanted to, that Lyrah had forced the next best alternative.

What Lyrah hadn't considered until the boy came walking in was that she now had to constantly see someone who was basically a younger version of...of *him*. Lyrah had enough trouble trying to control her anxiety when the subject of intimacy came up, let alone when thinking of *that* monster. How was she not supposed to think of him when looking at his own son?! The boy not only had the exact same height, posture, and gait, but he sounded *exactly* like him. He was like a younger twin!

Lyrah's arms instinctively crossed to hug herself as she thought of the confrontation at the dock, where she had called him a pretender. He had answered back, *"Hey, I was protecting people!"* The anger in his voice, his expression... In that moment, it was as if she had been looking at Dayless the Conqueror himself, and she had cowered. For that small span, she had been back in his bed, helpless, afraid, completely under his terrible power, being constantly abused once more.

She had fought off the reaction quickly, her sense of duty and determination winning the battle; but still, that image was so frightening. It was that part of the boy that frightened her, his ability to become the Conqueror in her eyes.

"He is not his father," Lyrah said again to herself. "He's just a lost and confused little boy who doesn't know how to use his powers..."

But then again, he did defeat that famous pirate, Lyrah thought. *That certainly tells of a capable and strong young man. He also freed those kidnapped girls...*

Oh, how Lyrah's heart ached for those poor girls. She knew exactly what they had gone through, having experienced much the same...except that *she* had never been rescued, she thought bitterly.

Then Lyrah noticed something: her regard for the boy was different in that moment. The boy, Daylen, had saved a group of girls who were much like she had been, and had done exactly what Lyrah would have done in the same situation: kill every last one of the sex slavers.

That was something to appreciate in him.

"This is how I need to see him, for who he is. The papers say he's a hero, and for those girls, at least, he is."

Lyrah breathed a sigh of relief, for when picturing Daylen in her mind, now it was much harder to see his father. One was a rapist and monster, while the other was apparently someone who killed those types of people.

Someone that Lyrah could not only put up with, but also someone that she might even be able to like.

CHAPTER THIRTY-SEVEN

*The whole world had fallen into war and the Archknights
petitioned me many times to stop.
I ignored them, as I knew they had no right to intervene in
matters regarding nations. They continued to bother me,
eventually assigning a personal counselor from their ranks.
I called him Puppy.
The continued resources that maintained my armies were more
crucial at that time than ever before. This was the reason why I
reacted so strongly when Daybreak, one of my larger Hamahran
cities, rebelled.*

D aylen entered the sitting room to see Lyrah on one of the
couches.

A sharp stab of guilt struck him with such force that his legs
lost strength for an instant. Catching himself on an armchair,
Daylen paused to breathe in before managing to stand. Bracing
himself, he looked back to the woman. The guilt surged again—but
this time, being prepared for it, he stood strong.

"I've seen you use your powers to heal, so why are you still
injured?" Lyrah said.

"It's not that kind of injury... I just didn't sleep well."

She nodded, her face softening for a moment.

Daylen walked to the tray of cloche-covered plates that was

near the door. Apparently breakfast had been delivered. He took one and walked to the dining table, glad for the excuse to get away from the woman.

Sitting, he removed the cloche and found a meal that had to be Tuerasian cuisine. It looked *really* good, but even that couldn't brighten his mood.

The seat in front of him was pulled back and someone sat. Daylen looked up to see Lyrah and his guilt surged again.

She was still so young, but then again everyone looked young to Daylen; to most people, he supposed Lyrah would appear aged and hard.

"You need to watch me eat?" Daylen asked.

"You can eat a shoe for all I care. We need to talk."

Daylen glanced at her and heartache ripped through his chest so pure that he grunted under his breath. He would just have to bear it. "Then talk," he said with half a breath.

"The Bringer says you won't reveal how you became a Lightbinder."

"Correct."

"Will you tell me where you were when it happened?"

"No."

She studied him for a moment before asking, "Why are you keeping the secret? You don't seem to like the Order very much."

"The Arch Order of Light is the single most important institution in the world. You need your powers to do what you do, whereas others not bound to your cause would abuse it to their own benefit."

That seemed to surprise her, though she was certainly doing her best to keep her face a mask.

"And *you* won't abuse them?" she asked.

"No more than you," Daylen said, not flinching from the woman's gaze. She stared back at him as if their eyes were in a duel.

"And you'll keep knowledge that might threaten the Order to yourself?"

"Hmm… I wonder what you're referring to," Daylen said, triggering the spring-loaded dagger in his gauntlet. He casually raised his gauntlet and reset the dagger. "But if there was anything that might threaten the Order—say, something that could nullify their powers—I would be pretty Light-cursed stupid to reveal it to anyone, considering it would affect me too."

She frowned deeply, clearly understanding the not-so-subtle subtext.

"How did you know my name?"

Black. He had hoped she would have forgotten that.

"My father," Daylen said reluctantly.

Lyrah's jaw tensed and she took some very measured breaths. Her hands gripped the edge of the table and she replied with a voice quivering in anger. "He mentioned me by name?"

"Yes," Daylen said softly. "You probably don't want to hear this, but no man has ever borne as much guilt than my...my father. One night, he spoke of the people he felt he had mistreated most. He didn't say what he had done specifically, but for some reason most were women, you one of the more prominent among them. He even described your appearance, which was why I recognized you. I don't know what my father did to you," Daylen lied, "but he..."

"Stop!" Lyrah said, her hands white from gripping the table so hard. Her head was bowed and she seemed to struggle to regain control of herself.

She hates me so much... Well, no wonder.

Lyrah eventually calmed. "Are you really a master of the sword?" she asked, clearly forcing a change of subject.

"Yes."

"How?"

"My father taught me."

Lyrah briefly paused before saying. "You'll be going to the constabulary infall."

Amazing that even with someone whom Daylen felt he had done so much wrong, he could still resent them if they tried to boss him around.

He ate some food and swallowed a disrespectful retort with it. Instead, he chose a much more managed response, but even then, it was laced with more force than he intended. "You don't need to tell me my business. I've said I'll turn myself in, and I keep my word."

Lyrah stared back at him; and again, for the slightest moment, there was a hint of the poor frightened girl he once knew in her expression. It vanished quickly, replaced with hardness. What had caused that flash of vulnerability?

"That's yet to be determined," Lyrah said.

Daylen breathed out long and slow as he tried to cope with the guilt from being so close to this woman. "And will you trust me once it is?" he asked.

"A first step."

She was smart to be so cautious. Lyrah certainly hadn't grown up to be a fool.

Lyrah was looking back at him, but her eyes eventually broke from his gaze, glancing to the side. Others might have thought that sideways glace meant nothing, but Daylen could read people, and he saw that tiny flash of vulnerability again.

Lyrah looked back at him angrily. "What?"

He realized he had been staring. He looked away. "It's nothing."

Daylen wasn't going to tell her what he had just realized: that she was afraid of him. She was fighting it, and most people wouldn't have noticed—but Daylen did, and there was only one thing that Daylen could think of that would do that. It was who he looked like, who he sounded like: *himself*—just a much younger version. Daylen could only imagine what this poor girl thought of the monster that had imprisoned and raped her every low for a month, but judging by these reactions, Lyrah still struggled with what he had done to her. It wasn't just the anger and hate she had struggled with when Daylen had lied about how he knew her name—it was fear. Daylen had permanently damaged this poor woman, he realized with a sudden surge of guilt, and he could think of no punishment painful enough that would adequately administer justice for that crime. No wonder the Light tormented him so relentlessly, and all this simply served to reinforce Daylen's knowledge that he deserved it. The pain he felt, the guilt, the heartache at seeing the damage he had caused, to see the fruit of his sins... He deserved it all.

"Nothing?" Lyrah said accusingly. "Just look at your face. If you have a problem with me, spit it out."

Well, Daylen couldn't exactly say he had just realized that she was still damaged from him raping her. He had to make something up. "It's just that..." He hesitated; he couldn't think of a good reply. He needed to say something that would satisfy her accusation and also make sense as to why Daylen would try and hide it. And if his reply came too late, it would only look like he was thinking up another lie.

He looked down, and nothing clever came to him. Looking up, he was struck by the image of Lyrah's face, and ended up blurting out the very same thought as it came into his mind: "You're beautiful."

Well, that had stunned her—as well as Daylen.

Lyrah's face was frozen in quiet consternation, a reddening blush heating her cheeks.

I'M SUCH A LIGHT-BLINDED, BLACKENED IDIOT! he thought at himself in horror.

There was a reason people said to think before one speaks. What Daylen had said was true, of course—she really was beautiful —but only a *bloody idiot* would blurt it out like that, especially considering what Daylen had done to her. It had been a *profoundly* stupid thing to say.

Lyrah had completely withdrawn mentally. Her breathing had increased and she was clearly feeling anxious. She closed her eyes and, clearly taking stock, slowly stopped looking so nervous. Instead, she looked merely uncomfortable.

Yes, indeed the air felt very awkward now, and Lyrah was looking at everything but him.

"Sorry," Daylen eventually said. "I didn't mean it that way."

"I don't want to know what it meant. I'd rather we not talk about it."

"Good… So, the weather."

"What about it?"

"It's very weather-like."

Lyrah held a gaze on him for a moment before a small smile cracked her expression. "Yes. Similarly, I've noticed that for some reason trees act a lot like trees."

Daylen smiled. "The world's full of mysteries."

"Mysteries like why a pubescent troublemaker is trying to make small talk with someone who clearly doesn't like him." Lyrah was glaring at him and Daylen was stunned by the massive mood swing. "Hurry up and eat, *kid*," Lyrah said, leaving the table abruptly. "I'll be taking you to the constabulary within the hour," she added before walking to the sitting room and finding a couch with its back to Daylen.

Daylen's surprise was quickly melted away by anger. Keeping control of his tongue was all he could do as his shaking fists clenched his cutlery, pressing them into the mahogany dining table.

He remained in that state for a good minute, breathing deeply and letting his rage come under control.

Daylen eventually dropped his knife and fork, leaning back in frustration and saying under his breath, "Bitch!"

———

Around ten minutes after Lyrah had left, Ahrek emerged and joined Daylen at the dining table with one of the plates.

Daylen hadn't eaten anything.

"I'm pleased to report that Archknight Cueseg is a wonderful man. He made that breakfast you're eating. It's a traditional Tuerasian dish called capaden…"

"I don't really care."

Ahrek sighed. "What's put you in such a foul mood?"

Daylen didn't reply.

Ahrek glanced to the sitting room. "Ah, not getting along, I see."

"Really? You sure?" Daylen bit out. "Ahrek, this was a bad idea."

"It was the only peaceful solution."

"Yeah, well, right now I'm feeling like a little less peace would be nice. I need to hit something."

"You're frustrated—"

A knock came from the door, cutting Ahrek off.

"I'll get it," Daylen said, happy for a reason to end the conversation.

Opening the door, Daylen found Sain on the other side. The boy had cleaned himself up considerably. He had bathed and his hair was cut in a stylish fashion. He was wearing black boots over brown slacks and a vest over a loose white shirt with a backsword at his side.

"Speaking of hitting something," Daylen said with a smile as he folded his arms.

"What?" Sain replied.

"Oh, just wishful thinking. It's good to see you."

That comment seemed to surprise the snot. "Really?"

"As big a pain in the ass as you are, you're worlds better than what I've had to put up with. Come in."

Sain entered. "Look, I know you don't want me around, I just wanted to let you know that the salvage claims have been processed. It's all approved." Sain held out the same leather envelope that had kept the *Maraven's* registration. "The *Maraven* is yours."

Daylen took the envelope. "That was blackened fast! It should have taken a week."

"Well, I think the group of kidnapped girls that needed to be returned to their families, the death of a famous pirate, and the capture of his ship put us higher in the queue."

"Good point."

"There're a lot of people who really want to speak to you."

"I'll be visiting the constabulary infall."

"Oh, not the conners—reporters. There were, like, twenty of them trying to get past the security at our stack."

Daylen groaned. "They've already heard of it?"

"You're famous. It *was* Blackheart you killed, and one of the girls you saved is the daughter of some important senator."

Daylen looked to Ahrek.

Ahrek nodded. "Senator Terain, if I remember."

"She's no more important than the other girls," Daylen said, looking back to Sain.

"That's not how they see it," Sain replied with a shrug.

Daylen groaned. "Great."

"So…about the *Bloodrunner*," Sain began to ask.

"It's yours."

Sain pulled out a folded document from his coat. "Well, that's what this paper says…but really, you should have the ship."

"I don't need it. Stop feeling guilty. It's yours, as is the rest of the money."

"I…just don't know what to say."

"Don't say anything. Go and make a life for yourself."

Sain stood, looking at his registration, and after a moment suddenly walked to Daylen and hugged him tight.

Daylen stiffened, feeling very uncomfortable.

"Thank you," Sain said in a quivering voice.

"That's… Um, that's fine," Daylen said, hugging him back awkwardly.

Sain pulled away, wiping tears from his cheeks and sniffing.

"I'd go with you, you know. Help you in whatever it is you're trying to do."

"No, all I'll be doing is looking for trouble. You've had enough of that in your life. Go buy a nice house, invest the rest of your money and start a business, get a girl pregnant and raise a family. Live a good life, Sain."

Sain sniffed again and wiped his nose. "That sounds nice."

"It is, for those who can do it."

Sain smiled. "And I might be closer to having a family than I thought."

"How so?"

"Well... I've met someone."

"When under the Light did that happen?"

Sain suddenly looked guilty as sin. "She's... Well, she was one of the girls you saved."

"*What!*" Daylen erupted. "You bowlegged little *snot*, you took advantage of one of those girls!" Daylen's arm flew back to strike the idiot, but Sain's cowering reply stopped him.

"She has nowhere to go! Her family will disown her for what's happened!"

Daylen calmed and his arm lowered. "Sharra. She jumped your bones, didn't she?"

Sain wilted, blushing conspicuously. "How...how did you know?"

"She tried the same on me."

"*What?*" Ahrek said from the table.

"I didn't do anything, Bringer, so loosen your knickers, will you?"

Sain's face was red with embarrassment, and also jealousy, by the look of it. "She... She tried..."

"Yeah, but not out of affection. She wanted to go with me, looking for security in her ruined life. She was willing to do anything for that, which was why she threw herself at me. And I'm guessing that's why she threw herself at you."

Sain folded his arms. "So what if it is? I'm not an idiot; I know she can't love me, we've just met. But I like her, and I can give her the safety she wants. If she wants to ride me because of that, it's her choice, but I'd take care of her anyway."

Daylen sighed. "It's not so much her choice but an instinctive and destructive way of coping with what's happened. She needs to come to terms with it and not continue the same type of abuse, even if it is self-inflicted."

"I'll... I'll talk to her about it."

"Sure you will, because you'd *love* to be celibate again."

"I will! I won't lie—I like, you know, *that*. She's the most beautiful thing I've ever seen. But if it's bad for her...I'll stop it."

Daylen was still skeptical, of course, but Sain's commitment was more than he could demand. "All right, good. Who knows, you two might work out; but regardless, that girl has been abused in the cruelest of ways, Sain, so if you're taking her under your wing, you *better* do right by her."

"I will, I promise."

"Good...and I'm sorry for flying off the handle."

"It wouldn't have felt right if you hadn't."

Daylen chuckled. "Yeah."

There was a silence and Sain eventually nodded. "I... Umm, I guess this is goodbye, then."

"It is. Don't waste this, Sain."

"I won't."

Sain stood there for another moment before eventually nodding to Ahrek and leaving, closing the door behind him.

Daylen stood there looking at the closed door, feeling...joy? Not just feeling enjoyment from passing pleasures or comforts—he actually felt genuinely happy. He couldn't remember the last time he had felt like this.

That boy's life had just been saved, not just physically, but morally and emotionally. It would have been so easy to kill him; he was a pirate on a crew that had attacked them. But there was such light in him. How many people who do terrible things only do them because of the circumstances of their life? Out of everything Daylen had achieved since becoming young again, stopping crimes, punishing villains and killing tyrants, this was the best and most noble act of them all. Redeeming a life from evil.

"You did a very noble thing for that boy," Ahrek said, having walked to join him.

"I gave him money. He's the one who's choosing a better life from it."

"You did far more than just give Sain money," the Bringer told him quietly. "You didn't let him get away with any misbehavior while in our care, and showed by your actions that a man can fight against the circumstances of his life."

"Really? I broke his arm, remember?"

"Well, apart from that," Ahrek acknowledged with a slight chuckle. "Sain's light was shining when he left just now. He's going to do good things with his life. Sometimes all a boy needs is the right type of kick up the rear to see the error of his ways, breaking bones excluded. What you gave him was the discipline he had needed all his life. You'll make a good father someday, Daylen."

That last comment stung. Daylen had been a good father before his life was ruined—a great one. But what about all the other countless children he had fathered since, without even knowing? He wasn't a good father, nor would he let himself be one ever again.

Daylen then noticed Lyrah staring at them in consternation. "What?" he said.

Lyrah said nothing and turned back to sit facing away from them.

"Oh," Ahrek said, suddenly looking to Daylen's new backsword, "I can't believe I hadn't noticed till now. Where's Imperious?"

Daylen smiled and held out his right hand. Light began to shine from it and quickly formed into Imperious.

Ahrek gasped, and even Lyrah, who was still listening in, looked and then stood in shock, her mouth hanging open.

Their reactions made revealing his new trick *so* worthwhile.

Daylen raised Imperious and looked at the blade as he spoke. "Seeing the Archon over there do this gave me all the clues I needed. Sunucles are essentially solid-light objects, and as a Lightbinder I can draw light into myself. It's that simple."

"So it's not creation but light absorption," Ahrek said, looking to Lyrah.

Lyrah was visibly perturbed.

"Another secret of the Archknights, as it turns out," Daylen said, looking at Lyrah. "I wouldn't be surprised if all Archons kept a sunforged sword stored within them, as well as a few other sunucles."

Lyrah sneered. "If you tell *anyone*, I'll…"

"Hey, I wasn't the one who used this ability in public."

"That was different."

"Exactly," Daylen said. "If my life is being threatened, to hell with your secrets!" He gripped Imperious tightly. "Anyway, even if people see me do it, no one will figure out that I can store sunucles within me. They'll just think I can create swords in the same way as the Bringer's miracle. I'm guessing you've used that ability in front of people before, and yet the secret is still kept."

Lyrah grimaced at him and didn't reply.

"Glad to see that we understand each other."

"You've clearly finished breakfast," Lyrah said. "Get your things. We're leaving."

"No."

"I said—"

"Oh, shove it up your ass!"

"Daylen!" Ahrek warned.

"You shove it too, Bringer," Daylen said before turning back to Lyrah. "I'm no one's whipping boy, and you better not try and order me around, *girl*, or we're going to have a *big* problem. Got it?"

Daylen felt guilty as soon as he had finished. It was so easy to forget who Lyrah was when he became angry or frustrated. His appearance had a very unfair effect over her, and it was cruel to use it even by accident. It was clear that whenever he did, something retreated within Lyrah. She was still broken and afraid. Even now, her face was an image of consternation and hidden anxiety.

Lyrah held her gaze on Daylen for a moment before turning and walking to her room, shutting the doors behind her.

Lyrah's head rested on the doors of her room as she wept bitterly.

He was more like his father than she could bear. He looked exactly the same; his height and posture, even his way of speaking, were all identical. And when he got angry or annoyed, that was the hardest of all.

When he spoke that way she was a trapped little girl again, completely under his power. No matter what she tried, that voice cowed her as completely as if she had just been raped all over again.

Lyrah gasped as her sorrow grew. How could she do this? It was impossible. She had thought she could separate the boy from his father, but he was too similar to the bastard.

A knock rung on the door, causing her to jump back. She sighed in frustration, angry at how weak she was. She hated being weak and helpless more than anything.

She tried to take stock and walked away from the door, straightening her posture and wiping away her tears.

She turned back to the door. "Yes?"

"It's me," came the voice that had been burned into her memory. Without seeing where the voice came from, it was is if the monster himself had spoken, and in that instant her strength vanished.

Lyrah slowly fell to the floor as she began to cry once more.

The doors opened and the boy entered, closing them behind him.

She hadn't locked it. *Idiot.*

"Go away," she said pathetically through her tears.

He crossed half of the floor between them and stopped.

Silence.

She eventually looked and saw that the boy was crying, too. Why would he be crying?

"I'm sorry for how I spoke to you," he said. "There's no excuse for it."

The idiocy—she wasn't upset that a teenage boy had spoken strong words to her, and in reality he had done nothing wrong. Her hostility was purely because who he looked like, which wasn't his fault.

"You don't understand," she said.

"Actually, I do."

What did he mean by that?

"I lied when I said I didn't know what my father did to you. I can only imagine what seeing my face must do. You deserve to be free of that bastard forever, and I'm...I'm *sorry.*" Tears came back to Daylen's face as he said this, impassioned and heartbroken. "I'm so very sorry for what happened to you."

She looked up at him, and saw no lie in his eyes.

The boy's sorrow was so keen that it was as if he blamed himself for what his father had done.

And it was in that moment that something changed within Lyrah. This boy—no, this *man*—was nothing like his father. The image of Daylen, the young man torn apart by pain, sorrow, and such profound guilt, was such a contrast to the image of the Great Bastard that she had within her mind.

Lyrah stood, feeling calm for the first time in his presence. "You don't need to apologize, Daylen."

His self-deprecating look conveyed that he didn't think so.

"I'm sorry. You don't deserve to be judged because of your father."

"Perhaps I do," he said with a cryptic twist of his lips.

"No, I knew your...your father. He was a cruel and heartless wretch. You're nothing like him."

Daylen laughed, to Lyrah's confusion. "That's good to hear. It's really the whole reason for my life at the moment."

"That's as good a purpose as any, I suppose."

They stood in silence, and Lyrah saw something in the young man's eyes; Age. His eyes looked old and had a depth in them that she couldn't understand. With those eyes, how he talked and handled himself, and his greater height, it could be very easy to forget how young he was.

And then Lyrah realized something. For the time they had been looking at each other, Lyrah hadn't seen the young man's father. Instead, she saw who he really was: Daylen, the young man, just trying his best to be the best man he could.

"Would you mind if we left for the constabulary now?" Daylen asked. "I think it's about time."

Was that a veiled concession to her authority? "Yes, that would be good," Lyrah said, and Daylen opened the door for her as they left.

CHAPTER THIRTY-EIGHT

*I needed all my people to obey me and support the war effort,
but in the rebellion they did the opposite; and just as if they were
fighting for the other side, they had made themselves my
enemies. Indeed, their rebellion broke the crucial supply chain to
one of the main fronts, causing a massive defeat and
withdrawal.*

Thousands of men died, and you can guess who I blamed.

*I pulled out four of my annihilators from the front lines and
traveled with them to Daybreak. Once we arrived, in rage and
madness I commanded them to level the city with everyone inside.
I murdered over a million men, women, and children that fall.*

L yrah had said he was nothing like the Conqueror, and though
Daylen was all too aware of how ironic that was, he *was*
trying his very best to be a different man. Hearing these words
from a woman with such a personal understanding of who Dayless
the Conqueror was brought such light and joy into Daylen's heart
that it was hard to describe.

Maybe he could actually do it; maybe he could be a different
man.

Thus Daylen was in a very good mood when he left with Lyrah
to go to the Prime Constabulary, Ahrek being all too happy to see
them off, saying he had some personal errands to make that fall.

Lyrah's companion, Cueseg, said he wanted to spend the fall at the Hold.

Daylen had even pushed his guilt back to the point that it felt like a soft weight on his chest. His good mood helped, but his guilt was still ever present in his subconscious and Daylen couldn't help but be constantly and unavoidably mindful of Lyrah and her every move.

She was such a contradiction; so strong, powerful, and sure, yet so fragile and vulnerable at the same time. Daylen felt totally responsible for that fragility.

As they walked down the hall to the elevator, he found himself being the perfect gentleman, letting her in the elevator first and opening each and every door they walked through.

It was as if he was trying to make up for what he had done, as impossible as that was, but the futile nature of the task didn't mean that he shouldn't offer this woman whatever recompense he could give, even if that was simply being courteous. He should really offer himself in slavery and let her do with him whatever she wished—but why just her? He had treated hundreds of girls as wretchedly, not to mention the millions he had murdered. The whole world had a claim on him for justice. Maybe someday they would get it.

With Lyrah being an Archknight and Daylen's mug printed on every broadsheet in the city, they drew the attention of nearly every person they passed.

Daylen was already reaching out with his light sense, something he tried to do constantly now, and because of it he noticed something odd.

Lyrah's inner light suddenly seemed to shimmer with brightness...and there was something familiar about it.

She's using her powers, Daylen realized.

Being as subtle as possible, he glanced about to try and figure out what ability she might be enhancing.

I bet she's listening in on their conversations, Daylen thought. *A good idea, in fact.*

Daylen enhanced his hearing and as soon as he did, Lyrah's head spun on him. "What're you doing?" she asked softly.

Daylen leaned down, as Lyrah was half a head shorter than he, to whisper, "I could ask you the same thing."

Her eyes narrowed.

"Oh, you didn't know I could sense our powers?"

She glared for a moment before repeating her question. "What're you doing?"

"The same as you, I'm guessing," Daylen replied. "Eavesdropping?"

Lyrah suddenly looked like a child caught trying to steal a cookie, and the light that was shimmering within her stopped instantly.

Daylen smiled. "Gotcha."

Lyrah glared at him, all haughtiness and authority, and her light shimmered once more as if to say that she had every right to eavesdrop even though she had looked as guilty as sin. She walked on ahead of him.

Daylen caught up and kept on enhancing his ears, knowing full well that she had lost any authority to stop him, and it seemed to bother her—which gave Daylen some type of juvenile pleasure. His courtesy only went so far. Lyrah the person needed endless recompense; Lyrah the overbearing and controlling Archknight, on the other hand, needed to lighten up.

I wonder how much the knights actually abuse their powers so long as others don't know? Daylen didn't really blame them, of course, as he was all too happy to abuse his powers in the same way. Who wouldn't like to hear what others said when they thought no one was listening in?

"That's him! The hero from Treremain," one person said as they passed.

"Paper says he defeated the legendary Blackheart and rescued a harem of captive girls."

Daylen sighed. The story had broken already? Sain *had* said that a heap of reporters had been crowded around the ships.

A quiet conversation caught his attention.

"Who's the knight?" one person asked.

"Looks like his mother."

"No, I read in the papers that his mother was some old widow. I bet the knights have gone after him because of his powers. They'll want to see if there's a connection with their own magic."

Well, the last part was true enough, but Lyrah? His *mother*? By appearance, Daylen looked young enough to be Lyrah's son, he supposed, but in truth he was easily old enough to be her grandfather.

Lyrah's face had become hard and bothered. This woman's face always seemed to reflect how she was feeling, and because of that her mood was very easy to read.

She must have heard the same comment, Daylen realized, and something about it had upset her.

She's concerned that people are seeing a connection between my powers and the knights.

"Don't worry," Daylen whispered. "If people figure out I'm a Lightbinder, I'll just say that I dedicated my life to your cause and the powers were given to me in my sleep. You know, a blessing from the Light or something."

"That will do, I suppose... Thank you," Lyrah said, yet her mood hadn't improved.

"You're welcome," Daylen said.

There must have been something else in the comment that upset her.

Daylen wondered what. Her regard toward him seemed to have improved a little since leaving their rooms. Still, Daylen didn't think it was the inference that he might be her child that bothered her...

Daylen stopped dead in his tracks.

Lyrah turned to him impatiently, but his realization was so concerning that he ignored it.

Daylen could have fathered countless children with the girls that had been forced into his bead, and Lyrah had been one of those girls...

Had she fallen pregnant?

If so, where was the child? According to the time Lyrah had been in his bed...well, the child would be in their late twenties by now. Were they a good person, or would Daylen have to stop their evil as he'd had to with Blackheart?

Daylen needed to know.

"What's wrong?" Lyrah asked.

"It's... Um, I'll tell you once we get a coach."

"Fine. Just keep up."

Daylen asked one of the valets outside to flag them a skycoach. The valet stuttered a nervous affirmative in reply.

Without asking, the valet made sure to flag the finest coach in the line, and when returning, said, "I'll see that the hotel pays for the expense, Lady Archon—and, um, Mr. Daylen."

Daylen was about to say this was unnecessary, but Lyrah cut

him off, saying, "Thank you," in a way that implied such service was totally expected.

Well, she *was* a knight.

Though far more expensive Skycoaches were more common within cities than their ground-based darkstone-driven cousins as they helped decongest the streets and were much faster. The skycoach that landed in front of them was fully enclosed with fine glass windows and gold-leafed carvings embroidering its body.

The valet opened the door for them and they entered after giving their destination to the pilot.

Once seated, the coach softly lurched as it left the ground.

"What was your problem just now?" Lyrah asked.

Daylen took in a deep breath, knowing that this was a sensitive topic and that he was going to have to lie through his teeth to learn the truth.

"Dayless. He had many women brought to him."

"Girls!" Lyrah spat back at him. "He raped countless young and vulnerable *girls*, Daylen."

"I know, all right? I'm not trying to lessen his crimes. Look, I've only recently learned that Dayless fathered children with those girls—my half brothers and sisters. Dayless himself had thought precautions were taken to prevent that. I want to meet them and see what kind of people they are. So..."

Lyrah interrupted him and answered in a cold voice, "I never had any children."

Daylen nodded, feeling such great relief. "Thank you. I'm sorry for asking."

Lyrah looked away and stared out the window. "You have a right to know of your siblings."

Daylen let silence settle for a time before saying, "Blackheart was one of them."

"What?" she said, looking at him with wide eyes.

"Yeah, I found irrefutable evidence. That's how I learned I have...that I have siblings." *Not siblings—children.* "I should have hundreds of them, and I just can't help but wonder how many have turned out like Blackheart."

"Some, maybe."

"Just like their father."

"No," Lyrah said. "I used to think that an evil parent would always produce corrupt children..." She struggled with emotion.

"But meeting you has proven me wrong." With wet eyes, Lyrah looked out the window of the coach, clearly not wanting to talk.

It wouldn't be right for him to pry, so Daylen let her be. He wondered about his children making their way in the world. He hoped that one day he would meet one who was a good person.

Or, in other words, meet one who was nothing like himself.

Lyrah and Daylen sat in silence until they arrived at the Prime Constabulary. Daylen was happy to be left alone with his thoughts and it looked to be the same for the knight.

The Prime Constabulary was a long building made up of several larger square-like sections that were all joined between. It was a brick building with stone frames over all the windows and doors. The largest square section sat in front and in the middle of the rest of the building, about seven stories tall with a large double door at the front.

Once out of the coach, it didn't take long for a constable to notice them and race inside.

And now I'll get to find out how much of my past they've discovered is fake. Light, this might go badly.

Daylen and Lyrah were greeted by several officials the moment they walked through the front doors.

Daylen looked about. They stood in a large marble floored foyer that had two wide staircases on either side leading to an upper hallway. A reception desk sat in the mid-back of the room. Daylen stepped forward. "My name is Daylen Namaran. I'm here to turn myself in and answer to the charges against me."

"We know who you are," a conner said, weighing a pair of manacles in his hand. "I don't suppose there's any point to putting these on you."

"Not really," Daylen replied.

The conner looked to Lyrah. "Thank you for escorting him, Lady Archon."

"I'm not an escort," she replied smoothly. "I'm his custodian, and as such will be remaining at his side at all times."

"Ah, yes. Of course," the conner replied, slightly nervous. "This way, then."

Many people stared at them as they were led through the constabulary, some even nodding respectfully. Daylen would have suspected this deference was aimed at Lyrah, but several people looked directly at him when doing so. One rather attractive woman even winked.

Daylen and Lyrah were shown to a small square room that that was plaster-white and brightly lit from sunstone sconces. It had a rectangular table in the middle with two chairs on each side and a large mirror to the right wall. They were directed to sit in the chairs facing the mirror.

Daylen could sense seven people standing in the room behind the mirror with his light sense. They were looking through the mirror as if it were glass.

The mirror must have acted like a window from the other side. *When was that invented?* Daylen wondered. If sound could travel into that hidden room, those people would be able to spy on everything. It was very clever.

Once sitting, one of the men in the spying room left and walked to enter the room with himself and Lyrah. He was a middle-aged man in a tailed suit and top hat holding a clipboard and a newspaper under his arm; a sturdy man with a round face. He had a trimmed dark-purple beard with soft streaks of green, wore a cravat and had a rapier at his side.

The man took off his hat, revealing evenly streaked hair of dark purple and green, and dropped the broadsheet on the desk in front of Daylen.

The paper had a drawing of Daylen front and center with the headline: *Daylen, Son of the Conqueror, Defeats Blackheart!*

"You made the front page," the man said as he sat in the chair across from them.

"And it only took a fall from when I arrived," Daylen replied, grabbing the paper.

"That's the press for you," the man said.

A subheading sitting at the bottom corner caught his attention. It read: *Delavian Council of Dukes Deny Rumors of Having Intimate Relations with Goats.*

Daylen burst out laughing.

"Something funny?" the man asked as he took his seat on the other side of the table.

"Oh, the spot about the Dukes."

"I thought you'd be more interested in the article about you."

"Nah, I know that story, but the Dukes getting knocked off their high horses...that's interesting."

"Yeah, sickening stuff. You think it's true?"

"Absolutely," Daylen said with a grin.

"We'd better get underway," the man said and nodded to Lyrah. "Lady Archon, might I ask why you're accompanying this young man?"

"She's my lawyer," Daylen said.

Lyrah didn't look at him, but smiled and stomped on Daylen's foot. Judging by the crack and searing pain shooting up Daylen's leg, she broken a toe or two.

Daylen grunted, drawing on the light from the sunstones in the room to heal. Lyrah had obviously used such force because of that, and honestly he liked that no-fuss strength about her.

Besides, getting in that little rib was worth it.

"I'm his custodian," Lyrah replied cordially, sounding quite satisfied with herself.

"Are you okay?" the man asked Daylen.

"Oh, it's just a little pain in the ass."

That one made her glare at him.

He smiled back with juvenile pleasure.

"Right... I'm Detective Dain," the man said matter-of-factly, "and I've been assigned to your case." He flipped through the papers on the clipboard. "Typically you would be shipped back to Treremain, as the crimes you're accused of were committed within that jurisdiction, but this isn't a regular case by any light. So here we are. Let's start with the most serious charge: murder." The detective put down his clipboard and placed his hands on the desk, one on top of the other. "Mr. Namaran, did you kill anyone while in Treremain?"

Good, Daylen thought, *he's focusing on the charges and not my past. With any luck, it won't come up.*

"Yes," Daylen said.

"Who?"

"Six people. Two men I caught in the act of rape, a woman sexually molesting a young girl, another woman trying to murder her husband, and a man who had just murdered some poor young boy." Daylen let his anger resonate as he added, "I didn't arrive soon enough to prevent that last one. There was also a beggar in the Freysian city of Laybourn. That one was actually self-defense. He tried to slit my throat as I slept."

"Reports say that the beggar was decapitated and his head pinned to the wall with a knife. Rather excessive for self-defense."

"I was in a bad mood."

Lyrah tsked next to him.

"Look," Daylen said, "that beggar was a murdering piece of drack. How many other people do you think he killed before he found me? He deserved what he got, and the world is a bit brighter for it."

"Then you're claiming justification?" the detective said flatly.

"Of course."

"Then explain each homicide in every step and why they were justified."

Daylen knew why the detective was asking this—he wanted to see if Daylen's account of the events would match the evidence at the crime scenes, which they would. All he had to do was tell the truth, but that might complicate things regarding his powers. Daylen turned to look at Lyrah. "I would like to, but that would mean talking about some sensitive information regarding my abilities."

Lyrah's mouth pressed into a thin line. Her eyes glanced to him, clearly weighing up her options, and then she looked at the detective. "Daylen is a Lightbinder," Lyrah said. "He dedicated his life to our cause and received the powers. This is why most of the crime scenes were left in such an unnatural state."

Daylen smiled. Lyrah clearly understood that people would quickly figure out that his powers were the same as the knight's and lying now would only cause problems later on.

"Hmm, that would explain the holes in the walls and the eyewitness accounts," Detective Dain said, "and the Order's interest in this young man. I thought you had to be a knight to have such powers?"

"You do," Lyrah said, "in practice at least. You have to dedicate your life to the cause of the Archknights." Lyrah looked at Daylen. "This young man did, and then received the powers…"

"In my sleep," Daylen said, butting in. "I just woke up one day and had them."

"Do you still have these powers?" the detective asked.

"Yes."

"I need more than just your word."

Daylen sighed. He placed his left hand flat on the table and hammered his fist down on his thumb with enhanced strength, crushing it. He groaned in pain, holding his eyes shut tight, blood having sprayed out like spilled ink. Then, opening his eyes, he raised his fist, revealing a bloody mess. His thumb then slowly began to reform.

Once it was healed, the detective breathed in and nodded. "Right, that settles it. I expect the charges will be dropped by the end of the fall."

"What do you mean dropped?" Lyrah asked.

"He's an Archknight, or effectively one, and therefore has power of arrest and sentencing."

"But there are some charges that have no witnesses to validate Archknight intervention. We work in twos for a reason."

"Yes," the detective said, "but because of the precedent of the witnesses to the other interventions, I don't see any reason to challenge Archknight authority in this case."

"But he is not technically a knight," Lyrah said.

"He could only have his power if he hadn't broken his oath, right?" the detective asked.

Daylen looked to Lyrah, smiling cheekily. She wanted him to be found guilty of murder so he could serve out his sentence with the knights, but being guilty would mean the killings were unjustified, revealing the ugly truth that anyone with a knight's powers could break the oath that supposedly granted them, which might lead to the greater truth: that anyone, regardless of oath, could become a Lightbinder.

Lyrah was doing her best to hide her frustration, not acknowledging Daylen at all. "Yes," she said flatly.

"Exactly. There's plenty of corroborating evidence, as well as direct witnesses, proving that most of the criminals were engaged in the same crimes as Daylen claims. And on top of that, there's evidence that Archon powers were used in each intervention, meaning that Daylen was keeping his oaths by intervening, which is fighting evil, I believe. What better witness than the Light that his actions were justified?"

"My thoughts exactly," Daylen added.

Lyrah said nothing.

"Typically you would be free to go, but there's a separate standing order to keep you in custody."

"What?" Daylen asked.

"There's a lot of people wanting to question you about your father."

"Oh, that."

"Personally, I don't care, as it's not your fault who your father was, and the papers seem to have explained enough—if what they say is true?"

"It is," Daylen said before adding in his mind, *not*.

"You're supposed to wait here while we fetch whoever wants to question you, but seeing as you have an Archknight custodian, you're technically already *in* custody. If you let me know where you're staying, I'll pass it up the chain and you can leave."

"The Fallton."

"Nice place, that. You're free to go, though officially you can't leave the city until the charges have been formally dropped."

"Thank you," Daylen said, rising. Those people wanting to question him had probably already dug into his fake past. That conversation was going to be tricky.

"Pleasure," Detective Dain said while standing, "and might I say, you're a fine addition to the knights' ranks. I can see why the Light chose you. Killing *Blackheart!*" the man suddenly exclaimed with a fierce smile. "We've been after that bastard for years. Well done, lad. Well done indeed." And with that, Detective Dain nodded and left.

"Now there's a lad who's good at his job," Daylen said, turning to Lyrah, "don't you think?"

Lyrah didn't respond, and left the room without him.

Daylen took a moment feeling very smug about himself before he followed. Every person he passed was looking at him, and some even gave him a pat on the back, congratulating him for killing Blackheart and freeing those girls.

It was great to see that law enforcement considered him to be on their side.

Lyrah was waiting for him in the foyer, of course; no chance that he would be rid of her so easily.

"Look, I'm sorry for being a smartass, but you haven't exactly been a ray of sunshine, either."

"You got off because I lied," She hissed under her breath. "A lie that you knew I *had* to say!"

"I would have gotten off anyway and you know it—it's just that now your Order's secrets are kept."

Lyrah looked at him with hard eyes. "It's time we have a proper conversation."

"Fine."

"Follow me."

Lyrah walked out of the building, and once on the sidewalk, she crouched before suddenly shooting up into the air in a massive jump and onto the roof of the large constabulary building.

Daylen was gazing up. With her sudden acceleration, she must have done the same jumping trick Daylen performed through manipulating mass.

Daylen crouched and increased his mass with one bond, which seemed to make him weigh about a ton, and then jumped, releasing the bond an instant before his feet left the ground.

Wind suddenly rushed past him as he shot into the air, clearing the building's height entirely. He slowly began to arc, and when he reached his greatest height he enhanced his strength and landed with ease.

The roof above was terraced and flat. Lyrah was standing with crossed arms, looking at him. "Who taught you how to do that?"

"I figured it out."

"No one just *figures out* how to power jump."

"That's what you call it, power jump?"

"Yes, now answer the question."

"I already have: I taught myself. I also figured out how to absorb sunucles, remember."

"Absorption is different. It can be done by accident. Power jumping is far more sophisticated."

"I agree with you there. Look, all it took was a good understanding of physics and a bit of experimentation."

"Then stop it! Experimenting with mass, as well as some other properties, can be *extremely* dangerous."

Daylen laughed. "Yeah, I found that out the hard way."

Lyrah sighed in frustration. "What happened?"

"Oh, I made my feet explode."

Lyrah looked confused. "That could only happen by reducing your mass with a level-four bond."

"Yeah, what of it?"

"You've *specialized* mass?"

What did she mean specialize? Lyrah looked genuinely surprised. "Are you talking about stacking bonds?" Daylen asked.

"No, I'm talking about specializing. Don't tell me that you've specialized a bond without knowing."

"Why don't you tell me what specializing is?"

Lyrah paused, smiling. "No, not until you join the knights."

"Oh, so it's going to be like that, is it?"

"Exactly. If you want to learn how to use your powers properly, and safely, you'll join the knights."

"I've done all right by myself so far."

Lyrah's eyebrows rose. "Exploding your feet is 'all right'?"

"I survived."

"And what if you were around innocent bystanders?"

"I'm more careful than that."

"Doesn't look like that to me."

"I didn't ask you."

Lyrah sighed. "I'm not going to teach you anything until you join the knights, but I can't have you be a danger to others."

"Danger is subjective."

"Can I test something?"

"It depends."

"Light, you're as stubborn as a goat!"

"The feeling's mutual!" Daylen said, raising his voice.

"Argh!" Lyrah yelled and paced back and forth. "Look, just channel all of your bonds into strength, will you?"

Daylen shrugged. "I can't see any harm in that," he said, and did so. "There."

Lyrah smiled. "Good, you've just lost your specialization. Now you won't be able to make a level-four bond in mass."

"What are you talking about? Of course I can make a level-four bond."

"Then try it," Lyrah said, folding her arms with a smug smile.

"Sorry, I don't exactly want to risk exploding any of my body parts again."

"Then *increase* your mass."

"How would you be able to tell the difference between four ton and eight?"

"I'll lift you."

Daylen knew she could make herself incredibly strong, but enough to lift eight tons! She should only be able to increase her strength sixteen times, which wouldn't even be close to strong enough. Maybe she could still get a read on his weight by how difficult he would be to move.

"Whatever," Daylen said, and walked to the end of the building. He stepped onto the brick barrier that encircled the edge which would put the main wall underneath him and support what his weight was about to become. Daylen then stacked all four bonds in mass, making himself weigh about eight tons, one for the first, two for the second, four for the third, and eight for the fourth. The top tiles of the brick barrier cracked underneath his now massive weight.

Lyrah approached and stepped onto the barrier next to him. After a moment the tiles underneath her feet cracked, indicating she had increased her mass too. Daylen noted that they didn't crack as much as the tiles underneath him, meaning she hadn't increased her mass as much.

She then grabbed him underneath his armpits and lifted him with only the slightest effort showing on her face. The tiles cracked even farther under her feet now that she was also supporting Daylen's enhanced mass.

Daylen was utterly speechless. When stacking all his bonds on strength he could lift at most a little over a ton, but not eight! At least Lyrah looked as surprised as he felt. "You weigh a little over seven tons, not eight," she said, putting him down and stepping off the barrier. "You could only be so heavy with a level-four bond."

"Ah, yeah. That's what I've been saying."

She turned to look at him. "That should be impossible."

"Evidently not."

"You can't just specialize at a whim...unless your bonds are granting a greater enhancement than normal."

"How much are they supposed to grant?"

Lyrah eye's narrowed on him.

"You can at least tell me that much."

"So long as you tell me the strength of your bonds."

"Done."

She huffed. "The first bond in mass will multiply or divide your normal weight by ten. Each bond after that will double the previous enhancement."

"That sounds right. I weigh around ninety kilograms, so the first bond makes me weigh very close to nine hundred. Which means you're right, with all four bonds that would make me seven thousand two hundred kilos or seven point two tons, not eight."

"*Four* bonds?" Lyrah asked, reacting as if Daylen had just turned into a woman before her eyes.

"Umm, yeah."

"You have *four* bonds?"

Daylen realized he might have just revealed something he shouldn't have. *Well, it's too late now.* "Doesn't everyone?" he asked.

"*NO!*" she screamed.

"Oh."

"How under the light do you have *four* bonds?"

"I don't know. I've had four ever since receiving my powers. How many am I supposed to have?"

"Three! Every Archknight, for as long as we've had our powers, has only ever received three bonds and that—is—it. No more, no less. *Four* should be utterly impossible!"

"Then how're you supposed to make a level four bond if you only have three?"

"Through specializing, and no, I'm not going to tell you what that is."

"Fine."

"I don't understand this…unless you got your powers through a different process."

"Well, that's a problem, because I'll never tell anyone how I got them."

Lyrah paused and a slight smile crossed her face.

Daylen narrowed his eyes at her. "I meant it when I said I wouldn't tell anyone."

"Okay then," she said. "You have four bonds. Don't think that makes you powerful or something. You still don't know how to specialize or use your powers properly."

"Then teach me."

"Join the knights!"

"I will. I just have some loose ends I need to sort out first."

"And they are?"

Daylen paused for a moment, wondering if he should tell her, but considering that they were stuck with each other, he relented. "When I was digging through Blackheart's records, I discovered that he was dealing with the Dawnists from this city, selling them all the skyships he had captured. I want to find out why. There's also the matter of the sex-trafficking trade that I intend to destroy."

"You intend to destroy the entire human sex trade?"

"Eventually."

Lyrah studied him.

"You like the sound of that, don't you?" Daylen asked.

"I can't say that I haven't wanted to root out those scum ever since I joined the knights, but we fight the Shade before anything else, and they've been getting more active these past years."

"You're not assigned to hunt the Shade right now."

Lyrah smiled. "All right. How do you plan on going about this?"

"One thing at a time. The Dawnists should be easier to deal with before an entire criminal enterprise."

"I can't say that I'm very fond of the Dawnists, either."

Daylen grinned. "Good—then it looks like we're going to have some fun."

CHAPTER THIRTY-NINE

*That unspeakable act of genocide was the beginning of the end.
At the time I issued the order to destroy Daybreak, the Archon
who accompanied me, Puppy, could not believe what he had
heard. It was then that Puppy realized the truth: that I was a
madman. He attacked me with a sunforged sword whose hiding
place, to this day, I still cannot discern. I was suspicious of
everyone but my most trusted servants at that time, so I had
expected this betrayal and had made preparations. The knight was
quickly run through by several shotspikes. Amazingly, he began to
heal, and still advanced to kill me. I fought him sword-to-sword
with Imperious. Even while healing from his wounds, the knight
was easily twice as fast as a regular man, but I was a master of
the sword, and took his head after a great exchange of blows.*

I want your word that you'll join the knights once we deal with
these loose ends," Lyrah said, still standing on the constabulary
roof.

Daylen sighed. "Right now I can say with absolute honesty that
I fully intend to join the knights once these loose ends are sorted
out."

"Right now," she parroted, "meaning your intentions might
change?"

"Of course," Daylen replied flatly. "I can't predict the future, so I won't discount something arising that affects my intention. Thus, I won't fully commit."

Lyrah sneered. "You speak like a politician."

"I won't back myself into a corner. In the end I'll join the knights when I see fit, and right now, that's after these errands."

"They're more than errands: they're self-appointed quests. Why does it even matter to you?"

"Because with these powers I can actually do something about it… It's how I've chosen to live my life."

Lyrah was silent for a moment. "You've made the pledge."

"What pledge?"

"To fight evil for the rest of your life. The Archknight's Oath."

Daylen nodded slowly. "I suppose I have."

"Did you make it before you received your powers?"

"I know what you're getting at, and no, I didn't. Trust me, there was no one as unworthy as me at the time I received my powers."

"As unworthy as you?" Lyrah asked as her eyes narrowed.

Damn it. "Don't expect me to elaborate."

"I need to know if you were some kind of criminal before receiving your powers."

"My past is mine to keep," he demurred. "You won't know of it, and neither will anyone else, so don't worry—the reputation of your precious Order will be safe."

"So is what you're doing some kind of penitence?" Lyrah asked.

Daylen looked away dismissively. "Something like that."

"Because of something you did or because of your father?"

He returned his gaze to hers before saying, "Both."

"You're not responsible for your father's crimes. And what could you have done to cause giving up your life out of guilt?"

"Nothing that anyone will ever know."

It was clear that Lyrah wasn't satisfied with that, but she must have known that there was nothing she could do about it.

"All right then," Lyrah said eventually, "the Dawnists. What's your plan?"

"My plan is to find one of those Dawnist soap boxers and get them to tell me where their leader is."

"And why do you think they'll tell you?"

Daylen looked at her knowingly.

"Ah."

"Exactly."

"There should be Dawnists in one of the city squares."

"Or I could just listen for the nearest one," Daylen said.

"That's right, you can stack four bonds whenever you want. So effectively you're a weak Listener."

"Weak?"

"A level-four bond can be impressive, but it's nothing compared to what a strong Listener can do with a level six, or a high Listener can do with a level nine."

"*Nine*? There're Archknights that can make level-*nine* bonds? I thought you knights only had three?"

"There's far more to our powers than you know, though very few get that strong."

"What can they do, hear words spoken on the other side of the continent?"

Lyrah smiled.

"Really, they can do that?"

"I'm not telling you."

"Oh come on!"

She smiled at him haughtily.

"You *like* teasing people, don't you?" Daylen said accusingly.

"Only when they deserve it."

He would have tried to guilt her about that, but considering he liked teasing people too, he couldn't bring himself to do it.

Daylen channeled as much light as he could into his hearing, focusing on any speech about the Conqueror.

At first the noise nearly deafened him, but he quickly focused, noticing something troubling. His head spun in that direction.

"What is it?" Lyrah asked.

"A cry for help," Daylen said and, without hesitating, he ran toward it. The Dawnists could wait.

Lyrah was following him without any objection, and with a few well-aimed power jumps they reached the alleyway where a woman was being chased by two men.

Daylen and Lyrah landed right in between the woman and the two men, who pulled up looking utterly shocked.

"It's...it's him," one of them men whispered to the other. "The guy in the papers."

"Oh, Light," the other moaned.

Daylen approached the scum while Lyrah saw to their trauma-tized victim.

"We haven't done anything," one of them said as they backed away.

"Judging by that woman's torn dress, you were certainly trying," Daylen growled, sensing that there was barely any light within these depraved men.

Then they fell to the ground, decapitated, but not from anything Daylen did. Lyrah had ran forward in a flash and killed them both.

The woman screamed at seeing the carnage.

"How is that any different from what I did in Treremain?" Daylen growled at her.

Lyrah sent a sideways glare at him before pulling out a cloth and cleaning her two-handed warsword. "We found them in the act of attempted rape, their hearts were nearly as black as Shade, and as a *real* Archknight I have judicial authority to carry out sentences. And to further distinguish myself from you, we're going to find a nearby constable to let him know what has happened."

"But if you came across the criminal grubs that I did in Treremain, you would have killed them just the same as me. You never thought my actions were unjustified—it was all about forcing me to join the knights!"

Lyrah lowered her hands and turned toward him. "Your killings being justified or not was the difference between trusting and not trusting you. I had no idea what you were like."

"But you do now?"

"I'm starting to."

That was about as good an admission of trust as Daylen would get, so he was happy to let that subject rest. "All right, let's find that constable and I'll try and listen for a Dawnist again. But in a city this big, there'll always be someone else in trouble."

Lyrah walked back to the woman who was now sobbing on the ground, "If you hear someone calling for help, then we help."

Daylen smiled. "I wouldn't have it any other way."

Three rapists, eight muggings, a murder attempt, and two wife-beaters later, Daylen was holding their ninth mugger by the neck. "What should we do with this one? Chop off an arm?"

"No," Lyrah said. "How could he serve out his sentence properly with a missing arm?"

The mugger squirmed and constantly tried to get free. Daylen punched him in the stomach so hard that he would struggle to breathe for the next few minutes. "Well that depends on what type of slavery he'll be sentenced to. You only need one arm to wipe someone's ass."

"That's if he's lucky enough to end up a manslave. The other option is the mines."

"Well, he couldn't work the mines with one arm," Daylen said and turned to the mugger, who was still struggling to breathe. "So we can either chop off your arm and thereby increase your chances to become a manslave, or leave you in one piece where you'll rot as a mineslave."

"P-please…"

"I think we've scared him enough," Lyrah said.

Daylen dropped the miserable idiot, who crumpled to the ground, crying.

"So, why'd you do it?" Daylen asked.

"We're starving," the man groaned.

"And threatening someone with a knife is the way to fix that?"

"I'm sorry," he sobbed. "I'd never really have hurt him. I just needed the money."

Daylen sighed. It was a sad and common story, an otherwise good man turning to crime because of poverty. Both Lyrah and Daylen had been gentler with this one on account of the light they both sensed inside him.

Daylen fished out a crown from his pouch and dropped it on the cobblestones.

The man stared at it. "W-what?"

"Use it to feed your family. Don't ever be so stupid again, got it?"

"Thank you, I…"

"Get out of here."

"Really, I…"

"GO!" Daylen growled.

The man jumped back and then ran away.

"That was generous of you," Lyrah said.

"I'm surprised you let me, with how by the books you are and all."

"Actually, if you had tried to arrest him, I would have stopped you. That man deserved a second chance."

Daylen couldn't help but smile at that. As hard as Lyrah was, she was also compassionate.

"On to the next one?" Lyrah asked.

"My powers are getting sluggish and I won't be able to use them for much longer, so this time we really do have to go to the Dawnist."

"Huh, you can use your powers so proficiently that it's easy to forget how green you are."

"I'm not green."

"Yes you are," she replied smoothly. "Your bonds are as raw as they get, only being able to maintain them for an hour. You really need to do some conditioning."

"So I can get them to work for longer?"

"Of course."

"Well, thanks for telling me. And I didn't even have to join the knights."

Lyrah's expression dropped and then she glared at him. "Savor it. You're not getting anything else."

Daylen smiled. She had let her guard down because she was actually enjoying his company, and the truth was that Daylen was enjoying hers, too. Far more than he deserved. Lyrah was intelligent, compassionate, and strong, and in the short hour that they had been working together to do good, he had almost been able to forget their past.

"Why don't the knights do this?"

"You mean what we've been doing?"

"Yeah."

"The Shade."

"That can't take up all your time."

"The Shade are far more numerous than you think," Lyrah said, and then added in a softer tone, "and the knights far fewer... I wish I could help individual people every day, believe me. But fighting the Shade helps the world more. Also, apart from the Shade, you need at least a level-four Listener to hear distant cries for help. They and Sniffers are the best ones for digging out Shade nests, so you can guess what they're most often assigned to. The problem is that few knights choose to specialize in listening or sniffing because those abilities can't be used in combat. Thus Listeners and

Sniffers are some of the most valuable and vulnerable members of the Order."

"I see," Daylen said, grateful that Lyrah had been so open with him. In fact, it made him want to join the knights sooner. With his four bonds, just how strong could he really become? He could truly help the knights, and thereby the world.

Daylen enhanced his hearing and listened for those lost idiots that *actually* loved his past self. He couldn't help but notice several cries of distress, but at the end of the day he was one man and he couldn't save everyone. It made him sick, but this was just like the choice the knights had to do: to fight the Shade or help regular people. Whatever the Dawnists were planning wasn't good, and it needed to be rooted out.

"There's a soap boxer around three kilometers that way."

"Do you need a rest before we go?"

"I'll manage," Daylen said, and then launched himself into the sky with a power jump.

———

Daylen landed in an alleyway about a city block from the Dawnist, Lyrah right behind him.

"He's on the corner of the street over," Daylen said.

"Lead the way," Lyrah replied.

They left the alley and it didn't take long for them to draw a decent amount of attention.

"Is it you or me that everyone's looking at?" Daylen asked.

"I'd say it's both. As a knight I always stand out, and then there's you with your Grand High Master's Mark. You're also becoming quite recognizable thanks to the press."

"We're quite the potent combination."

Lyrah glanced at him with a slight smile.

"You'll have to stay at a distance while I talk to the Dawnist. They're less likely to trust me if you're around."

"Agreed," Lyrah said, and walked off.

Daylen approached the Dawnist who looked to be a factory worker. He was calling out to the passersby—no crowd around this one.

He stopped mid-speech as he saw Daylen.

"You!"

"Yes," Daylen said, glancing around to make sure no one was listening. Several people were, so he stepped in closer. "I want to join."

"You do!"

"Quiet! But yes. I need to speak with your leader."

The skinny man leaned down and whispered, "Go to fourteen over thirty-two in the Brickhollow Tenement community on Nail Street, Maraden District. They'll definitely let you in."

"Thanks," Daylen said before walking back to meet Lyrah.

"Fourteen over thirty-two, Brickhollow Tenement on Nail Street in Maraden District," Daylen said once Lyrah had rejoined him.

"You don't really think that's where the Dawnist leader is?"

"I don't know. We'll have to wait and see."

"Even if their leader isn't there, if you can find something that belongs to him, you'll be able to track him by enhancing your scent."

"Tracking, of course," Daylen said, feeling stupid. "That makes sense. I mean, hounds can track people through scent. Honestly, I had forgotten about enhancing it ever since I experimented with it falls ago. I just hadn't needed it since then."

"Well with a level-four bond on scent you can do more than track people."

"You're talking about emotion."

"Yes."

"I find it easy enough to read people's emotions, so I've had little need to smell them out."

"Unless people are trying to hide their feelings. I'm only saying this because it might be useful to know the emotions of the Dawnist leader."

"That's good advice," Daylen said, giving Lyrah a suspicious look.

"What?"

"You're teaching me about our powers. I thought that wasn't going to happen until I joined the knights."

Lyrah's eyes narrowed. "It's for the sake of the mission, so take it as a small sample of what the knights can *really* teach you."

"I understand completely. So, while you're being forthcoming and all, is there anything else that might help me?"

"One other thing," she said disdainfully. "If you're going in to try and get them to inadvertently reveal information, channel all your bonds to your voice. One bond to the voice can increase the volume in which you speak, but you can reduce the volume to a normal level even while channeling. Regardless of the volume, channeling light to one's voice has a supernatural effect on your words. The more bonds you channel to your voice, the greater influence your words will have on people. It can increase people's disposition to agree with you, do what you suggest, or help them understand a concept you're trying to explain."

"Wow, that's amazing."

She nodded. "You can stack four bonds to voice, which will be very potent. Just remember that it's not mind control," she warned. "If they don't want to talk about something, like a secret, or if the person is aware of the influence, they can resist no matter how many bonds are used—it's just harder. But if they're unaware, and their guard is down, especially if they trust you, with a level-four bond you can get them to reveal nearly anything."

"Thanks."

"I didn't do it for you."

"Not even just a little bit?"

Lyrah didn't answer and walked ahead.

Daylen caught up. "So, how often have you enhanced your voice around me?"

"Like it's had any effect. You're as stubborn as a mule."

"Stubbornness is a factor in how effective it is?"

"Of course."

"So we're both immune to it then," Daylen said, smiling.

Lyrah glared at him. Daylen just smiled back.

He really was enjoying this.

CHAPTER FORTY

The countless discontents throughout my empire saw what I did to those who rebelled, and so they didn't dare do so openly. Instead they acted with more subtlety. Rayaten Leusa had grown in great influence over the years preceding the Daybreak Massacre, but after that, something changed. So many things in my empire stopped running smoothly, with breaks in supply lines, production problems, and attacks on government buildings and barracks, all being run by a group of underground rebels. I later learned that all these efforts were organized by this one man, Rayaten, who had become wholly consumed by his opposition to me. Despite the bounty I put on his head and the men I sent to hunt him out, I never found him.

Instead, most of my men came back dead.

They decided to catch a skycoach, which let Daylen's powers recover somewhat from the excessive use.

Once the coach landed, Daylen looked out his window at Brickhollow. The tenement community was a collection of tall, thin buildings squeezed together that boarded a single short lane in a U-shape. The street was littered with small bits of rubbish, scraps, and debris, with dirty children playing in the lane and the elderly sitting on old chairs out front.

Clotheslines were strung over the central lane from building to building with linens hanging in the still air.

"From the look of it I almost understand why the Dawnists want a revolution," Lyrah said.

"There were far more slums like this during the Dawn Empire," Daylen replied. "Enough to fuel a nation's rebellion."

"Just because there's less poor now doesn't mean that there should be any poor at all."

"Yeah," Daylen said with a sigh. "You'll need to wait here."

"I know."

"See you soon," Daylen said, and exited the coach.

The smell in this part of the city was offensive, and Daylen wondered when the last time the council had sent some slaves here to clean the streets.

He enhanced his perception and quickly noticed many distrustful eyes on him, as well as three dirty young men skulking in the shadows of an alleyway looking as if they were ready to rob him.

He released his bond and was met by a soft headache in return. "Yep, my head really doesn't seem to like me bonding light to it." He channeled to heal himself which, once again, didn't push the pain away completely.

Daylen walked into the tenement block and was pleased to see that he wasn't followed. Making his way through the piles of rubbish he came upon a very aged man sitting on a damaged chair in front of one of the buildings. The image stopped Daylen in his tracks, for looking upon the old man Daylen could only see himself. They must have been close in age. An oddity, for few people lived so long, what with the Fourth Night, Daylen's rule and the bloody second revolution—a person was very lucky to survive all of that, or unlucky depending on how you looked at it.

Daylen approached the man who stared at him uninterestedly.

"Excuse me." Daylen said, "But could I have a moment of your time?"

The man's eyes twitched and he seemed to register Daylen for the first time. "What, who're you?" he said in a slurred voice, most of his teeth missing.

"I'm no one," Daylen said. "I was just wondering—did you live through the Fourth Night?"

The man's focus switched, gazing into his own memory. "The

Fourth Night, terrible it was... I fought them, you know—the monsters, I fought them."

"Then you're a hero."

"No, it was those that went into the Underworld, they're the heroes."

"Even Dayless the Conqueror?"

"He was Daylen Namaran back then, before he became the Great Bastard... A good man, once."

It was hard for Daylen to control his emotion at hearing this. The mere fact that this man had lived through so many terrible things made his life worth honoring. Yet here he was, cast off, sitting amongst trash. It was heartbreaking. This man had certainly lived a better life than Daylen—yet who would be remembered?

"Please tell me your name."

"Parpen."

"It's good to meet you, Parpen," Daylen said, kneeling down and handing the man two crowns.

"What's this for?" Parpen said in amazement.

"For living a good life."

Parpen huffed. "I don't have much to show for it, and I don't have much life left, either."

"Such a long life is a burden few people bear. Have you lived in light?"

"I tried."

Judging by the man's inner light he had more than tried. Light, he must have been a saint. "Then I can't see why the Light wouldn't welcome you into its rest."

"I guess I'll find out soon enough."

"I'm glad to have met you, Parpen. I hope you find peace." And Daylen left the old man on his chair, wishing he had time to befriend him properly.

It was easy for Daylen to find the thirty-second unit of flats.

Those three thugs had skulked out of their alleyway and were now hiding around the corner that led into the main central lane of the block.

Daylen entered the flat, climbed the stairs to the fourteenth apartment, and knocked on the door.

A tall bulky man answered, and his eyes widened as soon as he saw Daylen.

The man must have been in his thirties, meaning he would have been ten years old or so when Daylen had been deposed. How could anyone who lived during the Dawn Empire want to bring it back? Just going off statistics, everyone from that time would have had at least had one relative or friend executed, if not more.

Daylen stacked his bonds to voice before speaking carefully and with control. "I'm the son of Dayless the Conqueror. Let me in."

The man was silent for a second before stepping aside.

Daylen entered to see three other tall men of varying muscle and girth standing near the door, each armed with a rapier.

Two of the muscled men looked young, but the last looked older than twenty, meaning he too must have lived during Daylen's rule. *Are these people mad?*

The apartment's walls and roof all had wet rot, the carpet stained and dirty. In the adjoining room several weathered chairs had been arranged in rows. They were being addressed by a woman who had pale blue hair with deeper blue streaks throughout in a short cut.

The woman paused when Daylen entered, staring at him with pair of sharp and truly stunning eyes. She was wearing a button-up white shirt and black slacks with a rapier at her curved hip.

She was gorgeous and must have been in her late twenties or early thirties, though still a pup to Daylen's older eyes.

"You'll have to excuse me," the woman said to the seated group.

"Jena," a seated man said, "we'll need to leave soon."

"I know," she said in a soft, almost timid voice, "but this might be important." A head shorter than Daylen, she was slight and curvaceous. She approached him with a look of awe. "It's true—you look exactly like him."

"Are you in charge?"

Jena's demeanor changed and she smiled, looking suddenly confident. "That depends," she said playfully.

"On what?"

"What you want. Last I heard, you weren't exactly sympathetic to our cause."

Daylen stacked all his bonds to his scent and wasn't prepared for how hard the putrid smells of this place would hit him. It nearly caused him to lose his composure, but he quickly focused his scent to smell for emotion and targeted the sense to the young woman.

This Jena was radiating a smell of...well, the only way Daylen could describe it was *sex*. His mind processes that smell into an understanding. She was attracted to him. Powerfully attracted to him, if this smell was anything to go off. There was also a prickly smell that Daylen instinctively knew as caution. Daylen switched his bonds back to his voice.

"I want to know why you revere my father."

"Simple," Jena said. "He was a great man. Do you know that he was a bona fide war hero before he even became Emperor?"

"Trust me, you don't know more about Dayless the Conqueror than me."

Jena shook her head, smirking. "No. You grew up in an orphanage and only lived with the Conqueror for a few years before he died. I've spent my whole life studying your father. I understand who he *really* was."

Daylen gritted his teeth. This idiot girl knew nothing. What would she say if she knew that the *real* Dayless the Conqueror was actually standing right before her?

"Didn't you read the letter he left? It's been reprinted in the papers. Dayless hated himself for all that he had done."

"If he really did write that letter, which I'm not convinced is true, he must have lost his way and forgot the vision he had for a unified and just world."

Daylen pushed down his growing rage and did his best to not choke on his own words. This girl was attracted to him after all, so he would certainly catch more flies with honey, as the saying went.

"You might be right," Daylen said, looking Jena in the eyes. "Father was very reluctant to speak of his past. He was a different man toward the end, and I want to know who he was. I think you're the one who can teach me on this...as well as many other things."

Jena smiled, her sharp eyes twinkling. "Then you've come to the right place." She nodded to the muscle surrounding them. They relaxed. "You can call me Jena. Come."

That was easy, Daylen thought. *I'll have to remember to enhance my voice more often.*

Jena led Daylen to a study with several portraits of himself hanging on the walls. "We've saved as many of these as we can," Jena said. "The Senate opted to keep a few for history's sake, but only ones that vilify the great man. None truly capture his strength, though your appearance has served to show the younger generation what the Conqueror truly looked like." She looked at a portrait and spoke softly. "He was probably the most handsome man who ever lived, not the scowling villain the Senate wishes to instill on our minds."

Jena turned back to Daylen. "And you look exactly like him..." She suddenly became shy and brushed her hair behind her ear. She walked to sit behind her desk. "What would you like to know?" she asked, waving a hand to the seat on the other side of the desk.

Daylen sat and asked, "You're old enough to have lived during the Conqueror's rule, seen what it was like; how could you have any positive feelings toward a man that oppressed you?"

Jena leaned forward, resting her chin on laced fingers. "Just the thing every woman wants to hear: how old they are."

Daylen choked back a snort. "Oh, trust me, girl, you're practically a baby on the larger scale."

Her mouth pressed together at that. Probably not the best response to a woman trying to flirt with him. "My question?"

"It's a matter of perspective," Jena said, leaning back. "They say the Conqueror starved his people, but the truth is that no one died of famine. He made sure everyone had enough, reserving the larger portion for his armies and storehouses, all to protect his people from invasion and the next Night."

"I doubt you would be saying that if he had executed anyone close to you."

"My parents," she replied flatly.

"What?" Daylen asked, shocked.

"My parents were executed by the Conqueror."

Daylen's mouth fell open and he couldn't think of anything to say.

"I was heartbroken, of course," Jena continued. "I *was* just a child, after all. But once I grew up, I wanted to know why they had been executed. In fact, that was the reason I started to search out the truth about your father. It turned out my parents were part of the rebellion and had tried to sabotage one of the Empire's battle-ships." Her mouth turned down in displeasure. "If they had succeeded, the entire crew of the ship would have been killed. Innocent soldiers only doing their part to protect their nation and families. It was a hard thing to realize, that my parents were murderers, and the truth is that they deserved to be executed," she finished tightly.

Daylen was lost for words. He had never expected to find a family member of one of his victims to be *happy* with what he had done.

Looking at Jena, this soft-spoken and slight-statured girl, Daylen now saw a cold hardness behind those discerning eyes.

Jena smiled at him. "You see, the real question isn't how we Dawnists can love your father, but why everyone else hates him so much." She started to speak matter-of-factly. "Dayless the Conqueror sought to make all men equal. His wars were fought to protect his people, his laws were fair and his punishments just. Do you know it was really the Guilds that promoted and funded the majority of the resistance against him? Think about that. They were hoarding most of the wealth in the nation from the majority of its citizens, and when the Conqueror sought to regulate their practices and redistribute their stolen wealth to those who rightly deserved it, they betrayed him for their own ends."

Her words grew in passion as she continued, a stark contrast to her natural soft voice. "Just look at how much the revolution has benefited the Guilds and craftsmen. They've expanded their oper-ations, making the wretched factories that we must work in like slaves. The Conqueror never would have allowed this—he would have protected his people. That should be his name: the Great Protector, not the Great Bastard. The Guild Masters have now formed their own Great Houses, where the true rulers of this nation come from. They're all corrupt!" she hissed. "Light, they've essentially resurrected the old oppressive aristocracy!"

Daylen could see her point with that one regarding the division of the rich and poor but it neglected the glaring differences between the aristocracy, the Dawn Empire and the modern day. These falls anyone could become rich and own land.

"Is there a single senator that's come from the factories or the tenements?" She continued, "No! The rich ensure that the rich are elected, who will serve their interests—and the rest of us, the majority of the nation, suffer in poverty."

Daylen had to suppress a snort. The rich ensured that the rich are elected? Was she actually paying attention to her words? The poor constituted the larger vote. The reason why the rich were in power was because *the poor were electing them*. Granted, there were more complex reasons behind this like access to education but it all ignored the fact that getting someone elected from the factories or tenements didn't ensure they would represent the poor any more than assuming someone who was rich wouldn't. She was making moral judgments upon people based on their social status rather than their individual actions, the same thing Daylen had done when he overthrew the aristocracy and executed them.

Listening to Jena—her intelligence, her conviction, her passion —it was clear that she was more than a pretty face. True anger resonated in her voice and it simply took enhancing his scent to confirm that her conviction was real. On top of that, there was actually a measure of light within her. She honestly believed what she was saying was the right thing whilst at the very same time excusing mass murder. Oh, what foul and corrupt things humans could be. With such conviction, it would be easy for others to fall for this woman's lies and half-truths.

It infuriated Daylen, for no one knew better than he how evil the Dawn Empire had been. In fact it infuriated him so much that before he even realized it, he had hissed the words out through clenched teeth: "I am Dayless the Conqueror."

Jena looked at him as if he had lost his mind.

"I *am* Dayless the Conqueror," Daylen said with every bond channeling light to his voice. "I never fathered a child while in hiding; instead I found a way to make myself young again." Daylen stood and Jena's expression showed that she was now taking him far more seriously. "And let me tell you, Jena, you're nothing but a deranged zealot. I despise everything you stand for. I didn't lose my way while in hiding; it was there that I finally found myself again. I rediscovered the man who fought through the Fourth Night, the hero you say you love, and that man would have been horrified at everything I did as Emperor. He would have fought with all his power to destroy him!"

Daylen glared at the woman, who was now staring at him in shock. "The problems in the current government don't validate the

Dawn Empire. Redistributing wealth is just another name for state-sanctioned theft. I stole everything from everybody—land, money, and resources—and then gave back just enough for the people to survive, hoarding the rest for my military and indulgence. I murdered anyone who opposed me, took away the people's right to speak, the very freedom you flaunt on countless soap boxes through the city. I would have slaughtered any group who spoke against me to the level you speak against the current government, so as bad as you say things are, they're a damn sight better than the Dawn Empire and aristocracy. You want a better life for the poor—*good*! But bringing back the failed and oppressive ideologies of the past is the most foolish thing you can do. The Dawn Empire is *not* the answer. You would be just as poor as you are now, but even more oppressed and miserable."

"The Conqueror would never say this!"

"I AM THE CONQUEROR!" he seethed. "I need to be remembered as the tyrant I was."

"You were a hero!"

"I was a *despot*."

"NO!" Jena screamed, rising to her feet. "You freed us from the aristocracy!"

"And I also slaughtered their children. Nothing excuses that."

Jena's eyes grew colder with each word. "You did what you had to do to ensure the safety of the empire. It was a just sacrifice."

Daylen stared at her. "You really believe that, don't you?"

"I would have done the same."

A clearer comprehension dawned in Daylen's mind of who this Jena really was, and what she was capable of. "What are you planning?"

"You think I'd tell you?"

I need to try a different approach, Daylen though. "Like I really need to know," Daylen said condescendingly as he turned away. "You're a bunch of pathetic peasants. A mob of angry children pose a greater threat."

"You won't be thinking that in a fall."

Daylen smiled. Belittling her had worked. Jena had just revealed that their plan was already in motion. Daylen suspected that Jena would never slip like this regularly but he had the benefit of a supernaturally enhanced voice.

Daylen pretended to look worried as he spun toward the

woman. "What do you mean?"

"Let's just say that this city will never be the same again."

"You don't have the numbers."

"We don't need numbers to punish our oppressors," she spat. "And who knows—once the government is gone, there just might be room for the Dawn Empire to step in and bring order." Jena suddenly looked confused as if surprised by what she had said. "Something's wrong. My head… It's fuzzy."

She was feeling the effect of Daylen's voice.

Daylen switched his bonds to strength and threw the desk aside like it was paper. He grabbed Jena by the shirt, enhancing his voice again. "How are you going to destroy the government?"

"It's too late."

"HOW!"

Jena seemed to struggle with herself, her eyes wide and fixed as she fought against the pull of Daylen's power. The thugs from outside burst in.

"I'll tell you nothing!" she said, snarling. "You're *not* the Conqueror. You're nothing," she spat at Daylen. "LONG LIVE THE TRUE CONQUEROR! LONG LIVE THE DAWN EMPIRE!"

Daylen screamed, switching his bonds to strength, and Jena's head exploded from one empowered punch.

Her lifeless body slumped to the floor, blood pooling everywhere as Daylen dealt with the thugs.

The Dawnists in the adjoining rooms either attacked him or ran. The four that attacked didn't last a second.

Enhancing his speed and reflexes, Daylen ducked their sword strikes and lunged forward into the middle of the group and sliced them in half with Imperious' enhanced edge in one broad full-circle slash.

Daylen paused among the dead bodies for a brief moment, feeling sick at how easy it was for him to kill so many, but he quickly came to his senses and raced out of the building and across the street.

Lyrah was standing next to the coach and obviously noticed his blood-soaked hand. "What under the Light?"

"The Dawnists are planning to destroy the Senate within a fall's time."

"Then we just have to move the senators to a safe place."

"No," he said, shaking his head. "They're planning something bigger, something that will change the city forever."

"What? How?"

"I don't know. They wouldn't have kept any plans here. It's too public, but I have the scent of their leader."

"Yes, good. They must have a secret meeting place."

"We'll take the coach, it's faster."

Lyrah ran to the driver's cabin, threw open the door and said, "Out!"

The driver stumbled out of the cabin as fast as he could.

Lyrah climbed in and Daylen joined, saying, "I'm driving."

Daylen pulled open the underside of the control levers and quickly ripped out several safety regulators.

"What are you doing?"

"We're going to need speed."

"For all you know, you just crippled the ship!"

"If I did, this should be impossible," Daylen said, pulling the ship's throttle and lift levers. The coach strained in protest as it launched into the air faster than it had ever been intended.

Daylen worked the levers with absolute focus, weaving the coach through the streets, buildings, smaller islands, and other skyships.

"You could have ripped the core from the coach!"

"I know how far I can push these things."

"Where did you learn to fly like this?" Lyrah asked.

"Let's just say I have a fondness for skyships and leave it at that."

With a level-four bond to the scent, Daylen could do more than track Jena's movements: he could sniff out her entire path for the past several falls, knowing each point she stopped. With Daylen's profound familiarity with the city—he had built most of it after all—he could easily tell which location for the true headquarters of the Dawnists was most likely: an old abandoned factory in a run-down and unused part of the industrial sector.

"What could they hope to achieve by destroying the Senate?" Lyrah asked as the skycoach flew at speed. "Doing so would never resurrect the Dawn Empire. They don't have the support."

"It's more revenge than a proper revolution," Daylen said. "The Dawnists want to destroy their oppressors."

"So I'm guessing that their leader is dead?"

"Yeah," Daylen said flatly.

"What did he do?"

"She," he corrected.

"Their leader was a woman?"

"Yep."

"And you killed her?"

"Without a second thought."

"Why?"

"Um, maybe the fact that she's planning to destroy the government?"

"I know, but we could have questioned her."

"That zealot wouldn't have revealed anything. She was too dangerous to be left alive."

"Okay... I'll trust you."

Daylen looked to Lyrah, incredulous.

"What?" she asked.

"You trust me?"

"Just focus on flying."

Daylen smiled and did so, eventually guiding the coach into a slide landing right in front of the old factory.

Jumping out of the coach, Daylen and Lyrah quickly found that this factory wasn't nearly as abandoned as it appeared.

Several armed men and women ran out and attacked them. Daylen drew his new sword and swung it into his left hand, summoning Imperious to duel wield and take out these idiots as fast as possible.

He literally cut them into pieces.

Lyrah was right next to him and her strength was incredible. Grabbing each person that charged her, man or woman, and throwing them into walls or one another like they were rattan balls.

How can she become so strong with only three bonds? Daylen wondered once again.

Seconds later, every Dawnist that had attacked them was dead.

"You would be really good at rattan," Daylen said.

"It's my favorite sport."

They ran into the building, Daylen enhancing his speed and noting that he was much, much faster than Lyrah. She was fast, of course, supernaturally so, but nothing close to the level-three bond Daylen had made, keeping his last bond on scent, which was enough to track things close by.

Daylen continued to follow Jena's trail, which led him through the factory rooms to the basement and a brick wall. Jena's path led through it, which meant the wall must be movable. Daylen didn't have time to look about for whatever mechanism moved the thing, so he enhanced his mass and strength, stepping back for a charge —but then Lyrah came running past and crashed through the wall as if it were paper.

Daylen followed, entering a large vaulted brick room with a primary central table and several desks facing the walls.

No one was in this room, but there were many papers scattered on the tables, the most interesting of which lay on the center table.

Lyrah and Daylen ran to it and leafed through the papers.

There were hundreds of notations, equations, designs, and schematics.

"I don't understand any of this," Lyrah said.

"They're designs to repurpose the sunstone drives of skyships," Daylen said.

"You understand all this math?"

"I know a thing or two about engineering," Daylen said as he flipped through a large design pad, before stopping at a detailed drawing of a large chunk of rock. From the shrubbery at its top, it was clearly a floating island.

"Oh, *Light*," Daylen said with dread.

"What?"

"Those bastards!"

"What is it?"

"That's why Blackheart was selling skyships to the Dawnists. They've been illegally buying ships and repurposing their drives to fit them to the core of this island," Daylen said, pointing.

"Is that even possible with an island that big?"

"With enough directed and intense light, any hunk of darkstone will move."

"But I thought there were limits."

"Only under the square of its mass. If the core of this island is small enough and they have sufficient drives, they can do it. It's how smaller sky islands are moved over the city. Dig through the rock, fix the drives, and if you're committed enough you could turn a larger floating island into a moving mountain." Daylen took a deep breath, staring at Lyrah. "They're going to ram a five-hundred-meter-wide hunk of rock into Highdawn."

CHAPTER FORTY-ONE

*I pressed on through my setbacks, hunting out the rebels while
waging war, eventually defeating Zantium, Lee'on'ta, and
Toulsen, with Lourane and Orden being the last nations that held
out against my might.*
*It was then that the Arch Order of Light finally declared war on
the Dawn Empire, decreeing that I was a threat to the peoples of
the world. This was unprecedented, for until then, the knights had
never taken sides in disputes between nations.*

T he shield might be able to stop it."

"Highdawn's shield was designed to stop annihilators,
and that was hard enough. This thing is a hundred times their size,
and thanks to the good old square-cube law, its momentum once
in motion is going to be *insane*. The shield's anchors are going to
be pulverized to dust!"

"If this thing gets through the shield it will completely destroy
the upper islands," Lyrah said in dread.

"That's where the wealthiest districts are. The Dawnists see the
rich as their enemies as much as the Senate, and they don't even
care that so many poor will get killed too, the genocidal bastards.
But now that we know their plan, we should have enough time to
stop it. We just need to board the island, find the tunnels, and take
out the drivers."

"Could it be that easy?"

"If I had planned this, I would have collapsed the tunnels once the drivers were in place as well as made as many defenses as I could just in case."

"You think they're that prepared?"

"I do—Jena was a zealot, but shrewd. She'll have made as many preparations as she could think of."

"Then we need to evacuate the city and get as much help as possible. I can do that from the Hold and gather the other knights. From there we can also alert the border patrols."

"You've said there are a few knights that can make a level-nine bond. Would any of them be powerful enough to just destroy the thing?"

"Um... maybe. Archeron Peroven has a level-nine lightning bond and can call down a storm of destruction, but that might not be enough to sunder the island. Anyway, he's at the Arch Hold and won't be able to get here in time."

"Peroven?" Daylen asked, recognizing the name. "Was he the one who destroyed the second fleet in the Empire War?"

"Yes, but that isn't important right now," Lyrah replied impatiently.

"Yeah," he agreed quickly. "So are there any applications of our powers that could destroy the island?"

"No. Neither of us are that type of Lightbinder."

"Cueseg, your companion, he can—he shot me with lightning."

"Cueseg can only make a level-three lightning bond, and like I said, I don't think a massive bombardment of lightning would even destroy the island."

"All right, are there any Lightbinders like Cueseg..."

"Worldbinders. You and I are Lifebinders. The others are Worldbinders."

"So we need a powerful enough Worldbinder."

"Yes, but even then they need to have specialized the right bond to be useful. The only type of bond that I can think could do it would be an earth bond. There's a few knights with that type of specialization, but none close to us, and their bonds might not even be strong enough."

"That leaves us with no other choice but to assault the island and take out the drivers."

"It seems so."

"I'll grab Ahrek and meet you at the Hold."

"Good idea, a Bringer will be useful," Lyrah said, and they both ran from the room as fast as they could.

Daylen watched Lyrah as she power jumped away. He took the coach and flew it to the Fallton.

I just can't escape my cursed legacy, Daylen thought to himself as he raced over the city skyline. *These blackened Dawnists want to follow my horrible example and start another revolution so that the bloody cycle of history might continue. Why can't they see that life here is so much better than the Empire? I won't let another nation fall in my name. It's appropriate, poetic even, that I'll be the one to stop them.*

Daylen lurched the coach to a stop at the penthouse patio and ran in, sensing that Ahrek was back from his personal errands.

He was sitting on one of the dining chairs in the middle of the foyer.

"Ahrek, we have to go."

Ahrek took a moment to answer. "I suspected you from the first time we met," he said in a soft, defeated tone.

"What are you talking about?"

"I thought my suspicion foolish, but I just kept noticing things. Like how you said you've visited the cities of the Floating Isles. You know enough about them for that to be true, but when I mentioned that I'd heard they were rebuilt, you said that you had *heard* the same, not *seen*, meaning you hadn't visited them since their destruction, which occurred before the time of your supposed birth."

Oh no, Daylen thought numbly.

"That might have simply been a slip of the tongue, but you speak with the knowledge and experience of someone far, far older. You possess skills that take a lifetime to develop and perfect. You face battle with the confidence and calm of one that has fought in war. The Shade thought you the Conqueror. You know the names of the girls he forced into his bed and every sunucle that was linked to him is linked to you."

Ahrek remained staring at the wall, his back still to Daylen. "Still, even with all this, I gave you the benefit of the doubt—that was until this fall, where I spoke to a sunsmith and paid a visit to the records office. The sunsmith told me that indeed a link has a very small chance to pass on, but only to the first-born child. We both know that Dayless fathered hundreds of children, and if you were one of them, you would be among the last born, not the first, which means there's only one way that Imperious could be linked to you. At the records office I found that every single thing you've said about your childhood was a lie. There is no birth certificate of you anywhere, and your name is missing from every single orphanage in all of Mornington."

Ahrek stood and turned to face Daylen with an expression as cold as death. "So, Daylen, I'm going to ask you a question—and by the Light, you will answer me honestly. Are you Dayless the Conqueror?"

CHAPTER FORTY-TWO

*After the knights declared war, things changed drastically for me.
No one really understands how powerful the knights are. I
certainly underestimated them after killing my advisor knight,
Puppy, but apparently Puppy wasn't particularly strong.
In one battle, a single knight defeated a whole fleet, summoning
an apocalyptic storm and calling down lightning that utterly
devastated my ships.
Once the Knights joined the resistance, who were well prepared
and equipped, I was beaten back again and again.*

Daylen's heart felt like it had been pulled down further and
further with each word, and he now looked at Ahrek feeling
nothing, his soul void and empty. "Yes," he replied.

Ahrek's face was as still as stone. "Which Bringer did it?"

"Did what?"

"Used his last miracle to make you young?"

"I didn't even know that was possible."

"You have lied to me every fall from the time we met, *Dayless,*"
Ahrek said, the last word dripping with venom. "STOP IT!"

"No Bringer did this to me," Daylen said truthfully. "I was
turned young when I received my powers, and trust me, it's not
what I wanted. If you recall from the note I left, I was actually
trying to kill myself."

"Yes, by casting yourself from the continent. Pity that didn't work out for you."

"Yeah. Now what?"

Ahrek huffed a bitter laugh. "It's funny that we've never truly met before the freak accident that turned you young. We have a long history, you and I."

"What do you mean?"

"Ahrek isn't my original name; it's the one I took up after becoming a Lightbringer."

"Really?" Daylen asked, wondering numbly in what way and to what extent he had hurt this man. "So who are you, then?"

Ahrek stared into Daylen's eyes, their faces locked. "Rayaten Leusa."

Daylen stumbled back, feeling as if Ahrek had just physically kicked him in the gut. His world reeled and he fell to the floor, catching himself with a hand.

"*You're* Rayaten Leusa?" Daylen asked, his eyes wide in utter astonishment.

"Yes. Every battle you fought against the rebellion, every alliance forged against you—I was behind it all."

Daylen's head was spinning.

"Do you know why I became the leader of the revolution?"

"No."

Ahrek's voice quivered as he spoke. "You *killed* my family. My wife. My son, my daughters! You killed them all, you *bastard!*"

"I…I'm sorry," Daylen said quietly.

"You think that means *anything?!*"

He shook his head. "I know it doesn't."

"Anara, my wife; Deston, my son; Arenna and Sereen, my daughters," Ahrek fumed bitterly. "Know the names of at least a few that you butchered!"

"I'll remember them."

"Good—and now you'll take those names to your grave." In a flash of light, Ahrek created a white diamond sunforged blade and kite shield, swinging the sword down at Daylen.

Without thinking, Daylen's sword arm shot up and he summoned Imperious from light, blocking Ahrek's attack.

"I've wanted to die for the last *twenty years,*" Daylen said through clenched teeth. "But the Light has denied me my wish. So please, Ahrek, *please*, kill me if you can. I want you to…I just can't let you."

"Lies! No pain in this life is close to what the Light has in store for you," he snarled. "All I have to do is ensure you meet it!"

Ahrek lashed out with the skill of a Grand High Master, but with Daylen's sunforged gauntlet and enhanced speed and reflexes he easily deflected each of Ahrek's attacks.

"Ahrek, this isn't you!" Daylen said amongst the singing sunforged blades as he withdrew step by step from Ahrek's onslaught.

"You don't know a thing about me!"

"Killing me will do nothing! My destiny is Outer Darkness, where my existence will be destroyed. That isn't a punishment, it's a gift!"

"For one such as you, the Light will see that you answer for every one of your sins before your existence ends!"

"Yes, by prolonging my wretched life!"

"I'll prove that false by killing you."

"Ahrek, we don't have time for this," Daylen said desperately as he deflected more and more strikes. "There's a half-kilometer-wide island about to ram the city and I have to help stop it!"

They had fought their way out of the penthouse onto the patio by this time, their swords chiming off one another again and again.

"You still think so highly of yourself," Ahrek replied harshly. "What can you do that the knights can't? That's where Lyrah has gone, isn't it?"

"I have to know that the city is safe!"

"The world will never be safe as long as you still breathe!"

Daylen reached the edge of the building and quickly performed a power jump to get away.

As Daylen soared through the air, he looked back to see Ahrek running after him, jumping from the edge of the Fallton.

"Ahrek, no!"

But Ahrek didn't fall. He flew directly toward Daylen with an outstretched hand.

Ahrek can *fly?*

Something suddenly grabbed Daylen around the waist, stopping him midair.

It was the invisible force from Ahrek's power. Ahrek was still flying toward him, his sword held back, ready to thrust.

Daylen grabbed the skimmer at his waist and moved it away from him with an outstretched hand. He locked the skimmer in place, enhanced his strength to maximum, and heaved. He ripped the handle clean off, not having come close to breaking Ahrek's invisible hold.

Daylen didn't have time for this. Luckily, he had a way to incapacitate Ahrek, and hopefully it wouldn't kill the Bringer.

As Ahrek reached him he swung, his sword leveled to take off Daylen's head.

Light, the man wasn't kidding around. Ahrek clearly knew that Daylen could heal from anything but a deathblow.

Daylen went to block with his gauntlet but feinted, triggering his darkstone dagger.

An invisible force grabbed Daylen's gauntlet the very moment he was about to touch Ahrek's sunforged sword. Daylen had suspected Ahrek would do this; there was no way the Bringer would let him shatter the sword, and his reply had just given Daylen a point of leverage.

With his strength still enhanced, Daylen heaved his arm outwards, his body braced against Ahrek's first hold, both breaking the hold on Daylen's gauntlet and blocking Ahrek's sword strike with it.

Ahrek screamed as a loud crack rung the air. He dropped his sword and shield to clutch at his chest as he fell.

The force holding Daylen's waist disappeared at the same time, and he fell with him.

Ahrek's eyes were closed and his teeth bared against pain.

Daylen reached out, grabbing Ahrek to save them both from the fall.

Ahrek's eyes shot open and he grabbed the darkstone dagger still sticking out of Daylen's gauntlet. Light flashed and the Bringer summoned a sunforged sword in his other hand before skewering Daylen without hesitation. Ahrek twisted the sword and slashed it out of Daylen's side.

Daylen screamed and tried to kick Ahrek away from him, but Ahrek held to the darkstone dagger like a lifeline, which also prevented Daylen from shattering the Bringer's sword with it. Ahrek went to slash at him again, but Daylen kicked even harder, causing the dagger to snap free and knocking them apart.

Daylen got a second of healing in before he increased his

body's fortitude and mass, which slowed him considerably. Stones shattered under him as he fell the remaining meter, making a deep depression into the ground.

He switched all his bonds back to healing and tried to look about.

His head was reeling from pain—but Daylen was used to pain, and he managed to figure out that he had landed in the middle of a main street, a large crowd of people startled by his sudden appearance.

Daylen crawled out of his crater and looked past them to see Ahrek floating just above the ground some twenty meters away, his eyes pressed shut and face scrunched in agony. His arm was pointed beneath him, palm open to the ground. In a second or two he drifted upright, his face slowly relaxing. He absorbed the sword in his hand, but Daylen's darkstone blade was nowhere to be seen.

Thankfully Daylen was almost fully healed and had climbed to his feet. He had nearly been cut in two.

"I don't have time for this!" Daylen hissed to himself.

Ahrek noticed him quickly and he flew in his direction like a shotspike. He reached a hand forward and force-grabbed Daylen, picking him up and throwing him with incredible strength at one of the buildings to his left.

Clearly Ahrek had learned not to grab Daylen with two tele-kinetic holds, thereby giving him a point of leverage. With only one force grabbing him, Daylen could do nothing to stop it.

Instead he increased his mass and fortitude, curled himself into a ball, and held Imperious tight.

He smashed through the entire building. Daylen hit the brick building behind the first, making a large spider-web crack in it and falling to the alleyway, where he landed uninjured.

"Glad that worked," he said to himself. He hadn't been sure enhancing his fortitude and mass would prevent injury to the level it had.

Daylen channeled all his bonds to speed and shot down the alleyway like a skyship in fight. He held his gauntlet in front as a windshield, yet the drag from his clothes still nearly ripped them off his body. Then he noticed that Ahrek hadn't snapped his dark-stone dagger free from his gauntlet but had ripped it clean out, wrecking the springs and leaving no darkstone at all.

Looking back, Daylen saw Ahrek hovering in the air. He seemed to spot Daylen easily.

At my regular speed, I can sprint at thirty kilometers an hour, making this speed four hundred and eighty. No—the wind resistance is slowing me, but surely Ahrek can't match this speed. Daylen had thought too soon, for he noticed something shining in Ahrek's hands as the Bringer flew at him easily closing the distance.

He's surging, Daylen realized. *What a good idea,* he thought before skidding to a stop, kicking in a door, and ducking into a building.

It was a stockroom for one of the stores that faced a main street. Daylen ran and grabbed the sunstones from the bracketed wall sconces. He tucked three under the glove of his gauntlet where they lay fixed on his skin.

As he did so, a loud whining siren rung in the air.

Daylen knew that sound: it was the Night Siren, usually used to announce the fall of night, but it was also used for other city-wide alerts. "Lyrah! She's started the evacuation," Daylen said to himself with some relief.

Daylen heard steps land on the cobblestones outside.

"All right, I clearly can't escape him, so I'll just have to end this."

Daylen increased his mass and then his speed, but not nearly as much as he could—he didn't exactly want to crash through the building on the other side. It was dumb luck that he hadn't hit anyone when Ahrek had thrown him before.

Daylen ran to the door, timing it so he would reach it at the same time Ahrek did.

He rammed Ahrek, knocking him into the brick wall on the other side, which splintered in a massive circular crack.

But Ahrek wasn't hurt at all; in fact, he hadn't even hit the wall. He had pushed himself off it with his powers, letting the force he could create absorb the impact. Ahrek must be pushing against anything that came near him, effectively making an invisible protective barrier.

"Oh, Light."

Ahrek's powers grabbed Daylen and smashed him back and forth into the side walls of the alleyway, the Night Siren whirling in the air.

Daylen had increased his mass and fortitude the very moment Ahrek grabbed him, surging off the sunstones at the moment of each impact. Large holes were shattered into the brick walls with each collision. Again and again he was smashed, moving up the alleyway in a zigzag of demolition.

He was eventually thrown to the cobblestone ground.

Daylen stood, dust and rubble falling off. "Haven't you figured out that that's not working?" he said, and power jumped away.

Daylen half expected to be grabbed by Ahrek's powers again, but it appeared that he had finally gotten the message.

Daylen soared over the buildings and landed in the middle of a main street.

There were a lot of people bustling on the street but they were clearly too preoccupied with the evacuation, announced by the Night Siren, to notice him or even care.

Ahrek flew after him and thrust his hands outward, light bursting from his hands and materializing into four sunforged swords, two on each. The swords moved forward with Ahrek, each one spinning to point at Daylen. Ahrek then threw his hands forward and the four swords shot at Daylen like arrows.

"Light!" Daylen said, jumping to the side, dodging the swords— but the swords flew around and attacked again.

With enhanced speed and reflexes Daylen blocked and parried with his gauntlet and sword, dodging those attacks that got through his defense.

It was the most intense battle he had ever fought. The attacks came at an unbelievable speed, one after another, several at the same time, and even with Daylen's enhanced speed and reflexes he was very hard pressed to keep them at bay.

Ahrek was incredibly powerful!

And then Ahrek himself attacked in conjunction with his other swords, adding more pressure to the onslaught.

Daylen blocked and switched all bonds to speed, lunging out of the fray in a sudden flash. He then power jumped on a long arc to get some distance and breathing room.

But Ahrek was right behind him, sending his swords forward.

Daylen landed on a high-rise rooftop, spinning to knock aside the swords that were right behind him with his enhanced sunforged gauntlet. That gauntlet had saved him from getting struck many times in this fight already.

The swords attacked again and Ahrek came with them.

It was too much and a sword passed his defense, cutting Daylen deep in the thigh.

Grunting, Daylen rolled out of the fray and yelled, "Back in Blackheart's den, you said I was a better man than the Conqueror! Can't you see I've changed?"

Thankfully Ahrek paused, the four swords hovering above him. "You think the little good you've done absolves you of your sins? You must answer for your crimes!"

Daylen took the pause to heal his wound. "How did I do it?" he asked.

"How did you do what?"

"How did I kill them?"

Ahrek sneered. "Of course you wouldn't know. What's another drop in a sea of blood? My family and I lived in *Daybreak*."

Daylen's heart sunk. Daybreak—of course.

"I was away during the attack," Ahrek added, "and returned to find the entire city destroyed with every man, woman, and child executed by your order."

Daylen's guilt welled inside, bringing with it a pain greater than any injury he had ever received. He closed his eyes, trying to bear it, eventually nodding as a tear ran down his cheek. "Now I know. Anara, Deston, Arenna and Sereen. I told you that I'd remember them, and I will."

Ahrek readied himself to attack, his resolve not looking to have changed a bit.

This might really be the end, Daylen thought with hope—but if he simply let Ahrek kill him, it would be exactly the same as if Daylen had done it himself, running away from his pain like a coward. Daylen was many things, but he was *not* a coward. The only way to know if it really was the Light itself that was granting him the release he desired was if Daylen fought with all his might to stop it. Then, and only then, when his death was caused by things completely outside of his power, would he know.

Ahrek burst forward and without thinking Daylen defended, moving like lightning, yet it was still barely enough.

Energetic chimes sounded in fast succession as sunucles clashed on each other again and again. Daylen spun and weaved, moving four times as fast as he was naturally able, like a super-human dancer pushing his skills to their very limit.

As much as Daylen wanted Ahrek to win, it wasn't hard for him to fight just as fervently for the same goal. He truly hated losing at anything, even when he wanted to. Damn his endless pride.

Thankfully this time, even in spite of his pride, Daylen might still lose. Ahrek was relentless.

But...if he could stack another bond to speed, he would definitely outpace even Ahrek, as it would double his current rate. Daylen had three bonds enhancing his speed but needed his last bond on his reflexes to keep track of all the blades swinging around him, and even with that, Ahrek had still tagged him just before.

Wait a minute—there is a way I can get greater speed!

In one last desperate move, Daylen sucked deeply on the sunstones under his glove for a powerful surge of speed.

Daylen seemed to just appear in front of Ahrek in a blur of movement, where he plunged his blade through the Bringer's chest.

Ahrek's face was a picture of incredulity. "No... No!"

Daylen withdrew his sword and Ahrek held a hand over his wound, healing it. Daylen pulled Ahrek up, holding him by the neck and ran him through another four times.

"That should take you a bit longer," he said, dropping the Bringer to the ground. Turning away, he continued, "I know this isn't over between the two of us, and by the Light I hope you'll do better next time, but right now I have to make sure the city is safe."

"You don't care about the city," Ahrek said with a spit of blood, "you care for nothing but yourself. You're a tyrant! A genocidal mass murderer, pedophile and rapist!"

"I was, but I've changed."

"Then answer for your crimes!"

"I am with every second I live, and while I live I plan to do some good." And Daylen walked to the edge of the building, ready to jump away, as Ahrek cried with the Night Siren sounding in the background.

"Don't you dare walk away from me! I'll find you and make you pay—you hear me, you murderous bastard?" he screamed madly. "I'LL MAKE YOU PAY!"

CHAPTER FORTY-THREE

*Seeing the open defiance of the knights gave the oppressed people
confidence, as many nations had been waiting for this very
moment, particularly Frey, and they all rose up in open rebellion,
even my own Hamahra.*
*Even Azbanadar, my most loyal allied nation, withdrew its
support, though it didn't actively fight against me. I would have
destroyed its people for that, but I was rather preoccupied.*
*The rebellion led by Rayaten had been stockpiling weapons and
whatever skyships they could get their hands on for years.
Suddenly I was faced with an army numbering in the hundreds of
thousands made up of the people I thought I was fighting to
protect.*

Lyrah landed in the middle of the Hold's ward, the part of the
castle enclosed by the outer wall. The Hold was a massive
coal-gray fortress built in the old style that predated the aristocracy. It sat directly under the First City Island. Its castle-styled
defenses were mostly useless thanks to skyships, but the Hold did
have its own shield net that surrounded the fortress in a dome.

There were some regular citizens making their way across the
ward as well as a few knights in the middle of training and several
squires—non-Lightbinder members of the Order who maintained
the Hold and handled the Order's administrative duties.

Lyrah startled them with her dramatic arrival. "Archallion Kennet," she called out with a bonded voice, her words echoing through the Hold. "The city is under threat!"

Cueseg was among the knights in training and ran to her. "Lyrah? How is the city under threat?"

Lyrah waved the rolled papers she was holding that detailed the Dawnists' plan. "I'll tell you when Kennet arrives," she said, watching a man jump from one of the Keep's windows. He seemed to fly through the sky toward her, though in reality she knew he was falling. Kennet was a powerful Graviten: a Worldbinder that specialized in gravity bonds.

He swooped down and landed in front of them with a level of precision and grace that only came from years of training. "Archonair, what is it?"

Lyrah dumped the rolled papers except one, which she unrolled and held out to show a drawing of a large tunneled island. "The Dawnists, they've rigged an entire island to ram the city, and then plan to take control after the destruction of the Senate. The island might already be in flight."

Kennet took the drawing. "The Dawnists? They're a bunch of political nuts, not revolutionists."

"Kennet, they fought me and the kid. The Dawnists are ready to fight and die for their cause."

"Speaking of the kid, where is he?"

"Gone to get his Bringer friend to help." She stared at him intently. "This is *real*, Kennet."

Kennet looked to the keep's main entrance, where it appeared that all the other knights in the Hold were emerging in response to Lyrah's call. He pointed a hand. "Seer Lem!"

Archonair Lem was the seer of the Hold. Lem nodded and Lyrah sensed Kennet channeling light. Lem's hair, clothes, and sword suddenly fell up as if he were hanging upside down, followed by his body and he fell high into the air in between the darkstone anchors that made up the Hold's shield.

All the knights near Lem knew to not step where he had been, otherwise they would get caught in the same gravity flow.

The fact that Kennet could manipulate gravity at such a distance, the keep's entrance being easily twenty meters away, spoke to his great skill.

Kennet eventually leveled Lem out a little before he would have hit the underside of the City Island above.

"Are there any islands out of place in the distance?" Kennet asked with bonded voice.

"Nothing close!" Lem called back. "It's hard to see a difference with the islands farther away."

"Are any of them moving?"

"Not that I can see."

"Look for any of the Dawnists you've seen in the past."

"Yes; just a moment."

Even from this distance Lyrah could see Lem bow his head, and though she couldn't see him close his eyes, she knew he was doing just that. A seer like Lem could use their powers to see the location of any person they had seen before, no matter where they were.

"There's only three that stick in my memory enough to find," Lem called down. "One is currently working in some factory. The other is with a group hiding in a warehouse. The last must be touching darkstone, for all I can see of him is darkness."

Kennet turned back to Lyrah, letting Lem fall. He would land easily with his free bond. "Archonair Lyrah, are you sure about this?"

"Yes, the island is supposed to hit within a fall."

"But we don't know which island."

"Correct."

"It would be one of the Floating Isles," Cueseg added, "where no one can see the work."

Kennet shook his head. "We can't know that for sure. If we set out for the Floating Isles to cut them off and the island we search for happens to be, say, Croprest, Hamenday, or Cityview, we could have put ourselves too far away to stop it. We run the same risk if we try and fly to the closer islands."

"Then we set a watch at the city border," Lyrah said, "with a speaker to alert us as soon as Lem spots it. Also, it wouldn't hurt to send a scout to take a look at some of the closer islands at least."

"Agreed. We'll also send a few knights to round up the group of Dawnists hiding in that warehouse. And even though this might just be an inflated dream cooked up by some idiots, a city evacuation order should be issued regardless." Kennet looked to the Hold's Head Squire. "Master Daymore, sound the Night Siren."

As Daylen leapt over the city, he could see countless people running about trying to evacuate. As Night clearly hadn't fallen, the people in the city knew that the Night Siren in this case meant to get out of the city.

Skyships queued in long lines to get through the city's shield. That was going to be a problem as the shield's exits were already making a bottleneck. The larger majority of people would have to leave the old-fashioned way along the ground, the hardest of all being those who lived on the City Islands.

Daylen could see several skyships ferrying people off the islands, but it wouldn't be enough. The High Road would also bottleneck people like the shield did with the skyships. Not good.

If all the skyships in the city were put to ferrying people off the islands, it could be done, but that clearly wasn't happening. There was too much confusion, and most of the larger ships leaving the city were traders more concerned with getting their cargo and goods to safety than random people they didn't know.

And people dared call *him* a bastard.

Daylen landed in front of the Hold's outer gate. Units of the city militia marched in and out, paying him no mind.

Daylen ran into the ward to find Lyrah issuing directions to another unit of the city guard.

"Sweep the tenements in Morninghome District and make sure they are clear," Lyrah ordered.

"You need more skyships to help ferry people off the City Islands," Daylen said without announcing himself. "As it is, there's a huge bottleneck on the High Road and those stuck on the upper islands won't get off in time."

Lyrah nodded and looked to a group of squires dressed in the knight's livery, then pointed to one. "Go to the Com Room and see they track a message to the Harbor. Order as many ships as possible to ferry people off the isles, and if there's any crew who resist, have the Harbor Guard commandeer their vessel."

The squire nodded and left as instructed.

"There's also a long line of ships trying to get through the shield, but there's too many of them. If we open the shield's war gate, that can be used to let more ships through."

"The war gate is already opened, but we have to keep it clear for our battleships. We can't have the gate blocked when we spot the island."

"You're right. I thought you would be off to find this blackened island," Daylen said.

"It's not moving yet. Scouts are checking out the closer islands and the rest of us are ready to deploy as soon as it's spotted."

"Where's your lookout?"

"Seer Lem. He's on the border patrol flagship above the mouth of the city."

"Only one?"

"Lem's got the highest sight bond in the city, level six. We'll just have to hope he spots the island soon after it moves."

"I'll help. I can stack to level four, remember?"

"Yes, that's right."

"How do we alert you once we find the island?"

"There's a speaker on the ship."

"Speaker? What, he'll just shout really loud?"

Lyrah smirked at him. "You still have a lot to learn. Go! And where is the Bringer?"

Daylen frowned. "Ahrek's not coming. He has some stuff to deal with." And with that, Daylen power jumped toward the city's mouth.

He was Dayless the blackened Conqueror! Ahrek thought once more as he struggled to fly across the city.

I had eaten with him, laughed with him, and the whole time he was the man who destroyed my life, the man who murdered nations! Alive!

This was why the Light had sent Ahrek to him: to give Ahrek the revenge that was rightly his, to finally free the world of the greatest tyrant it had ever seen. If only Ahrek had seen it sooner, before they had gotten to know each other. It made him sick that he had actually *liked* the wretched monster.

Now he would end it, somehow.

Healing himself from the brink of death had exhausted Ahrek greatly, however, and his body's ability to channel light was at its limit.

Another Lightbringer could heal his channeling fatigue, a type of healing that a Bringer couldn't do for themselves, and Ahrek knew the best place to find one—the very place that Dayless had been headed.

Dayless said he cared for the city, but Ahrek would never trust anything from that viper's mouth. Dayless was a lightless coward running from justice, and the only reason he pretended to do good was to fool people that he had changed, another attempt to escape his punishment. It was all to serve himself and prolong his horrible existence. He hadn't changed. Ahrek had seen enough of Dayless' true self these past weeks to know this—his arrogance, his rage and violence. And now, as a Lightbinder, he was more dangerous than ever before.

Ahrek reached the Hold, flying through its shield net and the wall to see it alive with activity. City folk, militia, squires and knights raced through the castle's bailey. There was a good chance that Dayless had passed through here even though Ahrek couldn't sense his light below. Luckily, there were two other lights that he recognized.

Ahrek landed in front of Lyrah, who stood in the middle of the bailey.

"Bringer," Lyrah remarked, sounding surprised. She raised a hand to whom she had been talking to and approached Ahrek. "Daylen said you weren't coming."

"One more lie among millions."

"What do you mean, and why are you covered in blood?"

"I'll tell you, but first I need another Lightbringer. I expect there's at least one here."

"There is," Lyrah said, and turned to one of the knight squires. "Go get Archus Heronta." Lyrah looked back to Ahrek. "Now, what do you mean when you say that Daylen has been lying?"

"He isn't who he says he is."

The knight narrowed her eyes. "Then who is he?"

"Lyrah, Daylen isn't the *son* of Dayless the Conqueror—Daylen *is* Dayless the Conqueror!"

The words struck Lyrah like thunder. "W-what?"

"He is Dayless the Conqueror, the Great Bastard himself. Somehow, he was turned young when he received his powers and has been lying to everyone ever since. Think about it! His skill, his link to Imperious, and the things he knows," Ahrek explained urgently. "I confronted him and he confessed. He *is* the Conqueror."

Lyrah couldn't breathe; no, she was breathing, panting even. Her hands were shaking. That man—that *monster* who had stolen her from her family to keep and abuse her again and again. Stripping her down to wear nothing but jeweled ornaments, her body exposed for all to see so she remained ready for his dark pleasure. He was alive, and more. She had been in his presence! He had *touched* her! The memories of the Conqueror that assailed her every time she looked at that boy weren't just because he looked similar, but because that's exactly who he was!

It was too much. He was alive and back in her life, making it seem as though she was there once more, powerless, helpless, the monster having all control.

She screamed, her hands shaking beside her head, her eyes gazing into nothingness.

She screamed again.

She wrapped her hands around herself as she fell to her knees, unable to think, pure terror overcoming her existence.

"Nooo!" she said in a horrified whisper. "No, no, no, no, no, no, no, no, no, no..."

Ahrek looked down at this poor creature, stunned beyond comprehension at her reaction. He held the woman, trying to calm her down amidst a deranged repetition of, "No, no, no," with intermediate panic-stricken screams.

Cueseg ran to them. "Lyrah," he said with great worry, kneeling down beside them. "Oh, Lyrah, no! I am afraid this happens."

Ahrek was at a loss. "I...just told her..."

"*What?*" Cueseg demanded in their shared language with a rage so uncommon to Tuerasians that it shocked Ahrek. "WHAT DID YOU SAY?"

"Daylen, my companion... He is really Dayless the Conqueror."

Cueseg's eyes nearly popped out. "*Alive?*"

"Yes," Ahrek said, nodding grimly, "and when I told her, she broke down."

Cueseg looked back down to Lyrah, speaking in Hamahran. "I

see signs of this, but that is with talk of sex." Cueseg's eyes became distant and he began speaking softly to himself. "It is sex that Lyrah is afraid of, and knowing the Conqueror is alive does this..." Cueseg's eyes suddenly focused on the broken woman. "Of course," he said in sorrow. "The Conqueror makes you afraid of it. This is why. You is one of his women."

One of his women? And then Ahrek realized, too. Lyrah, this poor creature, was one of the girls that Dayless, the wretched monster, had stolen away and raped. That's how he had known who she was, and that's why he had reacted so strangely when finding her at their hotel.

"Oh dear," Ahrek said.

Cueseg took Lyrah's face in his hands tenderly. "Oh, Lyrah, I do not know," he said with tears in his eyes. "I am so sorry."

There was a crowd of stunned onlookers.

"Go!" Ahrek commanded. "Don't you all have something important to do?"

They left quickly, looking embarrassed.

Cueseg gently pulled Lyrah's face in front of his own, but she didn't see him. Her face was a picture of terror.

"No, no, no, no, no, no, no, no, no, no, no, no, no, no..." she continued to whisper, her eyes wild.

"Lyrah," Cueseg said cautiously.

Lyrah fell into another fit of screaming.

"LYRAH!" he called out to her. "You are strong, you hear me! You are knight! I believe in you! Come back, Lyrah, *and be strong!*"

He was alive.

He had touched her.

He had said she was beautiful.

Once, the mere thought of the monster nearly brought on a panic attack, but now with this horrible knowledge that he was alive and had been so near to her, had *touched* her—it was too much.

She was that poor frightened girl once more, and there was no escape. He towered over her, abusing her, and she could do nothing to stop him. She cried, and he liked it. She was powerless, helpless, nothing.

And then when it was over, she had to follow him naked so his eyes could rape her all over until he took her to his bed again, where the nightmare repeated itself.

Powerless, helpless, nothing. Nothing except fear.

"Come back, Lyrah."

Other girls were brought in and there was nothing she could do but what he commanded.

"You are strong, Lyrah."

She wasn't strong. She was helpless, weak. Nothing but an object for a monster's sick pleasure.

"You are knight."

A knight could fight back, but she wasn't a knight. She was a weak little girl. If only she could be strong.

"Fight, Lyrah."

Maybe someday, if she ever escaped this nightmare, she could become strong; but that was the future, this was now. Right now she was weak.

"You are knight. You are strong."

A knight. A knight could fight back. She could become a knight, if she tried.

"You *are* knight!"

She…was…a…knight.

She was a knight?

She was a knight!

How could she be a knight if she was so helpless? That didn't make sense; but she was a knight, *she knew it,* somehow. And a knight *was* strong. A knight didn't submit to monsters, a knight *killed* monsters!

Her breathing evened out and her wild eyes stopped quivering. Awareness slowly came to her face and she focused on her companion, saying softly, "I'm a knight."

"Yes," Cueseg said with relief. "Yes, you are!"

"Thank you, Cueseg," she said and pulled herself from Ahrek's arms to stand. She looked back down to him. "The Conqueror, he's alive?"

Ahrek nodded.

"Then we'd better do something about that."

CHAPTER FORTY-FOUR

I was merciless in my tactics, yet even the most brilliant tactician can't win against overwhelming numbers and an order of knights wielding superhuman powers. At one point I even sent an annihilator to destroy the knights' Arch Hold, which it was more than capable of achieving. For some reason, however, the ship never reached it.

After months of fighting, I was forced to recall what remained of my armies to Highdawn itself, where I would make my last stand.

Daylen stood at the helm of the battleship, gazing out to the horizon with four bonds stacked to his sight, periodically switching one bond to his light sense, which increased its range significantly, just to feel out if anyone might be approaching.

It was like Daylen could see everything and focus in on details far in the distance. He wondered what this Seer Lem could see with a level-six sight bond. It must be incredible.

Still, neither he nor Lem noticed a single island move.

Daylen switched one bond to his light sense and noticed three lights on their way toward him.

Gee, I wonder who that could be, Daylen thought sarcastically.

Daylen turned to one of the crewman of the battleship. "I lost my skimmer recently, and while I'm onboard, I'd like to have another one."

"But, aren't you an Archknight?" the crewman said, which caused the Archknight speaker who was with them to turn his head with a disapproving look. "You jumped on the ship like you could fly. Why do you need a skimmer?"

"Just give me one."

"Uh, sure, take mine. I'll get another from the quartermaster."

Daylen took the skimmer and walked away from the helm. The skimmer's steel sphere, which encased the small sunstone drivers and darkstone core, was split into two halves which were threaded together. Daylen unscrewed the top half and put it in his belt pouch. Out of necessity the lid held the top driver but the five other drivers sat in the bottom half. The darkstone core was now exposed but still had uniform light on all sides. Daylen hooked the skimmer to his belt. Without the lid the skimmer wouldn't work, of course, but that wasn't why he asked for it.

Daylen then took out all the sunstone beads he had in his pouch and tucked four under his glove and the rest under his shirt, ready for use. He turned to face Lyrah, Cueseg, and Ahrek as they landed on the deck of the ship.

Ahrek looked much the same as he had before, and the Tuerasian was staring at him curiously, but Lyrah... Daylen couldn't express the hate he saw in her eyes.

She knew.

"There!" Archon Lem called out. "Hamenday Island is moving."

So the island was not from the Floating Isles. How under the Light had the Dawnists managed to mine their way into Hamenday's core without anyone noticing? And with Hamenday being so close, it would get here much sooner than he had feared.

The battleship jerked into motion, flying to join those ships with the knights.

The speaker was whispering something, and then said loudly, "The Archallion has been alerted. We'll meet them in flight."

So with voice, a knight can whisper messages to another person, Daylen thought. *Good to know.*

Daylen looked back to Ahrek and the others, sighing. "We don't have time for this."

"I'll stay," Cueseg said to Lyrah. "I know why you cannot. We will stop the island. You go and stop *him.*"

Lyrah nodded once, slowly. Cueseg walked to Lem and the Speaker, who were looking very confused at what was happening.

"You would think that if the Light wanted me dead, it wouldn't have renewed my life," Daylen said. "I hate it for that."

Ahrek sneered. "Your delusion is amazing."

"I'm not the one who's deluded, Ahrek," Daylen urged. "You don't want to put me on trial, you want to kill me! This isn't about justice, it's about your own selfish feelings. Who cares that everyone else I've wronged, who've also had loved ones die at my hands, don't get any satisfaction so long as you do?"

"No," Lyrah said, her clear and emotionless voice a stark contrast to Ahrek's, "we'll kill you in the name of all your victims! You are a monster, Dayless the Conqueror, and I kill monsters!"

"What?" Lem exclaimed in shock as he stood at the helm watching. "Dayless the Conqueror?"

Lyrah advanced slowly, summoning her yellow sunforged warsword.

She pulled back and swung her sword, not even bothering to try and mask it.

Why was she making her movements so obvious?

Daylen casually raised his gauntlet to block with a confused face, and the moment the sword connected he realized his terrible mistake. *Her strength.*

She was relying on his own arrogance and her diminutive stature to throw him off.

The sword hit the gauntlet with so much force that Daylen's arm snapped. By that time Daylen had switched all bonds to fortitude and mass but it was too late. The gauntlet hit the side of his body, the sword behind it, knocking him off the ship to flail through the air in a thirty meter arc.

Ahrek was flying right atop him not having wasted a moment, creating four swords which shot at Daylen without mercy.

Each sword impaled him.

Gritting his teeth and falling through the sky Daylen unhooked the skimmer at his belt. He looked at Ahrek, whose eyes widened as he saw what Daylen was doing. "I'm sorry," Daylen whispered, and he touched the open darkstone core of the skimmer to one of the swords sticking through his chest.

It exploded and Ahrek screamed in agony.

As Daylen suspected, the swords were linked to him.

Shattered sunforged shards flayed Daylen, but with each bond already healing him, he recovered quickly.

His arm had healed, too, and Daylen pulled the other swords from his chest so he could recover fully.

He grabbed the skimmer lid from his pouch and quickly twisted it back on so it would function again, using it to pull him sideways to the falling Ahrek.

"Please be alive," he pleaded as he grabbed the Bringer and locked the skimmer in place just before they hit the ground.

With enhanced strength, Daylen's arm resisted the mighty jerk from the sudden stop. He unlocked the skimmer and dropped to the ground.

They had landed in the courtyard of some rich person's manor house.

Daylen lay Ahrek down to find him unconscious and breathing raggedly. Breaking a link never killed a person instantly, but it was akin to being stabbed in the chest: the blow would either kill them in a few minutes, or they would wallow in agony for a fall or so to eventually recover.

Daylen gently shook the Bringer. "Come on, Ahrek, heal yourself!"

Ahrek groaned, light softly glowing around him. He was healing, thank the Light. It must be a subconscious reflex like Daylen's own healing ability.

A thud sounded nearby.

Daylen looked to see Lyrah standing at the other end of the courtyard.

He jumped away.

She followed him, of course, but Daylen could move faster, being able to stack his bonds.

Daylen raced and leapt through the city, easily putting several kilometers between the two of them before finally stopping in a deserted street.

Most of the lower city had been evacuated by now, though the upper islands were a much different story.

Daylen walked to lean on a building and catch his breath. He could use his powers for another ten minutes, maybe, but if he rested for a moment, he could get more out of them. And then he could find a skyship and help stop that island.

Only a few minutes later a thud sounded to his right.

"I can track you, remember?" Lyrah said coldly. "No matter where you go, I'll follow—and, eventually, you'll reach your limit and lose your powers completely."

She was right; if Daylen kept running, he would just waste the remaining power he had.

"You can't escape," she said with sword in hand, walking toward him.

Light burst from her whole body to materialize into a full suit of sunforged plate armor, with helm and everything else already fixed in place.

Light! Just how many sunucles can Archknights store within themselves?

Being sunforged, the armor glowed faintly and was only slightly translucent like thick glass or diamond, Lyrah's armor having a deep pink tint to it. Her face was a shadow underneath, but the banner of her white mantle swayed outside the armor.

Daylen had seen Archknights wear such armor before. Light, he'd had his own suit in the past, but that was only when they weren't fighting the Shade—and even then, such armor held the same fatal weakness, as all sunucles did. Touch it with darkstone, and it would shatter, potentially killing the one linked to it.

Still, apart from that, sunforged armor was practically indestructible. It weighed so little that it was like you weren't even wearing it, and it enhanced the physical abilities of the person wearing it, making them twice as strong and fast as they were naturally. This was the supernatural enhancement the armor bestowed from the sun-forging process.

Would that stack with lightbinding? Daylen asked himself. *If the armor made one twice as strong, would the first bond double that?* If it did, Lyrah was going to be ridiculously strong.

He sighed. *Here we go.* There was no other choice—he would have to fight.

Daylen held his sword up and walked away from the building to get some room to move.

Lyrah attacked, and this time Daylen was sure to not let the blows connect. With his enhanced speed and reflexes, he dodged each of her sword swings and struck back when the openings presented themselves.

A few of his hits landed.

Lyrah was very skilled, of course, but Daylen was a Grand High Master moving at four times her speed. The problem was that Imperious couldn't get through that blackened sunforged armor.

As he fought and dodged, moving like the wind, he knew he had only one way to get through that armor.

He spun around an attack and grabbed his skimmer from his belt. Not having time to unscrew the lid, he sliced it in half with his sword, Imperious making the sound of shattering glass as it cut though the darkstone core.

Seven hundred and eighty-eight.

Daylen didn't hesitate, and as soon as the skimmer was cut he punched it to Lyrah's armor.

Lyrah reacted suddenly, and in a single burst of speed she had dropped her sword and grabbed both of Daylen's arms before his attack landed.

She had surged.

Her sudden speed was only a little greater than Daylen's, and he could have dodged, but he hadn't been ready for it.

Daylen struggled, but couldn't move. Lyrah's strength and weight were incredible; it was like her hands were made of steel, her body an immovable statue.

"Who's weak now?" she hissed at him, and then booted him in the chest.

Even though Daylen was enhancing his own mass and fortitude, his ribcage was crushed and his arms ripped cleanly off as the rest of him was kicked into a huge fifty-meter arc.

His whole existence was pain, and he healed what he could as he flailed through the air, switching his bonds to mass and fortitude before hitting the ground.

Daylen made a small crater in the street where he landed. Amazingly, he was still alive.

Blood was pouring from his torn off arm sockets.

Daylen switched all bonds to healing, but it was going to take a while, unless...

He drew on the sunstones tucked under his shirt for a huge surge.

In a flash of light he was suddenly fully healed, his arms completely regrown, though his chest hurt and he could still barely move. That surge was obviously close to the limit of what he could process—good thing he hadn't sucked in all the sunstones.

He clawed his way out of his small crater to see Lyrah already standing nearby watching him, sword in hand.

"Do you have any idea what you did to me?" she said softly.

Daylen nodded. "I do."

"Really?" she said mockingly. "You know what it was like, to have strangers come into my home and threaten to kill my family unless I let you rape me, again, and again? To strip me naked and parade me around? To force me to participate in the most perverted acts until you grew bored, threw me out and moved on to another?"

Daylen's shame overwhelmed him, and he broke down crying, for it was true: everything she had said was true.

"I... I..." But Daylen could think of nothing to say. There was no excuse for what he had done to her.

"I fell pregnant," Lyrah said quietly.

Daylen looked up, his heart breaking. "*No,*" he said in horrific agony, "you said..."

"I said I never had any children," she said fiercely, "but I still fell pregnant. I couldn't bear the thought of carrying a monster inside me, so I cut it out...only to find that I had ripped out any hope of ever bearing another child again."

"No..." Daylen said through his tears.

"*You destroyed me!*" she screamed, before her face grew cold once again. "And now I'm going to kill you."

Lyrah marched on him, raising her sword.

"I've never wanted that more than I do now," Daylen said, and Lyrah hesitated. "And it's because of that that I can't let you. Don't you see that being alive, seeing what I've done to you, gives me more pain than death!"

Lyrah sneered. "Then you clearly don't know what I'm capable of," she said, and she attacked.

Daylen channeled light to his speed and forced his body to move.

His pride truly knew no bounds.

He power-jumped away and, once in the air, bonded light to his links with Imperious and his gauntlet and pulled, calling them to his hand.

He caught the sword, but one of his severed arms came with the gauntlet.

He pulled the arm out of the gauntlet, a surreal experience, and then slipped it on before he landed.

Lyrah was right behind him and didn't pause at all, attacking with a fury. Daylen enhanced his speed, making sure to not let even a single strike land, but then Lyrah's own speed suddenly jumped again. Daylen wasn't fast enough to dodge, but he did manage to block.

Fighting the force was pointless, so Daylen let Lyrah's strike push his gauntlet into him, which then knocked him into the air. Even enhancing his fortitude and mass, several bones still broke. He did a low surge, which pushed his healing ability even further, making him whole before landing in one of the city's marketplaces.

The market was empty, of course: a bare bricked field surrounded by buildings.

Lyrah also landed in the open square and charged Daylen.

Daylen took Imperious in his left hand and as they engaged he surged his speed, spinning around Lyrah's attack to press his open bare palm on her breastplate.

And then he tried to suck it in.

It worked—the breastplate, which was a sunucle, turned into light, which flowed into him.

Daylen smiled, jumping back.

Without her armor, Daylen would be able to win easily, having landed many strikes already.

But then something pulled on him with such strength that it picked him up off the ground, and he flew toward Lyrah. It was kind of like Ahrek's power, except that it pulled on his whole body.

Lyrah set her sunforged warsword for a massive swing.

Daylen channeled mass and fortitude, pulled up his gauntlet, and braced his whole body against it as he reached the knight.

Lyrah struck and Daylen's bracer nearly broke as it screamed in a high-pitched chime of protest, the impact knocking him off at a spinning angle.

Daylen's arm, ribs and back had broken from the colossal impact, his body becoming a ragdoll as he arced through the air, Imperious thrown from his hand.

And then the same force pulled on him once more.

It could only be one thing, and Daylen summoned Lyrah's breastplate.

As soon as the breastplate materialized, it shot toward Lyrah, and the pulling on his body stopped.

It had been the *blackened link*. Absorbing a sunucle that was linked to another person meant that when they pulled on the link, they pulled on him.

Daylen crashed on the ground, rolling several times before coming to a stop.

Well, that didn't work...

Daylen drew on his sunstones for a low surge, causing his broken bones to snap and click back together after a few seconds.

His powers were really straining at that point.

So far this fight had been nothing but an intimate lesson in pain as Daylen went from losing in one way to losing in another.

He dragged himself to his feet to see Lyrah walking slowly toward him, her breastplate back in place.

He pulled Imperious through the link to his hand.

"There's no chance you can win," she said.

"Yeah," Daylen puffed, "I'm starting to see that."

"Then stop fighting and die."

"I...I can't. Trust me, I *want* to. I've wanted to for years."

"Then I'll grant you your wish."

Daylen hoped so, for there was no way he could see himself winning. Lyrah was just too strong, and he was all out of ideas.

She attacked, and Daylen was grateful that she wasn't relenting, for given enough time to think and plan, he could always come up with a new idea or strategy to grasp victory from even the most hopeless situations... *Time to think.*

Damn myself, he thought, realizing exactly what he could do.

Hating himself, Daylen jumped back to get a second's pause, where he channeled each bond of light to his intelligence, thinking of any possible way to win.

He had not thought to do this before because he had been so focused on those attributes that directly affected combat like speed and mass, but his intelligence was a part of his body as all his other attributes he could enhance, so there was no reason he could see it wouldn't work.

In an instant everything became clear: new ways he could use his powers sprung in his mind with a succession of inspirational thoughts. He instantly knew how Lyrah could be so strong with only three bonds, and why his resistance was so much greater when combining both mass and fortitude, and there was one use of his powers that would be the most significant of all. It was a strange use, one that he might never have thought of—maybe no one ever had—but now he could see it clearly and just like it was with his intelligence, there should be no reason why it wouldn't work.

His second was up and Lyrah reached him.

Daylen switched his bonds, bracing himself for the huge headache from channeling light through his intelligence, to channel three bonds into his *skill with the sword*, and the last to his speed.

Surely enough his head burst with pain but Daylen gritted his teeth and pushed through it, ready to unleash the full force of this different type of bond.

Sword skill effectively plateaued when one became a Grand High Master and any small increase usually took years of additional training, but suddenly Daylen was eight times as skilled as his natural ability with the speed to match.

Daylen was already one of the most skilled swordsmen in the world, but now…he was absolutely incredible.

When a man got to the skill level Daylen had, swordplay was more a matter of reading your opponent and accurately predicting how they would attack. Now, with his skill enhanced so much, he knew every single way Lyrah would attack seemingly before she did.

Lyrah struck at him but Daylen dodged them all without even trying. Lyrah surged her speed to get the drop on him like she had twice before, but he predicted it perfectly and was already out of the way.

This fight had suddenly become more trivial than he could express.

"What!" Lyrah said as her attacks hit nothing but air. "How are you doing this?"

"I wonder if even the great Archknights have figured out what I just have," Daylen said, dodging Lyrah's last attacks and spinning around here to place his sword tip on her shoulder.

Lyrah screamed in rage and lashed out with her sword, but she could do nothing. It was as if Daylen had precognition.

"It's over now, Lyrah. You can't win."

"All you've done is figure out a way to increase your reflexes more. What are you doing, surging?" she asked, and then shook her head. "It doesn't matter; once I touch you, you're dead."

That wasn't going to happen.

Daylen moved around Lyrah's attack with ease and pushed the tip of his sword through the armpit under her armor.

Lyrah screamed in pain and swung, but hit nothing as Daylen put his sword through the gap at the back of her leg and sliced tendons.

She fell to a knee and swung vainly, Daylen stepping out of range. She fell onto her arms, panting.

"I'd never kill you, Lyrah, but stop now before I injure you so much that it'll take a fall for you to heal with your single bond."

"Damn you," she said, weeping. "*Damn you.*"

Daylen took that moment to channel light and heal his aching head but this time the pain only halved.

Feet tapped on the brick ground to Daylen's left. He looked to see Ahrek having landed nearby.

Daylen stepped away from Lyrah.

Ahrek walked to her side.

"I'm fine," she said to him. "I'll be healed in a minute."

Lyrah forced herself to her feet.

"You can't beat me, not even the both of you, not with what I've learned."

Ahrek was glaring at him before eventually letting his head sag. He sighed and then looked to the sky.

His eyes narrowed and his face became concerned as he noticed something.

Daylen turned to face the same direction and see what it was.

There was a sphere of shadow in the distance slowly moving toward the city—and it was exactly where Hamenday Island should have been.

"No," Daylen whispered.

"The Shade," Ahrek said, his eyes locked on the approaching horror.

CHAPTER FORTY-FIVE

Do not fault those soldiers who remained loyal to me, for I treated them well. They did not experience what caused most people to rebel; and remember that most of my men deserted to join the rebels, anyway.

Countless skyships flew in from all nations with numberless rebels and every Archknight in their Order, and they laid siege to Highdawn. What followed was the largest battle in the history of Tellos. It went on for falls with endless engagements, withdrawals, redeployments, feints, flanking, and more engagements. I later learned that it was Rayaten who was commanding the attacking forces, which made sense, for only a master tactician like he could have matched me at every turn.

Lyrah looked to Daylen and then back at the moving shadow. She bared her teeth in frustration and finally screamed in anger, her sword and armor flashing back inside her body.

"I can't stay," she said softly to Ahrek. "If the Dawnists are willing to use the Shade, then they've just become an even greater threat. My brothers need help."

"Go," Ahrek said, not even bothering to lower his voice. "I'll see to the Conqueror."

"How? He's doing something with his powers that make him untouchable. It's like he can predict the future."

"I'll figure something out. This must end."

"Fine," Lyrah said. "His powers can't last much longer. Just be careful."

Lyrah walked a distance, shooting Daylen one last glare of hatred before reluctantly leaping away.

Daylen and Ahrek stood alone, facing each other. "I've beaten you already, Ahrek, and that was before I learned this new trick. You can't kill me."

"Yes, it's clear your powers are greater."

"Then what are you doing here?"

Ahrek summoned a single sword from his powers and pointed it at Daylen. "Dayless the Conqueror, I challenge you to a legal duel. No powers, one sword each, and to the death."

Yes. That was the right answer, poetic even. A true and fair fight between two Grand High Masters. The Light would *have* to accept that, even if Daylen didn't use his powers to heal.

It would be a proper duel to the death.

Daylen slowly nodded. "You're wise, Ahrek. I could think of no better way to settle things between us. I accept."

Ahrek took his sword stance.

Daylen pulled off his gauntlet and dropped it to the ground. He raised Imperious, ready to fight.

They circled one another, gauging and planning.

Ahrek's eyes were firm and unwavering, hatred and determination on his face.

They attacked—two of the greatest swordsmen in the world in a fight to the death.

Their swords chimed as they clashed, parrying, thrusting, striking, seeking leverage in the bind, throwing feints and counters. Daylen had to bring every technique he knew to bear, and Ahrek was clearly doing the same.

The intensity of this fight was a step higher than their first duel. That time seemed so long ago, but in truth it was only several falls past. So much had changed.

Daylen feinted and struck; Ahrek pulled back, countered and thrust.

Why had the Light sent Ahrek to him? Was it really to see Daylen killed? If so, why hadn't it let him die when he had thrown himself from the world?

Ahrek blocked with a riposte, pushed, leaned into a low duck to lunge and struck at Daylen's legs. Daylen jumped and flipped over Ahrek, spinning his sword down mid jump, but Ahrek rolled to the side and brought his sword back for another attack.

There was more between them than revenge and hatred, for even after everything that had transpired that fall, Daylen still saw Ahrek as his friend.

Daylen attacked and swung his sword around for a series of aggressive forward thrusts, parrying Ahrek's counters at the same time. Ahrek parried each one with perfect precision before eventually pulling off a counter that halted Daylen's advance.

If he was to die now, what had it all been for? What did the Light really want from him? To see him suffer from a prolonged life, or to die at the hands of those he had wronged?

Counter and riposte, riposte and counter—back and forth they danced the deadliest dance in the world.

Ahrek performed a perfect series of interchanging attacks which Daylen deflected and countered with his own.

Ahrek defended himself with true mastery and risked a very aggressive advance with three deadly strikes followed by a thrust. Daylen deflected the first three strikes, losing ground each time, and attempted to counter the last attack with a dodge and thrust of his own.

And then it was over.

Ahrek had predicted the counter and was able to sidestep Daylen's blade moving in, preforming the exact maneuver Daylen had attempted. The blades flew past each other and ended pointing in opposite directions, Imperious having been thrust under Ahrek's sword arm striking nothing but air, Ahrek's blade finding its mark, running Daylen through to the hilt.

Daylen fell to his knees with a gasp.

Had Daylen been too tired from his constant fighting that fall? Was his heart just not in it? Or was Ahrek simply the better swordsman?

It didn't matter. Ahrek had won.

The Bringer pulled his sword out and stepped back. Daylen held a hand over his stomach, but it did little to stop the flow of blood.

His bonds instinctively tried to heal the wound, but he stopped them.

"You did it," he said groggily. "Well done," he added, and then fell onto his back.

Ahrek walked to stand over Daylen. "I've dreamed of this moment for so long. Even when I thought you dead, I regretted that I hadn't done it with my own hands."

"And now you have," Daylen said softly as blood pooled under him. "Enjoy it."

Ahrek pulled his sword back to finish it, but then Daylen spoke, interrupting him. "You know, we're the same you and I."

Ahrek paused. "I'm *nothing* like you!" he said, enraged.

Daylen laughed bitterly. Even at the end, he couldn't resist aggravating the man. "Really? Because looking at you right now, I see myself as I had been right before I killed the old Queen. Both of our families were murdered by those in power, and we both did everything we could to destroy them for it," Daylen continued with a twisted smile, "eventually leading a rebellion that would overthrow that government."

"But after that, you became a monster," Ahrek snarled, "and I embraced a life of service to atone for those I killed."

"A much better choice, true—but look at you now! Tell me, after you thought I was dead, did it really change anything? Did it make you happy?"

Ahrek's bared his teeth and pulled his sword back to end Daylen, but his sword did not fall.

"That's what I thought," Daylen said, looking into Ahrek's now uncertain eyes. "I've been through it too, remember? As good as it will feel to kill me now, you know that soon after you'll feel as bitter and miserable as before. There'll be momentary relief, but it won't last. Your family will still be dead and killing me won't bring them back. You'll still hate me as much as you ever did—only now there'll be nothing for your hate to be inflicted on. I can see how serving others would help, but you can't tell me you haven't been carrying a deep and seething hatred for me through all these years."

Tears came to Ahrek's eyes as he hissed, "It has been eating me *alive*! I thought befriending his son would finally see it gone, but it only made my hate resurface, and then I find out who you really are…" He screamed. "I just want it to *end*! I WANT TO BE RID OF YOU FOREVER!"

"There's no end," Daylen said, his head moving sluggishly

from side to side. "After eighty-two years of life, I know. I *still* despise the aristocracy, you know, and would kill them all over again if I could. Who wouldn't hate those responsible for killing their loved ones? It's our right." He nodded, his eyes wide with desire. "Do it. Do what you have to do…and find what little relief there is in it."

Ahrek was silent for a time, raising his sword to strike only to stop and let it slowly fall several times. He struggled with himself, before turning away to pace back and forth.

Daylen knew his struggle. Ahrek wanted to be free of his pain, but killing him wouldn't lead to such a release. Ahrek would still kill him, of course, and there was momentary satisfaction in revenge. Daylen knew it; Ahrek deserved it. He needed it.

Daylen gazed at the sky, the faint blurry image of the continent high above, still able to make out Ahrek in his periphery.

Ahrek looked to the sky and sighed. "There is a way to be free of this," he said with his back to Daylen.

"Really?" Daylen said as he choked on blood. "Well, you would be the first to know."

Ahrek turned to him. "No… Not the first."

Daylen's vision had blurred. "Then what is it?"

Ahrek didn't answer right away, but his whole frame shook as he wept. Eventually he heaved one last sob and said, "I forgive you."

Daylen looked to Ahrek in true disbelief. He could not have heard what he just did. Tears came unbidden to his eyes as he tried to make sense of those incredible, impossible words. "Wh… What?"

"Daylen Namaran, Dayless the Conqueror…I forgive you."

"You… You do?"

"Yes."

"How?"

More tears came to the Bringer's eyes as he shrugged. "I don't know. I thought it impossible. I even thought I was lying when I spoke the words, but as I did, it became true. Dayless… I feel no hate for you anymore. I truly do forgive you."

Such a thing was more amazing than Daylen ever thought possible, and he burst out crying, looking back to the sky in wonder.

Ahrek approached and held out a hand to Daylen.

Daylen hesitantly raised his hand, not sure to trust his own perception of reality.

As their hands grasped, Daylen felt light envelop him. His body seemed to sing in praise as all his pains left. He gasped at the sensation.

Looking to his body, Daylen realized what had happened.

Ahrek had healed him.

The Bringer then pulled Daylen to his feet, where Daylen fell into the man's arms, crying with more passion, relief, and gratitude then he ever had before.

CHAPTER FORTY-SIX

*In disbelief, I saw there was no way to win. I was defeated. And so
I fled, escaping Highdawn as the rebels took the palace.
Amazingly I felt like the fallen hero at that time, the true and just
ruler of the empire betrayed by his own people.
I hated them for that, and swore revenge on everyone who dared
oppose me.
I would return and kill them all.*

Daylen didn't know how long he stood there, crying into
Ahrek's chest. After all that Daylen had done, especially to
Ahrek, he never, not once, thought he would ever hear those
words.

It was amazing, impossible, but it had happened, and all he
could do was weep in gratitude and relief. It was like a terrible
weight had been lifted from him, and for the first time in twenty
years, his guilt was actually lighter.

After a time, his tears eventually dried and Ahrek took him by
the shoulders. "The island is getting close. You need to go and see
what's happened."

Yes, he was right. Daylen would wonder at the miracle that had
just transpired for the rest of his life, but for now, there was a city
to try and save.

Daylen wiped away his tears. "No, *we* need to go."

Ahrek shook his head. "I would, but my channeling ability is exhausted."

"I don't have much left, either... No, wait. I can feel them. They're back at full strength!"

"My healing," Ahrek said.

"It replenishes power too?"

"It heals the body, and it's your body's ability to channel that was exhausted."

He really has forgiven me, Daylen thought in wonder, the feelings of illation and relief distracting him. "Couldn't you have just healed yourself first?" Daylen asked pulling his focus back to the present.

"Healing myself doesn't replenish my channeling ability as it's that very ability being used to do the healing. It's like trying to repair something that's being damaged at the same rate, achieving nothing. But another Bringer could do it."

Daylen looked about at the empty city. "Yeah, I think we'd have trouble finding one. Black it, your powers would be useful right now." Daylen turned to the ominous shadow in the sky. "The island will hit the city before I can reach it by jumping. We need a skyship, and a fast one at that."

"We can signal one of the ships ferrying people off the upper island."

"Maybe," Daylen said as he bonded light to his sight. Instantly, he could see every ship before him in detail—and he recognized one.

Daylen pointed. "That ship heading back to the upper island. It's the *Bloodrunner*."

"Sain?"

Daylen smiled. "It has to be. The kid is helping people evacuate."

"But it's too far away," Ahrek said and pointed to another ship. "We might get the attention of that one."

"Nowhere near fast enough. If we want to reach the island before it hits, we need something like the *Bloodrunner*."

"Then how do we signal it?"

"Well I did just see the knights perform a nice little trick. Let's see if I can do it, too."

"Do what?"

"You'll see."

Daylen switched all his bonds to voice and whispered, thinking of Sain, focusing on him as if the lad were standing right near. "Sain. This is Daylen. We need the ship. We're standing in the middle of the closest market square to the ship's left—just look for a large empty city block among the buildings."

"You can speak to people at a distance?"

"I hope I can, as otherwise that would have looked rather stupid."

"It looked stupid regardless."

"Thanks," Daylen said sarcastically as he watched the Bloodrunner.

The ship didn't move and Daylen could guess that if it worked Sain might be questioning his own sanity at hearing Daylen's voice from nowhere.

Daylen tried it again. "You're not crazy, you idiot—this is one of my powers. Now hurry up and get your ass over here."

The ship jerked to a stop, hovered in the air for a second, and then turned to fly in their direction.

"It worked," Ahrek added.

"Yeah, and the kid's gotten fairly good at flying that thing."

"You calling everyone kid makes a lot more sense now, seeing you're about as old as a fart can get."

"Before I changed, you should have smelled them. They were a power unto themselves."

The ship dipped low to fly in on their side. It pulled to a stop with Sain at the helm and Sharra at his side.

"Do you have any idea how disturbing it is to hear a voice speak to you in your head?" Sain called out to them. "Especially when it's yours, Daylen."

"I can imagine," Daylen said as Ahrek climbed aboard. Daylen pulled on the link to Imperious and his gauntlet, calling them to his hands and then jumped high into the air to land at the helm of the Bloodrunner.

"Hello, Daylen—Bringer Ahrek," Sharra said as she took Sain's arm.

"Hi," Daylen said flatly. He still didn't know what to make of Sharra, but now wasn't the time to wonder.

"It is good to see you, child," Ahrek said.

"What under the Light happened to you?" Sain asked, looking at Daylen.

Daylen looked down at his clothes. He really was a mess. His sleeves were completely torn off, nearly every inch of his clothing was bloodstained and tattered, and his skin was covered in dust and bits of dried blood.

"Nothing I didn't deserve," Daylen said back.

"Okay," Sain said with a shake of his head. "You want to take the helm?"

"You're doing a fine job as it is."

Sain looked stunned. "Really?"

"Yes, now hurry up and get this girl moving!"

"Where're we going?" Sain asked as he worked the levers, which pushed the ship into motion.

Daylen pointed to the approaching shadow.

"That thing? I had guessed it's what's caused the evacuation. What is it?"

"Hamenday Island," Ahrek answered as the *Bloodrunner* quickly gained speed. "It's flying toward the city and infested with enough Shade to cloak it in darkness."

"*The Shade?*" Sharra practically squeaked out.

"Yeah, you might want to be dropped off somewhere," Daylen said.

Sharra breathed in and held Sain closer. "I'm staying right here."

"Fine, we'll try and keep the ship at a safe distance."

"All the registry stations are blocked up by other ships trying to leave the city," Sain said.

Daylen pointed to a section of the shield, "The war gate is in that direction and should be open."

"It is?" Sain asked. "There's a lot of people trying to leave the city who would like to know."

"Good point," Daylen said. "There was an order to keep it clear for the warships but that's useless now." Daylen bonded light to his voice and started to whisper, focusing on the captains of any nearby skyships repeating the words, "The war gate is open, let everyone know."

"What are you doing?" Sain asked.

"Sending a few direct messages like I did with you."

"I hope they listen." Ahrek added.

"Me too," Daylen said. "Maybe they'll think the light is speaking to them in their time of need."

"Not with your voice." Sain said with a smirk.

"This is very troubling, Daylen," Ahrek said. "The knights should have reached the island ages ago, yet it looks to be within a kilometer of the city—and the Shade still remain."

"Yeah... Something's gone wrong."

"If a whole troop of Archknights have failed what could we do to stop them?"

Daylen looked to the Bringer. "I'm Dayless the Conqueror, remember? I'll think of something."

"Hang on, *what?*" Sain said incredulously. "You're *Dayless the Conqueror?*"

"Yeah, tyrant of ages, oppressor of nations, enemy of all, especially family pets," Daylen said dryly. "Oh, and I purposefully redirect people's mail at every opportunity."

Sain was looking at him open-mouthed before finally saying, "All right, then, that explains a lot." Then he looked back to the horizon as he piloted the ship.

Sharra was taking the news a little more seriously, her eyes wide with shock and fear. "I thought you would have looked older..." she said slowly.

"Eating your vegetables can do wonders."

The Bloodrunner was really moving now, the city flying by them in a blur.

Sain really was doing a good job at piloting. The kid had an impressive knack for working things out.

Daylen still offered Sain the occasional correction in his piloting to which Sain seemed genuinely grateful.

They flew through the war gate and thankfully there were skyships following behind. They had got the message.

A great shadow in the sky loomed before them as they approached.

"We have minutes before that thing will reach the outskirts of the city," Daylen said.

"Won't the shield stop it?" Sharra asked.

"Not a chance."

"Then it's going to destroy the whole city!" Sharra said in despair.

"Most of it, at least," Daylen said, "if I can't stop it."

Ahrek was standing by the side railing and pointed before

calling out, "Look, there! A ship approaching the island ahead of us."

Daylen walked to the side of the ship as the one Ahrek pointed to was flying low, and enhanced his sight. "It's Lyrah," Daylen said. "She's commandeered a trader. The thing is a quarter as fast as ours, so we should actually reach Hamenday at about the same time."

"We should be close enough for your light sense to see what's on the island," Ahrek said, "if you enhance it, that is."

"You're right!" Daylen said, and channeled all bonds to his light sense. He'd never enhanced it so much, but with it he could sense everything on the island. The rock and ground was hardest to make out, the grass and trees on the surface much easier, with people being bright and distinct.

And then there were the dark voids.

"The Shade are on the surface. They'll all Lesser Shade, which isn't as bad as it could have been. There seems to be people there, grouped in threes and fours, but I can't sense any lightbinding powers being used. The Shade are trying to get to them, but are being stopped. It's hard to make out by what, but I think they're bunkers or something. The rest of the people are deep within the island near the back of the core."

Daylen put a hand on Sain's shoulder. "Fly us above the island and then match its speed. Whatever you do, do not cross into the darkness. Remember, you'll always be safe in the light."

"Got it," Sain said as he angled the ship upward.

Daylen pulled off his gauntlet and held it to Ahrek. "This isn't going to be much help. It's not like Imperious."

"I would create a strong shield made of steel for you if I could, but..."

"There's a shield below deck," Sharra said.

Daylen spun around. "What?"

"Yeah, that's right," Sain added.

Sharra ran off. "I'll go get it!" she called out.

"And grab as many sunstones from their holdings as you can find!" Daylen called after her. He looked to Sain. "Blackheart, he had a backup shield?"

Sain nodded. "Sharra found it while helping me clean out the ship. Blackheart loved using a shield, after all. I think he trained with this other one."

Daylen nodded. "It's useful to train with a heavier weapon than the one you fight with."

They quickly overtook Lyrah's ship and flew above the shadow.

Sharra returned with the shield and sunstones in hand. It was a large steel center grip kite.

"Thanks," Daylen said, taking the shield in his left hand and tucking most of the stones under his shirt with what remained from his first lot. He held two other stones in the hand that grasped the shield. "I could really use your help, Ahrek."

"I'm sorry, but it's up to you and Lyrah. I have faith in you, Daylen. You've fought these monsters before, and that was as a regular man. Now you're a Lightbinder. Go—bring the light back!"

Daylen nodded, summoning forth Imperious, and ran to the edge of the ship, where he jumped and fell into the darkness.

It brought back dark memories. The shadow was unnatural; not merely the absence of light, it was a physical thing that pushed light back, making it weaker.

Daylen closed his eyes to fully rely on his light sense. He had never really done this before. He had used it, of course, but not embraced it like this; and as he did, something remarkable happened. Darkness was all around but every object below him on the approaching surface, especially the plants and trees, had a faint glow around them in a way that he could make out their shape and appearance. It was a world of soft illumination.

Even in darkness, there was light everywhere.

Daylen landed on the surface with shrieks sounding close by.

He searched with his sense and saw the flayed, rent bodies of the Archknights laying all around him.

"Light, no!" Daylen said. *How could this have happened?* he wondered in horror.

And then Daylen saw several things sticking out of their bodies.

They were the backs of shotspikes.

Kneeling down, Daylen pulled one out.

The spike's head had four small sunstones fixed around an obsidian point.

Darkstone.

Daylen's rage mounted. Those Dawnists, the ones huddling in the bunkers, must have shot the knights with these darkstone-tipped spikes, nullifying their powers and making them easy prey for the Shade.

"Bastards!"

How did they learn of the knights' weakness?

He shook himself. Thankfully, the Shade were still too preoccupied with the Dawnists huddling in the bunkers to have noticed Daylen.

Lyrah's ship suddenly appeared as it flew into the range of Daylen's light sense. With it, Daylen could see the whole thing; it was faint, but there was a shimmering outline that defined it. Lyrah had flown the thing directly into the shadow.

Light, that woman had balls.

She jumped from the ship to land at his side, steel war sword drawn.

"Careful," Daylen said to her, "the Dawnists are using darkstone-tipped shotspikes. Also, from the look of it, these Shade have only recently been turned, which means no greater powers."

Lyrah looked about at her fallen brethren, her face becoming an image of pain and rage.

"*No!*"

And then her face froze on one body in particular. She ran over to it, screaming, "Cueseg!"

Oh, Light—it was her Tuerasian companion.

His body had been ripped apart, his head and bright yellow hair lying lifeless.

Lyrah fell to her knees, crying. "No, Cueseg, no…" she sobbed.

Daylen sensed the Shade turn to them, finally realizing that two humans were out in the open. They took to the black sky, shrieking and flying toward them.

"Lyrah, I'm sorry, but you don't have time to mourn," Daylen urged. "They're coming!"

Lyrah heaved a final sob and growled, "*I'm going to kill them all!*"

The Shade reached them and Lyrah screamed in rage, swinging her sword with incredible strength and cutting two Shade completely in half.

Daylen drew on the light from the sunstones in his shirt and channeled one bond to his sword skill, one to his speed, one to his reflexes, and the last to his hearing.

He lashed out with fury, and using this new combination of enhancements was unstoppable.

The Shade swooped and shrieked, but Daylen jumped and dodged like an acrobat, weaving in between them and cutting them apart, Imperious shattering with sound at each strike.

Lyrah was just as effective. She wasn't as fast as Daylen, but the Shade could barely even hurt her. They might as well have flown into a rock face instead of attempting to charge at the woman. With her incredible strength, her sword slashed through the Shades' thick flesh as if she were felling a tree with each swing.

And then with Daylen's enhanced ears, he heard what he had been expecting: the clicks of shooters.

With his enhanced speed he was at Lyrah's side in a flash, dodging the spikes shot at him and blocking those that would have hit her with his shield.

Unfortunately the spikes were shot from multiple directions and Daylen could only defend one direction with his shield. He could sense that there had been at least another thirty spikes that whistled past them in their general vicinity, including the one that struck him in the back.

Daylen grunted in pain as each of his bonds were severed, the light he was drawing into his body being sucked right back out by the darkstone. Before he could do anything, Lyrah pulled the thing from his flesh and threw it away while fending off another two Shade in the process. That gave Daylen the time he needed to heal, and he stood before deflecting another Shade.

"They can't see us, so they're shooting volleys in our general direction," Daylen said.

"We need to take out those bunkers!" Lyrah growled.

"Then follow me!"

Daylen charged the nearest bunker where his sense outlined four people crouching within, Lyrah running right behind him.

The Dawnists must have been able to hear him, for they shot blindly in his direction. Daylen held his shield in front, blocking those spikes that were on point with several pinging sounds and bright sparks as they hit.

The moment before he reached the bunker, he jumped and flipped back, letting Lyrah pass under and crash through the whole bunker with an explosion of debris.

The Dawnists inside were crushed.

Daylen rejoined Lyrah at her side.

The room-sized bunker had been made out of some type of

mortar-like stone, its roof slab having broken into three large pieces.

Lyrah picked up the largest piece, Daylen knocking aside three Shade as she did, and threw the whole thing at the next nearest bunker, which was still a good thirty meters away. The bunker exploded from the sheer force of the impact.

Under constant attack, Daylen and Lyrah ran to the two remaining bunkers, switching back and forth between defending the other from either shotspike or Shade, and destroyed the wretched Dawnists hiding within.

"There's three Shade left," Daylen said, as the last few shrieked and attacked.

Thankfully the Shade rarely ever used any tactics, not unless directed by their more intelligent Lords, and would never retreat.

Daylen and Lyrah cut the monsters to pieces and Daylen wondered at who they had been before being turned.

Daylen sighed as the darkness slowly faded. He held up Imperious before him. "And that brings us to seven hundred and sixty-three."

The glorious light returned to the island. The sky shone with its brilliant blue, the city, which they were very close to hitting, great and majestic before them.

"We're too late!" Lyrah said hopelessly. "We can never reach the core in time to stop this wretched thing."

"I... I..." Daylen didn't know what to do. In moments, they would cross over the city and hit the upper islands.

"I'm a wretched fool!" Lyrah said as she wept, falling to her knees. "If I hadn't chased you, I would have come here in time. I could have saved Cueseg and my brethren. I put my own vengeance before the fate of the city... My hatred has doomed us all."

"No," Daylen said, "if you had left with the knights, you would have been caught off guard alongside them."

"You don't know that—I might have made the difference!" she screamed. Her shoulders fell as she looked down at Highdawn. "Now *nothing* can be done."

Daylen looked to the city. The island was flying right over the main highway and would cross the city's primary throughway, directly aimed at the High Road and upper City Islands. Thousands of people were still crowded on the high road trying to flee the city—not to mention those still on the islands.

"NO, there has to be a way!" Daylen cried. "I could figure it out it if I had... Light, I'm an idiot!" Daylen braced himself for the pain he knew this would bring and channeled all his bonds to his intelligence, closing his eyes. Given enough time, he could always come up with a plan. He prayed it would hold true.

With his mind working sixteen times faster and more efficient than normal, he asked himself what could he do? What had he not thought of yet?

Plan after plan flashed in his mind as it worked at superhuman speed, each one useless. *I have to think out of the box*, he thought. *Is there any other way I can use my powers that will help, any way at all that I've never considered?*

What could his powers do? They could enhance anything that was a part of his physical self. Anything that was a *part* of physical self.

Daylen opened his eyes and said, "I know what to do."

"What?" she asked disbelievingly. "How?"

"No time to explain," he said releasing his bonds and being assailed by a wave of pain. It was even worse this time. Using two bonds to power jump to the Bloodrunner, which was still flying high above keeping pace with the island, Daylen used his other two to heal his headache.

The pain barely subsided this time, but Daylen was used to pain, he would just have to ignore it.

He landed on the deck with Lyrah right behind him.

"We're out of time, Daylen!" Ahrek called out urgently.

"Not yet!" Daylen said, running to the helm.

Sain jumped aside, letting Daylen take control of the levers. "Everyone strap themselves in, because this is going to be rough!"

They did so, sitting on the inbuilt side benches and buckling the leather straps.

The seat straps were there in case of storms and bad weather, for skyships rarely ever flew dangerously, especially with the inbuilt safeties—but Daylen had disabled the *Bloodrunner's* safeties falls ago so it could be towed.

There were straps for the helmsman, but Daylen didn't need them. Instead he bonded light to his feet's grip, which practically fused him to the deck.

Daylen yanked down the accelerator lever and the whole ship audibly groaned as it shot forward like a shotspike, the darkstone core threatening to rip itself from the ship's supports. She had never been built to accelerate so fast, but Daylen knew what she could handle.

Everyone was thrown sideways in their seats as the ship accelerated incredibly fast, and as it reached the island's front edge Daylen steered the ship to fly up in a flip, the g-forces truly intense, and then straight down, point first, like a plummeting arrow.

"Oh light, oh light, oh light, oh light," Sharra panted in panic, squeezing her belt straps with white knuckles.

"I'm about to piss myseeeeellllfffffff!" Sain screamed.

"Daylen, I hope to the Light that you know what you're doing!" Ahrek called out next.

"So do I!" Daylen called back, pushing the ship to go even faster, the island's side flying past them in a blur.

Daylen yanked a back lever, kicking the ship into a wild rotating spin which caused everyone else to scream, even Lyrah.

Daylen worked the ship's flight levers like a madman, fighting against the strain and directing the ship to the exact place he needed it to be before pulling the ship to a very quick but smooth halt.

Well, not quite a halt—the ship was still moving, of course, in perfect pace with the island, the helm five meters from the island's side.

"Okay," Sain said with a totally pale face, "now I really have pissed myself."

"Me too," Sharra said, sitting next to him.

"Daylen, I had no idea you could fly so..." Ahrek trailed off in amazement.

Daylen ran to Sain, and with enhanced strength ripped his straps off and dragged him to the helm.

"When I swing my sword you kick this thing into reverse, you hear me?"

"Yeah, yeah, sure!"

Daylen jumped off the helm and increased his mass so much that he came to a stop in the air and then fell crashing through the deck and the floors under it all the way until he reached the core, having reduced his mass incrementally with each impact so he could land without issue.

The core room was where one could get access to the sealed darkstone core of the ship, and the sunstone drivers fixed all around it.

Daylen summoned Imperious and cut out one of the sunstones inside a driver. A large hunk of brilliantly shining rock the size of a melon fell into his hand.

Daylen jumped out of the hole he had made, and in a great burst of speed ran to the bow.

He held the large chunk of sunstone in his left hand, Imperious in his right. He pulled his right arm across his chest, Imperious pointing behind him, and clenched his teeth as he channeled each bond *into his sword*. Daylen sucked on the sunstone's light for the biggest surge he could manage, channeling *everything* he had into Imperious.

Imperious shone with blinding light and power and Daylen screamed in rage and passion, slashing out at the island before him.

As he swung, a line of white light shot out of Imperious in the shape of a blade over two kilometers long which cut into the island, leaving a trail of light behind.

The sound of shattering glass filled their air again and again; a deafening chorus as Daylen pushed his blade on.

The pain was *unbelievable*, the Light inside pushing on his body like he was getting torn apart.

Bright, thin lines of sapphire blue webbed across the white light where Imperious's true blade swung, forming a web of cracks that appeared and then disappeared in quick successive flashes.

Shattering and shattering and shattering, the sword chimed until the enormous blade of light slashed out the other side of the island.

The massive island rumbled loudly as it was cut completely in two.

With a final deafening rumble, the island's bottom half fell off.

As the underside of the island's now exposed darkstone core was uncovered more and more, the light pushed the top half *upward*.

The bottom half plummeted to the ground. The upper half still moved forward, but now at a steep upward angle heading over the city's shield entirely.

Sain had done as he had been told and flew the ship away from the two halves of the island.

The sunstone was now the size of a marble in Daylen's hand and he staggered, falling to his knees.

The stone and his sword dropped to the deck, Daylen losing all control over his body.

He could feel that his heart had stopped beating, his strength completely sacrificed.

It had been too much. Ahrek had warned him about surging, but he had needed that massive boost, as otherwise he would not have been able to cut through the whole island.

He sagged and then slumped over, dying—and at the bow of the ship, there was no deck to catch him.

He fell.

Lyrah watched on in disbelief as the Conqueror did the impossible. Somehow, he was channeling light into his *sword*. She had not known that was even possible. None of the knights had.

And the power! He was surging too much—he was going to kill himself!

Dayless finished his strike, which had all only taken an instant, though the vibrations and the sound had been deafening.

He collapsed.

Lyrah pulled her straps off and stood to see the man who had just saved hundreds of thousands of lives fall from the ship.

"Daylen!" the Bringer called out, running to the ship's siding. "DAYLEN! A *skimmer*, I need a skimmer!"

Time seemed to slow down for Lyrah. This was what she wanted, wasn't it? That evil monster had stolen her from her family when she was only fourteen years old and abused her constantly. He had murdered *millions* and he deserved to die...didn't he?

She honestly didn't know. If she'd been asked a few hours ago, she would have answered yes without hesitation. But now...

With tears running down her cheeks, Lyrah raced to the side of the ship, calling out her sunforged sword and dropping it on the deck and then diving off headfirst, increasing her mass.

She plummeted like a shotspike, her increased mass pushing her though the wind resistance and falling with much greater speed than normal.

She easily gained on Daylen, but it would still be very close for both of them.

At fifty meters from the ground she grabbed him, reversing her mass and switching her free bond to the link with her sword, and then *pulled*.

Their fall quickly slowed and then stopped a meter from the road under them. Lyrah then gently slackened her link so that they drifted down the remaining distance.

They landed right in the middle of the highway out of the city a few hundred meters from the border of the shield. A massive crowd of evacuees were amassed here and were looking at them, utterly stunned.

Lyrah lay Daylen on the ground.

He was dead.

Why did I even bother? she thought to herself. *No Lightbinder would be able to survive a surge like that. I didn't save his life...but still, he didn't deserve to become a mess on the ground.*

He didn't deserve? What was she thinking! He deserved that and more—he was the great monster of her existence.

Then why had she done what she had just done? Why, when looking at him, did she not feel as much hate as she once had?

The massive throng of people had made a circle around them.

The bottom half of the island had crashed onto the ground behind Lyrah, forming a new broad hill. Lyrah has seen these people trying to move out of the way of the island as it had flown over the land, the ominous shadow clearly scaring them away so hopefully no one had been crushed by the bottom half.

"We're saved!" a woman said off to Lyrah's side.

"You saved us, Lady Archon!" another person said.

"No... Not me," Lyrah said softly. "He did."

"Wait... I recognize him," someone else said. "He's that hero. The son of Dayless the Conqueror."

"No," Lyrah said, standing. "He *is* the hero that you've all been hearing about recently, but he isn't the son of Dayless the Conqueror. This young man *is* Dayless the Conqueror."

The crowd gasped in unified disbelief. "The Light is capable of many great and wonderful things," Lyrah called out. "Just look at the Lumatorium, or my own powers... For reasons I cannot fathom, the Light saw fit to make the Conqueror young again, and he has been living each fall since then trying to do good. Ultimately, he saved the whole city." She sighed. "I don't know what to make of him any more than you do."

The people were silent apart from the murmurs spreading the news to those who hadn't been able to hear.

Shifting wind caused Lyrah to look to her side and see the ship they had been aboard come in low, a rope ladder being dropped.

Ahrek and the two children climbed down, the purple-haired boy carrying the Conqueror's sword.

The Lightbringer ran to the fallen tyrant, kneeling beside him and pulling him to his chest. "Daylen!"

"Why do you cry, Bringer?" Lyrah asked. "You wanted him dead as much as I."

"I did...but not anymore," Ahrek said, weeping. "I've forgiven him."

"*What?*" Lyrah said, ignoring her own doubts. "How could you?"

"Because that is the only true path to peace," Ahrek said, looking at her with intense eyes. "This man was no longer Dayless the Conqueror."

"But if he really *was* Dayless the Conqueror," a man spoke from the crowd, "it's a blessing he's dead."

"What are you saying?!" another woman protested. "He just saved the city!"

"It don't change what he's done!" the man replied.

"Of course it does," another spoke out.

"And what if he had gone back to being the Great Bastard with those powers he had," yet another person said. "Look at what he just did! He sliced a huge island in half. He could wipe out the city in a second if he wanted to."

The crowd erupted into a massive argument.

"I don't know much about the Conqueror and what he'd supposed to have done," the young man who had flown the ship said softly under the riot of voices. Only those near could hear him. "All I know is that this man saved my life in more ways than I can count... I'll love him forever."

"This can't be," the Bringer said with quiet resolve. "I will not let him die… There is a reason why the Light sent me to him, I can bring him back."

"Your *last miracle?*" Lyrah exclaimed in shock. "You can't give your life for his!"

"I can, and I…" But the Bringer was cut off by a gasp of breath —from Daylen.

"Daylen? *Daylen!* He's alive!" the Bringer cried.

Daylen gasped again, his hand reaching to the sky.

The blue-haired girl with them sobbed in relief, and the crowd was a mixture of cheers and cries of fear.

"He needs to be healed," Ahrek said urgently. "We need another Lightbringer. Someone find a Lightbringer!"

"No need," Lyrah said, feeling completely incredulous. "He's channeling light. He's healing himself…but it's impossible. He surged so much," she continued uncertainly. "No Lightbinder should have been able to survive that."

Daylen, the monster, breathed in heaving gasps.

How could he have survived! Lyrah screamed in her mind—and, as she did, an answer came.

"He has *four* bonds," she said in awe. "His body must be capable of sustaining and channeling far more light than a regular Light-binder, which means he can surge to a much greater degree. That must be how he survived!"

Daylen sat up, holding his chest. "Ow…" he said expressively.

Ahrek laughed. "Light, you had me worried."

Lyrah felt sick. Oh, she felt less hatred when looking on this man, but there was still plenty of it left. He was still Dayless the Conqueror—he had still done all those terrible things to her…and yet she had helped save him.

"Oh, my head is *pounding.* Where am I?" Daylen asked.

"The highway out of the city," the Bringer answered. "Do you remember what happened?"

"*Remember!* Light, I'll never forget. That hurt like a *bastard.*" Ahrek helped him to his feet where Daylen noticed the crowd. "Ahrek, they're staring at me with a bit more intensity than I'm used to."

"They know, Daylen."

"Oh."

"Here," the boy said, handing Daylen his sword. "From the

sound you made when you struck the island, I thought it had shattered into a million pieces, but it doesn't even have a scratch."

"Thank you, Sain," Daylen said, taking the sword and looking at the blade. "I wasn't sure if the darkstone core of the island would have any effect since the actual blade didn't touch it, just its projected power. I guess the effects travel both ways, which means any other blade would have shattered as soon as the darkstone core was struck."

"It sounded like a million dinner plates being smashed," the young blue-haired girl said as she clung to the purple-haired boy.

"That was Imperious resisting the darkstone. Light, so many breakings were just used that I've lost count."

"Breakings?" Ahrek asked.

Imperious dematerialized into light that Daylen pulled into himself. "Sunucles can't *really* become indestructible, but I did find a way to give them more lives."

"Is that the secret?" the boy asked.

"That's just how it functions," the Conqueror said. "I won't be telling anyone how it's achieved."

"Daylen, you should go," Ahrek said, looking at the crowd. "Before word reaches the government of who you are." Ahrek then glanced to Lyrah. "After what you did in saving the city, I think even the Archon here will permit it—for now."

Lyrah still didn't know what to do or what to think. She hated this man, the Conqueror; yet just like the Bringer had said, he had saved the whole city, as well as Lyrah's life when they had fought together on the island, even after she had tried so hard to kill him.

Daylen looked to the crowd and didn't reply right away. He sighed. "No."

The Bringer tried to protest, saying, "Daylen…"

"You were right, Ahrek," Daylen said. "For twenty years I've been trying to punish myself; and in doing so, I've denied all those I've wronged the chance to confront me as you have."

"But, Daylen, they won't see you as a changed man! Look at what I went through before seeing it. They'll call for your head," the Bringer urged.

"Then I might finally get to rest. If I'm truly sorry for my crimes, I'll answer for them. I see that now. There's no other way."

Ahrek eventually nodded. "Very well, but I'll remain with you through this."

"Thank you, Ahrek," Daylen said, and stepped forward. "I am Dayless the Conqueror!" he called out. "Yes, I appear young, but that's because death was too good for me. I hate myself for all the evil I have wrought and living with the guilt has been unbearable. So don't think that my prolonged life is a blessing."

Daylen felt tears on his cheeks as he continued. "I can never undo the terrible things I've done... And for them, I'm sorry. I know my apology does nothing to fix things, and everyone alive has some claim on me for justice. And so I'll let you. Tell the authorities that I wait for them at the Fallton. I'll come willingly and accept whatever punishment you feel I deserve."

Lyrah watched as the monster walked away.

The crowd parted before him to make a wide clearing; whether this was out of respect or fear, she couldn't tell.

Nor could she understand her own conflicted feelings. Part of her still wanted revenge. But was that needed? She had confronted her monster, fought him, and proven to herself that she was not weak or afraid. She felt good for that.

Cueseg had been right. She had needed to confront her fears—

"Cueseg!" Lyrah said in agonizing remembrance as she looked to the island that was rising high into the sky.

Cueseg, Kennet, Lem... Every Archknight who had been in the city apart from herself, was now dead. The sudden pain was nearly too much to bear.

"Lady Archon, are you okay?" the young purple-haired boy asked.

Lyrah couldn't prevent a tear from running down her cheek, but when she spoke her voice was stronger than she expected. "No. I need your help."

"Ah, sure," he said cautiously. "What can I do?"

"Fly me back to Hamenday. My brothers must be remembered."

CHAPTER FORTY-SEVEN

I sought out a quiet place where I could plan, and there I was consumed by a rage which eventually turned into resentment, depression, and then regret. When the only person you have for company is yourself, you eventually ask yourself some hard questions. It took time, but slowly, I saw my mistakes; and then, even more slowly, I confessed them to myself. This took a few years, but it wasn't until the tenth that I truly comprehended the full magnitude of my crimes.

The agony of soul that came upon me in that fall is more than I could describe, and from that time on I have had no greater desire than for my wretched existence to end, to finally free the world of Daylen Namaran forever.

But that would have been the easy way out.

I t was strange how much Daylen appreciated Ahrek's company as they made their way to the Fallton.

They walked in silence through the mostly empty streets, but Daylen could see that people were already returning. The Night Siren had been silenced, and skyships were making their way back to the port.

Not too far away, Daylen could see the top part of the island he had cut in half. Light, he was still amazed that he had actually done that—*cut a whole island in half!* It had cleared the city entirely and had flown steadily away from the continent, where it had stopped its forward flight abruptly.

Daylen guessed that the city's border patrol had finally flown to the thing and had found a way to disable the drivers pushing it.

It would now perpetually fly upward, a rising island to contrast with the Plummet in the distance.

When Daylen and Ahrek did eventually speak, their conversation drifted to their pasts where they talked openly and freely for the first time. They shared all they had done, their joys and sorrows, their triumphs and failures.

When they reached their penthouse their talk continued, laughs shared and tears shed long into Low Fall when most people would find sleep.

It was at the mid of Low Fall, with the sun shining in a cloudless sky, when a squad of high-ranking constables accompanied by a full troop of national soldiers entered their hotel room.

Daylen made no protest when his gauntlet and steel backsword were removed and he was put in chains. They marched him out of the hotel and locked him in the back of a conner sky van. Ahrek insisted that he be allowed to accompany him, and surprisingly he was.

They were flown to the Prime Constabulary where Daylen was given a black and white striped prisoner's uniform and once he had changed, locked in their most secure cell. Thick windowless brick walls on three sides and solid steel prison bars ten centimeters apart and five centimeters thick walled off the side that faced the outer room to the cell.

Daylen wasn't sure if the officials knew that the cell and his chains would do nothing to hold him if he wanted to escape, especially now that he had figured out Lyrah's trick—how she produced such enormous levels of strength.

That was more than enough to rip this steel cell apart if he wanted to—not to mention that he still had Imperious safely stored within himself.

But Daylen had come willingly, so there he remained without protest.

It took a fall before two very stern-looking Archknights entered the adjoining room, a male with deep red hair and pale skin, clearly Frey, and a female Hamahran with hair of streaked blue and green.

The female knight looked at him through the bars. "Give me your hand."

Daylen approached, having a good idea what was going on, and extended his arm.

The knight pulled an odd-looking manacle from a pouch that had some type of fixture on one side. Light shone from the fixture's underside around a black marble that would press onto a person's skin when the manacle was applied.

She locked the manacle to Daylen's wrist, where the darkstone instantly prevented him from using his powers.

"I could have broken out at any time until now," Daylen said. "This isn't necessary."

The knights said nothing and took positions on either side of his cell.

They mustn't have known that Daylen still had Imperious stored within himself, for with it he could break out whenever he wanted.

Daylen didn't recognize the knights, which made sense, seeing as all the knights who had been in the city had been killed in the Dawnist attack, including Cueseg, Lyrah's companion. Daylen hadn't really gotten to know the knight, but Ahrek certainly seemed to like him and had already expressed deep regret for the Tuerasian knight's death.

It was a tragedy. Daylen could only imagine what the Order was going through having lost so many knights, especially considering the fact that one of their secrets, their weakness to darkstone, had gotten out.

Daylen asked them about Lyrah, where she was now and how she was doing, but the knights didn't so much as look at him.

Daylen's first real visitor was a senator who had been assigned to handle Daylen's questioning. He was rotund and old, Daylen's junior by only twenty years, yet still strong of voice. He wore a tight suit, and his blue hair, now fading to gray, lay mostly hidden under his top hat.

"Rayaten?" the senator exclaimed when he entered the outer room that Daylen's cell faced. "Is that really you?"

Another man entered behind the senator, holding a large notebook.

"Darenlight," Ahrek said with familiarity. "Still a senator, I see."

"It's been nearly *twenty years*! I had heard you had gone off on some pilgrimage—but to become a Lightbringer? I never would have guessed."

"It's a good life for me. I go by Ahrek these days."

"Rayaten, some of us have been seeking you out for years," Darenlight continued excitedly, ignoring him. "I had nearly decided you were dead. We could use you in the Senate—do you have any idea how influential you would be?"

"Don't do it, Ahrek," Daylen said casually as he leaned on the front bars of his cell. "Bad things happen when the leader of a revolution takes a role in government."

"Rayaten is nothing like you, scum!" the senator hissed.

"That's enough, Darenlight," Ahrek said.

The man turned back to the Ahrek. "Rayaten, what in the Light's grace are you doing here with this monster?"

"Please, Darenlight, my name is Ahrek now," the Bringer reminded him quietly. "And Daylen is not the tyrant he once was."

"What are you talking about? We fought together to overthrow him. He murdered your family!"

"No one knows of his crimes more keenly than me. Daylen is truly penitent; that is why he has turned himself in, and I have forgiven him."

"*Impossible*," Darenlight replied, clearly shocked.

"It's true," Ahrek said. "I know it's hard, but if I had taken my revenge when I'd had the chance, Daylen would not have been alive to save the city. Hate creates nothing but more hate, and in some cases it leads to tremendous heartache and sorrow. Peace and forgiveness is the only thing that will heal the pains of the past."

Darenlight appeared truly awed. "You have changed, Rayaten... I mean, Lightbringer Ahrek."

"For the better."

Darenlight was silent for a moment before nodding and turning to Daylen. "Dayless. I've been sent to question you."

Daylen waved a hand. "Question away."

The senator nodded to the suited man behind him, who opened his book and pulled out one of those new-style pens with internal ink.

"First of all," Darenlight said, "how did you survive the destruction of your flagship in the Battle of Highdawn?"

"Easily. I wasn't even on the ship."

The man with the book had begun writing the moment Darenlight spoke—a scribe to record his answers.

"But several eyewitnesses placed you at the helm of your flagship."

"A body double. I was overseeing the battle from the palace. When I saw that defeat was inevitable, I ordered the execution of all the attendants and low-ranking officers who had seen me. Only my most trusted servants knew I escaped, and they were all killed off by..." Daylen looked to Ahrek.

Ahrek nodded in resignation. "I killed several of your officials as we stormed the palace, and then oversaw the execution of your head officers once the battle was won."

"I see," Darenlight said. "It's quite poetic that Bringer Ahrek was the one to turn you in."

"Daylen turned himself in," Ahrek said firmly. "You will make that very clear to the Senate, Darenlight."

"Ah, yes, of course," Darenlight said, before turning back to Daylen. "How did you escape the palace when every exit was being assaulted?"

"Through the sewers," Daylen said, not mentioning the many secret passageways he had built in the palace and around the city. "Once in hiding I planned to retake my empire, but being alone and having ample time to reflect, I slowly saw it was a vain endeavor. The people were visibly happier after my defeat. Then, as the years passed, I realized my rule was more criminal than just, which led me to understand the true magnitude of my crimes."

"It's hard to believe that you're truly penitent," Darenlight said dubiously.

"Really? You'd think the more serious sins would be easier to recognize."

"Or harder to confront in themselves, as that would mean acknowledging one's own evil."

Daylen raised an eyebrow. "I have more of a knack for causing confrontations than running from them."

"Indeed," Darenlight said. He then proceeded to ask question after question about the time Daylen spent in hiding, wanting information on every single detail, even though there wasn't much to say. Daylen had lived as a tinker and he had been miserable, and that had been just about it.

"How did this change come upon you, and how did you receive the lightbinding powers?" Darenlight finally asked.

"I went to cast myself from the continent like my letter says," Daylen said, preparing his lie. "But before I reached the edge, my body gave in and I collapsed, ready to die. There at the very verge of death, I desired more than anything to have lived my life differently. I told myself that if I could do it all over again I would spend each day fighting against those people who were like I had been. The desire was so strong that it was effectively a vow to fight evil. Later, I awoke young, and found myself to have these powers. The Light saw that my desires were true."

That had made his two knight guards twitch, but they said nothing.

Darenlight stared at Daylen and said, "Out of anything you've said, it's the witness of the Light itself that convinces me you might have changed. You have the powers, so your vow must be true."

Daylen glanced to Ahrek, who was looking troubled. He clearly didn't like that Daylen's change of heart was being supported through a lie. But it was a lie that even Ahrek knew was necessary, as otherwise the whole Archknight Order would be at risk.

"I'm satisfied with what you've told me regarding the time you spent in hiding. Now there are some other questions I need to ask."

Daylen cocked his head. "And they are?"

"Since your defeat, we have found a few stockpiles that you presumably built."

"Preparations for the next Night."

"List them."

"There's four vaults under the palace, or Senate, now. There's also a vault in each city district. You'll find them under the district square, market or council office. I saw that similar stockpiles were built in all the major cities and smaller ones in the larger prefecture towns."

Darenlight's mouth was hanging open. "We...We had only found the ones under the Senate. I didn't realize there were so many."

"Do you think I ate all the surplus after the people got their share? You'll find food, supplies, tools, seed, building materials, and weapons, enough for a whole nation. I suggest you leave them for their original purpose."

"I will pass that to the Senate. Now, what of the Imperial Reserve?"

"Oh, so you found out about that?"

"We're very thorough."

"Well, I've just told you where it is," Daylen lied. "The Imperial Reserve refers to the whole system of storage vaults I built throughout the empire."

"Oh," Darenlight said, somewhat disappointed, but looking convinced.

Thank goodness—Daylen's Imperial Reserve wasn't something he wanted anyone to get their hands on. Apart from the fleet of battle-ready skyships and enough weapons to arm a nation, as well as all of Imperious' breakings—however many remained—there was also the device he had dug up from his expedition into the Floating Isles: the thing that had enough power to destroy continents. Oh, what the Senate, or any nation for that matter, would give to get their hands on all that.

"What have you done with Imperious? There's many a Guild member demanding to see it."

"Imperious shattered when I cut the island in two," Daylen lied again. "Seems like even that sword had its limits. I only survived the broken link thanks to the Bringer."

"A great loss, but used to save the city, so a fair trade in my mind. That's all I have for now," Darenlight said. "It has been an... interesting experience."

The senator then bid his fond farewells to Ahrek, with a few more attempts to bribe him into the Senate.

After that, five other senators visited Daylen's cell within that first week with their own questions and agendas. Darenlight visited another two times as well—his final visit to share what the Senate had decided to do with him.

"There's going to be a public trial."

"Very well," Daylen said.

"Calling it public doesn't really communicate just *how* public."

"All right, then. How public?"

"The heads of state of every nation have been invited to take part in the proceedings. They will all have a say in your sentencing. In addition to this, every person over the age of twenty seems to have grievances against you, as well as many even younger when you take into account lost parents and siblings. Considering the magnitude of your crimes, we the Hamahran Senate have deemed it appropriate that every man, woman, and child be given the opportunity to face you and lay their charges at your feet, where their testimony will be heard and recorded. The trial will be held out in the open, in the center of the city's Fair Grounds."

Daylen sighed. "This isn't necessary. It's an overelaborate exercise that will lead to the same conclusion. We all know this ends with my execution."

"We do," Darenlight said, "but every person alive deserves to know that your execution is for whatever individual wrong you caused them. None should be forgotten."

"Fine. So you're not going to hold anything back. I get it, it's what I deserve..." He sighed again. "This is going to take a while."

"It's going to take weeks to organize, let alone carry out. A proclamation is being sent to all nations to come and take their turn in the proceedings. We have scheduled the trial to begin next month, to give those in distant lands time to travel."

"Very well, then. Is that all?"

"No. You're entitled to representation."

"I'll have no one make excuses for what I've done. I plead guilty to all charges."

"You can pronounce your plea after each charge is issued."

"Fine. Are we done?"

"Yes. I don't expect we'll see each other until the trial."

"It's been a pleasure," Daylen said with masked sarcasm.

"I'm sure," Darenlight said with a nod and left the cell.

"You don't look too happy," Daylen said, sitting on his cot and speaking to Ahrek.

"This isn't what the Light intends for you."

Daylen looked to the knights on either side of his cell. "Hey, Archons, I don't suppose you could give us a minute."

The knights didn't move.

"It's perfectly safe," Ahrek said. "You've suppressed his powers and standing guard in the next room will be sufficient for the time we talk."

The male knight looked to the woman, who nodded, and they left the room.

"We can sense you using your powers," Daylen called out to them as the darkstone restraint only stopped his channeling, not his light sense. "So we know you're listening in. Stop it!"

The inner light of the knight stopped shimmering.

All right," Daylen said to Ahrek, "what do you think the Light intends for me?"

"To live! If it had wanted you dead, it would have let you die earlier."

"I've done what the Light wanted me to and saved the city, preventing another bloody revolution. Now it's over, and I'm going to answer for my crimes. The Light's will has been fulfilled."

"But how do you really know that it's over?"

"Well, if I'm truly sorry for what I've done, I *need* to face my crimes—and doing so will mean my execution. There's no other way I live."

"There's another way. I was sent to you for a reason."

"You were sent to me for your own sake as much as mine."

"That's a part of it, but…"

"No buts," Daylen told him. "I know what you're thinking. You have the miracle of creation and you're just stupid enough to consider using your last miracle to sacrifice yourself to bring me back."

"Daylen…I can't help but feel you have more to offer the world. Letting you die would be a waste."

"And giving up your own life wouldn't?"

"I would perform it at the end of my life, as all Bringers do."

"And then I'd just let them execute me again."

"No you won't, not after you've answered for your crimes already, knowing there's more good you can do."

"If you bring me back, you deny everyone I've wronged the very punishment they deemed I deserved. You'll thwart justice, Bringer, and that can't be the Light's will, can it?"

Ahrek mouth pressed into a thin line.

"Can't you see that this is what I want?" Daylen sighed, and his head sagged. "I'm so tired…"

Ahrek didn't reply.

Daylen lifted his head. "Swear to me, Bringer! Swear to me that you will *not* bring me back!"

He still didn't say anything.

Daylen looked at him with accusing eyes. "You bastard. That's *exactly* what you're intending."

Ahrek bowed his head and turned from Daylen, walking to the door.

"Don't you dare," Daylen growled ferociously, running to the bars and pressing his face to them, "If you resurrect me, I'll hate you forever, you hear me! You. Will. Let. Me. Die."

Ahrek opened the door and left, not uttering a single world.

"Don't walk away from me, you blackened bastard. You will let me die! You *will* let me die!"

CHAPTER FORTY-EIGHT

I wanted to die and escape the horrible pain of my guilt. I decided on many occasions to turn myself in and face the justice of the world, only to stop, knowing that if I did I would definitely be executed, which would grant me the very thing I had desired for years. So instead, I chose to prolong my pain, and it has been exactly that: years of pain, suffering, and regret.

Ahrek didn't return, and Daylen didn't know what that meant. Regardless, the falls passed slowly with only the odd visitor, until the time came that Daylen was marched out of his cell and flown to the trial.

The Fair Grounds were the largest clearing within the city, and were completely enclosed by buildings.

When the van landed, Daylen could hear the rumblings of what must have been an unthinkably massive crowd.

The doors opened and Daylen stepped out to see an innumerable number of people blanketing the clearing, all standing shoulder to shoulder watching him. Hundreds of skyships had also been flown in and were sitting low around the grounds, their decks packed with people.

Incredibly, the near-deafening chatter quickly died as Daylen appeared.

The people and ships surrounded a large wooden platform that had been erected toward the northern end of the Fair Grounds. It was on this platform where the van had landed. On the left, right, and back of the platform were rows and rows of pews, each consecutive one raised higher than the pew in front.

In these pews sat the dignitaries and rulers of what appeared to be every nation in the world. With these rulers sat other high-ranking officials, including some of the Hamahran Guild Masters and higher ranking Archknights.

The whole Hamahran Senate was there, as well as the minister of the Mayn republic. The Tuerasian Yonsen, the Head Matriarch of Frey, the King of Toulsen, the Lourian Jhan, the Delavian Council of Dukes—Daylen had to restrain a chuckle at seeing them—as well as many more. Light, even the Magnate of Lee'on'ta was present, who rarely even left his secluded palace, his braids of ridiculously long purple hair falling all around him.

Daylen had conquered most of the nations these people represented, killing so many of their sons and daughters. They had as much right to see him brought to justice as any.

Conspicuously, Daylen could see no representative from Azbanadar, once his greatest ally, which might explain their absence. They had less hatred for the Conqueror and weren't on particularly good terms with Hamahra these days. What with how much Hamahra wanted to separate themselves from Daylen's legacy and their strong political differences, war between the two mighty nations was beginning to look very possible.

The red-haired Freysian Matriarch was looking at him with particular venom. To say they had a history was an understatement.

Quallandra was one of the rulers who had been in power back when Daylen had been Emperor. She had been a beautiful yet naive young woman back then, sixteen years old, and had sought peace with Hamahra on many occasions, even offering herself in marriage to him. Daylen never had any intention to marry Quallandra, but he seduced her anyway. She only went along with it because she was young and inexperienced, thinking marriage was the next step before an alliance. Still, she had fallen in love with him.

Then Daylen blackmailed her, refusing any marriage proposal. With Frey's very specific traditions and beliefs regarding sex, Quallandra's fornication would have seen her deposed—thus, under threat of exposing their relationship, Frey finally submitted. And then Daylen told her people about their illicit relationship anyway. How she had stayed in power was beyond him.

Needless to say, Quallandra had been all too ready and willing to lead her people in rebellion when the time came.

Light, Daylen had been such a bastard. He had justified those actions to himself, having still been pissed at Frey for not honoring older treaties with Hamahra and not backing them in their war against Delavie.

Of course there were one or two Delavian Dukes present who were old enough to remember him, too, as well as several members of their Senate.

So many of these leaders were scowling at him.

Daylen's life had been such a mess.

Seated on benches in front of the pews were ten scribes who had portable desks assembled. Clearly everything in the trial was going to be recorded, and it seemed that every ruler would have a say in Daylen's fate. With people like Quallandra included in that, the verdict was very obvious.

There was a single steel chair in the centre of the platform that faced the crowd. Daylen was directed to sit in it. Once he had complied, his manacled hands and feet were locked to the chair.

To the side of the chair was a phonotrack with darkstone vibronic amplifiers attached.

Two other amplified phonotracks were set up, one on a small dais five meters in front of the chair and the other behind a desk to the left of Daylen's seat.

It seemed that every word spoken in this trial would be broadcast to the crowd and telegraphed to many other cities as well.

It was a very elaborate setup.

A senator left the pews and walked to the desk on Daylen's left. It was Darenlight. Once seated, he spoke into the phonotrack's microphone. His voice sounded across the whole field of people, amplified and carried by hundreds of phonotrack speakers assembled through the grounds.

"We will commence the proceedings," Darenlight said. "We find ourselves in unique circumstances, and as such this trial won't follow regular procedure. As the crimes committed by the defendant are so numerous, the charges against the defendant will be issued in rounds. Also, because there are many crimes not officially known, those who wish to charge the defendant with a crime that has not been listed, committed in the time period of the given round, may do so and give testimony of the same. This trial is to also provide those who feel wronged by the defendant an opportunity to confront him and express what sentence they feel appropriate to his crimes, for all people deserve a say in the fate of the man that oppressed the world. Because of this, it has been decided that the plea of the defendant will be taken *after* all charges have been issued for a given round and the witnesses who wish to testify have done so. If the defendant pleads not guilty, he will be given the chance to make his case.

"Presiding at this trial are the state heads of every nation with grievances against the defendant—and I, Darenlight Brighten, will be acting as moderating judge. The defendant is Daylen Namaran, more commonly known as Dayless the Conqueror. Daylen Namaran is accused of numerous war crimes during his tenure as Emperor of the Dawn Empire that will henceforth be presented. It is the sixty-seventh fall of spring, year fifty-one of the Fifth Day. Does the defendant wish to make any opening remarks?"

Daylen shook his head. He would make no excuses.

"I will offer opening remarks on behalf of the defendant," an all-too-familiar voice called out from the side of the platform.

Daylen looked to see Ahrek walking toward him.

Once Ahrek was at his side, Daylen glared at him. "Ahrek, I'll have nothing to do with you until you answer me."

"Very well," Ahrek said. "If you are sentenced to death, I will accept it as the Light's will and not bring you back."

Daylen sighed contentedly. "That's all I wanted. It's good to see you. I need a friend right now."

"What are friends for otherwise?"

"Now, why do you want to give my opening remarks? You won't change anything."

"It might not change the verdict, but it will change people's perception. They need to know who you really are, and by the looks of it, *you* certainly aren't going to tell them, are you?"

Daylen tsked and looked to the moderator, nodding. Darenlight raised an inviting hand to the small dais.

Ahrek stepped atop it and gazed out to the crowd, saying into the microphone, "I am Rayaten Leusa, Leader of the Second Revolution." Gasps of shock and awe erupted all around them. The officials seated on the pews were looking to one another in confusion, those Hamahran senators old enough to have lived during the revolution nodding in dumfounded confirmation.

"I speak on behalf of the man I once fought to destroy. Why? Because the Light directed me to this man before I knew who he was, and in that time I learned of his goodness. The man seated here isn't the same as the tyrant who oppressed the world. He has changed. I say that knowing full well that it was this man who murdered my family." Ahrek gazed at the many faces in the crowd. "I *know* what he has done…and after the greatest trial of my life, I have forgiven him. If I can, then so can you. Daylen Namaran bears more guilt and sorrow than any man alive. That is why since becoming young again he has dedicated every moment of his new life to help people and fight back the darkness that is so rampant in the world. And ultimately, his change of heart is why he is on trial right now. It was he who turned himself in, and nothing but his own submission keeps him seated. He has *chosen* to answer for his crimes—the greatest sign of true penitence there is.

"Does his change of heart undo the crimes we will hear in this trial? No. But will his death?" Ahrek asked, to grumbles from those arranged before him. "What is *true* justice? Is it revenge, so that we can inflict the same pain and suffering on he who gave as much to us? Or is it restitution? Would justice not want to teach those who do wrong of their own evil, to make them truly penitent? If so, then justice has already been done. Only when the hearts of villains cannot be changed can I see the need to protect the world from such unrepentant evil. As for Daylen, I understand that there is still a debt to pay for true restitution, but I implore you to consider carefully: will this man's death pay more than a life dedicated to such a cause?"

It was amazing that even with such a huge amount of people, silence filled the air. Ahrek paused a moment before adding, "You will find greater peace in forgiving this man for what he has done than you will trying to punish him more than he already punishes himself. Believe me. I know."

The silence continued even after Ahrek had finished speaking. The Bringer left the dais and walked to stand beside Daylen.

"You did more than tell them who I am, Bringer," Daylen said. "You're still trying to save my life. I thought I made it clear that I don't want you to."

"No, you made it clear that I wasn't to bring you back if you're executed, not that I couldn't try to save you beforehand."

"Whatever," Daylen said dismissively. "It doesn't matter. It's not going to change the verdict."

Ahrek nodded. "Perhaps."

Daylen nodded to the moderator, who then announced, "Let the first round of formal charges commence."

A Hamahran senator rose from his pew and walked to the dais with a large ledger in hand. He opened the book and began reading. "We, the Hamahran people, formally revoke the authority of the Dawn Empire and classify the previously sanctioned executions of the aristocratic children and extended family members of the former ruling officials as murder in the first degree, and charge Daylen Namaran with two thousand five hundred and eighty-four counts."

"May the witnesses come forward," Darenlight said.

Around twenty people were lined up off to the side of the large platform and they came to the dais one at a time. The first few were simply Hamahran officials reading from the Dawn Empire's execution records. It was a lengthy process, and they were honest enough to admit that there must have been many executions that were justly carried out in the name of legitimate crimes. The problem was the charges of treason, for it was a known fact that Dayless the Conqueror had charged people with treason for merely annoying him. For that reason they decided all treason executions, as with all executions sentenced to people for opposing or fighting against the Dawn Empire, were murders committed by the defendant. Naming all those victims would have taken weeks, so they summarized them with the estimated civilian and military casualties of the Empire Wars. The final estimate accused Daylen of some twenty-eight million murders.

Hearing the staggering number sent a pain into Daylen's heart so sharp that he gasped and then panted for breath.

Twenty-eight million people. People with lives and loved ones, many young with their own hopes and dreams, all killed by a genocidal madman. As horrible as Daylen's guilt was, it seemed too small in comparison to the magnitude of his crimes.

The next witness was an older man with faded gray hair.

"State your name for the record, and then offer your testimony," Darenlight said.

"Augusday Felentius the Third."

Daylen didn't expect to hear *that*. Felentius was an aristocratic name.

"I am the son of Augusday the Second who served Queen Jasmeena as governor of trade. This man," Augusday, said pointing at Daylen, "sent his soldiers into my home where they *murdered* my parents and sisters, and would have murdered me had I not escaped. I was forced to live in hiding for most of my life."

Daylen had honestly thought he had hunted out and executed every member of the aristocracy.

The old man looked at Daylen through tears of hatred. "You ruined my life, and for what? What did I ever do to you? What did my sisters ever do? They were just children! What did my parents do? My father was the governor of *trade!*" he screamed bitterly. "I'll *never* forgive you for what you did to me. This man is a monster and must *die*. Saving the city doesn't change what he's done. Let the world be done with him—and good riddance."

Daylen expected the man to say as much, but hearing the words cut deeper than he expected. He couldn't hold back his tears of shame.

"You see, Ahrek," Daylen said, "few people are as forgiving as you, and I don't blame them."

The six other surviving aristocrats shared similar stories to the first. They all called for Daylen's execution, and though one acknowledged that Daylen seemed to have changed, he claimed that he was too dangerous to go free regardless. They ultimately felt that he would go back to his old ways if he was allowed to live, and the world would be safer with his death.

Once all the witnesses had given testimony, Darenlight asked, "How does the defendant plead?"

"Guilty," Daylen said softly.

"Has anyone come forward to lay additional charges against the defendant that were committed during this time?"

There was another moderator standing off to the other side of the platform where four people stood. The moderator nodded.

"Let the first witness come forward and make their charges."

It was a very elderly woman who took the stand.

"State your name for the record, lay your charge, and bear your witness."

"My name is Maratess Telatell. I was a livery maid on the

serving staff to the Queen. When the Conqueror took the old palace, he also executed each head servant and many of the lesser ones. They didn't do anything to deserve it. I went into hiding, which is why I survived. So, I, um, accuse this man of murder. Ten people at least." And she listed their names.

Well, Daylen *had* executed them, that was true, but it wasn't for doing nothing. One had tried to kill him—the Head Mistress of the serving staff if he recalled correctly—so he had promptly executed her. He then placed spies on each former upper servant, having seen how loyal they were to their former masters and found that several were working together to smuggle aristocrats out of the city. That's why he had executed them, as well as the aristocrats they had been protecting. Even though Daylen felt he had acted justly at the time, they were still murders. Those servants had only been trying to save the innocent lives of the aristocratic family members that Daylen had sentenced to death.

"How does the defendant plead?"

"Guilty," Daylen replied.

"Let the next witness come forward."

CHAPTER FORTY-NINE

But I cannot live forever. Beyond my control, death finally draws near. I wonder what it will be like. Will my existence end as some claim is the fate of those destined for Outer Darkness? If that's the case, I see it as a gift.
I'll soon find out.

It took four falls for all of the charges to be laid out and the witnesses to give testimony. If every single person who could have given testimony against him had done so, it would have taken months, but only those most wronged felt the need to confront him on the stand.

Daylen had never cried so much in his life, had never felt so wretched or so remorseful than he did during those falls, where each of his most terrible sins were listed before him. Light, did it paint a truly horrible and tragic picture; and throughout it all, Daylen's voice echoed:

"Guilty."

Amongst the worst and most painful list of charges were those of rape against the girls forced into his bed. There were four hundred and twenty-seven girls in all, multiple counts of rape against each.

From that deplorable number, only seventy of those girls had appeared to stand witness against him. As they had all been in their teens when Daylen had abused them, they now ranged between thirty and fifty years old. Confronting them was as painful and difficult as it had been when he had come face to face with Lyrah.

Even more troubling were the younger men and women who stood with them. Each one seemed to either stand next to or comforting one of the older women, none younger than twenty years old, most with dark-blue hair.

My children.

Daylen's heart broke at seeing them. They looked on him with differing expressions: hate, curiosity, awe, fear, resentment, or even longing.

There were some that wore the uniform of the National Guard, a few even the uniform of an Archknight. The rest wore common or respectable dress, every single one with a beaded tassel in their hair and functional sword at their side.

Daylen had let them down in so many ways, but would they want to change the past? Had he not slept with their mothers, they wouldn't even be alive, and he was confident they had at least appreciated being born. It was a very strange clash of emotions.

It seemed that several of the girls he had raped had the same feelings.

"He was cruel and perverted," one of the older women said as she bore witness on the stand. "And from it I fell pregnant. But even hating him so much, I could never hate my own child. People from the palace made sure we were taken care of, and we've had a good life since. I...I do not think he should be executed for what he has done."

"I wasn't ready for what was done to me," another woman said, "but he was kind in his own way, and from it I was blessed with my daughter, who's been the greatest joy of my life. So I wouldn't change the past—and even with all the other terrible things this man has done, I can't say I want to see him dead. I think he probably deserves it with all the people he's killed, but not for my part."

That woman and only three others shared such moderate testimonies. The rest were far more willing to express stronger feelings.

"I hate him," a more fragile woman said, quivering as she struggled to get through her testimony. "The fact that he's still alive to torment me and my son is too much. You must kill him and let our suffering end."

Strangely, it was the women who didn't have any children by him that seemed to despise him more than the others. To them, Daylen had truly ruined their lives, many not ever finding marriage, and a few still bearing deep psychological pain.

Daylen wept with his head hanging in shame as they spoke.

"State your name for the record," the Judge Moderator for that fall's proceedings said.

"Archon Lyrah. Knight, Archonair, and Lifebinder in the Arch Order of Light."

Daylen's head shot up.

He had not thought he would ever see Lyrah again.

She didn't look at him. "I was only fourteen when this man's servants took me from my home by force. My parent's lives were continually threatened if I didn't willingly submit myself to the Emperor. What he did to me over the next month was disgusting...vile...and the abuse has left me emotionally scarred ever since. I've never been able to be close to another man because of him. I've hated the Conqueror with more passion than I can express, and I even tried to kill this man when I learned who he was. I still hate him," she said bitterly, and then sighed. "But it's wrong to not consider what Daylen has done since he received his powers. He singlehandedly uncovered the Dawnist plot, and then defeated them, saving the city and countless lives in the process. He should be remembered for the good he has done as well as the evil. Apart from that, let him live or die. I don't care. All I want is to never see him again."

It stung more than he expected to hear Lyrah's testimony, more so than the other women. But what had he expected—that she would forgive him like Ahrek had? Yes, he had saved her life while they fought together, but Ahrek had explained how she had saved Daylen's life, too, when he had fallen from the *Bloodrunner*, and that was more than enough. She owed him nothing.

A deep pain remained in Daylen's heart as Lyrah stepped off the dais.

The remaining women bore witness, and as painful as that was, the trial still had a long way to go.

When Queen Quallandra came forward to list the crimes that

Daylen had committed against the Kingdom of Frey, she didn't hold back, and accused him of raping her, too.

Now *that* he hadn't done—it had been consensual between them, but it was clear she considered it coercion, as she had only slept with him at first for an alliance, which he didn't give. But still, she had come to enjoy their nights together and be very affectionate to Daylen before his betrayal. Was it through the claim of rape that she had kept her throne?

She hadn't been the only one to give an unbalanced accounting of Daylen's crimes; but even then, when the time came for his plea, his answer remained the same.

"Guilty."

As the falls passed Daylen was flown back to his cell and then out again for each session. The city and indeed the whole world were in a riot of debate. Everyone discussed what they thought of each round, the witnesses they heard, and what verdict they felt should be issued. No one could go anywhere and not hear a heated discussion about these things.

The trial started to take its toll on Daylen. He was so emotionally destroyed that it was hard to even walk. He didn't know how he could have gotten through it without Ahrek's support. Just having the Bringer there helped tremendously, but he did more, offering words of comfort and even helping Daylen up and down from his chair and bed—for so great was his pain.

Finally the last witness concluded his testimony, explaining how Daylen had used human shields in the Battle of Highdawn.

The moderating judge, who was Darenlight that fall, asked how Daylen pled.

Daylen felt numb. He had lived a long time but had never endured anything as traumatic and painful as this trial. He could barely speak, but he forced his mouth to open, and the soft strained word came out. "Guilty."

"Are there any more witnesses who would wish to make a charge against the defendant?"

"I do," a timid voice called out from the official pews.

He was spindly man of middle age with a balding head of thin blue hair. He wore an expensive suit and cravat with a cutlass at his side and walked with a hesitant step to the stand.

"State your name for the record and issue your charge."

"Senator Terain Daybright."

Why was that name so familiar?

The senator looked at Daylen. "I herewith charge this man, Daylen Namaran, formerly known as Dayless the Conqueror, with *heroism.*"

A murmur reverberated through the numerous crowds from that.

Daylen didn't expect to hear anything like that.

"Senator Terain," the moderator said, "heroism is not a crime that one can be charged with."

"But acts of heroism are officially recognized under the law," Terain countered. "And they must be proven through witnessed accounts. What better place to see that done than here? Also, if we do not conduct the ratification now, this man might not be alive to receive the honors he rightly deserves."

"A Senate vote to recognize acts of heroism cannot be done during a criminal trial."

"And what about this trial has been regular? We've basically rewritten the law for our convenience, so what grounds do you have to deny another change? You will not take me from the stand willingly, Darenlight."

Though the man was slight and soft-spoken, there was a hardness in his eyes that was easy to read. He truly meant what he was saying.

Darenlight was glaring at Terain, but eventually said, "Continue."

Daylen remembered reading about this law. It had been introduced a few years into the Senate's rule and was mainly an honorific. Those people recognized as national heroes had their names, portraits, and stories displayed on a featured wall in the Senate. Ahrek's real name, Rayaten Leusa, and how he had led the revolution, was one of the first to be put there.

"Those close to me will know that a year ago I sent my daughter away to her uncle," Terain said. "The truth was that she had been kidnapped by the infamous pirate Blackheart, who held her hostage to control my vote in the Senate."

Now Daylen knew where he had heard that name before.

The people seated in the pews looked to each other very uncomfortably when hearing that.

"I'll willingly stand trial for my duplicity and admit that every vote I took part in should be void," he said, "but I am not here to speak of myself. This man saved my daughter's life and rid the world of one of the active tyrants that plagued it. He fought his way into Blackheart's hidden lair to save her as well as other girls. No one asked him to, and he received no formal reward. He did it because he had the power to help, and because it was right. As we know from the press, at the very time he did this he also freed fifty other young women who had been stolen away from their homes to be sold off as sex slaves. Then there are the crimes he stopped in the city of Treremain, the lives he saved—and it seems that he has been busy here in the capital as well, especially in stopping the Dawnists from destroying our entire city! He saved millions of lives, mine included, for I, too, was stuck on the upper islands during the evacuation."

Terain paused to look across the pews. "These actions are clearly heroic and exceed many other acts that have been previously ratified. I propose we officially recognize them as such. I stand as an official witness and will happily call on as many other witnesses as needed. They stand ready beside this platform."

Daylen looked to see a group of people standing near the steps to the platform, Sharra and Sain among them.

"That's not necessary," Darenlight said. "These actions have been well documented by the press and we all saw the Conqueror stop the island. We shall put it to a Senate vote. All those in favor that the actions heretofore described be officially recognized as heroic?"

A single senator stood and said, "Yea."

Then another stood, repeating the sentiment, followed by the rest, some looking very reluctant.

"All those opposed?" There were none, and Darenlight added, "The vote is unanimous. The Senate may be seated." Darenlight looked to Daylen. "Daylen Namaran, you are now an official hero of the nation," he said, and then turned to the pews. "Before we continue—and seeing that we have allowed Senate voting in this trial—I would like to propose another vote to the Senate," he said shrewdly. "I suggest we revoke Daylen Namaran's status as a national hero for crimes committed against the Hamahran people. The specific acts that gave him the status will remain as heroic, but the individual who committed them will not. All those in favor?"

Most stood and said, "Yea."

"All opposed?"

Remarkably there were several senators who stood and said, "Nay," Terain's soft voice being amplified through the phonotrack in unison with the handful of others.

"Those in favor win the vote. Daylen Namaran's status as hero is hereby revoked."

"Well, that was short-lived," Daylen whispered to Ahrek.

"At least your recent actions have been acknowledged."

"Senator Terain," the moderator began, "you may retake your seat."

"As someone who has placed a charge against the defendant," Terain said, "I would like to take my turn and express the sentence I feel this man deserves and explain why."

Darenlight waived an impatient hand, indicating acceptance.

"I would first ask," Terain began, "what evil has this man wrought since he was deposed? We all know: *none*. And if this is the case, his life from that time has been a blessing to the world. How many of us would be dead right now if he had died when we thought he had? And how many will die if we execute him here, seeing that he is so determined to make right the wrongs he has committed? This man possesses great magical powers, but what many don't realize is that his powers are those of an Archknight!" Terain proclaimed, the crowd murmuring in response. "He received them through making a solemn vow to fight evil for the rest of his days, a vow that the *Light itself* ratifies. Apart from this man's every action since he received his powers, there is no greater witness that he possesses no threat to anyone than the Light. Yes, he has pled guilty to the crimes outlined, but we *must* take into account his recent actions. Therefore, I say that all charges issued against the defendant should be dropped and the defendant released so that he might continue to fulfill his vow."

An eruption of protest rippled across all those who heard Terain's extreme and ridiculous suggestion.

Amazingly, however, there were some cries of agreement.

"Order! We will have order!" Darenlight announced.

Daylen huffed. "Terain might as well demand the Shade serve him morning tea while he's at it," he said under his breath.

"But his words *have* had an effect," Ahrek whispered back.

Daylen looked to the senators and the other heads of nations. They either looked troubled, reflective, or outraged at Terain. "No.

It was nice of him to try and defend me, but I don't deserve it, nor will it change things."

"Thank you for your witness, Senator Terain," Darenlight said with unmasked resentment. Terain retook his seat in the pews. "Is there anyone else who would wish to make a charge against the defendant?" Darenlight added.

They all waited for a while, but no one came forward.

"Does the defendant wish to make any closing remarks?"

At this, Daylen nodded.

His two Archknight guards approached and unlocked him from his chair. Daylen pushed himself up, Ahrek taking him by the side as he had to do several times already, helping Daylen walk. Daylen summoned what strength he could and gently pushed Ahrek away. Ahrek placed a hand on his shoulder and nodded. Daylen walked to the stand.

The total silence in the air felt strange. Every set of eyes was on him.

All Daylen could say was two soft words, words that echoed across the city: "I'm sorry."

Daylen then left the stand and retook his seat.

It seemed like the people didn't really know what to make of his words; even Darenlight was looking at him with a conflicted expression. The moderator eventually cleared his throat and spoke once more.

"As Judge Moderator, I officially bring the first international criminal trial to an end. We will reconvene outfall for sentencing."

CHAPTER FIFTY

I could lie here in this hovel and wait for the inevitable, but that doesn't seem right. My life has been a plague on this continent, and leaving my body here strikes me as wrong. The world deserves to be rid of Dayless the Conqueror once and for all. Perhaps I should cast myself from the continent... That does sound poetic. Whichever way my life ends, know that it's an undeserved mercy. If the Light truly wanted to punish me, it would curse me to live. This has been the life of Dayless the Conqueror, written by his own hand. I have not written this to make excuses, but to confess my countless crimes.

I was a tyrant, and let the world remember me as such. Farewell.

Daylen lay on the bed in his cell, feeling more emotionally drained than he could express.

"You endured it well," Ahrek said, sitting on his chair in the adjoining room. "I can only imagine how hard that must have been for you."

The two Archknight guards stood in their regular position.

"Though I can't help but think," Ahrek said, "that every single charge issued against you could not have been entirely just. After all, people tend to paint a lopsided story when wronged."

"Of course," Daylen said, resigned. "There were heaps of

charges that were trumped up, not to mention the other ones that were misrepresented. There was a couple that had actually been committed by some of the more unscrupulous Guilds."

"What?" Ahrek said, sitting up.

"Oh yes—the unjust execution of the Knife Maker's Guildmaster, Boloten-something. I didn't have a thing to do with it. That had been a paid assassin by the Sword Guild. They had an agreement with the Knife Guild's second that if they removed the Guildmaster, the second, who would become the new master, would renegotiate the legal sword and knife crafting definitions."

"I...I had sat in as an arbiter in that negotiation. I had wondered why the Knife Makers had finally reneged on their stance."

"Well, if you remember, it didn't last. The Guild deposed the new master and claimed the new definitions were invalid. But in any case, the Guildmaster who issued that charge against me was just using me as a scapegoat. Not all Guildmasters were as respectable as you."

"Why didn't you say anything?"

"I can't prove anything. Anyway what's one more drop in a sea?"

"But it's not just!"

"No, my sentence will still be the same regardless. I'll be executed and that *is* just."

"Not if you're remembered for more crimes than you actually committed. And what of those who committed the murder?"

"Long since dead most likely, and as to being remembered for crimes I didn't commit it doesn't make any real difference. At least what I've done recently has been properly recognized. I'll be remembered for some small good by the end, which is far more than I deserve."

"Not more," Ahrek replied, shaking his head. "It's barely enough, especially if people can't see your service and sacrifices as grounds to forgive you or at the very least for the good you can still do."

"I'd never force anyone to forgive me. If my death is the only way they'll get a measure of peace, then I accept it happily."

"But we both know that this peace is false."

"Yeah, but *they* don't, and it's not like we can just tell them that.

I'm eighty-two years old, remember? You learn a thing or two about people in that time. When a person's heart is set on revenge, it's profoundly difficult to turn them from that path." Daylen looked in the Bringer's eyes. "You of all people know that, Ahrek."

Ahrek didn't reply, and they left each other to their thoughts for a while.

"I was wrong, you know," Ahrek said softly.

"That you can't make a good joke to save your life? Good, I've been telling you that since we met."

"Hah, no. I was wrong about where you're destined to go. You won't be going to Outer Darkness."

"Are you trying to upset me?"

"Surely you still don't want your existence to *end*."

"If it releases me from my guilt and pain, of course I do."

"Is it still so bad, even after facing your crimes?"

"Having heard every terrible thing I've done and coming face to face with those I've wronged? Yeah, I feel great."

Ahrek grimaced. "Oh… Sorry."

Daylen sighed. "It's fine. I'll always bear my guilt, but lately, apart from actually sitting through the trial, things do feel better. Knowing that I'm about to answer for what I've done does make me feel at peace."

"Then what would the Outer Darkness offer you?"

"Fine, if not Outer Darkness, then what? Do you think the Light will take me into itself?"

"I think you have more of a chance of redemption than you credit."

"Hah! Finally a funny joke."

"I mean it."

"Really? Well… I suppose I'll find out soon."

High Fall dawned, and no one came to collect him. Daylen waited with Ahrek, and by mid High a messenger came to tell him that the recess was extended until the next fall.

"I wonder what's taking them so long?" Ahrek said.

"Probably waiting on the right type of executioner. I wonder how they'll do it? Hanging, guillotine, impaling, a chopping block?"

"That's a morbid thing to consider."

"Personally I like the way that the old Kreen did it."

"The Kreen?"

"A society of mountain barbarians who were eventually conquered by Dererian the Mighty. They would execute people by throwing them into a pit of beasts with a sword in their hand."

"With a sword you could just fight off the beasts."

Daylen shook his head. "Not with the amount of beasts they used."

When the next fall came around, Daylen was marched out of his cell. He had gone through this so many times recently, but this time it felt different. He was walking to his death.

He had meant what he'd said to Ahrek—finally, after so many years, he felt at peace.

Ahrek was silent as the two of them were flown to the Fair Grounds.

As Daylen emerged from the van, he found that the grounds were even more packed and crowded than any fall before.

Over a thousand national soldiers surrounded the large wooden stage.

Daylen was led to his chair, which faced the opposite direction this time, toward the pews.

Ahrek stood at his side.

Once Daylen was locked into his seat, Darenlight took his place on the moderator's pulpit. "All to order," he said, and waited for the crowds to quiet down. "The sentencing will now begin. As the defendant has pled guilty to all charges, a verdict does not need to be issued. After much, *much*, debate, we the rulers of Tellos sentence Daylen Namaran, more commonly known as Dayless the Conqueror...to lifelong imprisonment and service in the custody of the Arch Order of Light. A suspended sentence of death is in place, pending any crimes he might commit."

"*What?*" Daylen said in total disbelief.

Shock and amazement exploded from the huge crowd.

The rulers looked resigned, disgusted, accepting, angry – and some few even seemed pleased.

They're—they're actually letting me live? Daylen thought incredulously.

The crowd was screaming so loudly that it was hard to make

out if the majority were pleased or outraged. Daylen guessed outrage, but it was definitely a mix.

"Order! ORDER!"

The command had no effect and the soldiers all stood on guard as the people jeered and shouted.

So that was why there were so many soldiers in attendance.

"WE WILL HAVE ORDER!" Darenlight demanded.

Finally, the massive throng settled somewhat, making the last few cries discernible.

"You murderous bastard!"

"Kill him!"

"He saved the city, let him live!"

"Death to the Conqueror!"

"I understand that this sentence deserves to be explained," Darenlight said loudly, finally bringing the people under control. "Most of us agree that this man deserves to die for what he has done, but we have ultimately decided that it would be too great a waste. Daylen Namaran has shown by his actions that he truly intends to fight evil for the remainder of his days. Of course, that doesn't change what he has done or the fact that we cannot be sure he might regress into his old ways. Thus his freedom is forever stripped, and he will remain under the watchful eye of the Archknights until the day that he finally dies."

Daylen slumped in his chair, feeling true dismay and dread, tears escaping from his eyes. Though these rulers didn't know it, they had actually inflicted the most terrible punishment possible for him. *He* had *to live*.

The Light truly had no mercy.

Ahrek placed his hand on Daylen's shoulder, but Daylen didn't look at him. It wasn't Ahrek's fault that Daylen had received this sentence; it wasn't even Senator Terain's. It was Daylen's. He was the one who had performed those actions that were now the reasons why his life had been spared. He had chosen to help people and fight darkness, and now even though he desired rest more than anything, he would have to continue to do just that.

Back when he had cheated death the first time round and received his powers, he had told the Light that he would live his new life fighting evil and saving people. Well, more than anything, this seemed to indicate that the Light had accepted his offer. At least he could still do good—it wasn't like they were throwing him in a cell for the rest of his life. So that was something.

"I know this is hard for you, Daylen," Ahrek said.

"Yeah, well, that's life."

"You *were* planning on joining the knights, anyway. That's just going to happen sooner than you thought."

Daylen looked up at the man. "After all I've done, how can they let me live?"

"Because of what you did these past falls, and what you'll do in the future."

"We release the convicted into the hands of the knights and end the sentencing," Darenlight said. "You may all go about your business."

The rulers stood and made their way off the stand. The crowd started to rumble with conversation.

Daylen's Archknight guards were joined by three others of the Order before they unlocked his shackles from the chair.

"You're coming with us," the female knight said.

Daylen forced himself to stand, not totally convinced he was lucid. This was a reality that shouldn't exist.

"Could you give us a minute?" Daylen said to the knights, while indicating to Ahrek next to him. They nodded and stepped aside.

"You don't need to come with me, Ahrek," Daylen said. "My freedom is gone, and it's not like the knights will let you hang around."

"Then they don't know how insistent I can be...but you're right. As I slept last Low, the Light released me from my charge. I have fulfilled its will. Part of me longs to accompany you still, but my place is not with the knights."

Daylen nodded heavily. "I'll miss you, Ahrek."

"And I you, but please don't think that I won't be visiting. We'll be friends forever, you and I."

Daylen smiled, and his heart warmed. "Out of everything that's happened, that strikes me as more a miracle than anything else: two men who were the worst of enemies, one with mighty cause for that, now the closest of friends."

"The Light works in mysterious ways. It clearly knew that we needed this. I could have never overcome the darkness in my heart without your help."

"And I never would have confronted my crimes. I'll be seeing you, Ahrek."

Ahrek smiled. "Oh, you can be sure of that."

And with that they embraced each other before Daylen turned back to the knights.

"We have a ship waiting," the female knight said. "This way."

Daylen sat above deck on the Archknight skyship, flying to the Hold in deep reflection. It was as if the chapter in Daylen's life as the Conqueror was finally closed. He realized that, though his rule had been ended long ago, the fact that so many of his crimes had remained unanswered meant that he hadn't truly been able to move beyond them, emotionally or mentally. As he had said to Ahrek after saving the city, if he was truly sorry for his crimes, then he should answer for them. Now he had, and though the debt remained, which he would be paying for the rest of his new life, he could finally say truthfully to himself that he was sincerely sorry for his sins. He had proven that much—and for the first time in a long time, it made him feel good about himself.

As with his guilt, who the Conqueror had been would still be a part of him for the rest of his life, forever there as a constant reminder to never approach any thought or practice that might lead to the same mistakes. Indeed, the Conqueror's memory seemed to act like a bulwark against his weaknesses, like the revulsion he had experienced when Sharra had tried to seduce him. The Conqueror in Daylen now ensured that that very same person would never come back. He felt more in control of himself and his weaknesses than ever before.

And now a new chapter in his blackened long life was beginning. He was to be a slave. That was the sentence inflicted upon him, and he would accept it...so long as being a slave meant he could continue to fulfill his new life's purpose to hunt out the evil of the world and destroy it. That was the only reason the Light had spared his life. Daylen had made his offering, the penance for his sins, and the Light had accepted. The leaders of the nations, the Archknights, and his sentence of slavery could jump off the edge of the world if they would try to prevent him from that purpose.

The ship descended and docked next to a large balcony that was built on the back wall of the Hold's main keep.

The gangplank was lowered and Daylen disembarked to find someone waiting for him.

"Lyrah?" he asked in shock.

Lyrah was *not* looking pleased.

"Take those manacles off," she ordered to the other knights, "as well as the inhibitor."

The female knight who seemed to be the leader amongst his attendants replied, "But…"

"They're useless; he could break free at any time if he wished."

"Um… As you wish, Archonair."

"Good," Lyrah said once Daylen's restraints had been removed. "Now, leave us."

The knights looked to each other hesitantly and then did as commanded.

"Because of my experience in dealing with you, I'll be your custodian and guard."

This was the *last* thing Daylen had expected, as Lyrah had made it very clear that she never wanted to see him again. Pain and guilt swelled within him, but incredibly, part of him was glad to see her. "But don't they know…" Daylen began.

"The *whole world* knows my history with you," Lyrah said.

"Oh yeah, right. And you were still assigned to be my custodian?"

"I was asked if our history would affect my service. It won't." She looked at him intently. "It might have in the past, but not anymore. You have no more power over me. You mean nothing, and you'll not speak to me in any familiar way. Understood?"

"I understand," Daylen said, and waved a hand to the mighty Hold. "So where do I fit in with all of this?"

"That'll be determined by the Archain and the Archeron Council, who I'm to take you to once things are sorted out here."

"I look forward to it," Daylen said as Lyrah turned. He followed, feeling the despair over his continued life subside as purpose grew in his heart. It was the same sense of purpose he had felt when committing his new life to do good shortly after receiving his powers. It was interesting that in every choice Daylen had ever made it was with the intent to do good, but his life was proof that intent didn't mean spit. Ultimately it was his actions that defined who he was, and this time Daylen's actions actually mirrored his initial intent. It made him feel better about himself than he had in a long, *long*, time.

Daylen could actually do it. He could do good and fight evil without making the same mistakes of his past.

He could be a better man—and in fact, he thought with a bitter-sweet smile, he was.

ABOUT THE AUTHOR

He likes swords.

youtube.com/shadmbrooks

facebook.com/shadiversity

twitter.com/shadmbrooks

CPSIA information can be obtained
at www.ICGtesting.com
Printed in the USA
LVHW032339160719
624353LV00002B/134/P

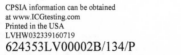

9 780648 572916